Degrees of Darkness

Tony J Forder

Copyright © 2017 Tony J Forder

The right of Tony J Forder to be identified as the Author of the Work has been asserted by him in accordance Copyright, Designs and Patents Act 1988.

First published in 2017 by Bloodhound Books

Apart from any use permitted under UK copyright law, this publication may only be reproduced, stored, or transmitted, in any form, or by any means, with prior permission in writing of the publisher or, in the case of reprographic production, in accordance with the terms of licences issued by the Copyright Licensing Agency.

All characters in this publication are fictitious and any resemblance to real persons, living or dead, is purely coincidental.

www.bloodhoundbooks.com

Print ISBN 978-1-912175-58-1

Also by Tony J Forder

Bad To The Bone

Praise For Bad To The Bone

'A classy thriller with great characters in the form of DI Bliss and DC Chandler' – Maggie James, author of *Guilty Innocence*

'Books like *Bad to the Bone* breathe new life into a sometimes stale genre.' – *NovelGossip*

'Tony has brought us a new Police Procedural Series, that has a powerful start and impressive characters.' –*Bookstormer*

'The pace is fast, the characterisation superb, and the storyline is full of twists and turns.' – Anita Waller, author of *Winterscroft*

'I enjoyed the story very much and kept me guessing to the end and didn't see the ending coming!!!!' – *Breakaway Reviewers*

'This is a cracking police procedural extremely well researched.' – *Books From Dusk Till Dawn*

'Takes a lot to shock me. This one actually made me exclaim out loud.' – Ross Greenwood, author of *The Boy Inside*

'Great descriptive writing that gets into the minds of the characters' – *Ali The Dragon Slayer*

'A highly enjoyable read and can't wait for more in the series.' – *By The Letter Book Reviews*

'A pacey, invigorating read.' – Mark Wilson, author of *Ice Cold Alice*

'The combination of realistic police procedural combined with dark humour, intrigue and suspense literally had me up all night!' – *Feminisia Libros*

'Forder is clearly a writer who cares about words and getting them in the right order and using the right word in the right place. And he's good at painting word pictures too.' – *Book Lovers' Booklist*

This book is dedicated to Alan Garner, Stephen King, Charles Dickens and Michael Connelly. Garner for unlocking my imagination with *The Weirdstone of Brisingamen,* King for consistently showing us all how it should be done, Dickens for the ability to add colour to minutiae and Connelly for being the guv'nor of crime fiction.

To my wife and daughter again – always.

Chapter One

The two-storey detached house was impressive, generously proportioned. Built in smooth red brick and finished with stained dark wood, its gardens were large and lush, lawns neatly manicured. A magnificent willow crouched by the tall wooden fence in the back garden, behind which ran a driveway that serviced all six houses in the row. This was an affluent neighbourhood and its inhabitants were cocooned in a blanket of self-assured security. The quiet street was dark and silent shortly before midnight on that third Sunday in July.

When Janet Rogers switched off the downstairs lights and went up to bed that night, she first checked on both her son and daughter as they lay sleeping in their separate rooms. Gary was a motionless mound buried beneath the covers. Laura lay on her side, both hands clasped as if in prayer beneath her cheek. Janet blew kisses at her children before making her way along the landing to her own bedroom. As she pulled back the lightweight duvet and slipped between the sheets, she paused, one foot still resting on the floor. Her toes gripped the carpet pile as she considered what she had done. It had been several years since she'd felt the need to be assured of her sleeping children's health and safety in that way, so why tonight? From where had such an impetus come?

A moment of consternation threatened to overwhelm her, but it passed swiftly and she felt a little foolish. Nevertheless, Janet rose from the bed and padded across to the door. She opened it a few inches, and immediately began to relax. Irrational, yet comforting. She glanced across at the motionless form on the other side of the bed, glad he hadn't been awake to mock her.

She would not have been able to explain her actions. He would not have been able to understand them.

She lay awake longer than usual, face turned towards the bedroom door, wondering how that tiny gap between the edge and its frame could be so reassuring. *What is wrong with you?* she chided herself. *They're not babies anymore.* The days of listening to monitors, heart skipping beats and pulse racing every time a child's breath was snatched away, were long gone. *Go to sleep, you stupid woman. The kids are safe and well, and will be their usual zombie-like selves in the morning.* Her lips curled upwards at the thought, and she nuzzled into her pillow. *That's better. Nothing to fear after all.* Janet's eyelids began to flicker, the first stages of sleep starting to weigh them down. Her mind repeated the mantra until conscious thought was lost: *Nothing to fear after all. Nothing to fear after all.*

When she awoke three hours later and saw the figure standing above her, she realised for the first time in her life what fear actually was.

*   *   *

In the third bedroom now, and here was his prize. What had gone before was merely a precursor. This was the reason he had come.

Naked, save for the plastic covers taped around his feet, and white cotton gloves pulled snug on large hands, he paced the room like a caged animal. He felt good, so loose and alive, a busy night's work behind him, the best part yet to come. As he moved he kept his face turned towards the sleeping girl, his eyes as unblinking and glassy as those of a reptile. His tongue snaked out to moisten thin lips.

He stopped pacing and stood quite still for a few moments, allowing himself to focus. Sweat slid from his body as though his flesh were made of glass. After running a hand across his forehead, he smiled crookedly and moved among the shadows towards the girl's bed, feet hissing on thick carpet. She was quite beautiful, strawberry-blonde hair draped around her oval head like a silken halo, lips parted as if preparing for a kiss. Moonlight bleeding through her bedroom window cut a pale slash across her arm. He stared at her exposed flesh, and what he saw there took his breath away. For although the room was warm, her skin had erupted in a rash of goosebumps.

She had felt the chill of his approach.

The girl was dreaming, eyes flickering just as her mother's had an hour so earlier. The rapid eye movement fascinated him. Softly he called her name. His smooth voice whispered like a gently flowing stream. Twelve-year-old Laura Rogers stirred in her sleep but did not awaken.

'Laura?'

The voice like a sigh came again. This time he gently shook her warm body. The touch was electric, his long thin fingers jerking reflexively, prompting an explosion of images in the darker regions of his mind. His hand maintained the contact longer than was necessary. Only the thickness of the thin cotton gloves separated them. It was still almost too much to bear.

The girl began to emerge from her slumber. She blinked the fog of sleep away, drank him in with widening eyes, yet said nothing. Fear had eroded her capacity for speech.

* * *

The intruder's hand reached out toward her. 'You have to come with me,' he said. 'Right now.'

Terrified, Laura Rogers shook her head. There was a cry of horror within her, but it was buried deep down and she could not find a way to it. Her mouth flapped open uselessly, and a white-gloved hand clamped over her parted lips. A gleaming, bone-handled knife appeared before her eyes as if from nowhere.

The intruder lowered his head close to hers and his eyes became dead black pools.

'Don't cry out,' he warned. 'When I remove my hand from your mouth, you must not scream. If you do, your family will suffer unimaginable pain. Do you understand me?'

She gave a single nod. He withdrew his hand.

'Good. Now then, pay attention. I want you to come with me, and you will. Whether you come walking by my side, or gagged and trussed over my shoulder, I really don't care. But you *will* come with me.'

'Who are you?' Laura managed to ask in a tiny voice that was scarcely more than a whisper.

He smiled terribly. It was intended to be disarming, but was merely predatory. 'Are you afraid of the dark, Laura?' As he asked the question the man waggled the knife back and forth. His voice remained easy and light.

She nodded, mute once more.

His smile broadened. He touched the knife to the tender flesh of her cheek, sweeping the long steel blade along its smooth curve with delicate strokes.

'That's good, Laura. That's very good. Because I am the dark, and you *should* fear me. Do you hear me? Do you understand? I *am* the dark, Laura.'

A low, whimpering sound filled Laura's ears. At first, she thought that someone – or some*thing* – else had entered the room, before realising that the pitiful moans were escaping from her own lips. If this man truly was the dark then she would live in fear of it for the rest of her life.

Suddenly her scattered thoughts reassembled themselves, a jigsaw completed in a flurry. 'What about my ...?'

'Your family will be safe provided you come with me. Provided you don't cry out or give me any problems. If you don't do exactly as I say, I'll kill them. I'll kill them all. I'll make you watch as I do it, and then I'll kill you, too. But believe me, Laura, I will take my time about it.'

Laura saw she had no choice. She found it hard to believe this was not a dream, some terrible nightmare from which she would soon awaken, sweating and scared, yet dripping with relief. A small voice inside her head told her to run, to fight, to scream loud enough to wake the dead. Another reminded her of his warning. With great reluctance and enormous resolve, Laura pushed back the sheets and twisted around. She wore only a thin sleeveless nightdress, and felt naked before his unswerving gaze. He smiled and nodded.

'That's a good girl,' he said. 'I knew you'd understand me, Laura. I just knew you would. I can see we're going to get along just fine.'

'What do you want with me? Why are you doing this?'

'All in good time, Laura. For now, you only have to focus on doing as you're told.'

She stood, swaying unsteadily for a moment, betrayed by her legs as she reached for her dressing gown, but the man yanked on her arm and pulled her away. He leaned forward, eyes fixed upon hers. 'Did I say you could have your robe? Did I ask you to get it, did I give you permission to put it on?'

Laura shook her head stiffly. 'No, but I ...'

'But nothing. Do only as you are told. Now, come with me.'

By the hand he led her along the landing, down the stairs and into the kitchen. As they moved beyond the breakfast bar, Laura peered down at a strange dark shape on the quarry-tiled floor. It took her fully twenty seconds to recognise what remained of her cat. Her eyes flew open and she glared at the man through a welling of tears.

'Why did you have to kill Simba?' Her voice was small, shocked by the brutality.

The man grinned, shrugged and replied, 'Why not?'

As they left the house through the back door, he stopped to pull on a cotton tracksuit, before stepping into a pair of soft canvas shoes. The bags that had been on his feet disappeared inside a small holdall. He did not wash first, and it wasn't until they were outside in the sultry night air that Laura fully realised what had been smeared across the man's face and naked body.

Blood. Dark and slick. Too much blood for one tiny cat.

In that instant, she knew the truth. But by then it was too late. 'You told me you hadn't hurt them!' Laura cried.

He slapped a hand over her mouth once more. 'I know,' he said, leaning in. 'I lied.'

Chapter Two

The morning sky was blue and bright and impossible to look at without squinting. Not a single cloud worthy of the name could be found anywhere. The sun had been up for just a few hours, yet already its heat was fierce. Across the land, people were going to skip work and head out to the coast, fields were going to be scorched, tarmac was going to melt, and flesh was going to toast. The day held all the promise of greater glories yet to come. Summertime. But the living was far from easy for Frank Rogers.

He stood gazing out of his first-floor office window, peering down at the nose-to-tail stream of traffic trickling by, the air rippled slightly by choking exhaust fumes. Like the spine of some fossilised creature, the line of vehicles curved away into the distance and out of sight beyond a bend. An occasional horn punctuated the din made by growling engines and squealing brakes. Every year it seemed to take longer to get nowhere, Frank thought. He shook his head and took a sip of coffee from a chipped mug bearing the legend 'World's Greatest Dad'.

'What a day to be cooped up,' he said, turning to his young administrator seated at the office's only desk. 'There has to be more to life than this.' He gave a curt laugh and glanced back out of the window. 'Or that.'

Zoe Thomsett, nineteen years old and gloriously single, leaned back in her chair and nodded. 'Give me the day off and I'll find out if there's more to offer,' she said, flashing a wide, toothy grin.

'The Alpha Debt Collecting Agency not exciting enough for you, Zoe?' Frank asked, grinning. 'I'll have you know I've put my heart and soul into this business.'

'You're the one who started going off on one about there being more to life,' Zoe complained.

'True. But I'm the boss. I may come here every Monday morning to do all those mundane chores like make calls, plan my schedule, write up my diary and discuss the business with you, but I don't have to. On a beautiful day like today I can do as I damn well please.' He shrugged. 'So how stupid am I?'

'As you pointed out, you're the boss, so it might hurt my career prospects if I answer that. Anyway, what would you rather be seeing out of that window right now?'

'An ocean,' he said without pause, turning his head once more. 'Any ocean. Waves crashing in to the shore. And the window I'm looking out of is in a bar where I've just been sold an ice-cold beer in a frosted glass.'

The young woman blew out her cheeks. 'Bloody hell, Frank. Take me with you, will you? It sounds lovely.'

'Believe me it is. I sat on the outside deck of a bar overlooking Malibu beach one time. I've never felt so at peace. The sunset that night was just about the most beautiful thing I've ever seen.' Frank could see it still when he closed his eyes.

'Not much like Leytonstone High Road, then?' Zoe said.

He didn't have to look outside again to see the grime-stained buildings and shambling people whose eyes never left the cracked and litter-strewn pavements. Leytonstone, riding the cusp of humanity in east London, is a suburb uncertain of its place in the world, offering little but shelter and the passing of time.

Frank moved across to the desk he and Zoe shared. 'No,' he answered softly. 'Not much. But this is the here and now, and the agency pays the bills. Sometimes.'

The tiny office was functional – barely. Into it were crammed two large filing cabinets, a photocopier, computer station, and a row of three assorted soft chairs for visitors. A seam on one of the chair cushions had split open, revealing blisters of yellow foam. The folds of a brown ill-fitting carpet disguised a sloping floor, whose boards creaked and groaned like a ship's rigging when walked upon. Zoe had tried to make the place more appealing by hanging a couple of small prints on the stained walls, and setting out a display of colourful plants, but they served only to make the decor appear even more dour. Whenever Frank bothered to look at the room, he realised it must come across as a front for a half-hearted business closer to drowning than staying afloat.

Frank and Zoe faced each other across the wide desk – the only item in the room not bought second-hand. Her half was neat and tidy, while his was stacked with crumpled letters, unpaid bills and Post-it notes ringed with coffee stains. As he reached for his diary, Zoe slid her hand in front of him and left it there, palm upwards.

'What?' He looked up and frowned.

Her eyes narrowed. 'You know what. You paid Mr Hedges a visit on Friday evening. Did you get the money for Mannion's Autos from him? If not, I'll take the car keys instead.'

'I got the money. He was easily persuaded.'

'Really?'

'No. Not really.' Frank shook his head at the memory and smiled. 'He was a big bugger, too. Stood there by his front door in just a vest and shorts, scratching his crotch every few seconds and telling me to 'piss off if I knew what was good for me'. It was either back down and lose Mannion's business, or take Hedges on.'

'And you put the business first.'

'No choice. I grabbed hold of the family jewels, gave them a few sharp tugs and twists, and he coughed up the money ... amongst a few other things'

Zoe threw back her head and laughed, her whole face coming alive, gleaming with youth. Frank admired her easy-going nature. She was cute and knew it, though she tried her best to disguise the fact by sporting weird haircuts and even more bizarre clothes. Today her hair was tinted orange, and her thin peach blouse and leather micro skirt could not conceal the shape of a body in its prime. Behind the startling appearance lay intelligence and warmth, as Frank had come to discover.

'Great,' she said, still chuckling. 'I'll bank the money this morning and write out a cheque for our grateful client.'

Frank shook his head. 'It's a cash deal.'

Zoe rolled her eyes. Gave an indulgent sigh. 'Frank! I told you we shouldn't get involved in that kind of thing any more. You have to go about things the right way if you're going to get this business established how you want it.'

'I know, I know. But some people prefer to work with cash only. That's the way life is at this end of the scale. It greases the wheels, Zo. Always has done, always will do.'

'Well it's not good enough.'

'So, you don't want the cash, then?'

'Oh, no you don't, Frank Rogers.' Zoe beckoned with her fingers. 'Hand it over.'

He pursed his lips, stalling. The thick smell of fried onions from a nearby burger bar wafted in through the open window. Compared to the seemingly permanent odour of blocked drains, it was a welcome relief.

'I know that look,' Zoe said. 'What have you done with it this time?'

'Some of it. I have some of it. The rest I spent.'

'Don't tell me, you had the kids this weekend and you blew the money.'

'Something like that.'

She put back her head and made to pull out her hair. 'Ooh, you drive me bloody crazy.'

'Hey, hold on a minute. I *am* the boss. I thought we'd established that.'

'You'll be the boss of nothing if you carry on the way you're going.'

'I have our client's money.'

'But you spent our percentage.'

Frank nodded. He tried a smile, but Zoe wasn't having any of it. 'That money was needed for bills, Frank. The rent on this place has to be paid, we need stationery and our supplier won't give us any more credit. BT are screaming at us in big red letters. No office and no phone means no business. Do you hear what I'm saying?'

'Yes. Your voice is raised loud and clear.'

Zoe flapped a hand at him. 'Oh, sod you. You're hopeless. Whatever made you think you could run a business?'

'My wife.'

'Oh. Her.' Zoe's tone mellowed, and her scowl became less severe. 'Look, Frank, I'm serious now. We have to keep a tight grip on things for a while. This is my living we're talking about as well, you know. Think about it: if you go bust I won't be around to brighten your days anymore.'

'Oh, right. I'll really miss the ear-ache and that multi-coloured thatch you call hair.'

Zoe puckered up her lips. 'You'd miss my short skirts and my cleavage.'

'Can't say I've ever noticed.'

'Not much. I've caught you checking out the goods.'

Frank shook his head. 'Zo, just looking at you saps all my energy.'

'I'll bet it does, old man. And don't call me Zo.'

Frank was about to snap off another response when the door to the office juddered open, snagging on a ridge in the carpet.

A tall man, with thick black hair and a swarthy complexion, stepped inside. He wore a grey double-breasted suit, white shirt with a red silk tie. Black shoes gleamed like polished ceramic. His face was long and narrow and hard looking, with eyes that seemed cold and unforgiving. He looked like trouble.

Frank swivelled in his chair and his eyes and mouth opened wide as if synchronised. 'Nicky!' he cried. 'To what do I owe this honour?'

The man remained in the doorway, silent and seemingly anxious, like an actor who has fluffed his cue.

Springing to his feet, Frank walked quickly across the room. 'How the hell are you, pal? It's been a while. What brings you—'

Frank Rogers stopped, the words snagging in his throat. He and the visitor had been cadets together at the Hendon police training centre, and though Frank had risen through the ranks a little quicker, they had both reached the level of detective inspector before he'd decided to quit, little more than a year ago. He and Nicky remained great friends, whose unsocial working hours kept them apart more than they liked. But while he was thrilled to see his friend, Nicky's face was creased and weighed down by sorrow.

Taking a short step back, Frank felt his skin begin to crawl. He knew that particular look too well. It had been written across his own features often enough. Something cold gripped his insides, squeezing hard. The air became difficult to draw into his lungs, as though the entire room had been emptied of oxygen. A balloon filled with bile swelled around his heart. He felt as if someone had put a sawn-off to his temple, or punched his stomach with a knife.

'What is it, Nicky?' Frank's treacherous voice crumbled at the last moment, lending the name an extra syllable.

'I'm sorry, Frank.'

That was all his friend said. It was all he needed to say. Frank Rogers knew the rest.

Chapter Three

It was in Highams Park, on the very edge of east London where it bleeds into Essex, that Frank's estranged wife had chosen to rebuild her life without him in the home of another man.

Janet had taken with her their son and daughter, and it was the absence of the children from his daily life that had recently begun to strip Frank of any optimism regarding the future. He could not recall a day since the break-up of the marriage when his heart had not ached, his love for Gary and Laura impossible to calculate. They were sources of immense pride to him, their bright and witty outlooks forcing him to believe that not everything he touched became tainted. That something good had come of the life he and Janet had built together.

The short drive from Frank's office seemed to take an eternity as Nicky Loizou's two-year-old Mondeo stuttered through predictable multiple snarl-ups. The atmosphere inside the car was grim, laced with equal measures of incomprehension, overwhelming grief, and despair.

As Nicky weaved his way through the weary traffic, Frank stared straight ahead through the windscreen. Though of little more than average height and build, he had worked hard to attain a professional aura of someone brooding and menacing. His salt-and-pepper hair was cropped close to the scalp. A direct, narrow gaze had been perfected. Now he felt small and weak. A broken reed, flapping lifelessly in the breeze.

'Tell me again,' he muttered softly. He'd shed no tears, but he felt moisture in his deep-set hazel eyes.

Without pause, Nicky laid it out once more. 'The mother of one of Laura's friends who often takes her and Gary to school, was there as usual to collect them this morning. Today no one came out of the house when she tooted the horn. She thought something was wrong because both cars were still in the driveway, newspaper poking through the letter-box, and the curtains were drawn. At first, she thought they'd all overslept, but after a time she became concerned. The woman had her shit together. She called us.'

'Go on.' Frank nodded. 'I know you already told me, but I really didn't hear it first time around.'

'We found Paul Clarke and Janet upstairs in one bedroom. Gary was in another. All three were dead. There was no sign of Laura.'

'Any blood?'

'Of course. I mean ...'

Frank shook his head abruptly. 'No. In Laura's room. Was there any blood?'

'We can't be certain at this stage. Maybe some footmarks, but it doesn't look as if she came to any harm there and then.'

'So, she could have escaped ... run away?'

'We can't rule that out, but we can't assume it, either. Fact is, if Laura got away, why hasn't she come forward? Why wouldn't she have reported the crime? And wouldn't she have somehow found her way to you?'

For a moment or two there was silence. Frank's eyes had narrowed, but now he nodded. 'You're right.'

'I'm sorry to be so blunt, Frank, but I don't want to give you any false hopes. You know how this goes better than anyone. We believe whoever carried out the murders now has Laura.'

Frank felt his friend's continued appraisal, and knew that a wretched sense of impotence would be twisting Nicky's insides. He opened his mouth to say something else, but then suddenly they were there, and all at once words seemed obscene.

* * *

As the car nosed into the tree-lined cul-de-sac, Frank felt his muscles tensing. This was happening. It really was happening.

Police attendance was heavy, with squad cars and forensic science vans scattered everywhere. Detached homes, each different in style and size, peered down at them as if offended by their presence in such a tranquil setting. The modern, angular house and surrounding grounds where Frank's family had lived, were now bordered by white-and-blue tape. Behind a hastily erected barrier stood the media; notebooks, cameras and video cameras at the ready. The usual gawkers did what they did best, while beat coppers kept them under observation. Uniforms, suits, and overalls both green and white came and went through the front door of the house, while others on their hands and knees patiently scoured the front lawn and drive.

'No ambulance,' Frank noted as they rolled to a halt.

'The bodies must have already been taken away. The pathologist and his crew were about done when I left.'

Frank jerked his head around. 'Bodies?' His voice quavered, and he felt as if he had somehow misunderstood earlier. As if Janet and Gary and Laura were going to come running out into his arms. Frightened perhaps, injured even, but safe. Alive.

He felt Nicky's hand on his shoulder. A gentle squeeze. 'It's for the best. You wouldn't have wanted to see them like that.'

'No.'

As they got out of the car and walked across to the scene, Frank's mind spiralled into a whirlpool, dragging all manner of memories into its core. How many times had he done this before? How many corpses had he seen? How many people had he informed that their loved ones were dead? Then he had been detached, perhaps not as warm as he might have been, given the circumstances. Wanting to get on with the job of finding out who the perpetrator was, unconcerned with the husks of victims who would never be able to tell him what he needed to know.

Now it was his wife, killed in another man's bed. His eight-year-old son, killed in that other man's house. And Laura. Where in God's name was his daughter? Frank's mind continued to toy with his emotions. He felt as if all his thoughts were trapped in the hold of a tiny sinking ship, being sucked down into the murky depths of some fathomless ocean. It was all so unreal, someone else's nightmare.

'Are you filming the onlookers?'

He asked the question almost before the thought had formed in his head. His gaze veered off into the sun-drenched crowd, wondering whether the killer of his child was amongst them, gloating over his work as some of their kind like to do.

Nicky nodded. 'We'll run it by the neighbours afterwards, see if they spot any strangers.'

Looking up at the house as they approached, it didn't seem possible to Frank that he'd been here just last evening, dropping off the children after spending a wonderful weekend with them. He recalled that his thoughts had been filled with petty jealousies; his wife finding a better life elsewhere, his children living comfortably in another man's home, precious times together now grabbed only sparingly. But he had imagined then that his two children would be with him once more on the following Saturday morning, bringing warmth, a touch of brightness and a little sanity back into his world. Now there was only horror waiting for him, and the certain knowledge that his life would never be the same again.

He took one last look around, felt the weight of inquisitive eyes upon him, sensed a ripple running through the gathered media. They would want to know who he was, what he was doing there. His gaze also took in the onlookers, meeting their questioning stares.

Are you out there? he wondered. *Are you out there now, grinning behind your hand, mentally congratulating yourself at a job well done? Are you? Because if you are, be warned. You may not know who I am right now, but you will. That I can promise.*

Frank turned swiftly away and, with a heart so heavy he thought it might drag him down to his knees, headed inside to confront his demons.

Chapter Four

As they entered the house, Nicky paused on the threshold. 'Look, Frank, there's something I have to tell you. The special crimes team were called in for this, so they are running the show.'

Frank nodded and took a deep breath. 'Okay. That's good, isn't it? Why do you look so concerned?'

'The problem is we have no say over who's leading the team.'

'I still don't see ...' He paused, eyes narrowing. 'Who's heading the investigation, Nicky?'

'You're not going to like it. Believe me.'

Frank closed his eyes and used his thumb and middle finger to massage the lids. 'It's Foster, isn't it? Colin-fucking-Foster.'

'I'm sorry.'

'So what rank has he arse-licked his way up to?' Frank asked.

'Let it go, mate. It's history.'

'What rank, Nicky?'

His friend gave a heavy sigh. 'Superintendent. Roger Finnieston was the chief super on duty, he took one look at the scene of crime and assigned the case to Foster as the only senior investigator available at the time.'

Silence again. Then: 'Does he know I'm coming?'

'No. You have a right to be here ... you know, family involvement. But no questions, Frank. Don't try to get involved with the inquiry itself. He won't have it.'

'With a bit of luck he won't be around much. Who's your DCI?'

'I'm DCI now. My promotion came through a couple of days ago.'

'Detective Chief Inspector Loizou,' Frank said, tasting the flavour of each word. 'I'm impressed. Congratulations, Nicky. You deserve it. Why didn't you call me?'

'I was going to give you a bell later today, thinking we'd go for a drink to celebrate.' His voice tailed off, and he looked away. They both knew there would be no celebrations now.

They moved beyond the open front door and into the hallway. Detective Sergeant Warren Capel, an officer Frank recognised, stood in the hallway having an animated discussion with three other detectives. He broke away from them without a word, extending a neatly manicured hand.

'Frank,' he said, suitably sombre. 'What can I say? I'm gutted for you. I still can't believe it.'

Frank nodded and breathed deeply. 'Yeah, me neither. Thanks, Warren.'

He looked beyond the tall, sandy-haired man, openly appraising the house, for this was the first time he had set foot inside. Large and comfortable, money poured into it tastefully. Expensive prints adorned the pastel walls, lighting subdued yet exact, furnishings plush and colour-co-ordinated. Cream carpeting, mahogany woodwork, solid panelled doors painted with a soft sheen. He wondered whether Janet had advised Paul Clarke on the decorating. He thought it likely; it looked every bit the house she had always wanted. Fit for the glossy pages of a magazine.

Though not any more.

There was a rush of footsteps on the stairs, one person descending them hastily. Frank looked up and glanced across. Detective Superintendent Colin Foster stopped on the bottom tread. A thin, almost gaunt figure, Foster wore his authority with the air of one who believes it is nothing more than a stepping-stone to greater things. His myopic eyes seemed huge behind tinted, gold-rimmed spectacles. An unconvincing toupee perched on top of his head. He nodded once, a single gesture of compassion. When he spoke it was all business.

'Don't go up there. The forensic team are still busy. Any hairs or fibres you leave behind will only confuse the issue.'

'I think I still remember the drill. And thanks for your concern.' Frank's voice was louder than he'd intended. 'You're all heart.'

Foster clambered out of a white protective overall, removed both elasticated plastic overshoes, straightened his tie and swept back his hair with long, thin fingers. He shrugged into his suit jacket, reaching for a well-used comb in the breast pocket. An audience waited for him outside. Media hungry not only for answers, but for someone upon whom to focus their attention. Right up Foster's street.

'I'm sorry for your loss,' he said eventually, his voice clipped and unconvincing. 'But, right now, the investigation is my priority.'

'And not mine?' Frank squared his shoulders squared.

Foster rocked gently on his heels.

He's loving this, Frank thought. For too long he had worked in Frank's shadow. Now he was free, now he had the authority. Frank despised him, all the more, for that.

'No,' Foster said. 'Not any longer. This kind of thing is best left to policemen, not debt collectors.'

Although Frank had no intention of reacting to the jibe, he felt Nicky's hand in his midriff. He took a moment, then said in a low, even voice, 'I want you off this case, Foster. I'll talk to the chief superintendent about it. Commander Allen if I have to.'

Foster gave a thin smile. His lips were moist, like thick pink worms. 'You have to have a valid reason to remove me from the case, Frank. Dislike or… envy, simply won't be enough.'

'I have a valid reason.' Frank noticed that many of the milling uniforms and suits and overalls had stopped what they were doing, and he knew he was about to make a mistake. But he was on a roll and the bitterness of past feuds poured out. 'I want the bastard who did this found and caught, Foster. Trouble is, you couldn't find your arse in the dark with a torch, or catch a fucking cold in mid-winter. My valid reason is simple: you're not up to the job.'

A nerve pulsed around Foster's left eyelid. His gaze narrowed. A trembling hand pushed back the glasses on his shiny narrow nose. 'Do whatever pleases your tiny mind, Frank. I know what your opinion is of me, and rest assured it's reciprocated. Just don't come anywhere near this investigation or I'll have you for it. Obstruction of justice is still a crime.'

'So is the fact that you're heading this or any other investigation.'

Scowling now, Foster looked around deliberately. 'Any of you real policemen caught helping this man to interfere will find yourselves writing out traffic tickets in the shittiest hole I can transfer you to.'

His gaze returned to Frank, challenging him to continue. Frank slowly shook his head, had one last glance upstairs, then turned sharply and headed back out of the house. He needed fresher air to breathe, to put distance between himself and Foster, and from the house that now held such terrible associations.

* * *

Back in the heat he felt nauseous, and the fresh clamour from the media bored holes into his skull. He was vaguely aware of Nicky and Foster having a heated disagreement, but his mind was wilting beneath the assault of terrible images and irrational thoughts. Then Nicky was with him, gripping his arm, helping him stagger forward. Until then, Frank hadn't realised how much he'd needed the support to get him where he wanted to go.

'Trouble?' he asked as they made their way back out to the street.

Nicky shrugged. 'Nothing I can't handle. He didn't want me to take you back home. I said we'd do it for any other bereaved citizen, and I wasn't about to make an exception for you.'

Together they fought their way through the media who, while they had not been given a full briefing, were aware that Frank was a player somehow. A number of the elder statesmen recognised him and were calling out their questions, either unaware of his personal tragedy or perhaps not caring about the intrusion.

Several uniformed officers moved swiftly to head them off and form a human barrier.

When the two men reached the car, Frank slumped back in the passenger seat and said, 'Thanks, mate.' He allowed himself a hollow smile. 'Sorry to put you to all this trouble, but I can't cope with Foster around.'

'I'm sorry, Frank. I should have told you about Foster before we drove over here. Truth is, I was hoping he'd be gone by the time I got back. When I saw his car still here I knew I had to warn you.'

'Don't worry about it. I'll have to see the place another time, when he's crawled back under his rock. But thanks for sticking with me, Nicky. I'm glad it was you who …' Frank shook his head, helplessly.

'I couldn't let it be anyone else, mate. Too important. As for Foster, I should have known better than to bring you here while there was even the remotest possibility that he might still be around.'

Much of the short journey across to neighbouring Chingford took place in silence, Frank becoming wrapped deeper within his own mind, feeling himself retreat from the awful reality. At some point, he realised they had stopped and were parked up outside his house.

He turned his head. 'I need a drink. How about you?'

'Well, Foster said to head straight back when I was done. All things considered, I reckon I can spare an old mate some time. And Foster can go to hell.'

'*Superintendent* Foster.'

'Yeah. Ain't that the biggest fucking joke you ever heard?'

Frank's home was the standard three-bedroomed semi; the nuclear family's choice of dwelling. Built between the wars, at a time when space had not been at a premium, he felt himself dwarfed by the substantial rooms, still unused to the feeling of emptiness some eleven months after Janet had left him. Even with the children there at weekends, the resonance spoke more of a way-station than a family home.

In the kitchen, he yanked open a cupboard door and took down a bottle of Johnny Walker Black Label. His hands were shaking as he uncapped the whisky. Taking two tumblers from the draining board, Frank filled both almost to the brim, passing one to Nicky before leaning back against the sink. Two thirds of his own drink disappeared in one swallow. He felt the heat spread through his body and he welcomed it. Stared into space and let his mind go blank.

* * *

Nicky's eyes never left his friend's face. He searched for signs of recognition, of shock, but there was nothing to be found there. Frank had simply switched off.

The glare of the day hit both men as it spilled through the glass doors leading into to the conservatory, where wicker furniture had grown dusty and plants had survived only because of Laura's determination. Nicky took off his jacket, draped it over the back of a dining chair and sat down. He rolled his sleeves up to the elbow and loosened the knot of his tie. Taking careful sips from his glass, he waited patiently. It wasn't a time for words. Only if his friend spoke them. Several minutes passed before Frank seemed to come back from somewhere distant and melancholy.

'I was with the kids just yesterday, dropped them at the house around six in the evening.' He was talking to Nicky, but his eyes were lost in the past.' On Saturday we went to Margate with Janet's friend, Debbie, who seems to have taken a shine to us for some reason. Actually, she and I have got quite close recently. I like her, the kids like her. We've become something of an item. Yesterday I took Gary and Laura out to Epping Forest, showed them a few places where I used to go as a kid. We had a nice stroll in the woods, a good honest talk about our lives and our plans.'

He choked on the words, looked up at Nicky. 'It's almost a year since me and Janet split up, and I don't think I've been handling it too well. Somehow it all seemed to come right this weekend. Debs was an added bonus, but me and the kids ... we were great together. I can't believe they're gone, Nicky. I can't believe I'll never see my little boy again. Or Janet, for that matter. I still thought a lot of her, you know.'

Swallowing back on his own sorrow, Nicky nodded. This kind of grief was difficult enough when dealing with strangers. Now, with his best friend in such desperate need of answers, he felt particularly lost. 'It'll take a while to sink in. You should have someone here with you, Frank. How about I call your mother?'

'No.' Frank's shake of the head was certain. 'I need to be on my own. Like I say, it hasn't really got through yet. And I have to keep my wits about me for Laura's sake. She may need me. She *will* need me.'

'We'll find out soon enough. The lads'll keep working on this one till they drop.'

'I know what Foster said, what he threatened, but I want in on this, Nicky.' Frank looked across, pained. 'You're my best mate, and I shouldn't ask. It's your career, and I know what it means to you. But you're the only one I *can* ask.'

'Fuck Foster. I was going to offer anyway. Later. When you'd had a little time. I won't leave you out in the cold.' Nicky spread his hands and shrugged. 'I couldn't do that to you.'

Frank's chin began to tremble, his eyes blinked rapidly. 'I don't know what to say.'

'So, say nothing. What kind of a pal would I be if I let you stew every day, not knowing what the hell was going on? No, Foster's a grade-A twat, but I can handle him. He has the rank, but he doesn't have the respect of the men.'

'It's a bad dream, Nicky.' Frank dropped onto a high stool, rested his elbows on the breakfast bar and put his head in his hands. 'The worst nightmare of all. But I know it's one I'll never wake up from.'

Nicky stood and came across the floor. He pulled Frank to him, embracing his friend and inviting him to let go of his emotions. When he did, Frank's whole body convulsed. Nicky held him tight until the wailing and sobbing had subsided. When his friend was spent, Nicky pulled back a little, tears still sliding down his own cheeks.

'What a pair of old tarts,' Frank said. He laughed without mirth, knuckled his eyes.

'Speak for yourself. I'll miss my godson, too.' He clapped his friend on the arm.

'I know you will, mate. I know. Listen, you'd better drink up and get going. I don't want Foster coming down heavy on you.'

'Yeah. I'll head back, see how things are shaping up. Capel will have set up the incident room by now.' He paused, eyed Frank speculatively. 'Look, are you sure you don't want anyone here with you? There must be someone I can call? How about Debbie?'

Frank shook his head firmly. 'No. There are people I need to tell, of course. And I'll do that as soon as you've gone. Well, once I've pulled myself together.'

'You sure?'

'Positive.'

Nicky drained his glass. Grabbed his jacket, hooked it over his thumb and flung it across his shoulder. 'I'll be round later tonight with everything we have. If we get anything major, I'll call.'

'Thanks. You know what it means to me.'

Nicky nodded and smiled. 'Like I said, no trouble. I'll be here when I can.'

'Okay.'

'Take care, Frank. And…I'm sorry, mate. I really am so very, very sorry.'

Chapter Five

Nicky returned a little before midnight, by which time Frank had called Debbie, Janet's parents, and his own mother. Janet's father had been the most difficult of all to deal with, which came as no surprise. For a few seconds the man had said nothing. Then, as he always did in times of stress, he went on the attack.

'Was this someone with a grudge against you, Frank? Is that why my daughter and grandson died?'

Having expected nothing less, Frank bit down on any residue of bitterness he may have felt. An ex-RAF electrical engineer, Arthur Rankin had never hidden his dislike of Frank, and had constantly sniped at the police force: kindling to Janet's own rising flame of disenchantment. Frank had always wondered how much of an effect his in-laws had on Janet's decision to seek pastures new. He suspected they were responsible for a great deal of her dissatisfaction. Perhaps they had persuaded her into the very bed in which she died.

'No, Arthur,' Frank said without rancour. 'It wasn't at our house, was it? No one I've ever put away would know where Janet has been living these past ten or eleven months.'

'If you say so.' He paused; an uncomfortable silence that seemed to drag on forever. Just as Frank was beginning to wonder if the line had gone dead, Rankin spoke once more. 'She was getting her life in order. For the first time since before she met you, she was actually—'

'Arthur, I'm not going to go down this same old road with you. I'm suffering, too, and my grief is every bit as real as yours. I just felt it best that I should let you know, rather than having some stranger contact you.'

'Mary is out at the moment. I don't know how I'm going to tell her, but when I do we'll want to see Janet.'

'I don't think that's a good idea.'

'Don't you dare tell me what to think or do!' His voice rose in pitch, venom in the words. Frank could almost see the spittle flying from the man's lips. 'This is my daughter we're talking about. I'll do as I damn well please.'

You do that, Arthur. Maybe you deserve to go and see your precious daughter all cut up, butchered, lying on a mortuary slab. Maybe that's exactly what you need.

Frank exhaled slowly. The thought was unworthy of him. Nobody, not even Arthur Rankin, deserved to see their own flesh and blood so horribly mutilated.

'Arthur, even I haven't seen the ... Janet or Gary.' *Bodies. You were going to say bodies. Why is that so difficult for you?* 'My ex-colleagues tell me it would be too distressful. They were both brutally attacked and disfigured with a sharp weapon. I was only trying to save you from that pain.'

'Oh, yes. I'm sure you were. If you'd cared about our feelings you would never have married my daughter.'

'I'm going now, Arthur. I'll speak to you again when you've had time to let this sink in.'

'Speak to me? Speak to me? Now that my daughter's gone I don't want you to speak to me ever again, you murdering bastard. Do you hear me? Do you?'

As he cut the connection with his hand, Frank held the phone against his slick brow. Its touch was cooling. His head was pounding now, just above the eyes, where it always got him when it was feeling particularly vicious. The pain came in waves, the ebb and flow of a relentless tide. He swallowed a couple of paracetamol and allowed the headache to subside before making the next call.

His mother offered sympathy he found hard to believe was entirely genuine. He hadn't seen her in more than a year, and she had never taken to Janet or either of the children. Her reaction wasn't entirely unexpected; she hadn't exactly been the most maternal of mothers, and was a grandparent in name only.

Duty done, Frank's final call was to Debbie. Through her tears of shock and distress she offered to drive over and keep him company. Despite their growing fondness for each other, Frank gently refused. 'Tomorrow,' he said. 'I'll call.' Then he went back into the living room and sat down to wait, the bottle of Scotch by his side. The sun slid effortlessly across the sky, shadows lengthened, the room became tinged with grey, and finally fell into darkness. At some point, Frank switched on a table lamp, but his only other movements were pouring and drinking. He didn't eat, never once moved from the spot. He just sat and drank and weaved his way through time.

* * *

He'd had better days, and the light of those other days came back to brush against him now. Times when life was so much more than mere existence, when the way ahead seemed clear and full of promise. Times when he and Janet were still together, starting out, their plans still fresh and exciting. Then the children had come along, and each seemed to bless them more.

In his mind he saw every hug, every kiss, every tender moment shared, heard every song that ever meant anything to either Janet or Gary. Moments frozen in time, always there to be called upon, even when the pain of doing so was too much to bear, the pain of not doing so worse still.

It was some while before he realised that Laura hadn't yet figured in any of these snapshots from the past. There was a part of him still desperately clinging to the hope that his daughter was alive, that her return was only a matter of simple negotiation with her captor. And there was another part that reminded him of all the times he had seen distraught parents wrestling with the exact same emotions, only for fate to deal them the very worst of hands.

Around eleven-fifty he heard a car pull up outside. He peered through the curtains, and was at the door to meet Nicky before his friend had a chance to ring the doorbell. Nicky looked exhausted, his suit crumpled, eyes red-rimmed. Wayward strands of hair hung down over his forehead. At forty-three, Nicky was a year younger than Frank. Today, both men seemed much older than their years, sorrow a crueller enemy than either gravity or time. Frank offered him a Scotch, only to discover the bottle was empty. He fetched two beers from the fridge.

'So, what have you got so far?' he asked, sitting forward on the armchair, fingers of both hands raking his lap.

Nicky took a moment to gather his thoughts. 'You're not going to like it, Frank.'

'Just tell me. How much worse can it get?'

'It looks as though we have a serial killer and abductor on our hands.'

This was about the only thing that had not occurred to Frank. Murder investigations were never anything less than difficult at the best of times, but the two words that haunted detectives most of all were 'serial killer'. Not only were they usually the most malevolent of creatures, but they were also often the most elusive.

The majority of murders were committed in a brief moment of rage or passion, often by persons known to the victim, or for easily detectable reasons. Serial killers were unorthodox in every conceivable way. They played by their own twisted set of rules, in a game few were able to comprehend.

Things had got worse after all.

'Jesus,' he breathed, shaking his head. 'I didn't know anything about this. The news just depresses me these days.'

'A lot of the major details have been deliberately kept from the press, and the link between incidents kept low-key. But the media coverage has begun to get heavy-handed as usual.'

'And you knew this earlier? Knew this was more than a one-off?'

'Not for certain, no.' Nicky inclined his head. 'And I didn't want to worry you more by putting it forward as a theory.'

Frank nodded. He understood. Would have done the same thing in Nicky's shoes. 'How many times has he struck?'

'As far as we know, this is the seventh.'

'Seven?' Frank blew his cheeks out slowly. His heart raged. 'Seven families destroyed by one man?'

'It looks that way, yes.' Nicky ran a cupped hand across the stubble on his chin. 'In each incident, our man has killed everyone in the house apart from one child – always a girl. From what we've been able to establish so far, and bear in mind that the details are sketchy at the moment, all of the girls have been of a similar age: eleven to thirteen, with around eighteen months separating youngest and oldest. He's killed younger and older girls in the family, but always abducts one. So, a definite pattern has been established.'

'Have any of the abductees been found?'

Nicky shook his head.

'When was the first?'

'About six months ago. In Hove. And before you ask, the pattern is pretty irregular. He's not on a lunar cycle, and we can't match the incidents to any known religious or pagan ceremonies.'

'Apart from taking the girls, what's his MO?'

Nicky took a sip from his can, belched behind a clenched hand, let the can rest on his lap. 'Each attack has come during the early hours of the morning. In every instance, he's attempted to gain entry through the back door. He takes the lock apart. Clean, too.'

'A locksmith?'

'Could be. Experience of it, at least. Anyhow, if he finds the door bolted he uses the windows. None of the windows have had security locks fitted. He's either extremely lucky, or he knows what to expect.'

'Or he's tried others, failed, and gone elsewhere.'

'You haven't lost your touch, Frank.' Nicky gave a rueful grin.

'What then? Once he's inside.'

Nicky cleared his throat. If he was troubled by Frank's urgency, he made no mention of it. 'We have a pet killer. Best guesstimate is that he does the pet before his human victims. Animal blood has been found on stairways, landings and in bedrooms. He did Laura's cat.'

Frank closed his eyes for a moment. 'Were there pets at each of the victims' homes?'

'No. But if there was one, he killed it.'

Nodding thoughtfully, Frank used both thumbs to wipe his eyes.

Nicky edged forward. 'You want to leave this till the morning, Frank? It's been a hell of a day for you.'

'No. No, I'm okay if you are. Let's push on. So, he likes to kill the pet, but he doesn't need to. It's not a part of the ritual. He just enjoys it, some kind of a precursor to the main event. No dogs, I'll bet.'

'Right. Two cats, one rabbit, one guinea-pig.' Their eyes met. 'Frank, do you want to know it all? None of it is nice, as you can imagine. Most of it is just plain awful.'

'All of it, Nicky. You know how I work, what I need.'

'But this time I thought—'

'Just give me what you have.' He added weight to his tone.

'Okay. The way we figure it, he takes out the parents first, then any other children. Three of the women had been vaginally penetrated just before death, but we figure this is probably the work of the husband. Firstly, because there are no traces of our man's semen inside the vagina, and secondly, we know for sure that he masturbates. All of the women had semen on their faces. We haven't had results back from the swabs taken from Janet's face yet, but almost certainly it's our man's, and there's no vaginal match.'

Frank swallowed hard, imagining the monster ejaculating over his estranged wife, wondering if she were still alive at the time, imagining her terror. Taking a deep breath, he shut it away. For now.

'Even if he didn't come inside them, there would be some leakage, right?' he asked. 'Some secretion to tag.'

'It's possible, even likely, but it doesn't always happen.'

'So, he jerks off over the women. Post-mortem would be my guess. Nothing unusual there for these sick freaks. DNA?'

Nodding, Nicky took another sip of lager and eased back into the sofa, rolling his neck and shoulders. 'Tested and typed at all previous incidents. No match with anything on file, but we're still putting that together. No distinctive blood group either. He's just another 'O'.'

'Prints?'

'Nothing. Must wear gloves, but nothing that sheds fibres. Could be latex, but with all the high-tech stuff available to forensics these days we should have been able to get *something* if that were the case. They think it's more likely to be some kind of lint-free cotton.'

Frank raised his eyebrows, then frowned. He sat back, considering. 'Strange. He takes precautions by wearing gloves, but he doesn't mind leaving semen which, if we nab him and the DNA proves positive, is as indicting as any print.'

'Maybe in the heat of the moment he forgets himself.'

Frank shook his head vigorously. 'No. I don't think so. This man knows what he's about. He's good, not lucky. He has control. But maybe … Maybe he doesn't fear DNA. It's only useful to us if we have it in our database.' Frank shrugged. 'It doesn't quite fit.'

Nicky agreed. 'Come back to it,' he said. 'There's a lot more to consider.'

Frank nodded. It was starting to feel like the good old days; working closely together, hunting down the criminal. Only then he and Nicky had faced each other across an incident room desk, Janet and Gary were still alive, and Laura wasn't missing. The world hadn't turned to shit and his heart hadn't been shattered into a thousand pieces.

Chapter Six

The soft glow from the solitary table lamp cast strange shadows across their faces. The day's heat still radiated within the walls of the house, yet Frank felt a bone-numbing chill his heart recognised long before his mind. Weary beyond mere exhaustion, he sat back while Nicky fed him the rest.

'Forensics have just about cleared the scene, but the real results won't start coming through until tomorrow. They're still doing a few little jobs around the house, but nothing essential. You're right about him being good at what he does, though. Reports from the other scenes of crime say he hasn't left a thing. No fresh fibres that didn't match clothes or substances in the house. No hairs, no footprints outside, no tyre tracks. Not a single witness either.'

'This bastard's a sick freak, not a fucking ghost.' Frank shook his head and probed his eyelids once more. 'They all leave something, Nicky. They leave something and take something away with them. That's just the way it works. In his case, semen may be all we have. But it'll do for him when the time comes. More likely, though, is that something was missed by forensics. That's just the way it works, too. Either that or what has been found will only make sense once we have someone in custody. Okay, so we have nothing to go on with the physical side of the investigation at present. How about the psychological aspect?'

'Right. The local investigation is now being officially linked with the others, handled and co-ordinated here by SO1 East. The media will be informed first thing in the morning, so watch the shit hit the fan then. It's the first of the series in the capital and the Met have the resources to cope. By tomorrow we should have everything the other areas have on this bastard. As soon as we do, our own profile will be put together to merge with theirs.'

SO1 East is the major enquiry team for the eastern section of the Metropolitan area. Headed by a senior investigations officer – in this case Superintendent Foster – officers from division would be dragged in for the duration. Frank was aware that Nicky Loizou had volunteered immediately after the bodies had been identified.

He nodded. 'Okay. Print me out as much documentation on this as you can, please. I don't care who else has worked on this, I'll do my own eliminations.'

'Will do,' Nicky said. 'I'll get Capel on it first thing.'

'Good. But what do we have right now? Serial killers usually don't stray too far from home, but you say he's done the same thing in seven different areas. That suggests he doesn't pick the location at random, but has a purpose for being there. What does that make him? Salesman? Lorry driver? Do we have another Sutcliffe on our hands?'

'Those two are the most obvious occupations. But checks have been made nationwide, and all likely suspects who are or were in either of those jobs have been questioned. No one matches with this MO exactly. Fact is, no one comes even close to it. This appears to be a new sick puppy on the block, Frank.'

Frank snorted. 'The Yorkshire Ripper was missed several times, even after questioning, and despite being thought suspicious by several officers. An FBI agent from the Quantico Behavioural Science Unit, who was on a visit here at the time, made several suggestions that were very close, yet still the man was missed. Blind luck nailed him in the end, not detective work.'

'I know, I know. But we have to rely on the information at hand. We can't second guess every single statement.'

'We'll do a local search, of course?'

'Sure. The collator worked on it all afternoon. Nothing so far. It's all being put through HOLMES, which we've been hooked up to, but again no match as at eleven-thirty when I left.'

Frank hoped that whoever had been delving into the Home Office's vast crime database knew their stuff. There was definitely a knack to shaping the queries, and some people seemed to find what they wanted with supreme efficiency.

Frank massaged his temples. Blood pounded in them, and he felt his own pulse throbbing in his neck. 'You said the girls he took were all of a similar age and type. Yet another aspect that suggests they weren't random selections. He didn't just pick them off the street. He was specific in his choices.'

'Information will be sketchy until tomorrow, Frank. But what you say sounds about right.'

Frank got to his feet and walked across to the French windows. His legs felt heavy, body weary, mind pounded by surges of grief and outrage. He stared out at the night and sighed, misting the glass pane. When it cleared, his reflection stared back. A sorry sight. Ravaged, sagging face. Dark empty sockets.

'When that information comes in from the other six crime scenes, Nicky, I'd like a copy of each one.'

'Of course. It'll be interesting to study the similarities.'

'Not just the similarities. I want to itemise every single aspect. The similarities may give us the answer as to why he's doing this, but it's the anomalies that'll bring us closer to him.'

'I'll get it all to you as soon as I can.'

'Cheers. Now, go home, Nicky,' Frank said. He turned and regarded his friend fondly. 'I can't thank you enough for your help, but you go and get some rest, mate. You deserve it.'

Nicky stood immediately, clearly not about to argue. 'I'll see you tomorrow,' he said wearily. 'Maybe it'll have moved on a pace or two by then.'

Frank sniffed. The shadows gathered around him. He felt diminished by the pain he was feeling. 'I wouldn't bet on it. This fucker knows exactly what he's doing.'

'They all make mistakes eventually, Frank.'

'Not all.' Frank was shaking his head. 'Most, I agree. But not all.'

'We'll get him. I promise you.'

'I can't do anything for Janet or Gary now. They're both gone, and eventually I must come to terms with that. But I have to believe that Laura is still alive, that I'll get my daughter back. I have to cling to that belief as I try to know him. What I don't understand right now is *why* he takes them. What does he want with them?'

Nicky said nothing. Frank understood; there was little his friend could say that would be at all comforting. The two men headed out into the hallway. At the front door, Nicky paused, hand on the latch. 'Frank, I…I have to ask. We need a formal identification. I could do it, but–'

He raised a hand to forestall the question. 'It's okay. I'll go over to the hospital mortuary tomorrow morning.'

'Mr Clarke's parents have already made their ID.'

'Dickhead,' Frank said, softly.

Nicky frowned. 'What?' He shook his head.

'That's what Gary called him. Debs told me on Saturday that Gary didn't like Clarke, so out of earshot he would call him Dickhead. I told him off about it on Sunday, then we both had a good laugh.'

The two men chuckled, then were quiet for a moment.

'Would I have been able to save them, Nicky?' Frank searched his friend's eyes once more. The place where any truth would be found. 'I mean, if I hadn't fucked up our marriage, would Janet and Gary still be alive? Would Laura be here with me now?'

Nicky squeezed Frank's upper arm and shook his head forcefully. 'Don't do this, mate. Don't beat yourself up. You've had enough of a battering for one day, and putting yourself through the wringer won't do any good. Look at it a different way: if you'd been there, you may well be dead now, and then who would be helping us find Laura? No, the only one to blame here is the sick fucker who did it.'

Unconvinced, Frank nodded but said nothing.

'I'll see you tomorrow, mate. I'll get you into the house as soon as I can, let you have some time there alone. Take care.' Then Nicky was gone.

* * *

Within seconds of his friend's departure, the emptiness of the house spoke to him from every darkened recess. It reached out with familiar voices. He heard Gary calling down the stairs; Janet answering from the kitchen; Laura telling them both to be quiet because she was on the phone to one of her many friends. He heard their laughter echoing from every room, their tears, their joy, their sorrow. They were here with him now. All around him.

With an ache that threatened to cut him in two, Frank realised that he could smell Laura's sweet cheap scent. He sniffed the air, drew it in, not wanting to let go. He couldn't name the perfume, but he was able to place its origin: it was the first bottle that Laura had ever bought for herself, with her own money. It was kept here, not at Dickhead's house. Here. With him. Where it mattered.

Frank thought ahead to the formal identification. The act of purging oneself of any lingering doubts. People always wanted to do that right away, to see their loved ones as soon as possible, confirming the horror already held within their heart.

Not him.

He knew he ought to have done it by now, so that the post-mortem could be performed. But today they would have been horrific. Today the bodies of the people he had loved would have left a bitter, sour taste in the mouth that would have lasted an eternity. Tomorrow morning, Janet and Gary would be unrecognisable as corpses. Their wounds would be under wraps, faces twisted by pain and death relaxed once rigor had left them. He would see them as he always had in life, not how they were in their moment of passing. He had no desire to remember them that way. It was no memory to have.

Staggering slightly under the crushing weight of his loss, Frank locked the doors and windows, turned off the lights and dragged himself upstairs. Locking up was a ritual that seemed somehow perverse at this moment. What or whom was there to keep safe now? The thing he feared most could not be kept at bay by locks and bolts. The thing he feared most could rise up at any time from inside his own head. The thing he feared most was that single moment when merely believing he would never see his wife or son again became a certain knowledge. Nothing anyone could physically do to him could possibly hurt him more.

Before turning in for the night he ran a steaming hot bath, poured in the remaining few crystals, realised at the last moment that they were Laura's and wondered if the empty glass jar was a portent. He stripped off and lay back in the bath, eyes closed against the piercing light and an unrepentant, monstrous world. His hands drifted in the water and moved unconsciously against something solid. It was Gary's toy Minions frog. Frank held it up in front of his face, gave it a gentle squeeze. It offered a faint, apologetic croak.

Frank ran his hand gently over the frog's back, before placing it by the side of the taps. Then he slumped back into the water and wept until he was dry, finally realising that the thing he actually feared most had already happened.

Chapter Seven

At six-twenty the next morning, Frank Rogers struggled his way to consciousness through a pain so intense he thought his head might implode.

He hadn't thought to draw the curtains before rolling into bed, and now the glare from a rapidly ascending sun was stabbing him through the bedroom window. For just a fraction of a second he thought the headache was the worst thing he had to deal with that morning. Then he recalled how he had come by it, why he'd drunk so much in the first place. Truth rushed in to claim his soul once more. His wife and son were dead. Laura was in the hands of a madman. He didn't know whether he'd ever see her again, but he was certainly going to see Gary and Janet one last time.

Frank eased himself up and swivelled sideways, fingering small, dry nuggets from his eyes. He stood uneasily, body aching as it had never done before. He winced and whipped his head to one side as shafts of sunlight seared his bleary vision like molten razors. He padded barefoot into the en-suite bathroom, ran cold water into the sink and splashed it over his face. Standing upright once more, he let out a groan. Someone other than himself waited for him in the mirror: an old man with the pallor of a cadaver, eyes that have seen what awaits them in hell, and hair that looked greyer and thinner than it had just twenty-four hours earlier.

The cold water wasn't enough. Not by a long way. He took a long massaging shower, had a wet shave, and brushed his teeth twice. For the first time in more than six months he wiped on some aftershave. Then he put on his best black suit, and a blue silk tie that Laura had given him for his last birthday. As he knotted it with uncoordinated fingers, Frank saw Laura step into the bedroom. Looked at his daughter holding out the lovingly wrapped package, a proud smile beaming out of her face.

'Happy birthday to you …' she sang, laughing and clapping at the end. Getting as much enjoyment from giving a present as she did from receiving one. He forced the image away, but Laura continued to follow him around the bedroom.

No tears, Frank, he told himself. *Not now. But tell me, who are you getting dressed up for? Janet? Gary? They won't notice. Not anymore.*

It didn't matter that they wouldn't notice, he decided. It felt like the right thing to do.

The inside of his grubby Renault was already like an oven. He popped the sunroof, powered down his dusty window and cranked the engine. It was another beautiful day; brilliant blue sky, a few fine and wispy clouds, a gentle breeze that whispered and caressed. Just the kind of weather you'd want when visiting your loved ones.

He drove slowly, concentrating on the road ahead, a shimmer of heat-haze guiding the way. The rest of the world passed him by without a care. It was the usual summer fare; dresses were thin and short, flesh was browning, there were more smiles to be seen than at any other time of year, except perhaps for Christmas. Frank didn't think he'd ever feel like smiling again. For the rest of his life, summer would mean death and tragedy.

* * *

Sebastian Reeves was the Home Office pathologist who had attended the scene of the crime. He would now be involved with the police and various forensic teams until the investigation was complete. A heavy, rotund Cornishman, his face was permanently flushed and slick with sweat. Habitually he wore a bow-tie to work, the darker ones looking like squashed bats beneath a vast array of chins. He was known as the 'gentle giant', for despite his size he was timid and shy and awkward. More at ease with the dead than the living.

Frank had known him for several years now. As Frank came through the swing doors of the hospital mortuary, Seb happened to be standing at the reception area. He looked up from a clipboard. The expression on his face said it all.

'I know you'll do right by them,' Frank said as they shook hands. 'Let's just get it over with.'

Sebastian Reeves looked down at his feet. It didn't matter how many times he went through this, it obviously never got any easier for the man. Corpses were cold meat to him. It was the walking, talking live ones he didn't know how to deal with.

Frank preceded him down the cool, antiseptic corridor and into the viewing room. Seb passed through to another chamber, appearing moments later with a covered trolley at the long window. He waited for a nod from Frank before carefully peeling back the white sheet.

Janet's face was beautiful. Frank stared down at his estranged wife and saw all that he had once loved about her. His legs became heavy, he felt light-headed, and the tiny room seemed to pulse and throb with life. She wasn't, couldn't be dead, and still look so good. Seb was a master at what he did, personally applying cosmetics so that the decedent would not shock. But even he couldn't bring someone back to life.

'Is this Janet Anne Rogers?' Seb's voice came from a single speaker, yet whispered around the entire room, sibilants calling out like mocking spectres.

Frank nodded once. 'It ... yes, it is.'

'Are you ready for ... to go on?' the pathologist asked. Again he paused, waiting for Frank to nod, then dragged the sheet back up over Janet's face, and wheeled the trolley out again.

Gary was the one that did it for them both.

Frank identified his son, the boy's chubby face also unmarked. Frank stood stiffly, this time unable to prevent the tears from sliding down his face. He caught them in the palms of his hands, where they glittered like tiny jewels. *What might you have been, son?* he wondered. *I would have been proud of you whatever your choice, whatever you became. Because you would have been one of the good ones.*

His eyes hardened then, narrowing. *What was the last thing you saw? Did your eyes open when he came into your room? Did you see the man who did this to you? Did you smell his blood-lust? Oh, and what was the last thing you felt? Pain? Terror? Shock? Or did you wonder why your daddy wasn't there to save you? To keep the monster away from you. Just as he always promised he would.*

Appearing by Frank's side, Seb took hold of his arm and guided him back out of the room that felt like a cold-meat locker. Frank sat in the waiting area for several minutes, time washing over him, a helpless and broken man. The receptionist made him some strong, sweet tea. Frank didn't take sugar, but he drank it gratefully nonetheless, and allowed his thoughts to gradually reassemble.

Now that the identification procedure was over, he felt curiously detached. Janet and Gary were gone. He would mourn and grieve for his son until his own time ran out, but for now he had to think only of Laura. She was his sole reason for carrying on. While there was hope, some chance that she was still alive, he had to fight the sense of loss that was threatening to overwhelm him.

He made his way home, intending to wait the day out for Nicky. The sense of frustration was intense. He was aware that if he had still been with the police service, he would not have been allowed to join the investigation. His superiors would have deemed him too close, too involved. But he would still have seen the case unfold around him, would have been informed of every single twist and turn. Now all he could do was wait for Nicky to report in – something his best friend could lose his job over.

What made the situation all the more unpalatable was Colin Foster's presence on the case. The two men had clashed repeatedly when they worked together. In Frank's opinion, Foster was everything a good copper should not be. The man took credit for the work of others – something Frank despised him for. He had risen to his current rank on the sweat and blood of other men – some of whom were Frank's friends – and could not be forgiven for such actions. Now Foster was running this, of all cases. And he would screw it up. Frank was certain of that. Even if the monster was caught, no doubt due to the efforts of Nicky and the other officers, Foster would somehow let vital evidence slip through his fingers, or make the procedural cock-up that would see the case tossed out of court. But Foster came from the right side of the tracks, he had the breeding, a father who was a high-roller somewhere on the east coast, he said the right things to the right people, and he had been a Mason since the age of twenty-two. These were the only qualifications he needed.

Frank held the man and everything he stood for in contempt, yet vowed not to let Foster get in the way of what had to be done. There was the way of the book, and then there was Frank's way. And he knew that only his way would work this time. Only his way would get his daughter back.

Sometimes you had to bend the rules.

Perhaps soon would come the time to break them.

Chapter Eight

Frank decided to call in at the office before heading home. Zoe would want to see him, and there was business to attend to. He knew he wasn't up to it – not by a long way – but recognised the fact that he had other responsibilities.

The office in the High Road was one of two perched above a video store that also housed a pool room at the back, which seemed to serve as a meeting place for local small-time hoodlums. The office entrance was separate, but from time to time Frank would spot a face he recognised as he entered or left. He knew the building was monitored by plain-clothes police officers on a regular basis, but he doubted they would ever stumble across a criminal mastermind. They were all in Marbella.

Leytonstone had undergone many changes down the years. The A12 now wound through its heart like a concrete and tarmac artery, and many new houses had been built to replace council eyesores. But while much of it was efficient, some pleasing to the eye, the rest remained squalid and neglected. The area that bordered Stratford, where Frank leased his office, was perhaps the one that least remained in the mind. The council tenement homes were grey and uninspiring, shops and houses old and dark and devoid of style. The place was going nowhere and getting there fast.

Zoe was on the phone when he entered the office. Her eyes found his, before quickly darting away again as she continued her conversation. Frank had to remind himself of her age and relative inexperience in dealing with matters of such personal sensitivity. But after she cut short the call, his young office manager surprised him with a maturity beyond her years.

'You look as if you could do with a drink, boss,' she said. Everything else, all the compassion and sympathy, could be found in her open appraisal of him.

The Langthorne was the closest pub. It was a little after one-thirty, and on a stage, that comprised of four tables taped together and covered with a stapled dustsheet, a stripper way past her sell-by date was trying to look sexy while struggling to step out of her snakeskin thong. Frank walked past with barely a glance, ordered two pints of Stella, then he and Zoe moved across to an empty table on the far side of the bar.

Before they had a chance to make themselves comfortable, a cheer went up, and Frank turned his head. The stripper had fallen off the stage, thong wrapped around the heel of her right shoe. Frank paused, saw some of the other punters moving in to help her up; probably hoping to cop a feel as they did so. He sat down heavily, drawing both hands down his face.

'Bad day?' Zoe asked.

'Oh, yes.' Frank downed half his lager in one go, nodding as he wiped froth from the corner of his mouth. 'I don't think they come any worse.'

Zoe leaned across the table and laid a hand on his. 'I was worried about you. I was going to call you last night, but I figured you'd want to be left alone.'

'You're right, but I'm sorry. I'm the one who should have called you. Let you know what was going on.'

She waved his apology away with a flap of her hand. 'You had one or two other things on your mind. All I knew was what your friend told you when he came to the office, but you were out the door so quickly I never had the chance to tell you how sorry I was.'

Frank took another swig from his glass; the plastic container a sad reflection of the type of clientele that frequented the place. 'I didn't spend too long at the … scene. I don't exactly get on with the person in charge of the investigation. I'm going back tomorrow morning. Actually, I've just returned from officially identifying Janet and Gary.'

'Christ. That must've been an ordeal.'

'I hope you never have to find out.' Frank studied his assistant for a moment. Zoe's appearance was still somewhat clown-like, but the myriad of colours seemed unusually subdued. He wondered how she'd look in black.

'What do you want me to do about the business?' she asked, lighting up a cigarette.

Frank shrugged his shoulders. 'I can't think too clearly at the moment, Zo. Fend off any calls for the time being. I may have to hire someone to do my rounds, but let's see how it pans out over the next few days, eh?'

'You're the boss. Boss.' She blew out a cloud of smoke, fanning it away with her hand.

'I know you'll cope.' He managed a feeble grin. 'If you can't stun them with your natural charm, fax them a photo and they'll feel sorry for you.'

Zoe pulled a face, wrinkling her nose. 'I'll send them a bank statement. That'll have them wetting themselves with laughter.'

Without asking, Zoe fetched them two more drinks. By this time, the middle-aged stripper had hobbled off, swiftly replaced by one young enough to cause suspicion. The girl appeared nervous, entirely ill-at-ease, her movements rigid and uncoordinated as she shed her clothing.

Frank pushed his first glass to one side, picked up the second. Again, he put away half of the lager in two thirsty swallows. 'I have no idea where to begin picking up the pieces,' he admitted. 'I've been on the other side of this on many occasions, and though I've always felt a tug of sympathy, I've never really given much thought to how people carry on with their lives afterwards.'

'It's what we do, though.' Zoe shrugged, the movement causing her huge hooped earrings to jangle. She drew on her cigarette, the end flaring brightly. 'I remember when my old man was killed in a car accident. We thought we'd never get over it. Thought we'd never laugh again, never be happy. But we came through it, we do still laugh, and I even reckon we'll all be happy again one day. You have to have something to look forward to, don't you?'

Frank set down his glass and stared at her in amazement. 'Are you sure you're not a forty-year-old who's had some amazing cosmetic surgery carried out? You're a child, Zoe. How can you be so wise?'

'Me and Yoda, eh?'

Frank laughed, in spite of himself. 'What do you know about Yoda? You weren't even born when *Star Wars* came out.'

'You're forgetting the most recent ones. Plus, one of my exes was an absolute anorak on the subject.'

Frank leaned across the table, meeting what little of her eyes he could see behind the blue makeup. 'So, tell me, how do I go about it? How do I face up to this?'

Zoe paused only for a moment, stubbing out her cigarette. Then she gave a nod and said, 'Like you've met everything else since I've known you, Frank. Head-on. The one thing I know for certain is that you won't let this grind you down. You won't let whoever did this have that satisfaction.'

'The confidence of youth,' he said, shaking his head. But as he drained his glass, he felt Zoe's words strike home with a force that made him feel almost humble, and just a little less pessimistic about what the future had in store.

Chapter Nine

The first thing Frank did when he got home was to call an undertaker, spending the next fifty minutes making ceremony arrangements. It was a solemn, soul-destroying process that no grieving person should have to endure.

When he was done, Frank stripped off his suit and changed into jeans and a plain black T-shirt. Then he fixed himself another beer and called Debbie. He told her about the identification, the drink and chat with Zoe afterwards, how numb he was feeling. She asked if she could come to the house, and he didn't have the heart to say no. Although she had once been Janet's closest friend, a good friend to the entire family for that matter, she and Frank had grown much closer after the separation. When she arrived barely ten minutes later, Debbie fell into his arms without a word being spoken. They clung to each other. It was his family, but Debbie's ties with them were strong. He had no more tears to shed for now, but he comforted her while she sobbed.

What followed was a curious unease. For a short while they sat in the living room like strangers, awkward silences forming an unseen barrier. Instead of bringing them closer together as it perhaps should have, it seemed to have driven a wedge between them. It was as if their blossoming relationship had been acceptable only while Janet and the children were around to give it their blessing. Finally, when Debbie stood to leave, Frank took hold of her arm.

'I'm sorry,' he said. 'I know this should be very different, and I'm not handling it at all well. But things have changed and I'm just not sure of anything right now. I have to get it out of my system, Debs. I have to do my best for Laura, without any distractions.'

'I understand.' She kissed his cheek, wiped her pink lipstick away with the soft pad of her thumb. 'I know this is a terrible time for you, Frank. The worst of times. You do what you have to. If you need me, I'll be there for you. Just call.'

Frank nodded, uncertain how he felt right at that moment. The future looked so desperately bleak. There seemed no room for happiness in it. Not even with this lovely woman.

* * *

On his own once more, Frank switched on the TV and set the channel to Sky News. He didn't have to wait too long for the feature he'd known would figure prominently throughout the day. An official spokesman stood outside the revolving New Scotland Yard sign, reading from a statement. Essentially, he revealed to the nation what Nicky had spoken of the previous day: that the media had hitherto been kept in the dark about certain specifics relating to each separate investigation, both in order not to feed the killer with the kind of notoriety he may have sought, and also to lessen the chance of a panic. The spokesman dismissed all suggestions that this tactic may, inadvertently, have led to the more recent murders and abductions.

Frank had asked himself this same question. But as one who had walked the official side of the fence, he knew that if he had been the senior investigating officer, he would have wanted the same limited information released to the media. While he wasn't aware of the exact details not provided, he knew the kind of things investigators liked to keep away from the public.

The news item concluded with a reporter casting doubt on the Yard's assertions that the restricted release had been the correct procedure to follow. Frank had crossed swords with the media on several occasions, and his guess was that their self-serving attitude would be seen by the general public for what it was.

Instead of moving to an unrelated item, the news segued into a piece on the abducted girls. Frank found himself staring at a photograph of his own face, taken many years before during a particularly harrowing murder investigation. A female anchor gave a brief outline of Frank's work as a detective, before mentioning his more immediate connection with the item. Suitably sombre, the woman spoke about Laura as if they were old pals, finishing her spot by posing a question: just how involved would Frank Rogers be in the current investigation?

Frank swore and jabbed the remote's standby button.

* * *

By the time Nicky arrived, Frank had emptied the fridge of beer. He'd made a half-hearted attempt to eat, but food was no solace.

'You look like shit,' Nicky said as he came through the door.

'Thanks for those few kind words.'

'Well, you do. Got a drink?'

'All out of booze, I'm afraid.'

'No wonder you look so rough.' Nicky shook his head as he walked along the hallway. 'Frank, you need to keep a clear head. If you want in on this investigation, then you're going to need all your wits about you. We both know all about Foster, and he's nothing if not sneaky and determined. I've had to prise Capel away from me tonight with a fucking crowbar. By tomorrow he'll have to be surgically removed. Foster's told him to stick to me like shit on a blanket. He knows how far back you and I go. He's desperate to keep you out of this.'

'Can't you have a word with Warren? Give him the full SP on Foster?'

Nicky pursed his lips. 'To tell the truth, I don't how much I can trust him. I'm pretty sure he wouldn't go running to Foster, volunteering the information. But if it all goes tits up, I think he'd drop me right in it. I have a feeling he and Foster are like this.' He crossed the middle and forefinger of his right hand.

Frank gave a weary nod of resignation. 'You can't blame him, I suppose. You can't expect him to put his career at risk the way you are. I don't mean anything to him.'

'I'm not doing this just for you, mate. I'm doing it because of Janet and Gary as well. I'm also doing it because I think working with you will get us to Laura quicker than working with anyone else.'

They moved into the kitchen, where Frank made a pot of coffee. The two men sat at the dining table, smoke coiling from one of Nicky's occasional cigars. It clung to the ceiling like a low-lying mist. At times like this, Frank wished he'd never given up smoking. Chewing gum, as he was now, just didn't have the same soothing effect.

'Have you seen any of the news items?' Nicky asked.

'Yep.'

'How d'you think we came out?'

'Okay. There'll be the usual few who will disapprove of any stance made by the police, and some of the rags will make you all look like PC Plods. Most won't think about it one way or another.'

Stifling a yawn behind his hand, Nicky gave quick nod.

Frank stared hard at his friend, whose eyes were already ringed with bruises of neglect that were as familiar to Frank as his own heartbeat. Major cases had a way of leeching away your very essence.

'Do you have someone to go home to these days?' he asked.

Nicky's reputation as a womaniser was well known throughout the Met. He'd dated women from dozens of different stations in various areas, and his sharp looks and style were almost legendary. Nicky's family had come to England from Cyprus when he was just two years old. His dark good looks were complemented by a build that made him stand out in a crowd. He liked to look good, so he wore the best clothes he could afford. His laconic nature and overwhelming presence attracted women to him in numbers.

Nicky was shaking his head firmly. 'You know what it's like, old son. Believe me, there are times when I'd like nothing more than to come home to a family, meal on the table, chilled wine in a glass. But the job is a killer of relationships. I don't have to tell you that.'

'Maybe. But remember, Janet left me *after* I'd quit.'

'Sure, but the damage had been done by then. Not many women want a man who often shares her bed for just a few hours a night, who spends most weekends either working or thinking about work, who hasn't got time for her needs, who is hardly aware of her presence most of the time.'

Frank drank his coffee black and strong. Its bitterness drilled into him. 'We're fucking clichés. Maybe we should have stayed with the Woodentops, out on the beat. Sure, they do shift hours, but they're pretty regular. Wives tend to know when their husbands will be home. Anything above that, like CID, fraud, vice, and you become the invisible man.'

They fell silent for a while. Each had his own memories to call upon, his own thoughts and aspirations to wrestle with. Eventually, Frank drained his cup and asked how things were progressing.

Nicky rubbed his eyes, shook his head. 'This fucker is slippery, Frank. If we catch him, though, we'll nail him on the DNA taken from his semen. There was a trail of blood leading from the main bedroom, into the other two, down the stairs, and into the kitchen. None of it his, so it would seem. Expecting results from the lab later today. No blood outside, so he must have changed in the kitchen. But no good footprints, I'm sorry to say. Not one clear, recognisable mark. By the time he came down to the kitchen the blood had just about been wiped clean.'

'No hairs?'

'None.'

'Are forensics certain?'

"Fraid so. The fresh hairs they found belonged there, while others had been lying around too long for them to be our man's. He either wears something over his entire head, or he's bald. All we really have to work with is the blood type we got from the semen, and his experience with locks.'

'What about the MO cross-check?'

'Again, nothing. If he's an old hand, then he's changed his MO completely. You know as well as I do how unlikely that is.

The only thing we can be reasonably certain of is that he's not going to hand himself to us on a plate.'

Frank clasped his hands together and raised them above his head, trying to stretch some life into his body. Nicky was right: he had gone to shit, in just a couple of days.

Twilight cast gloom around the kitchen. Shadows pressed against the two men. Nicky pushed his cup to one side, cleared his throat and said, 'His psychological profile is interesting. There's a consensus of opinion, too.'

Frank blinked. 'Go on.'

'He's either a sociopath or a psychopath, not psychotic. There's no sense of urgency or panic in what he does, as there would be with a psychotic. He's very deliberate. The profile says he's white and probably in his early or mid-thirties. He will be holding down a reasonable job, or possibly be self-employed. He's a creature of habit: the time of each incident, method of entry, killing the pet even though it doesn't seem necessary to what he does after. There's the usual spiel about him being badly treated as a kid. They think he takes the girls in order to replace someone in his life. But not for sex. Sex isn't what drives him. Although he masturbates over the mothers, he doesn't appear to have sex with them, or any of the other females he's killed. Could be he's looking to either replace a daughter, or take one he's never been able to have.'

Frank sucked in air. Whoever had put the profile together was good, but they needed more. He closed his eyes. Saw a vague outline standing over Janet, spattering his semen over her face.

'Hmm. I think he likes to watch.'

Nicky raised an eyebrow but said nothing.

'He doesn't have sex,' Frank went on, 'but I think he gets his kicks by watching. I think he does his masturbating while they're alive, not post-mortem as I thought previously. The opportunity for rape is obvious, but instead he gets *them* to perform, to screw, or just touching each other, maybe. Before or after death he has the opportunity of entering the woman, but he resists. And I don't believe that jerking off over a dead woman is enough for him.'

'But not all of the women were vaginally penetrated.'

Frank opened his eyes. 'I'm not saying it's part of the ritual. I just think that on these occasions the need has come upon him. Not necessarily the need to see them screwing, but the need to demonstrate his power over them, his control of the situation. It's not a part of his psychological signature. Something triggers this in him. Maybe it's the woman's looks, or perhaps the attitude of the man. It could be a punishment for something said or done. And if he does force them to screw while he watches, is he a voyeur by nature? He must have built up to this point, so maybe he was done for peeping in the early stages, or even flashing. Try to link that with the rest of what you have, Nicky. Stick it into the system and see what comes up.'

'It's worth a try. Could be right.'

'We'll see. Nicky, I need to get inside the house.'

His friend regarded him in the gathering dark. 'I know I promised you, mate, but it's risky. The area's still sealed off by forensics.'

'No problem. You don't even have to do it underhanded. Remember, as far as two of the victims are concerned, I'm the next of kin. Go to Foster. Tell him I want to sort through Gary's things. I have a right to them.'

Nicky stubbed out his cigar and wafted the smoke away from his face. 'You cover all the angles, don't you? Did that just enter your mind, or did you have it all worked out?'

Frank thought about it for a second or two, then shrugged. 'I'll be damned if I know. I suppose it was there in the back of my mind.'

Nicky met his friend's even gaze. 'Are you sure you want to see it, Frank?'

'Certain.'

'Then I'll arrange it first thing. I hope to have all the documentation for you as well within a day or two.'

Frank nodded to himself. Nicky would be as good as his word. It was still early in the investigation, so there was nothing else to consider. The two men sat for a while talking about other, unconnected things. Neither touched on Frank's loss. The only other thing Frank discovered that night was that gum tasted like shit if you drank coffee at the same time.

* * *

Later, when he was alone and surrounded once more by familiar shadows, Frank sat in Gary's room for more than an hour. He knew it was morbid, and really didn't want to dwell on the boy's memory just then. But for some reason the simple act of being in the room filled him with purpose. The four walls ought to have encompassed life for many years to come, yet that life had been snuffed out by a stranger. Sitting there on the bed, staring at all the things Gary had held so dear, Frank vowed to avenge his little boy.

In every corner, lurking in every dark recess, the image of the killer began to form. He was unknown, yet already they had figured out so much about him. And while he had no recognisable features, his profile was taking shape. He was being assembled out of nothing, and Frank sensed they were working along the right lines. Time was their biggest enemy now. And time was as devoid of compassion as any killer.

He went to sleep that night in Laura's room, allowing her presence to slip around him, to enter his pores. He wasn't afraid of it. Instead he found it comforting. He felt Laura by his side, enjoyed her warmth merging with his body heat, felt her heart beat in time with his own. They even wept together.

In the early hours of the morning he awoke from a dream, tried to hold onto it, but it faded quickly, like a nervous laugh. He felt sure that Laura had been part of it, and that she was safe. Unharmed. For the remainder of that restless night he clung to the thought like a drowning man to a raft.

Chapter Ten

Nicky Loizou was as good as his word. By eight-thirty the next morning, Frank was stepping over the threshold of the home his wife had shared with Paul Clarke. The house was still bustling with activity, though the scene of crime investigation was gradually winding down. Media with nothing better to do continued to gather together across the street, waiting for a fresh announcement, some movement on the investigation. Though they had reluctantly agreed to a request from the chief superintendent that they keep clear of Frank's home during this time of enormous strain, out here he was in their domain and up for grabs. As one they jostled forward, elbows digging, calling out to him, cameras whirring, microphones thrust forward on long boom poles. Frank didn't so much as glance in their direction.

Inside the house, a few remaining detectives and the forensics team worked relentlessly, all with but one thought: to find the all-important clue, the one that was going to break the investigation. As Frank stood in the hallway, aware that his mouth had become dry, someone called out his name. He looked up to see the ruddy features of Detective Sergeant Tom Whelan.

It didn't matter where he went or in whose company he was, Whelan always had an MP3 player clipped to the waistband of his trousers, and a pair of headphones either wrapped around his neck or placed over his ears. The first time Frank had met him he asked to have a listen. Whelan duly obliged. Expecting something soft and lyrical and typically Celtic, Frank couldn't have been more surprised when he heard the thunderous crash of waves beating against a rocky shoreline. It was the only thing

Whelan ever listened to and, as crazy as it seemed to others, it kept him relaxed and on top of his game.

Frank shook the man's enormous hand. Whelan, a large, brooding Dubliner, clasped him warmly. 'Good to see you again, Frank. I only wish it were in better circumstances.' His lilt was as pronounced as ever, though he hadn't once returned to the Republic since moving across the water when he was fifteen.

'Thanks, Tom.' Frank nodded his appreciation. 'Good to see you, too. It's been a long time.'

'You never did come back for that drink you promised us.'

'No. Sorry. In the end, I just couldn't face it. Too many memories, good and bad.'

Whelan gave a gentle smile. 'Ah, I understand. I'd be the same, I suppose. Not that I'm thinking of leaving, you understand. What the hell else is there for an ex-copper? Security work?'

'You could try collecting debts.'

Whelan nodded. 'I hear your business is going okay.'

'Up and down, Tom. Like everything else. Where did you hear that?'

The man tapped a thick finger against the side of his nose. 'I ask around and I keep my ears open. You might be out of sight, Frank Rogers, but you'll never be out of this particular copper's mind.'

'That's much appreciated, Tom.' Frank peered up the stairway, angling his neck. 'Look, I need to go into the bedrooms. Is that okay by you?'

'Nicky told me to expect you. You want your family's things.'

'Not all, just a few items. To tell the truth, part of me just needs to see it. I want to get a feel of the scene.'

'Your call, Frank. I don't know as I would want any part of it in your place, but … well …' He shrugged.

'I know. Even I can't think why I would want to see where it all happened.'

Whelan accompanied him up the stairs. On the landing, where the corridor split both ways, he stopped and sighed heavily, shaking his head. 'It's a terrible thing, Frank. Bad enough what the bastard did, but when you know one of your own is involved ... Ah, listen to me. Never could keep my big mouth closed.'

'It's okay, Tom. I don't think it's really got to me yet. Thankfully. I suppose the knowledge that Laura is still out there somewhere is keeping me on the edge. If she had been murdered too, well, I don't think I'd be walking on this side of sanity right now.'

The DS nodded, then inclined his head. 'Foster said you were to collect a few things and then go. Said I was to stick to you like glue and make sure you did just that.' The big man grinned. 'So, you just take your time looking around on your own.'

'Are you sure?'

Whelan appeared wounded. 'Of course. Foster's a prick, and even if he weren't I could never turn you away from this. The end room the way you're facing is the one ... the one Janet was found in. First one was your boy's.' He turned to glance back over his shoulder. 'Laura's is back there, past the bathroom.'

'Thanks. I really do appreciate it. Give me a few minutes, Tom.'

'Right.' Whelan marched down the landing to the far bedroom. He leaned in and said something out of Frank's earshot. He came back with two of the forensic team in tow, neither of whom Frank recognised. 'I'll stop anyone heading upstairs until you come back down,' Whelan said. The balusters rattled at their descent.

Frank drew in a deep breath. Let it go in one long sigh. He moved slowly. Past Gary's room. Door closed. Past a picture on the wall: a Japanese Samurai warrior waging war against a dragon in flight. One of Janet's favourites.

Mine, too. Didn't even realise she'd taken it until now.

The door to the main bedroom was standing wide open. Frank paused on the threshold, craning his neck to peer in. First impressions were always important. The post-mortem results were in, and from Nicky he had earlier learned that Paul Clarke's carotid artery had been severed. If Frank hadn't known, he would have been able to guess. It was impossible to ignore such a huge quantity of blood.

His eyes strayed to the twin bedside cabinets. The one to the right held a lamp, a pair of wire-framed spectacles, a copy of *Time Out* magazine. Had to be Paul Clarke's side of the bed. On the one to the left was a leather-bound book, next to a glass with a finger of orange juice left in it. Janet often took a drink to bed with her. *Especially if she's going to make love.* The book looked like something from her Dickens collection. A thin film of scum floated on the surface of the juice.

The arterial spray was on the right-hand side of the room. Clarke had managed to move – or perhaps he'd fallen off the bed. Either way, he hadn't got very far. The spray cut a swathe across the far wall and the first two-thirds of the drawn curtains. Where it ended, there was a pool of blood on the thick pile carpet, congealed now to a black crust.

Janet had died where she lay. Her blood was concentrated on the sheets and pillowcase, with just a few spatters on the headboard and wallpaper beyond.

Did you fight him? Frank wanted to know, recalling his wife's loathing of monsters in any shape or form. *Or did you do what he wanted, hoping he would get his kicks and then leave you alone? Did you hope that if he got what he wanted from you, he wouldn't go near the children?* Frank looked for answers from the room and got nothing in return. Janet would have fought to her last breath to save the children, of that he was certain. Her life had been superficial in many ways, but she had worshipped Gary and Laura.

He pulled a small notebook out of his hip pocket; old habits. He flipped over the cover and glanced down. According to the report submitted by Sebastian Reeves, Paul Clarke sustained sixty-four wounds. Janet had received fifteen fewer. The weapon was a breadknife, heavy seven-inch serrated blade, matching the Sabatier set downstairs in the kitchen. Frank put an asterisk by the side of that notation. He wrote: *Breadknife? Does he always use victims' own knives?*

Stepping inside the room, Frank slowly began to pace its perimeter. He smelled Janet everywhere, even above the cloying coppery odour of her blood and that of her lover. Her silk kimono hung on the wardrobe door. The sight of it stabbed him. His gift to her, two Christmases ago. They had made love while she wore it that same night. Two black stockings lay draped across a pine ottoman. On the floor beside it were a black suspender belt and a black lacy bra.

So, you wore them for him, did you? You wouldn't for me. Not even when our sex life was on the wane. Not even when I told you I thought it would spice it up a bit for both of us. So why him, Janet? Why did you wear them for him and not me? Why?

Frank looked away, needing to get his mind back on track. There was no time for petty jealousies, and he saw now how futile such feelings were. His eyes flicked everywhere, narrowing in concentration as he tried to smell the beast, tried to know him. Not that he ever expected to get deep inside the man's mind. That would almost certainly prove too harrowing an experience. No, his own initial investigative methods were not intended to understand why someone did what they did, more to learn how they had discovered their victims. If he could find that out, then maybe he could also trace a route back.

One thing was clear: they hadn't been chosen at random. The abducted girls were the lure. All were of an age, similar build, similar hair colour and style. But where had the monster first seen them? At what point did he decide to kill and abduct? For that matter, why kill anybody, why not just abduct the child? There was far more risk involved in taking on an entire family, so why kill them?

Frank nodded to himself, the answer both obvious and familiar. The man killed because that was the part he enjoyed. The abduction was necessary, the reason for being there at all, but the killings were a pleasurable aside. And not even the blood spilled by two adults had satiated the beast. Gary would not have put up much of a fight, he could easily have been subdued and left alive. Instead the man had murdered him simply because it gave him a thrill. Because he could.

For a second, Frank felt something stir within him. For the briefest of moments, he felt as if he himself was a monster, looking down on this family in the dead of night, wondering who to slaughter first, smiling and laughing as he wielded the blade. In that instant he was no longer himself, but a man he did not recognise as human.

No person, no *sane* person, could possibly choose to inflict such horror upon an innocent family. No animal, either. Only a monster could do such a thing. And whoever had visited this house with such evil intent had been a monster, but a monster of the very worst kind.

A monster in human guise.

Chapter Eleven

Closing his eyes for a few seconds, Frank steadied his breathing, allowing the giddy moment to pass, slowly bringing himself back. In his mind, he saw the outline of a man edging through the garden, keeping to the shadows, slowly making his way to the kitchen door. A man of great cunning. A man apart.

You came in through the back door. Just took the fucking lock apart, didn't you? Then you killed the cat – Laura's cat. *Not just any cat, you fucker – and then you went hunting. You found Clarke and Janet asleep. Did you know they'd already made love? I do. The semen inside her was Paul Clarke's and had been there for several hours before she died. Sebastian Reeves says she may have been entered again later, when she was dry. Was that you? Or was it him? Did you make them do it, but he couldn't come a second time? Or did you do it and pull out at the last moment?*

He hung his head and shook it. *No. If it happened at all, it was Clarke. Had to be. If you had put yourself inside her, you wouldn't have wasted your semen on her face. You kept to your usual MO, but it must have been tempting. Janet was fit, she had a terrific body. Didn't you want to enjoy it? Be a part of it for just a few seconds? Be inside her. You had the control, you had the time. But just as before, you masturbated instead. Such a waste for you. Why? Why do you not rape them?*

Frank's eyes sprang open again. *So, after you'd shot your wad you killed them. Who first? No contest. Him: a quick slash across the throat. Then Janet: several quick stabs. Immobilise her while you run around the bed to finish him off. Clarke staggers away from the bed, but you reach him easily. You put him down, then back to her. Taking it in turns to ruin them.*

Why so many wounds? Though your purpose here was to abduct a child, you enjoyed every second of this violence, but even then, just killing them wasn't enough for you, was it? You had to butcher them, disfigure them, too. Are you disfigured? Is that why?

Angle of entry tells us you're right-handed and probably taller than average, and we also know by the depth of penetration that you are strong. Even managed to carve your way through a few bones. Some of your type like to mess their victims up even after they are dead, but apparently, you don't get your kicks that way. You enjoyed yourself for a while, but when they were gone that was it. Game over. Move on to fresh prey.

His mind tossed stray images and thoughts around like leaves in a gale. *You're damned good. You plan and execute with great precision, and you don't panic. You give us nothing, yet you give us nearly all we need in your semen. So why don't you care about DNA? Are you stupid? No, that doesn't feel right. Maybe you're clever. More clever than we are, at least inside your own head where it really counts. With nothing else to go on, your DNA doesn't matter a damn. It's worthless unless we catch you. So why so careful not to leave fingerprints? Because we have them on file. That's the answer. Are you aware of that? Is it that you're clever, and not a fool? Are you teasing us? Is that what you're doing? I'd like to know. I really would.*

Frank took in the room once more. Death lived here now, its fierce anger reverberating between the walls. *Did they cry out? If so, they failed to disturb either Laura or Gary, and the neighbours heard nothing. You were so cool to begin with, then so frenzied. A rage overtook you. But why? Or was it controlled aggression after all? Are we mistaking frenzy for pleasure? I think we may just be. You're an organised killer, not prone to emotion. However it was, you must have used up a lot of energy, so I suppose you took a breather. Then a soft-shoe shuffle down the landing and on into my son's room.*

Following in the monster's footsteps, the trail of blood was clear. *You didn't care about footprints, either. Why not? Fortunate for you that we weren't able to get a clear marking. Fortunate? I wonder. Or did you deliberately muddy them? Another tease as you thought ahead to the investigation that would follow? You know a lot about our procedure, that's all too obvious, but what does that mean these days? There are so many books on the subject, dozens of TV shows, it wouldn't be hard to discover how to hide your tracks.*

Gary's room was even more painful.

On the wall beside the boy's bed were his beloved football posters. Something snared Frank's attention, and when he stepped forward to take a closer look, the breath froze in his lungs. Gary's favourite player was Jack Wilshere. There was one drop of blood on the entire team poster. It covered the Arsenal midfielder's face.

Did you do that deliberately? Did you ask my son who his favourite player was before wiping his own blood across the player's face?

On a bookshelf was an autographed football. Frank blinked. He and Gary had waited outside the Arsenal training ground one afternoon for the players to leave. They managed to get eight signatures. Frank could still see his son's face, beaming as his heroes made their scrawls, some even taking time for a word or two. It was one of the few treasurable moments, from too few hours spent together. Frank turned away before the rest of the room fully registered.

Laura's room was next, and it was disturbingly normal. She obviously hadn't put up a fight. *What did you tell her to keep her quiet? Laura would not go with you willingly.* Here again there were so many things that had once been in her bedroom in his own home. *Would she ever see them again?* he wondered. *And if so, would they forever be tarnished?*

He stared for some time at the bed, quilt drawn to one side. Then he stepped forward and touched a hand to the bottom sheet. For one impossible moment, it felt warm to the touch, as if his daughter had left it only seconds before. When the moment passed, the sheet just felt cold and somehow repugnant to him.

Frank searched the wardrobe and found a small leather holdall, into which he carefully placed some of Laura's clothes. Enough for a few days. He was about to walk out when something seemed to leap out of her dressing-table mirror at him. Laura didn't have many stuffed toys left from her younger days, but the few she had kept were cartoon characters. Of these, her favourite was Tigger. Frank popped him into the bag, too.

Downstairs, in the large and comfortable conservatory, he found Tom Whelan once more. 'Okay, you can send the team back up now,' he told the sergeant, who swiftly passed on the message.

When they were alone once more, Frank felt the weight of Whelan's shrewd scrutiny for several moments. The DS eventually shook his head and said, 'No tears? That's bad, Frank. Very bad. You've just seen the rooms in which your wife and son were brutally murdered. It's okay to cry for them, mate.'

Frank looked at him and spread his arms. 'I know it is. And I will. When the time is right.'

'There'll never be a better time. And it's not just okay, it's expected. Let it go. You have to let it go, Frank. It'll eat you up inside otherwise, as well you know.'

'I will, but not right now, Tom. I've done some crying. The rest, the real grieving, will have to wait until I know about Laura. My life can't continue until then.'

With obvious reluctance, Whelan accepted the assurances. He walked with Frank back outside into the hazy sunlight of another hot June day, small trees in the garden providing pockets of shade on the lawn. Frank realised how dark and cold the house had seemed. Had death left its mark here? He thought so. He also believed it would remain for a long time yet to come.

He and Tom shook hands again. 'I have to complete the cremation arrangements later on today,' Frank said. 'Will you come to the ceremony?'

'Do you really have to ask?'

'I guess not.'

'What about the inquest?'

'It's set for tomorrow morning. Short and sweet. Seb Reeves is releasing the body to the coroner. He's satisfied with the post-mortem. He didn't say, but I think he hurried it through to spare me the delay.'

Whelan smiled. 'That sounds like Seb. You going to the hearing?'

'I doubt it. It's cut and dried. But at least I'll know I can go ahead with the ceremony.'

'Well, let Nicky know the where and when. I'll be there. Is it open invitation to the squad?'

'Yes.'

As Frank stepped towards his car, the media again swarmed forward, shouting questions, cameras zooming in on his face, a clamour of noise and confusion. Beat constables in blue short-sleeved shirts pushed back the tide, causing a great deal of anger and resentment once more. As before, Frank ignored them and sped away from the scene. He didn't look back.

He still felt so terribly detached, as though it were just another case. Someone else's wife and son. Some other poor bastard's misery. As he had told Tom Whelan, grieving would have to wait. The living, as always, took precedence.

* * *

It was during the seemingly endless drive home that Frank realised for the first time that, by the end, he hadn't loved Janet any more. Perhaps any residue of love had been torn from him during their months of separation. Maybe she had taken it with her into Paul Clarke's bed. Or, more likely, it had simply not been strong enough to linger beyond the walls of their relationship.

He would still mourn her, he decided. She had, after all, borne him two children, and they had spent many years together. But there would be no real grief. That he would save for Gary. Gary, but not Laura. Because his little girl was still alive, and he was damned if he was going to let death lay its hand on her shoulder.

Not while he had a single breath left in his body.

Chapter Twelve

Laura Rogers had blinked rapidly for several seconds when the thick woollen hood was finally removed from her face. She winced at the harsh intrusion of light, squinting at first, then took the room in with one careful sweep of her frightened, pitiful gaze.

The room was cavernous; long, wide and tall. It reminded Laura of the classrooms in her primary school. The ceilings were high, with moulded cornices and picture rails, and ranged along the wall opposite the door were several tall sash windows, now boarded up; wooden cataracts erected over glassy eyes.

Two rows of lights hung from the ceiling on long black cords, their shades laden with dust and cobwebs. Attached to each fixture were a number of green air-fresheners in the shape of trees, similar to those Laura had seen swinging from the rear-view mirror in her father's car. The walls had long since lost their painted sheen, and chunks of plaster had fallen to the floor.

Two tea chests lay overturned in the centre of the uncarpeted floor. Clothing spilled out of one, while inside the other lay scraps of paper, a plastic bag containing drawing equipment, and several dog-eared paperbacks. By far the most remarkable item in the room took up almost a quarter of the available space. It was a doll's house, immense and skilfully constructed from floor to ceiling. Curtains adorned all four windows, a painted display of creeper and flowers surrounded the perfectly hung panelled door. Great care and attention to detail had been lavished on it, yet its size, its sheer perfection, was somehow repellent. It was too big, too precise – and completely unwelcoming.

As her gaze swung full circle, Laura finally turned to face the man for the first time.

He smiled at her, though only one side of his face seemed to move. His thin lips became a jagged slash. 'What do you think, Laura?' he asked.

Laura said nothing. She continued to study him, natural defiance triumphing over fear. The man's appearance now looked far more normal than she had expected, much kinder than she had dared to hope. It was a face you might see anywhere, at any time. A face you would not look twice at. His bald dome gleamed, reflecting the glaring lights, picking up a hint of the pale green walls. The man who stood before her did not look at all dangerous, hardly the type to snatch a child from her room in the middle of the night.

Or to commit murder.

Even as the thought came to her, so the man's features changed. His eyes narrowed and hardened, became spiteful, his mouth a downward arc of displeasure. He repeated his question, only this time the tone of voice was harsh, perhaps even cruel.

That was when Laura felt the first flash of recognition. It wasn't just that she had seen this man before, or that she had previously laughed and smiled in his company – though she could not recall where or when. More importantly, she knew exactly what he was thinking: he wanted her to be pleased with her surroundings. Somehow, she knew that he had built the doll's house, and that he was desperate for her to enjoy what he had created. And while all Laura really wanted to do was break down and weep for her loss, she also knew it was important to please this man; that her life may depend upon it.

'It's very nice,' she said at last, trying to keep the terror from her voice. It wasn't easy. She had often received praise from her father for being mature beyond her years. Now, more than ever before, she needed to prove him right.

She was rewarded with the smile once more. It cast a different shadow across the man's face. Laura had no idea why he had taken her from her home, why she had been chosen by him, or what his intentions were towards her. But she intuitively knew that the only chance she had of emerging from the nightmare was to play along with him, to become whatever he wanted her to be.

'I'll leave you for a moment,' he said, making a small gesture with his hands. 'You can play with anything you find ... except for the doll's house. The doll's house is special and must be kept for later – when you have proven yourself worthy.'

'What about my mother? And my ...?' Laura bit her lip, eyes snapping closed in a vain effort to ward off the image of the man in her kitchen, climbing into the tracksuit. She saw the blood anyway. Black in the moonlight.

'What about them?' His eyes devoured her.

'What ... what did you do to them?'

He chuckled, eyes widening as if in surprise. 'Killed them, of course. All of them. Mummy and Daddy and brother Gary, too.'

Laura swallowed back her pain. She had known, of course. As soon as she saw the blood, knowledge filled both her head and her heart. Its awful truth seemed to swell inside her now, causing a sharp band of pain to squeeze and probe behind her eyes. Her body swayed, the room began to spin, and its peculiar odour suddenly seemed more apparent. For one dreadful moment Laura thought she might be physically sick. Her mind screamed at her, begging to be shut down, to close itself off against the misery. Her eyes filled up, but she refused to shed the tears, refused to faint, refused to throw up. Instead she latched on to the single crumb of comfort in his words.

Mummy and *Daddy*.

No. That wasn't right. He meant Paul, the man her mother had lived with these past ten months or so. He meant Paul, but he thought it was her father. This was the truth she clung to, the knowledge she embraced fully. It was the only truth she allowed herself to recognise. She had to be strong. Any weakness would be latched upon by this man, and God alone knew what he might do to her then.

As he retreated, the man blew a kiss, offered another smile, then stepped out of the room, closing the door behind him. Laura heard a key turn in the sturdy-looking lock. As his footsteps echoed and faded away, so a violent shudder ripped through her body, a spasm she thought might actually snap her bones and see them crumbling to dust.

She wanted to weep, to scream, to beat on the door with her fists and bellow her rage. But again, she somehow knew that crying would only weaken her resolve, that screaming would anger the man and send him rushing back to punish her. She would grieve later, when it was safe to do so. The overwhelming pain of bereavement could not be confronted now, or she would be lost.

The fear would concentrate her mind, however, and she did fear him. For he was the dark. And the dark could not be reckoned with.

Chapter Thirteen

Though drained by all that had taken place, Laura picked her way around the room, ignoring the open tea chests. She refused to touch a single thing. To do so would mean accepting them; accepting *him*. Laura shuddered at the thought. She wanted no part of them. As she moved, Laura hugged herself and rubbed her bare arms. The air was stale, tainted by the air-fresheners and a thick, cloying odour she could not identify.

Little more than five minutes had elapsed before she heard footsteps approaching the door. The man was not alone this time.

His voice: 'Wait until you see her. She's perfect.'

A woman's voice: 'I hope so. I really do.'

His voice: 'I said she would be, and she is.'

The key rattled once more and the tumblers snapped back with a loud clunk. The door opened slowly on well-oiled hinges.

Laura was again struck by the man's appearance. He had stripped off the tracksuit, and now wore a checked shirt tucked into black denims, bare feet encased in grey moccasins. His tall frame was slight, but well-muscled. A lean face, chin narrowing to a point. His eyes seemed too small for his head, and beneath a nose that appeared broad in comparison, thin lips were like a slit in the wan complexion. The man reminded Laura of a child's sketch.

The woman by his side was every bit as willowy, her face more orderly, though containing similar features. She wore a beige ankle-length dress of ribbed cotton, that hung on her like a sack. They both smiled as they stood in the doorway, two grinning Cheshire cats, Laura thought.

The woman nodded. 'Hello, Laura.' Her voice was shrill, buzzing in Laura's ears like a swarm of angry bees.

'Hello,' she answered at once. Laura felt no warmth emanating from this woman, no female empathy, no scent of humanity. Perhaps there was as much to fear from her as the man. She would have to bear that in mind.

The woman stepped into the room, holding out a bundle of clothing. 'Here, slip into one of these.'

Laura took the bundle without a word, careful not to make contact with the woman's hands. She felt the same way about the man and woman as she did the contents of the tea chests. Laura looked down at the tiny cotton dresses she had been given. There were four in all, each one plain and simple, old, threadbare, colour washed out. She glanced back at the woman, who nodded encouragement, her eyes dancing.

Laura turned her back and shrugged off her night-dress, then prepared to pull on one of the dresses.

'No,' the man said behind her. 'Take off your underwear first.'

Laura looked back over her shoulder. 'But you haven't given me any others.'

'Take them off all the same. And this time face us when you do it.'

As she turned, Laura felt herself grow hot in the cheeks. She was no longer comfortable being naked around her mother, and certainly would never have allowed Gary to see her that way. She felt embarrassed, ashamed and humiliated as she now stepped out of her knickers and let them fall to the floor. She guessed this had been their intention, rather than commanding her for the sake of a coarse thrill.

The couple observed her closely, almost reverently, as they might a precious object. Laura heard them both utter gentle sighs as her body was revealed. She swiftly tugged on one of the dresses, holding the others close to her chest. The dress fit reasonably well, except that it was far too short. Laura gave the man and woman a sidelong glance, wondering whether they were expecting to be thanked. Was the dress a gift?

'Perfect,' the woman said, moving closer. She brushed the back of one hand against the curve of Laura's cheek, ran tender fingers through her fine hair. She took a step behind Laura and wrapped both arms around her, burying her own face into the nape of Laura's neck. The girl felt the woman's warm breath, stale and foul, the gentle pressure of lips against her flesh. There was an unpleasant odour, like stale sweat.

Laura shivered, in spite of her control.

'Have fun, sweetheart,' the woman whispered softly in her ear. She kissed her once more, scooped up the discarded nightdress and underwear, then joined the man at the doorway. 'We are going to enjoy each other so much. All of us.'

'Find somewhere to sleep,' the man ordered. 'One of us will wake you in the morning.' He nodded and smiled magnanimously, like a kindly uncle who has taken in an orphaned niece.

The door swung shut. Locked. Footsteps moved away. Laura let out a soft groan and sank to her knees. The floorboards were warm to the touch. She felt disgusted by what the woman had done, wanted to scrub at the icy spot left behind by those filthy lips. For the first time since she had been abducted, Laura felt helpless, realising that her father would have no idea where to find her, and that she truly was alone.

Except for the man and woman.

One of them would wake her. She dreaded the moment.

Dark red blood and images of death came creeping into her thoughts. Her mother. Gary. Both now gone. Murdered in their beds. She would never see either of them again. And now these terrible people had her and she didn't know why. Did not dare to imagine what they wanted of her. The time was right for her to cry, and Laura did so.

Chapter Fourteen

The man and woman strode hand in hand back to the room they shared, along the passage from the one in which Laura had been left to contemplate her fate. Though much smaller, this room was equally stark, and infinitely less cheery than the one they had left behind. A double bed, an old TV set and a single armchair were the only items of furniture. Clothing and newspapers lay scattered over the carpeted floor, together with rotting food and discarded containers. The pervading odour was one of neglect.

The woman flashed a warm smile at him. 'She's very nice. So much better in the flesh. I think I'll enjoy her.'

He nodded eagerly. 'Me, too. Something about her I can't describe. Delicate, yet ... so aware for one so young. She has great presence. I genuinely believe she's the one, that we've found her at last.'

'Thank you, darling.'

'For you, my sweet, anything.' A slightly mocking edge filtered into his voice.

She kissed him on the cheek.

'Surely I deserve more than that.' He injected passion into his eyes. Eyes which, he was aware, seemed at once blue, grey, or even silver, depending on what light surrounded them. Whichever hue, none was warm.

The woman grinned wickedly, raising an eyebrow. 'I do feel rather excited.' She rubbed the soft pad of her hand between her legs, closing her eyes as a deep breath hissed through slightly parted lips.

Long fingers moving swiftly, the man unfastened her dress, letting it slip to the floor. She stepped out of it wearing only tan stockings. 'Keep them on,' he whispered, already climbing out of his trousers and underwear. 'I want to feel their softness slide around me.'

Together they walked across to the bed. Her hand slipped to his groin, held him, pulled at him. As his fingers sought her she said, 'No need. I couldn't be more ready.'

He grinned as he entered her with one thrust. They moved hurriedly. Together they grunted and panted like rutting animals. She licked the sweat from his brow, cursing him between flicks of her tongue. His teeth left marks on her breasts.

It was over quickly, yet he felt completely satisfied. It had always been that way. Ever since they were children. As they lay together afterwards on top of the bed covers, she held him in her hand, fingers toying with him until he was hard once more. This time she let her mouth do all the work.

Later, while she opened some cans of food, the man switched on the TV. He clicked between channels for a while, before settling for the news. Each item washed over him, until one of the presenters said something very interesting indeed.

* * *

Eyes sore and hot from weeping, Laura gathered her thoughts and concentration once more. She looked around at the room and again wondered where she was. After leaving her house through the back door, the man had pulled the hood over her face. Once out of the garden gate they had turned left. Along the rear alleyway. Into a car … no, it was a van. Before starting the engine, he had asked her that same terrible question.

Are you afraid of the dark?

She said 'yes'. He laughed.

Excellent. I am the dark, Laura. So, fear me. Fear me like nothing else.

Now Laura struggled to think, her face strained by the effort. Where had she seen him before? The voice was familiar, too. He knew her name. Knew Gary's name. How? And how would any of the answers help her right now? But she believed it was right to pose the questions. It might be important. Somehow, she had to be strong. Somehow, she had to get away from these dreadful people.

Laura glanced across at the door and felt her body shake once again. If anything, the woman had unnerved her more than the man. If he was the darkness, what did that make her? The touch of the woman's lips lingered still, a cold spot upon her neck. There was more to come, Laura felt sure. If there was any comfort to be found from this dreadful situation it was a sense that she would live for as long as she was useful to them.

But would she want to live through what they might have in mind for her? Would she want to live afterwards?

Laura found she could not answer that. She was alive now, and would be for a while yet. She had to draw strength from that, forget about the future and the past, concentrate on her present. Forget about the human wreckage she might be this time next week, forget about what he had done to Gary and her mother. See only the next minute. The next hour. Take each moment and try to draw strength from the most meagre of scraps. Somehow. Or she would not survive.

Laura willed herself to draw away from the negative thoughts, composing herself, steadying her breathing, which had become irregular. She picked herself up off the floor and moved around the room, trying to find a comfortable place to lay her head. She decided to use some of the clothing from the tea chest, together with the remaining dresses she had been given.

Sleep called to her, another way out, a haven of further denial. Still the thought of touching their things repulsed her, but Laura became aware that ultimately, she would have no choice. Finally, she came back to where her appraisal had begun: the doll's house.

It was so well crafted, even down to the beautifully made curtains, that she felt certain there would be a bed inside. Perhaps this was a test, despite the warning. Perhaps the warning had been intended as a lure. Either way, it couldn't hurt to take a look. They would never know. Carefully she turned the handle on the door, pushed gently and eased it open. The interior was less bright, shadows converging swiftly from every direction. Laura was not at all surprised to find a light switch on the wall. She flicked it down and a single naked bulb sprang to life.

The bulb was of low wattage, so the doll's house remained in gloom, though Laura could make out a small sofa in one corner, a table with four chairs arranged neatly around it, and on the far side a tiny kitchen range and a single bed. More of the green air-fresheners hung from the ceiling, held in place by drawing pins, while others lay scattered across the floor. The room seemed alive with them.

There were some dolls laid out on the bed. Huge, heavy dolls, the like of which Laura had only ever seen in the best department stores. Laura did not intend to play, and dolls were a part of her past. She was desperately tired and wanted only to lose herself in sleep. There was an urgent need to block out the misery of all that had happened, and all that her mind told her was to come. She walked across to the narrow bed, intending to push the dolls aside. It was as her hands reached out that Laura realised her mistake.

There were three of them. Not dolls at all, but other children. Girls like her. Very much like her. Only these girls were dead, and all in various stages of decomposition.

Chapter Fifteen

Frank killed the Renault's engine outside a bland, grey breeze-block building, yet remained for several minutes inside his car. A single storey high, the unit was long and wide, with a fabricated roof whose negligible slope held too much water when the rain fell. It was one of several similar buildings on the industrial estate he'd driven through. Over the blue steel-shutter doors was a white and blue sign that read:

Police
Leyton Annexe

The estate had been developed in the mid-seventies, much to the dismay of local residents. It was built on the site of a derelict factory, smack in the centre of a quiet block of houses. Residents now had to endure heavy vehicles moving up and down their narrow streets at all hours of the day. Beyond the far side of the estate, whose perimeter was fenced in by steel, playing fields stretched for dozens of acres. Those who travelled only the main roads would never have known the estate existed, if it weren't for the large sign attached to a single streetlight. The sign made no mention of the annexe, however.

Frank swallowed thickly and felt his pulse quicken. Adrenaline squirted somewhere in his stomach. He had to go inside, had to see this through. It wasn't going to be easy. Not now. Not ever again.

Too many memories. Too many scars left unhealed.

Still he sat and thought.

Little more than thirty minutes ago, moments before Nicky had called, Frank was seriously contemplating another drinking binge. The fridge and cupboards were bare, but the supermarket was nearby. They sold Scotch, they sold beer, they sold Chardonnay. It seemed like the sensible thing to do given the circumstances. He had even snatched up his car keys from the kitchen counter when the telephone rang.

Hope flared like a distress signal when he first heard Nicky's voice, but in his wildest dreams he could never have expected this new twist. It was more like being involved in a vivid dream. Things just didn't happen like this to him. In his world you got shafted, life was a pisser, and then you died. It never reached out a conciliatory hand in such a way. Life was unforgiving and brutal.

Frank snapped his eyes open. Someone was tapping on the car window. Where had he been? Where had his mind taken him? He climbed out of the car and, offering a thin, tight smile, slapped Nicky on the back.

'This is a joke, right?' he said. 'Has to be.'

Nicky held up his hands in mock surrender, shaking his head earnestly. 'It's no joke, mate. A short time ago someone called the information hotline, said he was the person we were looking for. He says he has Laura, and the other girls. He'll speak to us ... but only through you. He'll deal with you and no one else.'

'Why me, for fuck sake?'

Nicky shrugged. 'Who knows? He's never done this before. Maybe it's the link with Laura, maybe he's seen the stuff they've been running on the TV or in the newspapers about you being a copper.'

'Maybe.'

'Perhaps he sees you as a challenge. Foster didn't want to have anything to do with it, of course. He ranted and raved, saying you were off the force now. But for all his bluster and rank, even a few of the top brass know he's a prick. He was duly overruled. For now. So be warned, Foster is not a happy man. He reckons it's a hoax, anyway. Some nut.'

Frank took off his sunglasses, squinting in the glare of the sun. His eyes felt as if they had withdrawn even further into his skull.

'One sure way of telling. There are certain things you wouldn't have released to the media, right?'

'Of course. No mention of him doing the pets, no mention of his preferred method of entry.'

'Who put Foster's nose out of joint?' He was beginning to feel better about things. The SIO wouldn't go out of his way to make life easy for Frank, but he certainly couldn't be seen to be obstructing such a headline investigation.

'It was the chief superintendent himself.'

Frank nodded. 'Good old Lion.'

Lionel Badger was one of the few members of the elite hierarchy whom Frank had ever respected. The man was no bureaucrat, had never baulked at bending certain rules in order to get the job done effectively, and had never once, to Frank's knowledge, passed the buck. He was a man who stood up for his beliefs, and took both the plaudits and condemnations with the same good nature. A man after Frank's own heart.

He looked beyond Nicky. The Leyton annexe unit stood like some vast Pandora's box, waiting to unleash its terrible secrets. He cleared his throat. 'Feels strange being back. I wondered whether Foster still allowed it to be used.'

'Funny you should say that. This is the first time we've used the annexe since he took over. This operation is simply too big to handle down at Francis Road. We didn't fancy the Yard getting their hands on the case, so Superintendent Finnieston sanctioned this place again.'

'I wonder if Foster stopped using it because it was my idea in the first place?'

'I'd lay money on it.'

The annexe had only ever been used for major operations, mostly to house murder squads. Frank had always believed that the structural confinements of the old station buildings at Francis Road led to sloppiness, to documents and information being mislaid as it travelled from one room to another, even between floors. Here it could be condensed because once inside nothing left the unit, and there was room for all the officers to breathe and relax while they worked – a major factor given the tense atmosphere of murder cases.

Frank drew in one last deep breath. 'Let's do it.'

The two men walked across to a tall and narrow door set into the pitted steel roller-shutter. It was 11.55am, temperature in the mid-eighties, and Frank felt sticky and damp. Nicky, on the other hand, although he wore his shirt collar buttoned, tie firmly knotted, looked as cool as if it were a winter's day. Frank envied him as he felt the discomfort of his own short-sleeved shirt plastered tight against his back.

The incident room, as the interior of the annexe was known, was buzzing. Tables, chairs, desks and filing cabinets were scattered around all four corners of the huge area, a central snake-like plastic trunking housing all of the communications and power cables. A dozen men and three women were either speaking on the telephone, rummaging through files, consulting computer monitors, or grouped around the many incident boards. The cacophony of voices and background noise was deafening. The place had an edge to it; you could cut yourself on the atmosphere.

Frank's reputation preceded him into the unit. As he began to renew acquaintances or make new ones, there were broad and genuine smiles, words of welcome, expressions of sympathy and condolence for his loss. Behind it all he felt an overwhelming sense of enthusiasm for his return, no matter how brief it might be.

And then there was Superintendent Colin Foster.

The man glanced up from a file he was scanning, peering over the rim of his spectacles. He didn't offer to shake hands, nor was there any sign of welcome or even sympathy. If anything, his eyes spoke of open hostility.

Foster pointed to a phone and said, 'He'll be coming through on that line. *If* he calls again, which I very much doubt. I've arranged for a trace, of course. However, I presume your good friend DCI Loizou has already informed you of my misgivings.'

'You don't think the caller is kosher.'

Tight-lipped, Foster shook his head. 'No, I don't. You may recall yourself how many crank calls we get in situations like this.'

'Who took the initial call?'

'Sergeant Cunningham. I believe you know him.'

'Yes, I do. He's a good bloke. If he thought it might be our man, then I'd be willing to back his judgement.'

Foster glared at him. 'Well, I'll be sure to keep that in mind. Look, don't think you're getting your feet back under the table here, Rogers. You take the call, you deal with it in the correct manner, and then you hand it over to us to carry on with. Afterwards, you go about your business. Collect some debts, or whatever it is you do these days.'

Frank was aware of several faces now turned his way. If they were waiting for a reaction they were going to be disappointed. Whatever Foster had in mind here, it wasn't going to work. Frank wanted this. He needed it badly.

'I'll wait here by the phone,' he said. And smiled.

Foster turned away angrily, snapping an order at some poor unfortunate who just happened to be passing.

Frank turned to Nicky. 'What time is he due to call?'

His friend perched on the edge of a desk, rolling up his shirt sleeves. 'He didn't say. He just told us to get you here quickly.'

Frank nodded and looked around the unit. Nothing much had changed, either in layout or decor. The breeze-blocks had received an obligatory coat of white emulsion the day before Frank first opened its doors to the squad, and only the odd poster had been added since. His gaze fell upon the incident boards. Two rows of photographs were pinned to them. He jerked his head away before the images registered. He didn't want to see Laura's face up there with the others. His daughter was a part of this, he knew, but she didn't belong.

DS Capel wandered over, hands in pockets. He seemed a little nervous. 'How did the SOC visit go, Frank?' His thin, effeminate features belied a wiry strength. He was usually to be found at the forefront of anything that needed 'bottle'.

'Not too bad. There wasn't much to be done. Just picked up a few of my daughter's things, then let people get on with their jobs.'

'This must be a bloody awful time for you.'

'Yes. The hardest.'

'You think this caller is for real? You think it's him?'

Frank shrugged. Capel was harmless enough, a pretty good copper in his own way, but he was often too naive for his own good. 'No way of telling just yet, Warren. But I'll know. The moment I hear his voice.'

'Let's just hope he's the genuine article,' Nicky said. 'We could do with a break right now.'

'I know I could,' Frank whispered. He glanced at the incident boards one more time, then dismissed them with a shake of his head. 'There's a lot going on in here. Is it being well organised?'

Nicky nodded, eyes straying to the far end of the unit where the majority of officers gathered. 'Statement readers and receivers are ploughing through everything we've had faxed over from the other on-going investigations, in addition to the statement sheets our own people have brought in. Warren's the action officer for the squad, by the way.'

'Not a lot of jobs to hand out so far then? Not with the few crumbs this prick leaves behind.'

'There's enough to be getting on with. Teams have been sent out to speak with the other murder squads directly. There's the door-to-door around the Clarke scene. Liaison with forensics and pathology.' Nicky shrugged. 'All the mundane stuff, all actioned, any part of which might just give us that break we're looking for.'

'I'd forgotten how grinding and ordinary this work can sometimes be,' Frank admitted. 'Piecing all the tiny parts of the puzzle together.'

'Yeah. And without a picture on the box to guide us.'

Frank nodded thoughtfully. Everything that could be done was being done. Nicky and Capel were pulling all the right strings, overseeing the minutiae of the investigation. It was now just a matter of patience, and relying on your team to be thorough and alert. The bustle around him continuing, Frank sat down by the telephone to wait. He was used to waiting. He waited for ten more minutes before the call came in.

Chapter Sixteen

So lost in thought was he, that the first Frank knew about the incoming call was when an amber light flashing on the mini switchboard snagged his attention. The trace was already running, intervening some five seconds before the ringing tone could be heard by the caller.

Frank swallowed, wet his lips, drew saliva into his throat, then picked up the handset. He wasn't aware of anyone or anything else around him.

'This is Frank Rogers speaking.'

'Hello, Mr Rogers. Or may I call you Frank?' The voice emerged from speakers placed around the incident room. It was deep, calm and authoritative. It sounded a little off, and Frank suspected the caller was using a voice scrambler.

'You may.'

'I'm so glad they managed to persuade you to take my call.'

'I didn't need any persuasion. But I have to ask: why me?'

'Before I go into that, Frank, let me tell you that if you are tracing this call, I demand you stop doing so immediately. If you don't, and believe me I will know, I'll have your daughter delivered to you within the hour in a rubber bag.'

Frank froze, his testicles crawled and shrivelled inside their scrotal sac. The man meant every word. Frank cupped his hand over the mouthpiece. 'Stop the trace,' he said.

Foster looked up sharply. He shook his head, a terrible glint in his eyes. 'You haven't established the caller's credentials yet.'

'I don't need to. It's him. Now stop the trace.'

Foster's chest swelled. 'In case I didn't make myself clear to you before, Rogers, *I* am in charge of this investigation. *I* will decide how best to proceed. The trace will continue until *I* decide otherwise.'

Frank deliberately eased his hand off the mouthpiece. 'Superintendent Foster, if you don't order that trace stopped right now, I'll rip your face to pieces with this phone. My daughter's life is at stake here, and just at the moment I don't give a shit about protocol or rank. Believe me, Foster, if you lose her for me I'll end you. I'll have fuck all else to live for.'

There was a moment of complete silence. It was as if everyone inside the annexe had stopped breathing. The two men glowered at each other, the superintendent seething as a flush crept into both cheeks. Eventually, as if the enormity of the challenge had dawned on him, he lowered his gaze and barked the command for the trace to be stopped.

The voice came again over the speakers. 'Well done, Frank. You handled that very well. I'm impressed.'

Foster glared once more at Frank with open hostility, realising that the caller had been allowed to hear their side of the conversation. Frank turned away. He had won a battle, now it was time to give a little and play by a few of the rules.

'I have to establish your credibility,' he said into the phone. 'It's standard procedure.'

'But you know I'm not a crank, don't you?'

'Yes. Even so ...'

'Go ahead. Establish away.' The caller uttered a low chuckle. There wasn't anyone in the room who didn't feel chilled by the sound.

'Okay. You've obviously read the newspapers or watched the TV. That's how you latched onto me. You must know that the police didn't give all the information in their possession to the press. What I'd like are a couple of answers from you.'

'Fire away, Frank. I'm all yours.' The voice became deliberately camp.

'First, you have a particular method of entering your victims' property. One that you seem to prefer. Also, you like to do something before approaching your victims.'

How was he able to do this? The man on the other end of the line had murdered his son and wife, had abducted his daughter. How was he able to talk to him this way? So calm, so collected. If the man had been standing before him he would have killed him there and then without a single qualm. As it was he could feel a cold sweat spread across his back between his shoulder-blades, the hand gripping the phone growing clammy.

'For the record then, Frank, and anyone else listening in, I take the locks apart in order to gain access, and if there is a pet in the house I kill it before I move on to my human victims.'

There was an explosion of released air and tension. Now everyone else knew what Frank had known right from the first word. Faces turned his way. Some were frowning, others slightly wary.

Frank breathed easily. 'Okay then. You have the advantage over me right now. How about giving me a name?'

'Oh, Frank. You think I'm that easily had?'

'No, of course not. I don't expect your real name. Just one I can use when we're talking. I doubt this will be our last conversation.'

After a brief pause, the caller said, 'If you insist on calling me something, make it ... Oscar.'

'Oscar. Right. That puts us on an even footing.'

'Oh, you think so? I have your daughter, Frank. Like a god I control her every moment. I decide whether she lives or dies, I decide whether she suffers or slips quietly away. And you think we're equal?'

Frank closed his eyes. He wanted to slam the phone down, to cut off that dreadfully confident voice. But the man was correct in everything he said. 'Fair enough. You're right, of course. You have the advantage, Oscar.'

'You agree with me? When people agree with me, Frank, I always feel I must be wrong.'

'Not this time. Of course you have the edge. So, use it. What do you want?'

'Oh, you know how it is, Frank. Sometimes a man just has to turn the valve a little, release some of the pressure. What's the point of being a genius unless one is admired for it?'

'You believe you're a genius, Oscar?'

'Ha-ha. I have nothing to declare *except* my genius, Frank.'

'You ... you want to tell me something, Oscar?'

'Yes, I do. How wonderfully astute of you, knowing I want to *tell* you something rather than ask a question. I imagine you were a magnificent policeman. Can you guess what it is, Frank? I think you can. I saw your photograph. You look extremely capable. Go on, give it a whirl.'

'Let me have a moment.' Frank cupped his hand once more. He lowered his head, studying the floor as if searching its dusty, scratched-to-hell surface for inspiration. The silence in the room was overwhelming. Then he lifted his hand and said, in a tired, resigned voice 'You want to offer us one of the girls, don't you, Oscar?'

'Brilliant.' Applause rang out through the speakers. 'I knew you could do it, Frank.'

'Dead or alive?' Frank asked. He closed his eyes.

'Ah. Maybe that depends on you. Then again, maybe not. You will have to wait and see, Frank. You and your merry boys in blue.'

'Tell me where.'

'Don't rush me, Frank. You may be short of time, but I have plenty to spare.'

'I'm sorry. At your own pace.'

'We'll talk again, won't we, Frank? I've so enjoyed our little chat.'

'If that's what you want, Oscar. I'll be here for you if you want to let off a little more steam.'

'This could be the start of a beautiful friendship.'

'I doubt it.'

The man chuckled one more time. 'You could be right. Still, your loss. I can be fascinating. Tell me, Frank, where does it hurt the most? The pain of losing the mother of your children, the knowledge of how your son suffered before his life was ended, the uncertainty over what has become of your daughter …where does that pain gather most of all in the dead of night to gnaw at your insides?'

Frank took a deep breath. The truth was there was no single place. The pain filled him completely. It ate away at his heart and soul, rampaged through his blood and fed upon the marrow of his bones. 'I won't discuss that with you,' he said.

'Oh, I think you will. When the moment is right. I think you'll discuss anything with me given the right circumstances.'

Then he told Frank where to find the girl and ended the call.

Minutes later, Frank was still sitting at the desk, sweat running down from his hairline. The incident room was buzzing once more. Foster and several others were already out of the unit, tyres screeching and kicking up clouds of dust and gravel as their vehicles sped away. Frank felt a hand press down on his shoulder. He looked up, eyes moist.

'Come on, Frank,' Nicky said. 'Let's go. Foster will want to be the first on the scene. But there's no reason why you can't be in on it.'

Frank nodded and got to his feet. 'Yes. Let's go. But don't hurry. There's really no need. No need at all. She's dead, Nicky. We can't help her now, whoever she is.'

'You don't know that.'

'Oh, but I do.'

'Not for certain.'

'The girl is dead, Nicky. Believe me.'

Frank felt his friend's close scrutiny, saw him nod his head. He believed.

Frank knew he was right. The girl was dead. And part of him thought that just maybe the caller was being deliberately cruel and sadistic. That just maybe, despite the promise of more verbal jousting, the dead girl might be Laura.

Chapter Seventeen

Sebastian Reeves carefully sealed the child's hands and feet in paper bags – his chosen method of ensuring he preserved the oils on her fingers and any traces of dirt or debris that may have adhered to her skin or got caught up under the nails. A series of photographs had been taken of the body from several angles and distances. The area around her had been vacuumed and photographed, the entire scene-of-crime operation caught on digital video for later analysis. The evidence collected at this stage of any investigation often proved not only a vital link to the perpetrator, but also essential in their subsequent conviction. It was crucial to maintain the chain of evidence, and to provide as much visual information as possible. Verbal descriptions were one thing, but nothing made a juror reflect quite like seeing the scene for themselves.

The SOC was that of a surreal horror story. Bunting and tinsel in an array of dazzling colours hung from steel struts, streamers and balloons had been taped to brick columns, and dotted evenly across the floor stood candles of all shapes, sizes and odours. And in the centre, lay the naked, mutilated corpse of a girl yet to reach her teenage years.

It was not Laura Rogers.

The abandoned warehouse on the edge of a business estate in Tottenham, north London, echoed with the dull noise of movement and muted voices. Despite this, Frank was acutely aware of the sound DS Tom Whelan's leather-soled shoes made as he descended the concrete steps down to where both Frank and Nicky waited. Whelan's face was as white as the overalls that he and the scene of crime officers wore.

The DS swallowed hard a few times before saying, 'It looks as if the bastard may have tortured her unmercifully before she died, and then seems to have taken tools of some description to her dead body when he dumped her here. There's no blood to speak of, but plenty of tissue and what looks like … like bone dust.' He hung his head, shook it slowly, as if shamed on behalf of mankind. No crashing waves were going to pull him out of this. 'What kind of an animal would do such a thing?'

Nicky looked up from his notebook. 'An animal wouldn't. This bastard's the genuine article. A real fucking monster.'

Whelan slowly clambered out of his whites, leaning against a brick wall for support. 'What did he sound like, Frank?' He had been elsewhere when the call came in.

Frank thought about it for a second or two. 'Composed. Self-assured. Arrogant. Egotistical. Everything I'd expected, and more. He's too damned confident, Tom. Way too sure of himself. One thing I know for certain, he doesn't believe he'll be caught.'

The sergeant threw his coverall onto the warehouse floor. His face creased by anger. 'None of them ever do.'

'Sure. But he's up to number seven now. You're no closer to him than any of the other murder squads around the country have been. You and they have all the information at hand, but still there's so little to work with. He leaves you nothing. At least, nothing he doesn't care to.'

Whelan nodded, drew in a deep breath. 'Insane bastard. We'll have him, though, mark my words. That wee girl up there deserves some justice. Oh, and speaking of insanity, Foster was raging like a wounded bull earlier. What did you do to upset him?'

Frank inclined his head. 'Actually, I probably said more than I should've. It was a mistake on my part. I embarrassed him in front of his squad, and he'll neither forget nor forgive that. I can only imagine he'll now do everything in his power to work against me.'

Whelan gave a slight uneven grin. 'You knocked him off his self-erected pedestal, and it serves the tosser right. He's a forceful enemy, Frank, but you have some powerful friends on your side.'

'Let's hope it gives me the edge. I need to stay with this.'

'I don't see how they can keep you out. It was you he called, Frank. It's you he wants to deal with. Now, do you need to see any more?' He tilted his head toward the steps. 'Seb has just about finished, and SOCO would like to have the body removed so they can wind things down.'

Frank told him he was done, eyes hooded with sadness, wanting to get out of this place and breathe fresh air again. Once the dispatch warehouse for a chain of major newsagent's, the building had been stripped of everything but its skeletal structure and a little cabling and pipe-work that hung through the rectangular gaps in the false ceilings of both floors. The shell was located at the far end of the industrial complex, where its naked windows could be seen from the dual-carriageway that ran behind it. The body remained where it was discovered, in the centre of the upper floor.

At first glance, the girl had looked enough like Laura to make Frank's heart skip a beat. It took several seconds for both him and Nicky to realise their mistake. And if it wasn't his own child, then her parents were already dead and would never have to mourn or see what had become of their daughter. Their own deaths had at least spared them that.

'I'm done as well,' Nicky said. He exhaled slowly. 'I've seen enough for one day. Enough for a fucking lifetime, in fact.'

The DS nodded. 'Okay. I'll catch you later. Foster's left me to clear the scene with SOCO. Take care, Frank.'

Frank and Nicky walked back out to the Mondeo. Nicky leaned against the car and lit a cigar, drawing heavily on it, his hands visibly shaking. Frank chewed on a stick of gum, his face turned to the sky, lost in thought. It was Nicky who broke the silence.

'This sick fuck is losing it, Frank. It's gathering momentum. It all changed the moment he left that poor kid up there.'

Frank nodded. 'I know what you mean. It's taken time, but now something has made him move. He's gradually been working his way up to this. But now that he's given us this one, there'll be more.'

'You think he's keeping all of the other girls alive?'

'No. He keeps each one alive for a time, I'm pretty sure about that. But only for a while. Wouldn't surprise me if he takes a girl every time the last one dies, though.'

Nicky looked at him. 'If that's right, then Laura is still alive.'

'Probably. But for how long?'

***

As the two men got into the car and began to compare notes, a light summer storm drifted in from the east, casting the sky into an impenetrable ice-grey. Sheet lightning flared briefly in the distance, followed some moments later by a low rumble of thunder. The air remained warm and still, however, and Nicky kept his window open to allow the smoke from his cigar to drift harmlessly away. Minutes later, an initial light spattering followed swiftly by a heavy downpour hammered against the windscreen, obscuring their view of the abandoned warehouse. Both men were thankful for this small mercy.

'So, just what the hell are we dealing with here, Frank?' Nicky's face had regained some of its natural colour. 'I've seen all kinds of shit before, stuff that's made me physically ill, but this is something else again.'

'I know. I've never come across anything quite like it, either. But keep your emotions in check, mate. We need to focus.' Frank was equally horrified by what he had seen, and his words were as much for himself as they were for his friend.

He glanced down at his book. 'Apart from the semen at the abduction point, he never leaves anything to go on. Not one time in seven. He's kept the girls, dead or alive, right from the beginning. Now, for reasons I can't begin to fathom, he's changed the pattern and decided to taunt us. He gave us the impression that the girl might still be alive. But you saw her. The poor thing has been dead for quite some time. This fucker likes games, Nicky. He enjoyed playing with us today. He left her in such a state that normal identification will prove impossible. Eventually we'll find out who she is, but it'll take time, and we'll have to work all the harder. He likes the idea of that.'

'What did you make of her flesh?' Nicky asked thoughtfully.

'Another new one on me. It reminded me of the way a floater's skin looks after spending some time in the water. But that isn't it. Not quite. No bites taken out of her by fish, no soil or muddy deposits on her body. I'll be very interested to hear what Sebastian has to say.'

'Grotesque, wasn't it? The whole scene sent a shiver down my back. The candles, party stuff, the girl and what he did to her. We've got one sick fucker on our hands, Frank. This business with ... Ah, shit. Sorry, mate. What must you be thinking right now?'

Frank put back his head and puffed out his cheeks. 'I try not to think anything, but I can't help it, Nicky. You know, when I saw that girl properly I was so relieved that it wasn't Laura. Yet every time I looked at her, I saw Laura's face. I see her now as just another victim. My own daughter.'

Nicky reached for his shoulder, squeezed it gently. 'Hang on to it, Frank. It wasn't Laura, so be thankful enough for that. You have to believe we'll get to her in time.'

Frank gazed off through the misted windscreen. For a while he again became lost in thought. Nicky turned the engine over. The wipers cleared the windscreen's outer surface, and he set the demister to work. He nosed the car away from the dark shape of the warehouse. Frank felt a cold spot on the back of his neck. He always did when he left the scene of any barbaric crime.

They drove in silence for some time, before Nicky again broke into his thoughts. 'So, what did you make of his call?'

'I imagine Foster will have the tape played to a forensic psychiatrist. He'll probably draw up some impressions.'

'I know. But what did *you* think?'

'He's on some kind of power kick. That's why he spoke to me. He knows he has me by the balls. He'll be considering the pain he's causing, enjoying the thrill of messing with my mind. Also...I think there's a chance he's some kind of religious freak.'

Nicky frowned. 'What makes you say that?'

'Think about it.' Frank gave an icy grin. Behind it there was a deep loathing for their quarry. 'What did he do to that poor girl, Nicky? Ignore everything he did to the flesh, ignore the disfigurement, the holes he drilled into her skull. What else did he do? How did he leave her?'

Nicky shrugged, shaking his head. 'You mean the way she was laid out?' He gunned the Ford along a stretch of dual-carriageway. The wipers squealed on dry glass. Nicky snapped them off as Frank looked across at him.

'Exactly. He crucified her, Nicky. The bastard spread her out on the floor and crucified her.'

Chapter Eighteen

'Have you been inside my house?' he asked.
The man was standing by her feet, looking down at her with eyes that gleamed like reflective mirrors.

Laura shook her head. She sat cross-legged on a pile of clothes at the far end of the room, as far away from the house as she could get. She had slept only fitfully, nightmarish visions of dead children pulling at her senses, yet even through her exhaustion she knew she had to be convincing. It was obvious now that her life depended on keeping this man happy. But it was so hard. Harder than anything she had ever had to do. Everywhere she looked she saw those dead faces staring back at her.

Dead girls. Just like she would be if she made a mistake.

'I can't hear you, Laura. Speak to me.' He cupped a hand around his ear.

'No,' she said. Her throat was parched, and the voice came out brittle and cracked. 'You told me not to.'

His eyes pierced hers. They held her captive, seeming to sap the last of her remaining strength. She blinked and stifled a yawn.

'Didn't you sleep, Laura?' The man's smile touched only his lips.

'Not much.'

What did he expect? She'd been taken from her bed in the middle of the night, her mother and brother were dead, she'd been humiliated and left in a locked room for many hours with only three rotting corpses for company. What did this man expect?

Dried tears still stained her cheeks, and there would be more to come. She couldn't stop herself from wondering what this man had done to her mother and brother, whether they had suffered, felt much pain before they died. There had been time to reflect on that. Too much time. She was certain that another day had come and gone, her stomach groaning with hunger every so often to remind her of minutes and hours slipping by. Now, knowing what lay beyond the walls of the doll's house, she was concerned with what he had in mind for her. What they had in mind.

'Would you like something to eat, Laura?' he said now.

She nodded eagerly. 'And a drink, too.'

'Please! Where are your manners, child? I do so hate ill-mannered children.'

'Sorry. Yes, please.'

'That's better. Didn't cost anything, did it? I'll be back in a few minutes. Then we'll have a nice chat.' He smiled once more, turned and left her alone.

She waited for the rattle of the key in the lock. When it came, Laura blew air from her lungs. She looked down at the half-moon imprints in her palms, where her nails had dug into the flesh. Realising that she was not the first girl to be taken by the man in the dead of night, having seen for herself the fate of the others, knowing that she had to perform in order to survive, was taking a great deal out of her. She didn't think she'd be able to cope much longer. It was too much to ask.

But then, as when the initial rush of negative thoughts had risen up during the early hours of her captivity, her mind thrust images of those other girls at her. Instead of breaking her, it flooded Laura with even greater resolve. She would say anything, submit to anything, to prevent that happening to her.

As soon as she'd realised what they were, Laura had turned away and fled. But the shocking vision still burned on her retinas. They had not smelled anything like she'd imagined corpses would smell, and the flesh hadn't really been rotting. The skin seemed to sag on their skeletal frames, prune-like, as though they'd stayed too long in water. It was as if they'd collapsed in on themselves. They scarcely looked human any more, but they were. Laura was certain.

How did the girls end up that way? What did the man and woman do to them? Did they have their fun and then just leave the girls to die? Did they starve them to death? Simply pretend they no longer existed? And how long before they grew weary? Days? Weeks? Months?

Laura tried to thrust these unwanted thoughts aside, but they funnelled back gleefully, tormenting, teasing. Wicked questions that would not be denied: *How long before they grow tired of me? How long do I have before I became like those inside the doll's house?*

Somehow, Laura tore her way through. Such thoughts were parasites, gnawing at her resolve. Soon there would be nothing left with which to fight. Then it would be too late. Survival. That was what mattered now. Keep him happy. Keep him interested.

* * *

When the man returned he handed her a bowl of cereal on a tray, together with a jug of milk and a tall mug. Then he moved back a pace or two and perched on the edge of a tea chest. Laura thanked him, set the bowl on the floor and poured. Vile smelling lumps of clotted milk fell from the jug, spattering over the flakes of corn. Laura jerked her head to one side, instantly nauseous.

The man shifted. 'What's the matter, Laura? Don't you like cereal?'

She looked up at him. 'I can't eat that. The milk's off. It's foul.'

His face clouded over.

No! her mind screamed. *You made a mistake. Survival. You have to keep him happy. You have to.*

'It's kind of you,' she said quickly. 'And I am grateful. But the milk has turned sour.'

He stared hard at her for several seconds, saying nothing. For the first time, Laura realised that she hadn't seen him blink even once. His unswerving gaze intimidated her. She wanted to keep this man happy, but she simply could not even consider eating the disgusting mess now lying in the bowl.

The man slipped off the crate, which tipped and fell to one side with a loud clatter, and moved back across to her. His movements were delicate for such a big man. He glared down at Laura, who felt the blood seep from her face.

'I don't *have* to feed you, Laura. There's no one around to *make* me feed you. I do so because I'm kind, because I'm thoughtful. You wouldn't want me to be *un*kind, would you? You wouldn't want me to be thought*less*?'

She shook her head, offered a tentative smile. 'I'm sorry. I didn't mean to complain. If you have no more milk I can easily pick out some of the flakes and eat them dry.'

He leaned forward, put his face closer. 'Eat them as they are,' he said.

'I can't.'

'Eat the flakes as they are, Laura.'

'I can't. Really, I can't.' Her eyes welled and her voice broke.

'Eat the fucking flakes as they are, Laura!'

She reeled back as if slapped, but her heart refused to bow. 'I'll be sick if I do.'

His smile came again. He took his time, allowing the flush to fade from his face. His hairless head shone beneath the bank of lights. 'No, you won't. Because if you are sick, I'll make you clear it all up. And again, if necessary. As often as it takes. Now eat your breakfast!'

Hope dropped from Laura's heart like a lead weight, filling the pit of her stomach with the bitter taste of desperation. He wasn't going to let it drop. His threats were not idle ones. She picked up the bowl and the spoon, looked down, the sour milk lying like cottage cheese on the golden flakes. Her stomach lurched, and she swallowed quickly. She knew that he would be as good as his word if she vomited.

Survival, a lone voice whispered inside her head. One stage at a time. Get through each moment, then move onto the next. Then the next.

Survival.

No matter what the cost.

Chapter Nineteen

Laura closed her eyes as she scooped the breakfast cereal into her mouth. It was better to imagine than to see. She chewed quickly and swallowed, repeated the process as fast as she could. The more she dwelt on it, the worse it would be for her. The knowledge of what she was feeding into herself was worse than the actual taste, so she sent her thoughts in search of better things.

When she finally put the bowl down it was empty. Her face was twisted in disgust, her flesh crawling and prickling all the way down to the base of her spine. She looked up at the man, who towered over her still. He was grinning once more and his eyes were dead.

'There. That wasn't so bad, was it?'

Laura shook her head. She didn't trust herself to open her mouth, for fear of what might come back out.

He winked. 'See. Told you. Now, here's your drink.' He handed her the mug.

Laura knew what would be inside even before she looked.

'Milk is good for you,' he said, and chuckled behind his hand like a sneaky child. 'Good for the bones.'

'Please.' Laura looked up at him, face crumpling. 'Please don't make me drink this.' Her voice faltered, became whiny even to her own ears.

His features became stone again. The transformation was so swift that it was impossible for her to notice the change happening. 'But you asked me for a drink. I distinctly heard you ask me for a drink, Laura, and that is what I brought you.'

'I know I asked for a drink, but I just can't drink that. I really can't. I ate the food, I did as you asked, but I can't drink that, no matter what...'

The door opened behind them. The man snapped his head around, and for a moment Laura thought she heard him let out a low snarl deep in the back of his throat. He might have been an animal, disturbed from its kill.

'We have things to do, sweetheart,' the woman said from the doorway. 'Busy, busy, busy.' She threw Laura a wide grin, waved with her fingers.

'But she won't take her drink,' he complained.

'Leave it with her. Perhaps she'll change her mind when she gets thirsty enough.'

This seemed to appease him. He looked back at Laura. 'We have to go out for a while. Please don't cry out or try to attract attention while we're gone. No one will hear you outside. But I'll be leaving a recorder running. If I hear your voice on it when I get back ...I'll have no option but to deal with you.'

'I won't make a sound,' Laura promised.

He laughed as he straightened. 'I know you won't.' He walked over to the door and paused on its threshold. 'Oh, and by the way, remember what I said before. Don't go inside the doll's house.'

Laura's eyes flicked reflexively across to the vast wooden construction. Instantly her mind screamed in alarm, and her heart began to clamour so loud that she felt sure they would hear it from where they were standing. On entering the doll's house, she had switched on the light, but when she ran back out of it, she'd neglected to turn it off again. Dim bulb or not, if the man looked directly into the window, he would know she was lying. With her very existence hanging by the slenderest of threads, Laura forced herself to look back at him.

'I won't go near it,' she managed to whisper.

He nodded and took a couple of paces across the room towards the house. 'Are you sure?'

Laura froze in place. He was going to check. He was going to open the door, look inside. He would see that the light was on, know she was responsible. And know that she had lied.

'Honestly!' she said quickly. 'I ... I promise. I wouldn't do anything you told me not to do.'

He stopped. Glanced across at the house. Laura waited for him to notice the evidence of her deceit. From where he stood the angle might just prevent him from seeing inside the window, but Laura couldn't be certain. The girl swallowed back her rising bile and willed him not to notice. Her teeth jammed together so hard that her jaw began to hurt.

'Are you sure you haven't been in there?' He stared hard at her now. 'Perhaps I ought to take a look. Just in case.'

'I wouldn't lie to you. I said I wouldn't go inside, and I won't.'

He continued to switch his gaze from the girl to the house. Eventually he nodded and offered a smile. 'Good girl.' He swivelled and went back to the door. 'I think we're beginning to understand each other, my pretty one.'

Nothing else was said as he stepped outside and the door was locked once more. When they were gone, Laura dared to breathe. A barrage of thoughts and emotions filling her head, she pushed the bowl and cup away.

Having waited for a few minutes, she then sped silently across the room to the doll's house. As she nudged open the door and reached a hand inside, Laura's mind was suddenly filled with the chilling certainty that a child's corpse was standing just beyond her vision, waiting to claw at her hand as she groped blindly for the switch. Three times she checked her hand, before steeling herself and finally extinguishing the only sign of her betrayal. This done, she stepped back from the house, heart thumping and blood rushing inside her head.

This was all too much. She had to get away. Laura tip-toed across to the room's main door. Were they really recording her? It sounded like something the man would do. So, she wouldn't cry out, or make a noise. But she would work on a way of opening the door. The recording wouldn't help them much if she were gone by the time they got back.

Twenty minutes later, Laura was convinced that if she was ever going to get away, it would not be through the locked door. It was solid wood, as was the frame. No amount of pushing or pulling or throwing herself against it was going to make the door budge. The lock was sturdy, and could not be forced apart. Weary and dispirited, she moved back to the pile of clothes, threw herself down and rocked back and forth, head in her hands. She was alone and she was afraid and she knew she was going to die. Laura shuddered once, rolled herself into a ball, closed her eyes, and slept.

And dreamed ...

* * *

She was inside the house. This time it was immense, the biggest house of any kind she had ever seen. She was hiding behind something, though she could not be certain of what. Her eyes were open wide, and she was trembling. The man's voice echoed and boomed.

'Come out, come out, wherever you are. I'll find you. I'll fiiinnndd yooouuu!'

Laura began to pray. *Our Father, who art in heaven ...*

'If you show yourself, you little madam, I won't be quite so angry.'

... hallowed be thy name ...

'But if you make me come and find you, if you waste my time, I'll have no choice but to hurt you in ways you can't begin to imagine.'

... thy kingdom come ...

'And when you've taken all the pain you can stand, I will kill you. Just like I killed your mummy and daddy.'

... thy will be done ...

'Just like I did to sweet little Gary.'

... on earth as it is in heaven ...

'I'll open you up, slash you to ribbons.'

... Give us this day our daily bread ...

'I'll let the worms and the maggots and the beetles feast upon you.'

'Laura.'

This voice was different. It was her father's voice.

'Laura, where are you, sweetheart?'

Her mouth opened, and clammed tight again. Where was she? What was she hiding behind? It draped over her like … like a second skin. No. No, it couldn't be. She could never have … But it was. It was one of the dolls. No. Not a doll. One of the girls. Like her. Only dead. Dead and rotten.

'Laura. He's gone away, darling. Daddy's here for you now. You don't have to be afraid any more, baby bear.'

Laura pushed the body to the floor, where it fell with a dull thud. 'Daddy!' she screamed. 'I'm here. I'm here.'

And the words spilled out of her mouth just as a dreadful voice echoed through her thoughts: *What if it's not Daddy? What if it was him? What if he made himself sound like Daddy?*

She reached down to pull the dead girl back on top of her. But as her hands took hold of the corpse's flesh, its head turned and its face cracked and split apart, revealing a terrible grin and a gleaming, hairless head.

'Not this time, Laura,' it said.

* * *

She screamed herself awake. Looking around like a startled animal, her glance fell over the house and swept away in an instant. Weeping silently, her eyes dipped and the bowl and mug swam into view. She found it impossible to believe that she had actually eaten the disgusting cereal. Keeping it down was possibly the bravest thing she had ever done. Certainly, it was the most appalling. But nothing would ever induce her to drink from that mug. Nothing on earth.

She was wrong about that, of course. But there was still so much about herself that Laura Rogers had yet to discover.

Chapter Twenty

Frank spent the afternoon wandering aimlessly around the house. Needing to avoid the silence that had come to disturb him more than at any time before, he switched on the hi-fi in the living room, inserted a CD and set it to play random tracks in a continuous loop. The warm and vibrant strains of B.B. King moved with him wherever he went, and he was grateful for the distraction. A Gibson ES-335 and the old jazz and blues guitarist were a match made in heaven.

When the telephone rang, Frank answered quickly, hoping for good news. It was Janet's father. 'I want to arrange the funeral ceremony,' Arthur Rankin said without preamble.

'It's already in hand,' Frank told him.

After a lengthy pause, Rankin sighed and said, 'But it is a funeral, yes? Please tell me you did at least do that for her.'

'I did what Janet and I discussed and agreed.'

'You've arranged for my daughter to be cremated, haven't you?' The tone and manner were accusatory.

'Yes. It's what she wanted.'

'And what about what we want for Janet? We were her flesh and blood, after all.'

Frank felt heat rising up from his chest. 'Which is an accident of birth, Arthur. She chose to marry me. She chose to have children with me.'

'She also chose to leave you and take those children with her.'

'And if she hadn't, maybe she'd be alive now. Maybe they both would be.' Frank winced as his own words filtered through the anger. He had no desire to hurt the man further. 'I'm sorry,' he said quietly. 'That was uncalled for.'

But he was speaking to a disconnected line.

Without any great enthusiasm Frank fixed himself a cheese sandwich, but pushed the plate away after only two bites. Usually he ground his own coffee beans for filtering, but today he made do with instant Gold Blend. That, too, was set aside before the mug was even half empty. He watered the plants, cursing when he failed to find their food, and whiled away an hour sitting in the conservatory just staring out at the garden.

Try as he might, he could not turn his mind from the man he had spoken to on the telephone. The man who had murdered his wife and son. The man who now held Laura captive.

What drives you, you son of a bitch? Do you have a purpose? Or is this all just a game to you?

Having spent so many years in law enforcement, Frank had come into contact with scum so evil, so lacking in morality and compassion, that he assumed them capable of anything. What he had come to understand was that some people were not driven, that no psychological scarring led them to behave in such a depraved manner. Whether they were born that way – some genetic foul-up – or a chemical reaction in the brain caused them to live their lives beyond the understanding of the majority, Frank had no idea. The sorry truth was that, throughout history, men had devised sickening and barbaric ways in which to take the lives of their fellow man. Perhaps there had never been a time when human monsters did not exist, a time when acts of brutality and savagery did not take place. Perhaps there never would be.

That was the thought that got Frank back on his feet and into the living room once more. He muted the CD player and watched Sky News for a while. Superintendent Foster, looking as slick and slippery as usual, was interviewed outside the warehouse. In sombre tones, he related details of their grim discovery, but made no mention of either Frank's involvement or the telephone call. When asked how the body had been located, all he would say was that he had acted on information received during the course of the investigation.

Frank was well aware that Foster had kept the call from the media for one reason only: to keep Frank's involvement out of the public gaze. He was happy enough with this. The last thing he wanted was for the media to camp outside his door and follow his every move. Let Foster keep himself in the spotlight, let the prick take all the plaudits as the case progressed, just so long as Frank could involve himself.

* * *

A little after six that evening, the doorbell chimed. Frank guessed it would be Nicky, but instead it was Zoe who stood there in the porch. He was surprised to see her, as she had never been to the house before.

'Something up?' he asked, the front door angled between them.

Zoe shook her head. 'No. I just thought I'd pop over and see how you were doing.'

Frank stepped aside, then led her into the living room. Her body spray wafted a sweet, bubblegum odour that only young women of a certain age find appealing. She wore a short, leather skirt, into which was tucked a pink T-shirt that pressed tight against her breasts. She looked brazen, yet at the same time curiously innocent and naïve. Frank realised how fond of her he had become.

'Can I get you a drink?' he asked.

'No thanks. I'm good.' She threw herself down in an armchair, legs flung in the air by the impact.

'What have you managed to sort out at work?' he asked.

'We're okay for a day or two. I've put a few things on hold, made your apologies. Pretty much everyone knew what had happened, so there was plenty of sympathy. I've paid some bills, but to be honest we're in need of a little money, Frank.'

He nodded. 'I'll have some transferred from my own account.'

'And what about future collections?'

'We'll let it slide for the rest of this week. If I'm not back by Monday or Tuesday, I'll bring someone in to help.'

Zoe nodded her appreciation and looked around the room. 'Nice place,' she said. 'Whole lot better than my dump of a bedsit.'

Frank leaned forward, frowning. 'I hadn't realised you'd left home. When did that happen?'

'A few weeks ago. Had another argument with my step-dad, and this time my mum sided with him. I decided it was time to get out. I never realised how much you had to pay for a bloody hovel these days, though.'

Frank felt terrible. He'd not only considered himself to be a good employer, but also a friend and a confidante to Zoe. That she had taken such a decision without him being aware left a sour taste in his mouth.

As if sensing his concern, Zoe shook her head and smiled. 'I didn't tell you because I knew you'd nag me into going back home, about the area not being safe for a girl on her own these days.' Then she added, 'And I also knew you'd insist on giving me a raise to help pay my rent.'

Frank laughed. 'Good one. You really don't know me at all, do you?'

Zoe blew a raspberry. 'A girl has to try. Especially a girl making her own way in the world.' She lowered her head, eyelashes flapping beyond the curl of fringe that fell across her face.

'Oh, stop it. Will an extra score a day do you?'

Zoe tried to look serious, missing by a mile. 'Twenty quid a day? Oh, no, Frank, I was only joking. You can't afford it. I don't deserve it.'

'Okay. You've convinced me. We'll leave things as they are, shall we?'

'I'll take it.' She shuffled across to him on her knees and hugged him close. 'Thanks, boss. Have I told you lately that you're the best boss in the world?'

'I don't think so, no.'

'Well you are.' She looked up at him, and he could tell she was being sincere. 'Really, Frank, I do appreciate it. I'll work harder for it, too.'

Frank was now uncomfortably aware of how much he was enjoying being held by this vivacious and attractive nineteen-year-old. At that moment, she chose to pull away, and he was extremely grateful that she did.

'You just carry on doing what you do best,' he said, as she moved back across to the armchair. 'You deserve a salary increase, probably more than I can afford to give you.'

Zoe shrugged, grew serious once more. 'How are you bearing up?'

'As well as I can, I suppose. The investigation is at the information-gathering stage, and it can seem a slow process when you're on this side of the fence, believe me.'

'You must be at your wits' end. Do they have any news on who this maniac is?'

Frank hesitated, unsure how he felt about discussing this with Zoe. 'Not at the moment. I'm sure there will be some movement soon, though.'

Perhaps sensing his reluctance to divulge information, Zoe leaned back in the chair. 'How do you feel about Janet?' she asked absently, as if her question carried no weight.

Frank considered for a moment, reaching inside for a truth he had known for some time. 'Less cut-up than I ought to be, perhaps. She was my wife, after all, and we had two great kids together. We shared a life for a long time. And still...there's no real grief. Sadness, yes. I would never have wished such an awful thing for her, despite what she did to me. To all of us, really. But in the end the only thing we had in common was our children and our history.'

Zoe, who had met Janet on several occasions, but had known her only during a time when Frank and his wife were enduring desperate times, pouted. 'Of course, she didn't deserve what happened to her. But she didn't deserve you, either.' The girl lowered her gaze. 'I know I joke about you and me, the fact that I've seen you eyeing me up, and I also know I'm just a girl really, with a head filled with girl stuff. But I need you to know that I'm here for you. If you just want to talk, or take the piss out of my hair and clothes, you just have to let me know.'

He smiled. 'I know you would. Zoe, you're a larger-than-life personality, and you're a great kid. But you're also so much more than a kid. So yes, when I need to step away from the doom and gloom, you're my go-to person.'

Zoe exhaled deeply. 'Bloody hell. I've never been one of those before.'

They laughed together at that. Frank had imagined he would never be able to laugh again until Laura was back with him and safe, and was astonished to hear the sound echoing around the room. It felt wrong, but it also felt very good. Somehow it made him feel stronger, perhaps even a little more confident of a positive outcome.

'Thank you,' he said. 'Again. I mean it, Zo. Thanks for just being you.'

As usual, Zoe brushed aside any sign of praise. 'It's what you pay me the big bucks for, boss-man.' She gave a wide, happy grin, and cupped her breasts. 'And considering you also get to cop an eyeful of these puppies, you've made a wise choice I'd say.'

Frank couldn't help himself. He simply had to laugh again.

Chapter Twenty-One

The following morning, Nicky collected Frank early and drove to a café in Stratford that was frequented on a daily basis by builders and cab drivers – a true sign of quality. Over their standard fried breakfast of double everything, Frank asked Nicky to bring him up to speed on the investigation.

His friend explained that nothing of value had come in from any of their main sources, forensics were still hard at it, so the hunt had not moved forward at all overnight. Frank voiced his concern that the case was now more than seventy-two hours old, and little progress had been made. Nicky waved these anxieties away, reminding him that this inquiry was unlike most others.

They were on their way to the Leyton annexe when Nicky's mobile chirped. The phone was in its slot on the dashboard, so Nicky switched it over to the speakers and on-board microphone. It was Warren Capel. His voice betrayed signs of excitement. 'Sir, I think we may have a major break.'

Nicky glanced across at Frank before responding. 'Go ahead, Warren. What do you have?'

'A call came in about twenty minutes ago. A Mr Simon Redbridge believes the man we're after recently threatened his daughter in their own home.'

'Who's seeing them?'

Capel cleared his throat. 'You are, sir. You and Frank.'

Nicky frowned. 'Are you sure?'

'Yes, sir. Superintendent Foster was about to respond, but the chief super happened to be here in the annexe and he made it clear that he wanted Frank to be in on the interview. The superintendent then decided he had other business to attend to and passed it on to you.'

Frank glanced across, saw Nicky's broad grin. A thin smile touched his own lips. It was obvious that Capel was being extremely tactful. Between the lines, however, it appeared that Foster's nose had been well and truly put out of joint.

'What standing does Frank have, Warren?' Nicky asked.

'A special detective, sir. On attachment to our squad.'

'Okay, Warren. Give me the address.' When he ended the call, he turned to Frank. 'I take it you approve?'

'Oh, yes. I'm a bit rusty, but I think I'll soon get the hang of it again.'

* * *

The house in Chingford sat in a street opposite the public golf course, and was less than a ten-minute drive from Paul Clarke's home. It was also within spitting distance of Frank's own house. He gave that some real thought as he and Nicky introduced themselves to Simon Redbridge.

The man was tall and lean, with a gaunt face, reddish fringe falling across his eyes. His shoulders appeared burdened as he led them inside. They were ushered into a large and pleasant living room, with high ceilings, a broken-colour finish on the walls, and carpet that seemed to swallow feet whole. A young girl sat on the soft pale-blue leather sofa, close to a woman who was obviously her mother. Frank recognised the uniform worn by the girl: a local private day-school. Frank and Nicky sat in armchairs, while Redbridge joined his family on the long sofa.

Nicky edged forward, took out his notebook and got things moving. 'I believe you have some information for us, sir.'

Redbridge swallowed. He sat upright, fists clenched in his lap. 'Yes. That's right.' He nodded vigorously.

'Good. Will you tell me, in your own time, exactly what happened?'

'It was a week ago tonight. My wife and I were woken by Karen, our daughter, screaming. She was standing at the foot of our bed, shaking as she screamed and wept, quite obviously terrified. It was a terrible sound, the like of which I never want to hear again. When we had calmed her down she told us that a man had been in her bedroom. A man she described as looking like a clown. He told her he had killed both of us, and that he would think about doing the same to her if she cried out. Evidently, he just stood there for a while, staring down at her. Then he just turned and walked out of the room. Karen gave it as long as she could bear, then came running into our room. I had a good look around, of course, but eventually we decided that it must have been a dream.'

'Why was that, Mr Redbridge?' Frank asked. While Simon Redbridge spoke, Frank had sneaked surreptitious glances at the man's daughter. Her likeness to Laura was uncanny. There was no doubt in his mind that the man they were hunting had been inside this house. The question was, why had he left this family unharmed?

Redbridge turned to Frank, tensing slightly. 'A few reasons really. First of all, apart from the fact that no one was in the house, I could find no sign of a forced entry or anything out of place or missing. Secondly, Karen had said that the man had our carving knife in his hand, but when we checked the knife was still in its rack. What with that and Laura describing him as looking like a clown, well, we just assumed ...'

'I probably would have come to the same conclusion.'

Redbridge smiled gratefully. The burden lessened somewhat, as Frank had intended it should.

'Would it be possible to speak with your daughter directly, sir?' Nicky asked, smiling at the girl. 'I realise that having seen and read the news it must be disturbing for you to believe this man may have been inside your home. However, it could still be that you were right. It could have been a dream.'

The man looked to his daughter. His face softened. 'How about it, sweetheart? Do you think you can answer a few questions? These men are here to help.'

Karen Redbridge nodded. Her face was tight, pensive. She sank further into her mother, who wrapped a protective arm around her. Frank smiled at the girl. Though the same age as Laura, she was a little taller, her body maturing faster as she continued her journey into womanhood. The girls shared the same hair colouring, almost the same flowing style. Karen Redbridge fitted the pattern exactly. So why was Laura taken and not this girl? There had to be a reason.

Frank was gentle with the girl. 'Okay, Karen. We'll take this nice and easy. Anytime you want to stop just say so. There's no pressure. Now, there are one or two things we need to know. To begin with, your father says that you thought the man looked like a clown. Why was that?'

'His face was just like a clown's.'

'You mean painted white, with a big red nose, black shapes around his eyes?'

Karen thought about this. Then she shook her head. 'No, not quite. And now that I think about it, his expression was sad. I thought he was a clown, but ...' She turned her face toward her mother. 'He looked like one of the masks on your wall, mum.'

Allison Redbridge nodded and smiled at Frank. 'Theatrical masks. You know the kind, one happy, one sad.'

'Right. So, not a clown then, Karen, but something like the sad mask.'

'Yes. And he said he was the dark.'

'He said *he* was the dark? Are you sure those were his exact words?'

'Yes. He said I should fear the dark, because he *was* the dark.'

Frank smiled and nodded encouragement. The corpse they had left behind in a body bag only yesterday had once been soft and innocent like this young girl. A child blooming like a flower, ready to open and be appreciated by the world. Anger flared briefly in his thoughts, but he thrust it aside.

'Okay. Good girl. You're doing just fine. Anything else you can think of, Karen? Can you describe the man in any other way?'

Again, the girl looked at her mother, then her father. Her cheeks flushed. Simon Redbridge prompted her. 'Go on, tell the man. It doesn't matter what you say. It will all help.'

'He didn't have any clothes on.'

'No clothes at all?' This from Nicky.

'No. Nothing.'

Frank moved forward in his seat. 'Are you sure? What about his hands? Was he wearing gloves?'

Karen considered for a moment. Frank could almost hear her thoughts: the chill of his touch, not flesh against flesh. 'Yes. I remember now. They were white, I think. Thin. Soft. Cotton, maybe.'

He nodded. 'Okay. You're doing a great job. This is all so much more than we could have expected. Now, is there anything else you can remember about him? Anything at all?'

'I don't think so.'

'Well, was he tall? Fat, or thin?' Frank didn't bother to ask about the man's colour. If he had been anything other than white, Karen would have mentioned it immediately.

'He was kind of thin. Tall ... maybe. I was lying down, he was standing over me. It was hard to tell'

'And his hair. What colour was it?'

Her mouth formed into a large O. She sat up straight, became excited. 'He didn't have any hair. He was bald, completely bald.'

'Good girl! That's excellent.' Frank decided to give her a break. Instead he turned to Nicky and said, 'Do you want to check the back door with Mr Redbridge?'

Nicky nodded and stood. The two men left the room. When they were gone, Frank spoke to Allison Redbridge. The woman's face was drawn, rings of recent neglect around her eyes. 'I think you already knew this was no dream. I suppose you must be wondering why he left you alone.'

Frank noticed Karen trembling slightly, his words confirming her worst fears: that it had all really happened.

The woman nodded and shook her head in turns. 'After reading about what this man did to that other family who lived nearby ...' Tears welled in her eyes. 'I can't believe how close we came.'

Frank made no mention of his personal involvement. It would serve no useful purpose. 'To be perfectly honest with you, neither can I. You were either very lucky or he did this for a specific reason. To the best of our knowledge this is the first time he's entered a home and left the family untouched. It may be a great help if we can work out why. Tell me, do you have a pet.'

'No. Not now. Our cat, Timmy, died a while back.'

Karen's head jerked up. The O was back in place. Frank got up and sat next to the girl. He took her hand in his, smiling at her. 'What is it, Karen? What else have you remembered?'

'He talked about Timmy. The man talked about Timmy.'

'And what did he say? Can you remember?'

Karen bit her lower lip. 'Not really. Something about ... he said that Timmy not being around might have been lucky for me.'

Frank lowered his head until his eyes were on the same level as the girl's. 'Karen, this is very important. Did the man call your cat by his name? Did he actually call him Timmy?'

'Yes.' Definite. 'I remember thinking it was strange, because Timmy had been dead for a while.'

Frank again turned to Mrs Redbridge. 'How long ago did Timmy die?'

'About a month or so ago. Is it important?'

Just then, Nicky and Simon Redbridge came back into the room. 'He took the lock apart,' Nicky confirmed. 'Clean as a whistle. Just like the others. The back door had been recently decorated. You can see where the lock was forced away from the sealed edge of paint.' He held up a plastic freezer bag. 'I got the knife for forensics to check over.'

Frank nodded and stood to let Redbridge take his place. He didn't bother to sit back down. 'We've really got something here. The man mentioned Karen's cat by name. He knew it was called Timmy, but he didn't know that the animal had died a few weeks before.'

Nicky peered shrewdly at Karen. 'He actually said your cat's name?'

Karen nodded. She melted back into her mother's arms. Frank noticed this and immediately said, 'I think we've gone through enough for one day. Thank you, Karen. You've been a big help to us. And thank you, Mr and Mrs Redbridge. This could be our biggest lead yet.'

'Mister ...' The girl's voice was weak.

'Yes, Karen?'

'The man. The man who said he was the dark. I thought ...' She bit her lip again, shaking her head.

'Easy, Karen. We can leave it for another time if you like,' Frank said. He tried to hide his eagerness. There was more to be gleaned from this girl, but he didn't want her plagued by nightmares. The sooner she was allowed to forget her terrible ordeal, the better for her peace of mind.

'It's just ... well ... I thought he looked familiar.'

'You mean you thought you recognised him? Like a neighbour, maybe.'

'Not a neighbour. I know everyone around here. But I did think I'd seen him before.'

'Around the street? In your home?'

She shook her head. 'No. I can't think where, I really can't. But I'm sure I had seen him before that night.'

'Okay. Well done, Karen. Listen, if it disturbs you to think about that night then you try your hardest to forget all about it from this point on. Sometimes that's the best way of remembering something important. So, don't think about where you saw him before. In fact, try not to think about him at all.'

Karen smiled and nodded. Redbridge showed Frank and Nicky out. 'Have you had any tradesmen working here within the past two or three months?' Frank asked. 'Could that be who Karen recognised?'

Simon Redbridge shook his head confidently. 'No. Thankfully, my brother can turn his hand to most things. Saves us a fortune.'

On the doorstep, Frank paused. 'One last thing, Mr Redbridge. Did your cat have a name-tag, or a dish with his name on? Something the man could have seen inside the house before he went upstairs.'

'No. He had nothing like that. Besides, all of Timmy's things went to the RSPCA when he died. There's no way he could have known.'

'And yet he did.'

The man nodded. Fear cast a shadow across his face. 'You don't think he'll be back, do you?'

Frank shook the man's hand. 'Don't worry, sir. I don't think that's going to happen. But if you want to take a few precautions, put some dead-bolts on the door and security locks on all your windows.'

'I've already arranged that. And thanks.'

'No. Thank you for getting in touch.'

'I'm only sorry it was too late for you and your family.' Redbridge regarded Frank with true regret in his eyes. 'I … I recognised you from the TV. It could have been us, couldn't it? What happened to your family could have happened to us just as easily.'

Frank wet his lips and took a breath. 'It could have. Yet it didn't. You're all here, all safe. This man briefly touched your lives, and now he's gone. Let that be your comfort.'

'I'm truly sorry for your loss. Sorrier still that we didn't take Karen's story more seriously.'

Frank shook his head. 'You weren't to know, Mr Redbridge. And even had you reported the incident, it would have altered nothing that followed. You've done fine. Just take care of your family now.'

* * *

Back in the car, Frank considered this fresh information in silence while Nicky drove. Nicky gave him the time he needed. When Frank did speak, he was all business-like once more. 'I hope you don't think I was out of order back there. I realise I kind of took things out of your hands. Old habits die hard, as they say.'

'Hey, no problem.' Nicky shook his head. 'You're still the guv'nor when it comes to seeing things no one else can see. You handled Karen brilliantly.'

'Poor mite. I know kids grow up more quickly these days, but in my eyes, she is still a child. She'll have nightmares now for sure. I feel guilty about that.'

'If it saves the lives of others, Frank, then it has to be worth it. Just thank whatever god you pray to that Redbridge could be bothered.'

'I don't have a god.'

'Oh, you know what I mean.'

'Do you think she *had* seen him before?'

'Could be. If he was checking the house out, she may have seen him hanging around.'

'She said that wasn't it.'

'I know. But she's been through an ordeal. Her nightmare turned out to be real after all. Imagine how *that* is affecting her sleep.' Nicky jerked the wheel to the right just in time, as a bicycle came up on his nearside. He shook his head and glared at the cyclist as they drove past.

Frank let out a dispirited sigh. 'How did he know the cat's name, Nicky? Somehow, he found out. But he didn't know it was dead. He must have been researching them at least a month before he went in there. But who told him the cat's name? Who?'

No answer came. He'd expected none. Frank lapsed into another thoughtful silence, and Nicky drove on without a word. An earlier storm had long since passed over. The roads were sticky once more, hot tar pulling at tyres. The Mondeo's air-conditioning was working overtime. Frank's mind was on a continuous spiral, leading him time and again into dead ends. In silence, he asked himself the same questions over and over. By the time they pulled alongside his Renault, he still had no answers.

Chapter Twenty-Two

Within minutes of being left alone, Frank was restless once more. Nicky had a meeting to attend at the annexe, where he would update the team on what they had found out from the Redbridges. He would be gone for the remainder of the working day, and it was unlikely that there would be any news in the next few hours. Edgy and anxious, Frank made a call. Less than five minutes later he was out of the house and heading towards the coast.

An hour and fifteen minutes later he pulled into the drive of a beautiful detached red-brick bungalow that was set back off a quiet road in Canvey Island, Essex. Frank sat with the engine idling for a few minutes, uncertain now as to why he had come. Eventually he got out of the car, walked across to the front door and rang the brass bell.

'Hello, Peter,' he said, when the door was pulled open. 'It's been a long time.'

Once inside, seated in a large room long-since turned into an office, with a mug of steaming coffee by his side, Frank began to relax for the first time that day. The man he had come to see had retired from the force at the rank of chief inspector some five years previously. Peter Forsyth had been Frank's mentor and good friend. Despite that, the two men had not spoken since Frank had quit the job.

'It's good to see you, Frank,' Forsyth said, a gentle smile crinkling the flesh around his eyes. Now fifty-nine, he looked as fit as he had the day of his retirement party – a bash they still talked about in his old stamping-ground of Shoreditch. Grey hair was now almost white, but it was thick and there was still plenty of it. 'I realise it's in dreadful circumstances, but I hoped you'd contact me.'

Frank met the man's even gaze. 'Didn't you think of calling me?'

'Of course. And I would have, had you not come here. I was waiting for the right moment. Perhaps I misjudged when that would be. The assessment of timing is always so much more accurate in retrospect, my friend.' He frowned, tilted his head. 'Why are you here, exactly? Why now?'

Frank sipped from his cup, the coffee strong and hot. 'I was at a loose end, my mind getting bogged down. I needed some clarity. I thought of you.'

'I'm only glad I was home when you called.'

'I'd probably have driven out here, anyway. Blown away a few cobwebs. But you *were* home. You are.'

The older man nodded, eyes now hooded with sadness. 'I'm so sorry for your loss, Frank. I understand you and Janet were no longer together, but you must be hurting, my friend.'

'I am, Peter. If it weren't for the fact that Laura is still alive, well …' He let it hang there, the implication obvious.

'How's the investigation coming along? I've been following it in the media, wondering what's happening behind the scenes. I was going to make a few calls, actually, but now you can bring me up to date.'

Frank told him about the killer making contact, the call from Simon Redbridge, his own official connection with the investigation, the re-opening of the annexe.

'Why aren't you there now?' Forsyth asked, frowning.

'Nicky thinks the less time Foster and I spend together the better. I have to agree. I'll get involved when it suits me best, but Nicky will feed back the everyday items.'

'I imagine that worm Foster will be beside himself with rage. He'll hate having you breathing down his neck.'

'Exactly. I'll keep away when it's not necessary for me to be there. Foster doesn't worry me, but he can be such a vindictive little shit.'

Forsyth raised his eyebrows. 'After what he did to you and not forgetting what you did to him in return, I think he's afraid of you for more reasons than just your ability to crack this one before he does.'

Frank gave an icy grin. 'That's as maybe, but I'll work with him if that's what it takes.'

'This one's a bad one, Frank.' Forsyth raised a finger and shook it from side to side. 'This man you're after is not your average villain.'

'I know. I'll be careful.' He glanced around at a room that was both familiar and comforting. Little had changed in the past few years. Forsyth's wife had died of cancer just a few months before his retirement, yet despite the bungalow being too large for a single man, selling had never been an option. The office, with its beech furniture and subtle lighting, had always been Frank's favourite room in a sumptuous home that was the bricks and mortar version of a pair of old slippers.

'How's Nancy?' Frank asked, his gaze falling on a large photograph set in a silver frame that stood on a nearby desk.

'She's very well. I'm a grandfather now.'

Frank smiled, genuinely pleased for a man he had once thought of as a surrogate father. 'That's terrific. Did she have a boy or girl?'

'One of each. Born just seven minutes apart.'

'Twins! I bet they're a handful.'

'They are.' Forsyth gave a happy nod. 'They are.'

Nancy was Forsyth's daughter. For years he had tried to get her and Frank together, regarding Frank as the son he never had and wanting him to be a part of the family. Though they had spent many hours together, a relationship had never quite formed. Then Frank met Janet at a party, and Peter Forsyth's idle dreams had been swept aside.

'Have you got time for me, Peter?' Frank asked now.

'I've always had time for you, my boy. Always.'

Frank pursed his lips. 'Not always. Not when I quit the job.'

Forsyth put back his head and sighed. 'It was such a waste, Frank. If you'd stayed, fought it out, you could have risen higher in the ranks and actually had some influence. You could have still been in the thick of it, doing the job you were born for.'

'It wasn't the battles, Peter. You must know that. I always enjoyed a scrap.'

The other man chuckled. 'We had one or two of our own, as I recall.'

'That we did.' He and Forsyth had argued often, sometimes fiercely about a number of issues, but it had never affected either their working relationship or personal friendship. Now he wanted to explain his decision to leave the Force. 'The hierarchy would never have allowed me to rise too far, and I accepted that. I worked within the system and sometimes outside it, not worrying about whose toes I trod on. But eventually I had to put my marriage and my family first. I had to do what was best for us all, not just Frank Rogers. I had to quit in order to save my marriage.'

'Then what the hell was your wife doing in another man's home? Why were your children not with you, Frank?'

He had missed this kind of direct speaking. Only Nicky ever really got this involved, but even he never took things as far as the old guv'nor.

'What can I say, Peter? Shit happens.'

'Don't be so flippant.' Forsyth's tone suggested only a mild rebuke. 'Don't mask your true feelings and thoughts with false humour.'

Frank regarded his friend for a moment, then nodded. 'I'd left it too late, Peter. Janet had met another man. We'd grown too far apart to stop the rot. Somehow, great detective that I am, I'd missed it. As simple as that, I'm afraid. The man she fell for was successful, much more the kind of man her father approved of, in a line of work the old bastard could appreciate and understand. Janet met the guy at some social function she'd organised. A six-month fling was enough to convince her that she could walk out on the years we'd had together.'

He paused for a moment, reflecting, then added, 'Actually, I think she was right. Not the affair – I never forgave her for that.

But our marriage was essentially over. Perhaps she was the brave one in ending it.'

'Such a shame. I quite liked Janet.'

Frank barked a sharp laugh. 'No, you didn't, Peter. You endured her for my sake.'

The other man merely shrugged. 'You said you came here looking for some clarity. What did you mean by that?'

Frank spread his hands. 'I feel as if I'm being crushed under the weight of thoughts inside my head. Always with me is the memory of what happened to Gary, and of course the situation with Laura. But I'm concerned about my business, and how my office manager will cope if this drags on too long. I'm putting undue pressure on Nicky, just by being around, by my involvement. I have a relationship with one of Janet's closest friends, and I've no idea how to move forward with that, yet don't want to hurt her feelings by pushing her away. I'm neglecting my home, and myself. I suppose what I'm saying is, I feel lost for the first time in my life, and I don't know which way to turn.'

Peter Forsyth held the coffee cup to his lips with both hands, his piercing, intense eyes focused on Frank. When he set his cup down on a small, round wooden table, he nodded twice before sitting back in his chair.

'An old teacher of mine once brought a cardboard box into the classroom with him. When we were still, he took out a large empty glass jar. Into the jar he tipped some rocks, as many as he could squeeze in. He then held the jar aloft. He asked us if we considered the jar to be full. Well, you couldn't get another rock in there, so we agreed that it was. He proceeded to pluck a bag out of the box, and from it he poured some coarse gravel into the jar. He held it up again for our inspection. 'This time it's definitely full, isn't it?' he asked us. Now, Frank, I have to tell you this was a strange beginning to a lesson, even for old man Carter, but as one we nodded and told him the jar was, indeed, full.'

Forsyth hooked one leg over the other, obviously enjoying himself. 'Our teacher then poured in some fine sand right to the brim, spun the lid back on and held it up one last time. 'This jar represents your life,' he told us. 'The rocks are the important things: your family, your wife, your children, and your health – things that if everything else was lost and only they remained, your life would still be full. Add the gravel, that is to say your job, your friends, your home, your moments of joy, and your life is now stuffed with goodness. The sand represents all the other tiny nuggets that go to make up your existence. If you fill your life with sand, there won't be room for the important things. The rocks must come first, then the gravel. The jar would then be almost overflowing with everything you need. The rest ... well, the rest is just sand'.'

The man shook his head at the memory and regarded Frank intently. 'We knew exactly what he meant, too. That was more than forty-five years ago, and it's still fresh in my mind. Occasionally it slips away – as it did when I was petty enough to cut you out of my life after you quit the job – but the lesson remains with me, close at hand whenever I need it. Perhaps it will help you, too.'

Frank had listened with increasing wonder, imagining some bespectacled old teacher, wearing a mortar-board and gown, performing this metaphor for life with a few simple items.

'So, what I need to do is prioritise,' he said to Forsyth. 'Get the most important things in place, and let the rest flow in around them afterwards.'

Frank ran his own words through his mind once more, then shook his head. 'But one of my rocks is missing, Peter.'

'Precisely.' Forsyth edged forward in his chair, wagging a finger. 'So, if you worry about the gravel and sand, you'll leave no room for the last rock. Frank, your business will still be there for you, and if it isn't, you know full well you'll make a living in some way or another. Your friendship with Nicky is solid enough to withstand almost anything. And if this new relationship of yours is worthwhile, it, too, can wait until its time is due. Laura first, Frank. Then the other things can follow.'

'And anything else is just sand.'

'Exactly.'

Frank grinned. He regarded his friend fondly. 'You're a wise old coot, Peter.'

'The advantages of a private education, old son. Had to be more to it than just torture and buggery.'

'I would hope so. But really, thanks. It helped.'

Forsyth gave a bow and said, 'So ends your lesson for today, glasshopper.' He got to his feet and stretched. 'Another coffee, Frank? You hardly touched yours.'

'Got anything stronger?'

'Tut-tut. I thought you knew me better than to ask that. Single malt?'

'Sounds just about perfect.'

The two men sat and drank their shots of whisky. About to drain his glass, Frank held it up and said, 'Does this count as sand or gravel?'

Peter Forsyth laughed. 'Now, that depends on the individual concerned. Speaking personally, a fine malt is and always will be one of my rocks.'

Chapter Twenty-Three

Frank poured himself a brandy. Drinking had become something of a ritual for him during the past few days, and he was a hair's breadth from taking up smoking again. Nicky refused a refill, placing a hand over his tumbler.

'You going to empty that bottle?' he asked. Nicky's tone was disapproving, but there was concern and understanding in there, too.

Frank smiled evenly and raised the glass. 'Eventually.'

They sat at the table in Frank's dining room, its chairs well-worn and moulded to certain shapes. He was all too aware that the room no longer bore the marks of a feminine presence, and lacked its previous charm because of that. Not neglected, exactly, but not cared for either. Like a once favourite toy gathering dust on some top shelf.

Nicky shook his head. 'Don't let it get to you, mate. When we get Laura back you have to be here for her. I mean really here, fit and healthy, ready for the challenge of seeing her through tough times.'

The glass now poised close to his lips, Frank said, 'You know what they say, Nicky. When the going gets tough, the tough get pissed.'

'You don't mean that.'

'No.' Frank let out a sigh of resignation and lowered his hand. 'No, I don't. But you talk about getting Laura back as if we've actually got something to work with. In fact, the very opposite is true. This fucker's laughing at us, Nicky. Me in particular.'

'That's shit talk! We do have things to work with. The information we got from Karen Redbridge, for instance. More important, perhaps, is that the prick's in contact. For some reason, he's latched on to you, Frank. That could be the break we need. Make it work for you. For us.'

'How?'

Nicky nodded at the crystal tumbler, now held loosely by Frank's side. The light caught its edge, sparkling in a myriad of colours. 'A bit less of that these past few days and you'd see it for yourself.'

Frank set the glass down without sipping from it. He met his friend's steady gaze, his tone firm but understanding as he said, 'You think this is a matter of self-pity, or drinking to forget? Well, you're wrong. All this drinking is purely a defence mechanism, Nicky. It's just a way of passing time, of getting through the long hours. If I have a drink in my hand then maybe I won't think about my son lying in the mortuary with God knows how many stab wounds covering his poor little body. If I have a drink in my hand then maybe I won't think about my wife in the same sorry condition. And if I have a drink in my hand then maybe, just maybe, I won't think about Laura … somewhere out there, wondering how it is that all her nightmares somehow managed to be real. I'm not drinking to forget, just to stop me thinking about anything other than getting my daughter back.'

Nicky nodded once, gave him a moment, then said, 'When he calls again – and he will call again, Frank – I think you should tell him you won't play along unless he offers you proof that Laura is still alive.'

'I've considered that. But what if he tells me to go fuck myself?'

'You'd be no worse off. He already has you by the balls. But I don't think it'd go that way. He's on a power trip. He needs this hold on you. It means a lot to him.'

'Maybe. Maybe.' Frank yawned. He'd had precious little sleep, his eyes felt gritty, and his head pounded. 'Okay, let's take a final look at what we have. The more we go through it the more we may see. Agreed?'

'Agreed.'

'So, aside from the physical aspect, what else do we know, or think we know about this sick fuck?'

Nicky sat forward, the springs beneath him groaning. 'Donald Cooper, the forensic psychologist who heard the tape and went through our notes, thought that bit from Karen Redbridge about him being the dark was really interesting. He thinks it's a sign that the man spent a lot of time in the dark. Probably as a kid. A bad record with pets is also likely. He also agrees with you about the crucifixion.'

'Yeah.' Frank nodded to himself. 'I gave that some more thought. He might not actually be a religious freak, but rather some anti-religious nut.'

Nicky gave a faint grin. 'Don said that, too.'

'Good for Don. Did he happen to tell you how our man knew the name of Karen's cat?'

'No. It didn't come up. Could be he heard someone out in the garden calling for it.'

'Could be. Doesn't feel right, though, does it?'

Nicky shook his head. 'No. It feels as if he got the name elsewhere.'

'Neighbour?' Frank suggested. 'A friend?'

'Did you see the stickers along that cul-de-sac? A real neighbourhood-watch area. I don't think they'd give information to strangers.'

'Simon Redbridge dismissed the idea that it could be a workman, but perhaps someone called when only his wife was there, gave an estimate, something like that.'

Nicky pulled a sceptical face. 'Doubtful. We can check back with Mrs Redbridge, but it's reaching. We'll also check through Paul Clarke's accounts, but again, I'm not expecting anything from these lines of investigation. Strikes me this man wouldn't leave such an easy pattern to follow. On the other hand, we don't have too many people left to ask questions of.'

'True. And now that I think about it, it's also a bit too obvious. Our man is smarter than that. I agree that he wouldn't have left such an easy trail. Still, let's have it checked anyway. Can't afford to overlook anything. So, what about young Karen Redbridge? Do you think she really had seen this bastard somewhere before?'

'I don't think she made it up. She didn't appear confused, either. But I get the distinct impression that both of these things could be important.'

Frank nodded. He threw back the last of his brandy and re-capped the bottle. He placed it by the side of his chair. 'Something just occurred to me. If our man was abused as a child then maybe he was on an 'at risk' register with social services.'

'Possibly. How does that help us now?'

'We could have it checked out.'

Nicky looked doubtful. 'But we don't have anything concrete for them to go on. No name, age, or even location.'

Eager now, sensing another path to follow, Frank edged forward. 'So, let's see what we can give them. White male. Thirty to thirty-five. Abused, both mentally and physically. Locked away in the dark. Hurt or even killed animals as a child. Father possibly a carpenter or handyman or locksmith. Parents may be devoutly religious.' He counted them off on his fingers.

'It could just ring a few bells with someone,' Nicky agreed. 'I wouldn't imagine they'd still have details or files going back that far, but someone who was around at the time might just remember something.'

'It's another avenue, that's all. We check in the areas we know he's been in. Seven altogether. Begin with the first, and move on to the others. The first murder is usually the most telling. Circulate the approximate description. Also, we try areas just south-west of London. That accent ...'

'I'll get someone on it first thing tomorrow.'

Nicky leaned back into the chair, stretched out his legs, and looked around the room. Frank followed his friend's gaze. Newspapers, envelopes and letters lay scattered everywhere. There was an electric bill among them, printed in bold red letters and figures. On the coffee table stood a half-eaten tub of Pot Noodle, a fork embedded in the centre. Next to it was an apple core that had turned brown and was veined with wrinkles. The carpet was spotted with biscuit and bread crumbs, and the wastepaper basket overflowed with wrappings.

'I'd fire your cleaning lady if I were you,' Nicky said.

Frank grinned sheepishly. 'It's a mess, right enough.'

'It looks as bad as you do.'

'I'll clean it. And me. Anything else?'

'Eat more. Drink less.'

'Yes, mother. What with you and Peter Forsyth, I've got no chance' Frank had told Nicky about his visit to Canvey Island. Nicky had also been a great admirer of Forsyth.

The two men smiled, totally at ease. They both knew that anything could be said by either one without any offence being taken. They trusted one another implicitly. A rare thing in their line of business. Nicky reached out, snatched up the electric bill and waved it in Frank's direction.

'You really need to get back to work. We all have to make a living. The bills still need paying. Just come into the annexe after you've finished for the day, or whenever he calls.'

Frank shook his head, eyes vague as his mind began to drift. 'Zoe can handle things for a little while yet. I can also bring someone in to help out on a temporary basis.'

'But your business …'

Frank cut him off, his voice stern and determined. 'My business is to see that Laura comes back to me unharmed. To help her recover, to see her through the grief I doubt she's had time to give in to. To give my daughter some kind of stability and comfort. The rest is just sand, Nicky. Just sand.'

'Sand?' Lines converged on Nicky's forehead.

Frank shook his head. 'Just something a wise man once told me. Look, I have to see it through with you and the team right now. But I won't lie to you, mate. When I have enough to go on, I'm going to work it through on my own. I'm going to have the bastard for what he did to my family.'

Nicky held up his hands, frowning. 'Just you hold on. Let us do the work for you, Frank. We have more muscle at our disposal.'

'True. You're also hemmed in by bureaucracy and rules and red-tape. I'm a free agent. For me there are no rules.'

Nicky paused, but made no further comment. Then he said, 'That list, the profile … it all points to a seriously disturbed, deranged personality. We've already seen clear evidence of that. He's proved he has intelligence, a keen, methodical brain. But someone, most probably his parents or someone close to him, did something to him. To his mind. How do you feel about that?'

'You mean am I sorry for him?' Frank considered this, then nodded. 'Yes. Yes, I am. I feel sorry for any poor bastard mistreated as a child. But that won't stop me putting the barrel of a shotgun in his mouth and pulling the trigger.'

Nicky reacted this time only with a raised eyebrow. 'I don't know, Frank. That makes me uncomfortable. I see an abused child, I feel the need to protect them. If they grow up to be an abuser, is it really their fault?'

'We all have choices to make. Not every kid who was abused becomes an abuser. People have to take responsibility for their actions. They have to be held accountable for the things they do. Anything else is just anarchy.'

'I'm still not sure. It's an emotive issue.' His gaze held Frank's for a moment. 'That business about the shotgun. You're not intending to do that, are you, Frank?'

Silence hung between them for a second or two. It was almost a physical presence. Then Frank looked into his friend's eyes. 'I'll tell you this much. If I can get Laura away from him using minimum force, I will. If it takes a battle, then I'm going to fight. If Laura dies, then so does he.'

Frank felt Nicky's sharp gaze cutting through him, knew his friend would be concerned. Earlier he had caught his reflection in the bathroom mirror, where he saw eyes that had lost their sparkle, leaving them cold and hard and flat. There was anger and frustration in them these days. Darkness beyond. But he hoped there was also a grim determination. Frank realised he was being driven solely by the thought of getting his daughter back, and anyone who got in the way had better watch out.

The doorbell chimed, breaking the spell; the moment had lingered uncomfortably. Frank sank back in his chair. 'That could be Debs. She phoned just before you got here. I asked her not to pop over, but she might have ignored me. Get it for me, would you. I don't want to see her right now. Tell her I'll ... I'll call her tomorrow.'

Nicky got up and moved into the hallway. A minute or so later he came back, Debbie a pace behind him. Nicky shrugged and gave an apologetic grin. 'I tried. But this is one hard and wilful woman.'

Debbie barely glanced at Frank before she shrugged off her brown suede jacket and began straightening the room. Nicky made his excuses and turned to leave. Frank walked him out to the door, thanked him for all his efforts. When he came back into the dining room, Debbie stood by the window, hands raised defensively.

'I know I should've listened to you. And I know you said to leave it for a while. But ... well, I needed to be here with you. And despite what you said earlier, I thought you could do with me being here.'

Debbie and Janet had been like chalk and cheese, both in attitude and looks, yet had somehow forged a wonderful friendship. Debbie had none of Janet's athletic grace, her body a little too small and rounded for that, with a full chest and heavy hips. But she had a quiet, unassuming way about her that most men found alluring. In a heart-shaped face, her eyes were darkly intelligent, a glint of mischief and humour sparkling in them always.

Frank gazed into those eyes now. Again, there was a stab of pain. He saw the wonderful afternoon they'd spent at Margate together. Them and the two children. Sun. Sand. Sea. Gary and Laura. Him and Debbie. Four inane grins. Laughter.

Days ago.

A lifetime ago.

Now those same lives were either over or irreparably shattered. He wanted to endure his own suffering alone, and had not considered that a selfish decision. But now he saw Debbie's pain, too. Her own misery. And he recognised the simple need they both shared.

She looked cool as always. Her hair was tied up and held back with claw-like clips, flyaway strands hanging down across the nape of her neck. She wore a simple summer dress, and sandals slapped against her heels as she moved. But her usual carefree air was muted, eyes ringed, cheeks more hollow. The past few days had been hard on her as well, and he saw now that by excluding Debbie from his grief, he had wounded her deeply.

'I'm glad you came,' he said simply.

She offered a faint grin. 'Me too.'

'I was wrong. And I'm sorry.'

She tried to shrug it off. 'It doesn't matter. It's your way of dealing with things.'

Frank edged forward, his hands gripping her bare upper arms. 'Yes, it does matter. My way is wrong. It always has been, and now it has to change.'

'We'll see. But now that I am here, I'd really like to stay.' She looked up at him, eyes wide and open and honest.

Frank sensed the meaning of her words. 'I could do with a hug,' he told her, holding out his hands.

'So could I.'

Tears spilled from her eyes as they crossed the barrier.

Chapter Twenty-Four

The sun was a bright yellow orb, powerful and intense as it bled through the drawn bedroom curtains. The summer quilt lay on the floor, discarded as an inconvenience. The top sheet was thrown back carelessly, while the bottom one was twisted and wrinkled.

Frank leaned up on one elbow and studied Debbie's naked form. Her hair had recently been cut, and he found the tiny stubbles on the nape of her neck extraordinarily erotic. One arm was tucked beneath her head, while the other hugged a pillow. He traced the length of her spine with his eyes, ribs snaring his gaze momentarily. The curve of her hips was spectacular, and he wanted to kiss the triangle of whiteness on her buttocks. Short yet elegantly shaped legs were bent at the knees; firm calves, delicate ankles, and feet so clean and tiny they could have been a child's. His eyes travelled back along the way they came. He leaned up a little further to see the swell of her left breast, delicately tipped with a nipple so pink it could never have been mistaken for one that had been suckled.

He let out a long sigh, recalling the previous night. Their lovemaking had initially been frantic. There was no steady movement, no rolling of the hips, no gathering of momentum or attending to her needs. Instead there was frenzy and longing and lust. He drove and drove until he was spent. She met him there – just.

It wasn't perfect, he had to admit. But the first time rarely ever was. For Debbie, pleasure was a secondary consideration that first time. She had wanted to exorcise the misery within him, she'd said afterwards, all of which was reflected in his eyes. It all came spilling out in those few minutes, and when their eyes locked afterwards, she told him softly that he had changed.

Later, having moved upstairs to the bed, they took their time exploring each other's bodies. And in the early hours of Friday morning they discovered that reality surpassed their anticipation. They were good together. Better than good. They each found a rare excitement, a spectacular new lease of life. When their eyes eventually closed and sleep staked its claim, they remained entwined, glistening and at peace.

Frank wondered now how the morning would affect her. Their passion, no matter how natural, no matter how necessary, had leaked over into their friendship. When she looked at him for the first time again, would there be an irreversible difference?

'Hasn't anyone ever told you that peeking at naked women is considered vulgar,' she said suddenly. The strength of her voice told him she had been awake for some time.

He chuckled. As if by instinct his hand reached out and he trailed his nails down the curve of her spine. She quivered, rolled over, eyes searching his. There was no false modesty, no move to hide her naked form.

'Still friends?' she asked.

'Of course.'

'Still lovers?'

His eyes swept her body once more. 'Oh, I do hope so.'

She giggled. Her eyelashes flickered. 'Me, too.' Her fingers encircled him 'Am I a hussy?'

'Yes.'

'Good. A slut?'

'Yes.'

'Better still.'

He moved his hips and tried to enter her. She laughed and raised herself. 'Uh-uh. Not until you tell me something.'

'What?' He believed he would have told her anything at that moment, such was his desire.

'What do you really think of me?'

'You're a slut and a hussy.'

Her hand pulled at his velvety flesh. 'That won't do. I mean what do you really think of me?'

'You mean, do I hold you in great esteem? Do I quite like you? Do I love you?'

Her face grew serious. 'Something like that, yes.'

Frank breathed her in. Her body had always held an allure for him, and though they had indulged in several innocent flirtations while he and Janet were together, they had become more intimate these past few months. Now he had to consider just what his true feelings were. As a friend, she couldn't be bettered. As a lover, she was wonderful. As a person, she was funny and caring and warm and open and friendly. As a ...

'I love you,' he said. It was the simple truth. He had loved her for a very long time.

Debbie slowly lowered herself onto him, exchanging one grip for another.

'Debbie?' he said.

A finger pressed against his lips. 'Shush,' she whispered. 'You shouldn't have to ask. You must already know how I feel about you. How I've always felt about you.'

He thought about that, and decided she was right.

Chapter Twenty-Five

It was a little before three that Friday afternoon when Nicky phoned. Debbie had kissed Frank goodbye just after lunch, leaving him with a pleasant glow that warmed his body, soul and mind. He felt neither remorse nor guilt. Debbie had cleansed him. It was as simple and as wonderful as that. She had retrieved him from a precipice he wasn't aware he'd been teetering on until the moment she embraced him. He was grateful. And so much more. Anything was possible now that he had her to keep him sane.

'Frank, I've just come from the pathologist's office.' Nicky's voice betrayed his obvious fatigue.

'And?'

'It's bloody peculiar. As we thought, the bastard did much of the damage while the poor mite was still alive. Enough to have caused immense suffering. Most of the wounds were ante-mortem, though several of the most severe came after she was dead.' He paused, the line was silent for a few moments.

Frank waited for his friend to gather himself, force away the images of the child in utmost agony, to wade through the anger. 'Take your time,' he said gently. 'Leave it till later if you like.'

'No. No, I'm okay. The peculiar thing is why her flesh looked like it did. It wasn't water she'd been left in. Well, it was, in a way, but not just water. There were also large traces of formaldehyde.'

'What?' Frank's eyes sprang open. He dragged the phone across to the kitchen dining table and sat down. A half-eaten sandwich sat on a plate, the edges of the bread beginning to curl. He stuck some gum in his mouth and began to chew. 'I can't believe it. Formaldehyde?'

'I know. Crazy, sick fucker.'

'I don't understand.'

'You're not alone. Evidently he injected it into her.'

Frank blanched. He tried to find some saliva but the well was dry. He spat out the tasteless gum. 'Oh, Jesus. I mean, formaldehyde is a type of acid, right. The sick fuck pumped that into her bloodstream—'

'Ah ... No. Not into her bloodstream. By the time it was injected she had no bloodstream. That was all post-mortem.'

Frank's shoulders relaxed. At least the poor kid had been spared that. The agony it would have caused. 'It still makes no sense. Are you sure it was after she died?'

'Certain. Her arteries and veins weren't scarred or burned as formaldehyde would have done had her blood been circulating. He must've done it quite soon after, though, because there was enough inside her to cause the reaction we saw.'

'Did Seb offer an opinion as to why someone might inject acid into a dead body?'

'Yes, he did. Seb said, and I quote, 'the man must be a bloody lunatic'.'

Frank rolled his eyes. 'Thanks. That's very helpful.'

'Hey, I'm only telling you what the man said.'

'Yeah, yeah. Okay, you going back to the annexe now?'

'Yep. Foster has a squad meeting arranged for three-thirty.'

'Okay. Let me know when you have anything more on the girl.'

'Like what?'

Frank teased the phone's curly lead around his wrist. It beat doodling. 'Like her name, for instance.'

'Oh, didn't I say? We know who she is.'

'Jesus, Nicky!'

'Sorry, pal. The name's Jeanette ... ah ... Jeanette Morris. Seb located a small birthmark on her left ankle, from which we were able to identify her. Next of kin have been informed.'

Frank peered out at the garden while he ran over the list of abductions in his mind. The grass was getting long again.

Neglected. The last time it had been mown, Gary had helped out. Laura's flowers were desperately in need of water. He would attend to them. There were enough ill-omens as it was, without the flowers dying off.

'She was the first to be abducted. Right?' He switched back.

'That's her.'

'But that was almost seven months ago. She wasn't all that decomposed. Surely he can't have kept her alive all this time.'

'No. The wounds that killed her are, according to Seb's estimation, at least five or six months' old. Maybe more.'

'Then how ...?'

'Well, this is why the estimation could be off by some way. Seb believes the body must have been kept in a container of the same stuff that was injected into her. Formaldehyde is a pretty effective preservative. That's its primary use, in fact.'

There was a pause. The pause soon became a silence. Then Frank said, 'You mean Jeanette Morris was ... pickled?'

'Bingo. Buy yourself a hotel in Belgravia.'

Frank was aware that Nicky's apparent levity was a facade, a defensive wall erected as a barrier against all that he had seen and heard and could imagine. Such a barrier was compulsory if you were going to handle a case like this and emerge intact. Truth was that even some battle-hardened detectives came unglued during murder investigations, particularly when the killings were brutal, the victims children. Levity was often mistaken for callous disregard, but was a necessary evil.

* * *

A couple of hours later, impatient and at a loose end, Frank decided to join Nicky at the annexe. There were files he wanted to scour, information he needed to assemble in his mind. He also just wanted to be there, to be amongst it all again. Plus, he was desperate for Oscar to call again.

The unit was quiet that late in the afternoon, Nicky and Warren Capel the only detectives there. A couple of uniformed

PCs sat skimming through a huge stack of blue files, and a few civilian administrators sat at computer terminals.

'How did the meeting go?' Frank asked, easing into a chair at the desk he had used before.

Nicky shook his head. 'Pretty grim. Foster was his usual self. He's trying to disassociate himself from the investigation. He can see it going down the chute, and doesn't want to go with it.'

'Down the chute? The going might be slow, but there is some progress.'

'Exactly what I said. I think he wants to jump ship. It was the body that did it. I think he sees the other six as a career buster.' Nicky winced and clamped down too late on his errant mouth. He shook his head. 'Oh ... Oh, Jesus Christ, Frank. I'm so sorry.'

Frank caught the dismay in his friend's face and dismissed it with a shake of the head. 'No need. Laura *is* a victim, and there's little we can do about that right now. Don't walk around on eggshells, Nicky. Tell it as you see it.'

He meant every word, yet they had the power to wound him deeply. There was a pressure building behind his eyes that was becoming increasingly more difficult to deny. He was clinging on desperately, Debbie's love and Nicky's friendship somehow keeping him afloat. Even so, he didn't think they would be enough if it went on much longer. There had to be a way through. And he had to find it.

He looked across at Warren and asked, 'Anything on the social services check?'

'Nothing so far,' Capel replied. He wore no jacket, and rough circles of perspiration stained his shirt beneath each arm. One thing the annexe unit lacked was air-conditioning. 'It seems unlikely that he would still be on record. But what we are doing, with the help of local areas, is putting out the rough description to welfare people in case anything rings a bell. We're even digging into past employees to see if any of them come up trumps.'

'Good idea.' Frank nodded approvingly. He couldn't see what else they could do at present.

'Also,' Capel went on, 'you wanted info on the murder weapons in each case.'

'Yes. We know he had tools, used them to gain entry. I wondered if he ever used his own weapon to kill his victims.'

'The answer is no. Victims' own knives used in every case.'

'Okay. It was just an idea. Now, I'd like to go through the information we have on the other girls. Is it all on computer?'

Nicky, who was sitting at a terminal, confirmed that it was. He hit a few keys and drew the investigation's database onto screen. He stood and offered Frank his chair. 'All yours. Warren and I have some calls to make. Any problems, just yell out.'

Frank, who had never taken to the silicon invasion, yet was proficient enough for his own purposes, began skimming through the information. He used a number of searches to cross-check, trying to come up with one item linking all the girls that may have been overlooked. He found nothing new. The only thing that surprised him was the timing of each incident. Four came in the first two months, only three in the last five. This was most unusual. The reverse, in fact, of the majority of other serial killings he had known. The perpetrator usually got a taste for it, got better at it, and shortened the period between each victim in order to satisfy his desire for more. Either that or they were cyclic, based on the phases of the moon. This peculiarity intrigued him, though he couldn't imagine how it could possibly move the investigation forward.

Scrolling back, he first read the file on Laura. Karen Redbridge's details were now there, too, even though she hadn't been abducted. Then he came to the last known abductee prior to Laura. One detail here caught his attention. The girl, Samantha Penny, was taken like the others, her parents and a sister murdered. The significant difference was that one further sister survived because she was staying with a friend the night it happened. Frank pondered this for a while, then spun around on the chair.

'The Penny family,' he called out. 'April this year. From Peterborough. Either of you know whether the surviving sister, Tania, has been spoken to?'

'Ask the database,' Nicky said. 'Field number seventeen lists the people questioned by either the SOCOs or investigating officers.'

Minutes later, Frank had the list on screen. Tania Penny's name was there. He sat back and thought about it for a while. In her own way, Tania Penny was a survivor just like Karen Redbridge. Maybe it didn't matter that she hadn't been in the house at the time. Maybe she had seen some stranger or something odd prior to the murder and abduction that she hadn't recognized as significant.

By the side of her name, in closed brackets, was a file number. The file would contain her statement. Frank exited the database and called up the word-processing software. He requested Tania's file. Even as his fingers tapped out the codes, he reflected that the silicon chip had some advantages after all. How long would it have taken to establish and retrieve this information by hand?

He read the girl's statement three times. She was eighteen, working in public relations for the local branch of a major insurance company. Her statement was concise and literate. She was obviously bright. *Is she also observant?* Frank wondered. He flipped open his notebook and jotted down the contact telephone number and address. At that moment, he didn't know where it would lead – if anywhere. But he was starting to feel a familiar stirring in his gut that could not be ignored. He was about to discuss this aspect of the investigation with Warren and Nicky when the telephone on his desk rang and his heart almost stopped beating.

Chapter Twenty-Six

That's it, Laura. Play with the things we left for you. You can enjoy your stay now. You didn't want to before, but I can understand that. Could you smell me on them? Could you smell them? The other girls. I bet you could. I'll just bet you could smell us all.

So, you kept away from the paper and books and games, did you? Afraid, perhaps? Revolted ... definitely. But now you're bored, aren't you? You're a bright young thing and you need something to occupy your mind. So, play with the nice games, read the books, draw and colour; anything but step inside the doll's house again.

Oh, yes, I saw you in there. I was watching all the time, just waiting for you to disobey me. They all did eventually, so you're not alone. You can't see the cameras, Laura, but they can see you. They see everything. So much more than you ever will. And when I'm not able to watch you, I record every moment so I won't miss a single heartbeat.

I am such a tease, aren't I? Did I have you worried when I spoke about the doll's house? You left the light on ... such a giveaway. I had no need to look inside, but I thought it would be fun to have you fear me just a little more.

You're the best yet, Laura. Far and away the best. Your light shines so brightly, like a star, or even a sun. I could not have ignored its call. You were destined to be mine, we were destined to be together, and still you have no idea what an honour that is.

How calm you are. How serene and dignified. You haven't snivelled, you haven't screamed, you haven't cried out or tried to fight. The others were not as clever as you, Laura. Because you know, don't you? You worked it out right away. You know that pleasing me, pleasing us, means you will live longer.

Longer. But not forever.

But then none of us lives forever, Laura. Hasn't anyone ever taught you that time is an abstract concept? It defies all logic, flies in the face of reason. Time wears you down if you allow it to. You deserve better than that.

Your face was a picture when you saw my other guests. I tried hard to preserve them, but I am an amateur. An improving one, though. Perhaps you will be my first success.

You did well with the milk, too. I know it was tough when I forced you to drink that mug of spoilt milk. But finally, you kept it all down. It took a while, a little patience on my behalf, and enormous strength of character on yours. But in the end, we got there. I was proud of you. I loved you for it.

And I so love to watch you sleep. Admittedly, you haven't slept for long periods of time, but you are even more beautiful wrapped in the loving arms of Morpheus. Your eyelids jerk as if alive, attuned to the mysteries of your dreams.

Am I a part of them? I do hope so.

You are perfect for what we have in mind. We both want to use you – your body – in so many different ways. And we intend to. But if we had you now you would not do as we ask, and once again the object of your presence here will be defeated.

You believe that while you do everything we ask, the very worst nightmares your imagination is capable of conjuring will not come true. You are wrong, of course. Soon one of us, perhaps even both of us, will tire of what your life means to us, and we will move you on towards your destiny. There will be no hiding place for you then. And you will remain with us for all time, never wanting, never needing.

Ah. Yes, I have just remembered. You were sneaky, weren't you? So very sneaky. I thought I had killed both your parents, I even told you as much. But you neglected to inform me that the man I killed was not your father. Just a man who fucked your mother. Tut-tut, Laura. You will pay for that audacity. But that will come later, of course.

The media coverage focused on your father's time as a policeman. A very good policeman, by all accounts. I saw his photograph. I spoke *to him as well, and we have developed something of a rapport. The media have swamped the public with photographs. You resembled your mother more, my dear. But there is something about Daddy. Something behind his eyes. I would like to know your father better, Laura. I would like to know him very much.*

I wonder how he feels having spoken to me. Can you imagine his pain, Laura? Can you imagine its colour? So bright, so dazzling, so intense. The pain of a thousand cuts would pale into insignificance by comparison. I can cause him to die a hundred deaths, with mere words as my only weapons. Now that is power.

I must admit that I had never considered this avenue before. There may be enormous pleasure to be gained here. How amusing. Perhaps he will be useful to me in more ways than I can comprehend right now.

Ooh, such a big yawn. You have no idea what time of day it is, do you? Nor even how long you have already been here. Shuttered windows. Lights on all the time. It's not easy to sleep with the lights on, is it, my dear? But believe me, it's preferable to the dark. The dark is a hiding place for things we don't want to think of or even imagine.

Go on. Lay your head down. Rest. Sleep. I have things to do now. Places to go. People to see. Someone to speak to. Busy, busy, bee. Busy, busy me.

Do you have a message for your father, Laura? Would you like me to tell him that you love him? Or shall I just tell him that you're going to die and there's nothing he or anyone else can do to prevent it? Shall I tell him that I will kill you slowly? After I have made a woman of you, of course. And shall I let him know how much pain you will endure before I give you over to your maker? If he loves you, little one, he will crumble to pieces and I will wipe my hands of him.

I love you, too, dear Laura. In my own fashion. I can be good and kind, but I know I can also be cruel. I don't mean to be. It's just ... It's just the way things are. The way things have to be.

Goodbye for now, Laura.

My new love.

* * *

She waited for him in their room, wearing a flimsy nightgown and nothing else. Her untethered breasts were small, but firm, standing proud against the sheer material. Lank and dirty hair curled around her neck like the tails of a vermin brood. She slouched in a narrow armchair, one leg hooked over a threadbare arm, exposing herself to him. She smiled as he entered the room.

'How is our little beauty today?' she asked.

'As well as can be expected.' His eyes narrowed. 'You weren't thinking of ... visiting her, were you?'

She stretched languidly, the smile still in place. 'Why do you ask?'

'Because I don't think it would be a good idea. Not yet. I know you want her. So do I. And I want you to have her. But not until she's of no use to us. Then ... well, then her body is yours, my dear.'

Disappointed, the woman got to her feet and prepared to get ready. As her nightdress fell to the floor, the man felt something powerful flow through him. A surge of raw energy. She turned to him, her naked body teasing. 'We still have each other,' she said.

He adjusted his trousers. 'Later. I have things to do. Business to take care of.'

She blew him a kiss, while the other hand stroked herself. 'I'll be waiting. All wet and warm for you.'

'I need you to shave me.'

'I'll do that as well.'

He laughed, kissed her fully on the mouth, pressed his groin against hers, then broke away. Her eyes were bright, pupils enlarged.

'I love you,' he said. And then he was gone.

* * *

He had chosen each location long ago, realising that sooner or later he would have to dispose of the bodies. The first, Jeanette Morris, had been a real whiner. Cry, cry, cry. That's all she would do. She hadn't been much use to him, other than being his first attempt at playing God. As expected, she hadn't turned out that well. Still. He had time. And practice makes perfect, so they say.

His first victim, his first failure. He was improving all the time, however, but there were others who needed to be discarded. He was happy to do them one by one. No rush. They weren't going anywhere. And neither was he.

He recalled that first time very well. The body was sheathed in plastic, which in turn was wrapped in a heavy cotton dust sheet. He pulled it from the van, heaved it onto his shoulder and headed toward the site he had chosen. Using one hand to keep the body balanced, his other gripped a hand-made wooden toolbox. He managed both easily.

Once in position he unrolled the body and laid it out on the solid floor. Then he took a number of items from the tool box and spread them around the small figure. The last item he withdrew was a portable CD player.

Before death was merciful, he had subjected this child to a number of tortuous ordeals, recording the entire proceedings. Now he snapped the CD player on and it began to play the first track. He whistled as he went back to work on her. The screams and pitiful moans of pain and misery emerging from the device drowned out the sound, but it didn't matter in the least. He never had been able to carry a tune.

Chapter Twenty-Seven

Inside the annexe, all three men started when the telephone rang. Across the other side of the unit, the PCs turned to face them, and the room fell into complete silence. It was the same phone line that their quarry had used before, its distinctive tone sounding like a death knell. Frank walked slowly back to the desk, sat down, drew a deep breath and picked up the receiver.

'Is that you by any chance, Special Detective Rogers?' he heard. His eyes moved across to the two detectives. He gave a nod and flicked a switch that would start the recorder and put the conversation through the speakers.

'Yes, it's me, Oscar.'

'Ah ... you remembered. How kind. Congratulations, by the way. Officially on the team now. I heard about it this morning. You've become something of a celebrity, even though you continue to ignore the media's questions. Good for you, Frank. We all deserve our fifteen minutes of fame.'

'Is my daughter still alive, Oscar?'

'What do you think, special detective? I mean, using all your powers of detective reasoning, what do you really think?'

'I'm asking you to tell me.' He glanced across at Nicky, who nodded grimly. His heart screamed out, imploring him not to go ahead with what he was about to do. But his head told him he must. For his own peace of mind. 'And if you tell me she is, then I want some proof.'

'My dear Frank, do you really think you are in any position to dictate terms?'

'You seem to have a need to talk to me, Oscar. If my daughter is dead, then I have no need or desire to talk to you. Prove to me that she is alive and well, and we'll talk all you like.'

'And what if I kill her now as punishment for your impudence?' The voice hardened just a little.

Frank closed his eyes. His heart rose to impede his breathing, hammering like a woodpecker at a branch. 'Then don't bother calling again,' he said with as much force as he could muster.

'I might not care, Frank. Perhaps you've misjudged the situation, or have been badly advised. If I react in a negative way, you will have killed her, Special Detective Rogers. You will have killed your own daughter. Yet … does not each man kill the thing he loves?'

'No. *You* will have killed her, not me nor anyone else. Just you. Now either do as I say or this conversation is over.'

After a brief pause, the voice came back slightly lower in tone. 'I can't do that at the moment. Laura is not with me. However, perhaps we can strike a deal. The next time I call, I will provide you with the proof you want. Give me a question for her, something only she will have the answer to.'

'Okay. Give me some time to think.' He cupped the mouthpiece, his relief obvious in the huge sigh he let go.

'Well done,' Nicky said. 'It's what you needed.'

Frank nodded. A question. Could he phrase it in such a way that Laura might be able to give him a clue as to her whereabouts? He couldn't think. His thoughts were lost in darkness. Nothing would come to him. Pain tightened a narrow band across his eyes. He had to use this opportunity. It was all they had. He took his hand away and said, 'All right, Oscar. Ask Laura to tell me where her favourite place is.'

'That's it?'

'It'll be enough.'

'Very well. I'll ask. Now do we talk?'

'You've offered no proof … but, I suppose I can trust you this once.'

'Oh, that is so kind of you. So now tell me, how does it feel to be a special detective?'

'It's fine by me. Whatever it takes.'

'Good. Better than collecting debts, I suspect. Perhaps I've done you a favour, bringing you back to something so obviously dear to your heart. And how did you like my little gift?'

'Gift?' Frank frowned now, shrugging at Capel and Nicky who sat enthralled. Inside the unit, the atmosphere crackled with tension as several other officers wandered in and immediately became absorbed by the conversation.

'Yes. Little Jeanette. I had thought of wrapping her in pink ribbon for you, but I dismissed the notion as too much of a grand gesture. Ultimately, I think the decor said it all. Hadn't you worked it out that she was my gift to you?'

'I failed to see her that way. What you left behind was no gift, believe me. Why did you do it, Oscar?'

The words almost caught in Frank's throat. The image of the child's poor body rose up before him, strong and stark. 'Why did you torture her like that? And why deprive her of any dignity in death by using the tools on her after she was cold? What purpose could that have possibly served?'

A low, throaty chuckle echoed down the line. 'Creative of me, wasn't it? One has to have some amusement, Frank.'

'But she was already dead.'

'Ah ... something was dead in each of us, Special Detective Rogers. And what was dead was hope.'

'You're talking in riddles again, Oscar. Don't you want to explain? Don't you want to remind me of what a genius you are?'

'I made a mistake, all right!' His voice rose considerably this time. 'She angered me. She annoyed the shit out of me and she wasn't right. Now forget her. Let's move on. Don't you want to know whether I have another gift for you?'

Frank caught his breath. Fear lodged in his throat once more. Was this the animal's final twist in this bizarre game? He hadn't yet offered proof that Laura was alive. Was he now going to offer irrefutable evidence of her death?

'Yes,' he whispered finally.

'Of course you do. And this time I'll even save you some bother, make life a little easier for you. My gift for you this time is Geraldine McGiven.'

Frank heard Nicky mutter: 'The second abductee.'

'I suppose she's already dead.'

'That's for me to know, and you to find out.'

'You wouldn't be giving her to me if she were alive.' Frank ran the list through his mind of what they thought they knew about this beast. He recalled the religion angle. Pro or anti? 'Oscar,' he said quietly. 'Don't you know it's a sin to do what you're doing to these people?'

'A sin? A sin, Frank? There is no sin, except stupidity.'

'And you're not stupid, are you, Oscar?' *You're not religious, either. Anti, then. Which probably means your parents were devout followers of some religion or religious group.*

'No, I'm not. I'm glad you understand that, at least. Now, why don't you stop trying to enter my mind, Special Detective Rogers? The passages and corridors are much too dark for you there. It's time we spoke about Geraldine. Time may be running out for her.'

'She's dead,' Frank insisted.

'So you say. But what if you're wrong? You can't be sure, can you? You can't be sure about anything where I am concerned. What if she is counting down to her terminal breath even as we speak? You may yet be in time to save her.'

'I don't think so. I think this is all just part of your squalid little game.'

'But thinking isn't the same as knowing, is it? And you can't risk being wrong about this. And believe me, when I play games they are neither squalid nor insignificant. So, hurry now. Hurry, for Geraldine's sake. You and all your busy, busy comrades in arms.'

And then he told Frank where to find her.

Chapter Twenty-Eight

There were no candles or bunting this time, no crucifixion, no bone dust. The abandoned building, once a haven for DIY enthusiasts, had been gutted of all fittings, leaving only the utilities intact. The power had long since been turned off, so portable floodlights, powered by generators, lit the scene. Dust swirled in bright arcs, and the shadows held their secrets close.

The derelict superstore formed part of an entire block of similar units just off London's North Circular road, each left to die when the land was purchased in order to make way for an estate of executive-style homes. The new landowners, perhaps rethinking their strategy in this busy part of Edmonton, decided to sit on their investment instead. The streets around the block were now usually deserted, disturbed mainly by youths looking to dump and burn out stolen vehicles.

The girl, who would have entered her teens three weeks before, was in a somewhat better condition than Jeanette Morris. She was still quite dead, but this time there were no obvious signs of torture, mutilation or post-mortem wounds. Her flesh, however, had the same quality, texture and appearance. Beyond the ruin of her cadaverous features was a face that had known both terror and immense pain. These two dark angels had visited her, and had not been kind.

Frank was staring down at her body when his chain of thought was interrupted by Warren Capel. 'Do you think he's slipping?' Capel asked. 'I mean, leaving her in another abandoned building just a few miles or so from where he left the Morris kid points to him being a local.'

'It suggests nothing of the kind.' Frank's response was bitter. He felt helpless. Helpless and afraid. 'It could be that he merely passes through this way on a regular basis. But I don't even think it's that.'

'But he's established a pattern,' Capel countered.

'Right. A pattern he really would like us to buy.'

'Superintendent Foster thinks the way I do. That the man has local knowledge.'

Frank turned to the younger man. Once he would have withered Capel with a glare. Now he no longer had it in him. He simply shook his head and said, 'You and Foster buy what you like, but leave me out. The fact is that both sites can be seen from the main roads, and it's quite obvious that they are disused. This man is far too clever to do something so obvious. Warren, you were a good copper once, your own man. Don't be taken in by Foster. He may carry you along on the ladder of promotion, but he'll also drag you down into the mediocrity he wallows in. You're better than that. Or, you once were.'

Heat rushed to Capel's cheeks. Even in the dim light that leaked across from the floods, Frank could see the man's burning embarrassment.

'Warren,' he said more kindly. 'The man we're after is not the genius he claims to be, but he *is* clever. Yes, he is establishing a pattern here, but not one we should be interested in. Leaving the bodies here tells me he doesn't live anywhere close by. He only wants us to think he does, or to at least consider it. He wants us to search for him here, run a door-to-door inquiry. It wastes a little more time, that's all. All part of his game.'

For a moment, he felt Capel's scrutiny. Then the young sergeant drew himself upright and turned away. Over his shoulder he said, 'Now I can see why you were collecting debts, Frank. You should go back to it. It's probably what you're best at.'

'Warren,' Frank called out.

Capel turned, his hands balled into fists, expecting to be challenged.

Frank smiled. 'Be careful out there.'

Capel took a breath and relaxed, shook his head and moved closer once more. 'What is it with you and Foster, Frank? He's a decent super. Why is there so much animosity between you two?'

Frank closed the gap between them in three easy strides. He yanked his thin denim shirt out of his trousers and pulled it up to his chest. Three scars ran across his abdomen in the shape of the letter K.

'This is why,' he said. 'Around seven or eight years ago, Foster and I were working on a case together. We tracked down a couple of real nasty bastards, followed them to an abandoned lockup in Leyton beneath the railway arches. We split up. I got jumped, but I managed to call out. I got cracked on the head with a crowbar and I went down. My head was still spinning and I was only halfway conscious when one of the bastards carved his initial on my stomach with an eight-inch machete. They were both laughing as he cut me. I was screaming like a stuck pig. For good measure, they gave me a couple of hefty kicks with their Doc Martens, then they ran. I was left holding my guts in both hands. And Foster…he was standing about twenty yards away, watching every moment. He didn't even try to help me.'

Capel's eyes were wide in disbelief. 'You're certain Foster saw all this?'

'Of course. It's not the kind of thing you have doubts about. He knew I saw him, too. He came to the hospital a day or two after I'd got out of intensive care. He said he was sorry. Then he begged me not to tell anyone. I told him where he could shove his apology.'

'But what happened after? After you reported him?'

Frank's smile was thin and thoughtful. 'I didn't. He was the up-and-coming wonder boy, the man with the golden gonads. I was the black sheep. My guv'nor would have believed me, but most at his rank or above wouldn't have. So, when I got out of hospital, I repaid Foster my own way.'

'You gave him a hiding.'

'Oh, yes. I gave him some bruises, a broken nose, and loosened a few of his pearly-whites. It was immature, but it made me feel just a bit better. But he's a louse in so many other ways. He's a parasite. He'll feed off your good work, Warren. That's why I told you to be careful.'

Capel gave a sheepish grin. 'Thanks. Maybe I need to rethink a few things. And ... I'm sorry. You know, for what I said.'

'Yeah. I know. But maybe you were right.'

'No. It's this damned case ... seeing the poor kid like that.' He held out a hand.

Frank shook it. 'Just watch your back.'

As Capel walked away, Nicky wandered over, oblivious to the exchange. 'Strange one this,' he said, indicating the girl's corpse. 'You'd think he would have cut her about even more than the first. He got a taste for it last time. You'd think he'd want more of the same, but there's no sign of escalation.'

Frank nodded. 'That's exactly what was running through my mind. Maybe he's just getting better at whatever he's trying to do. On the phone, he said he'd made a mistake with the first one. That must have been in letting anger get the better of him. She wasn't right, so he took his frustrations out on her.'

'So how does that explain what he did when he dumped her body?'

'Oh, he did that to get our attention. And because he could.'

'But what wasn't she right for?'

Frank shook his head. His eyes were desperate. 'That's what we have to find out, and find out quickly. Two down, Nicky. If he sticks to the pattern, there are only four to go before Laura.'

Chapter Twenty-Nine

Frank and Debbie were sitting down to dinner when Nicky arrived unexpectedly. Debbie had fetched some clothes from her small flat in Snaresbrook, then returned to Frank's house, and was there to greet him when he arrived home, insisting that she cook, that he eat a proper meal for the first time that week. He was not strong enough to argue, nor was he inclined to. The food was good, her presence beside him even better. It was hard carrying on with life, with Laura never far from his thoughts, but he knew that not looking after himself would solve absolutely nothing.

As soon as Frank opened the door to his friend he knew that something was wrong. He felt himself go instantly cold.

'Don't worry, mate, it's not what you think,' Nicky said hurriedly.

Frank found his breath. 'You'd better come in.'

When Nicky saw Debbie in the dining room, the half-eaten meal, uncorked bottles of wine, and Debbie looking as if she'd spent several hours choosing what to wear, he immediately apologised and turned to leave. But Frank put out a hand.

'If it was important enough to drag you here, then it's important enough for you to stay.'

Debbie agreed. 'Do you want me to make myself scarce?'

'No.' Frank shook his head. 'Whatever it is I'd only tell you anyway.'

She gave him a grateful smile, pulled out a chair for Nicky, and fetched him a glass. 'Have you eaten?' she asked. 'We can stretch what's left to three.'

'No, thanks.' Nicky sat down heavily. 'I'm going out to dinner with a few of the lads.'

'Sure?'

'Positive. Some wine will be great, though.'

He poured himself some Jacob's Creek Chardonnay, took a couple of sips, then turned his gaze to Frank. 'I thought you needed to know why Foster spent less than ten minutes at the murder scene earlier.'

Frank took some of his own drink. He blinked over the rim of the fluted glass. 'I'm not going to like this, am I?'

'No. You're not going to like it at all. All I ask is that you hear me out before you explode.'

Frank put his head back and rolled his eyes. 'What has that prick been up to now?'

'You guessed right, it *is* one of Foster's stunts. The second call that came in … I'm sorry, Frank, but Foster went behind our backs. He'd arranged to have a trace put on any call coming in on that line.'

'A trace!' Frank slammed the glass down onto the table, spilling the contents. As he got to his feet he felt a vein in the centre of his forehead begin to pulse. 'But he heard what that crazy fucker said. He knew what it could mean.'

'Yes. Yes, he did. But he went and traced it anyway. I swear I didn't know, Frank.'

'I realise that. God, Nicky, you don't have to justify yourself to me.' He took a few deep breaths, calming himself sufficiently to ask, 'So what happened?'

'The trace itself was no good. Our man is using a mobile phone. They can only be traced to a large cell location within a grid unless GPS is functional. Foster got a team working on it, however. There is no GPS to activate remotely, so it's probably an old device. They did, however find out what address the phone is billed to. Foster went straight there. A glory run, I think, looking to close the investigation and get himself another gold star. It turned out to be an office space. Rented out to a Mr Black. It's one of those complexes where you can lease space, a separate phone line, mail drop, that sort of thing.'

Frank was nodding. 'Yeah, I know what you mean.'

'From the owners, Foster was able to establish the following: the office and line have been leased to Mr Black for the past nine months. The arrangements were made over the phone, the quarterly bill paid in cash via a hand-delivered envelope. No one has ever seen Black. The phone line is rented by the company, and they charge Black for calls and the line itself. It's a hiding place for small and often shady businesses, but it's not illegal.'

'In other words, we can't trace him any further than that.' Frank shook his head slowly. 'He might be a warped, sick bastard, but he *is* clever. Too damned clever for my liking.'

'The company who run the complex have been asked to continue leasing both the office and the phone line. They were reluctant, but the persuasion wasn't too gentle. There shouldn't be any repercussions because of Foster's interference. Our man need never know the call was traced.'

'The stupid, vengeful bastard. Foster did that simply to get back at me for showing him up. He put my daughter's life at risk just to boost his fucking ego.'

Debbie reached out a hand, her fingers linking with his. 'Easy, Frank. It's over with now. Nothing came of it, so no damage done.'

'We can't be sure of that. This guy may actually have a way of knowing his call was traced. It may yet come back to haunt us.'

'Well, there's nothing we can do about that. It happened. It's history.'

Nicky's eyes were drawn to their interlocked hands. He raised his eyebrows, smiling. Debbie smiled back. 'We're something of an item,' she admitted.

'Good for you,' Nicky said, nodding approvingly. 'Bloody good. Now perhaps someone can keep him on the straight and narrow.'

Frank glared at them both. 'You're not putting me off. That bastard Foster will pay for what he did.'

'Just leave it be, Frank,' Nicky said. 'What's the point in antagonising the situation all the more? Believe me, when he puts in his report, he'll be hauled over the coals by the chief super. Your insistence for no traces went on record. Foster went against your wishes, complained about your threat, but more importantly he went against the best interests of the investigation this time. He'll pay.'

Frank gave a wry grin. 'Nicky, that tosser will worm his way out of it somehow. He'll say I gave the go-ahead verbally, or something along those lines. But don't you see? I have to get him stopped. Next time we may not be so lucky. Supposing our man uses another phone, one that can be traced? What then?'

Nicky considered this for a while. He drained his glass. Finally, he said, 'Let me handle it. I'll go to the chief super and tell him exactly what happened. Let him decide.'

Frank shook his head. 'No. No way. You can't do that. You go over his head and Foster will finish you.'

'You're forgetting one thing. I have an extremely influential friend.'

'Who?'

Nicky grinned. 'You. You're highly thought of by the chief super. He won't let Foster walk all over me. But if you steam in there now, kicking up a storm, he and the other brass might just consider you to be too emotional, and throw you off the case completely.'

Debbie stroked the back of Frank's hand. 'Listen to him. Nicky's right. Don't make waves. After, when it's all over, do what you want. Chin the bastard for me if you like. But now isn't the right time.'

Frank looked between them again. He blew out his cheeks. 'The voices of reason,' he growled. 'Why the hell do they have to plague me?'

Nicky pushed his glass across for a refill. 'The post-mortem result on the McGiven girl should be in tomorrow afternoon, Sunday at the latest. I'll let you know as soon as I see it. The girl's grandparents are coming down to identify the body ... if they can.'

'If it's her.' Frank surprised himself, the words spilling from his lips unchecked. He shrugged at Nicky's curious glance. 'The way this sicko likes to play games I wouldn't bet on it.'

'I never considered that,' Nicky said, shaking his head. 'Damn it! I should have done more to confirm her identity before we notified them.'

'Don't worry about it. I only thought of it just then. The girls look so similar it would be easy enough to make a mistake. I know these people coming down for the ID are family, but be careful with them. Make sure they're absolutely certain. We don't want to go burying the wrong girl.'

'Right. Thanks for that.'

'Where are they coming from?'

'Fleetwood. They lived just a few minutes from where she was taken in Blackpool.'

Frank sat back down at the table, the remainder of his meal untouched and unwanted. The room seemed to have grown dark during the conversation. Colder, too.

'Blackpool. London. Hove. Peterborough. He certainly gets around. You know, if he keeps these kids so long he must have a big place somewhere off the beaten track. I was thinking of a farm, holding them in a barn or something like that.'

'Why a farm?' Debbie wanted to know. It was the first time she had asked him anything about the investigation, other than how the search for Laura was progressing.

'In part because of the formaldehyde. We once had a DC whose brother was a farmer, and I seem to remember him telling me that some farmers use it to disinfect certain areas. It fits. He'd need somewhere isolated, so that he could take the girls in, bring the bodies out, without being seen or heard.'

'It's a good thought,' Nicky agreed. 'I wouldn't mind betting you've hit the nail on the head there. It does fit. Better than any place I can think of right now.'

'Not that it's of any help to us at the moment. Still, it's something to mull over.'

'Any more thoughts about Tania Penny?' Nicky asked, draining his glass.

'One or two. I tried contacting her earlier, but got no joy. I'm going up to see her as soon as I can arrange it.' He explained to Debbie about Samantha Penny's sister. She agreed it would be a good idea to see the young woman, ask a few more questions, bearing in mind the fresh information they had.

Nicky left soon after. Debbie washed the dishes, Frank dried and put away. They were silent minutes, both lost in thought. When they were done, Debbie pulled him into her arms. They held one another for some time, breathing as one person, before moving to the bedroom. As Friday eased into Saturday, they made love with a slow and easy passion that took their breath away. It was a balm to their wounds; wounds still open and fresh and ready to weep again. But for those few tender and precious moments in time, each was able to cast doubt and worry from their minds. Fear may have lingered a little longer, but it, too, was soon lost to the moment.

Chapter Thirty

Frank's study was small and cluttered. It smelled of musty files, stale air trapped since the winter months, nervous sweat, cheap cologne, Scotch. It was 7.30 am Frank had come downstairs around four, sleep having eluded him yet again. The heat of the previous day remained, and he wore only boxer shorts. He felt exhausted, eyes gritty, mouth as dry as the bottle of Bells by his elbow. In front of him lay a sheet of paper, notes and scribbles and scattered thoughts spread across it. He tried to make sense of the scrawl, but failed miserably. His eyes refused to focus, his head hammered. There was so little to go on, and time was now the most uncompromising of enemies.

A letter, lying face up on the desk, snagged his attention. It was from his bank, requesting a meeting to discuss the business. Collecting debts was the last thing on his mind at that moment, but he knew that if it was ignored for much longer, he would lose the company altogether. Frank shook his head at the thought. The least of his concerns right now, perhaps, but a worry he could do without.

The telephone rang. He snatched it up, irritably.

'Frank Rogers.' His voice was harsh. Dry and brittle. He cleared his throat.

'Hello, my dear special detective.'

'Who is this?'

'Oh, you know who I am, Frank. I'm the man with the power.'

Frank's mouth was suddenly drier still. A chill, an insect's swift scuttle, passed between his shoulder blades. 'How did you get my number?' he managed to ask.

'Oh, it was simple enough. It's amazing how much information one can purchase these days.'

Shocked as he was by this intrusion, Frank remembered what had to be done. 'I told you I wouldn't talk again unless I knew my daughter was still alive.'

'Oh, yes. Your question. I assure you, Frank, Laura is alive. And well, given her unusual circumstances. Here, let me play you something.'

A moment later, the man could be heard asking, 'What's your favourite place, Laura?' His voice echoed, its pitch slightly higher.

'My favourite place?' A pause, then: 'School.'

There was a distinct click, followed by the caller speaking again. 'You must be proud to have a scholar in the family, Frank.'

Frank had closed his eyes. It was his little girl. His heart sang at hearing Laura's voice again. *But school?*

Frank was frowning, deep ridges sagging on his brow like paint applied too thickly and left to dry. It had to be a clue, because Disney World was her favourite place, and no way would this creep come up with such a bluff. Laura liked school well enough, but her favourite place? No. No, it had to be some kind of clue. But what? Is that where he had her, in a disused school? Such a place would be big enough, out of the way even, perhaps in a rural location.

'Still there, Frank?'

'Yes. Yes, I'm just relieved to know my girl is okay.'

'Don't worry yourself about that for now. Worry about this: another gift has been left for you.'

'Where?'

'Oh, no need to rush, Frank. It's far too late for you to help my latest piece of work.'

Frank closed his eyes, callused fingertips tracing their edges. There really was no rush. This bastard was as good as his word. He'd let them know where to find the body, right enough. It was his way. Part of his MO. But he would do so in his own good time. Two so far. Number three wouldn't be any more dead for the delay. But what did he mean by 'piece of work'?

You have to know, Frank. This has gone on too long. You have to know this man. You have to see him in your mind.

'What work?' he asked.

'My art, of course. One can do so many wonderful, creative things with the human body, special detective.'

Frank's face began to burn. The two previous examples of this madman's creativity still haunted him. The question was, did the monster truly believe in his own words, or was he merely playing to an audience? The beat of a drummer no one else was able to hear.

Frank wrestled with his thoughts for a heartbeat or two.

'Some would say you have other, less aesthetic reasons for what you do,' he said.

'Oh, I know them all, Frank. Believe me, I've heard the tired ramblings of expensive meddlers. But no, I have no desire to sleep with my mother. Even if I had, necrophilia is not my style. You know that. I don't fuck 'em once they're dead, special detective. Not in the given sense. I just work on them. I am not impotent, nor am I shy around women. I had a decent childhood, I was kind to our pets, and I am not a loner. In short, I am not a stereotype. I am me. My own man. I remain true to myself. But tell me something, Frank. Do you?'

'I think so, yes,' he muttered, distracted by the man's words. 'Expensive meddlers'. The phrase stuck in his mind. 'Expensive meddlers'. Psychiatrists?

"Think so'. Come, come. That's nowhere near good enough for a man of your calibre. Be more positive.'

'I am, then.'

'Really? Perhaps. We shall have to see. I have a feeling your true worth will be put to the test before long. I see your face in the newspapers, Frank. I like what I see. And no, I am not a homosexual. I prefer the female of the species. You only have to see what I make of them to know that. But you look to be a worthy opponent. Women, alas, are not. Your new woman looks nice though, Frank. Capable, I'd say. Quite a candid picture one tabloid ran of you and … Debbie this morning. The name suits her. Nothing flash or whimsical. Nothing above her station in life.'

Frank felt himself shake with anger. The press must have been watching him from a distance since the case broke into the news. Grubby people spying on him, waiting for that first photograph of him breaking down. Instead they got some dirt.

'You leave Debbie out of this.' His voice was low, imbued with controlled aggression.

'I don't know that I can. She interests me. But then, so did your wife, though for entirely different reasons. The new floozy is so much nicer than Janet, Frank. Your good wife's photo may not have done her justice, but you're better off out of it, I'd say.'

'Now listen! I'm warning you …' Frank's hand squeezed tight around the receiver.

The cold, mocking voice interrupted him. 'A natural reaction. But a waste of your precious energy and emotion. Why not save it for Debbie? I'm sure she's demanding. Is she, special detective? Does she like to experiment in bed?'

'I told you to leave her …'

'Her breasts. About a thirty-six C-cup?'

Exactly, Frank had time to think.

'Do her nipples taste good?'

Frank continued to fight it. The urge to slam the phone down, to shut out that terribly confident voice, was almost overwhelming. But he couldn't react. He had already shown far too much weakness.

'I bet they do, Special Detective Rogers. I bet if I ran my tongue over them they would taste so sweet. But tell me, how do you think those milky white breasts would look and feel if I took a nice sharp chisel to those darling buds?'

Snapping point. The pencil Frank had been balancing between his fingers broke in two with a loud crack. 'You bastard! You low-life, scum-sucking …'

'Now, now. Is that any way to talk to a taxpayer?'

'You and me, filth. Just you and me. I challenge you to meet me face to face, you fucking cowardly prick.'

'You sound so sincere, Frank.'

'I am. Believe me, I am.'

'A little sincerity is a dangerous thing.'

'Don't fuck about, you coward. Meet me. Do it. If you're man enough'

'Oh, I don't think that would be wise.'

'So, I was right. You're just a common coward.'

'I am anything but common, Frank.'

Frank clamped down on another outburst. No. Goading this man would not work. Never, no matter how often he did it. He was playing into the bastard's hands. *And he still has Laura. Don't forget that. Never forget that.*

'Okay.' Softer now. Controlled. 'Have it your way. Tell me where I can find the latest victim.'

'I'll tell you in a moment. First, I'd like to find out how well you know the delightful Debbie.'

'Forget it. I won't discuss her with you.'

'You already are. Still, I'd watch out for her dark side if I were you, Frank. She must have one. Why else do you interest her? You're so dark yourself. Only you don't know just how dark. That's why you are working on my case. Kindred spirits, you and I. Kindred spirits.'

Frank let it wash over him. He waited until the silence had soaked up all the menace. 'Where is she?' he asked.

This time the madman told him. Then he laughed. 'As for doubting my manhood earlier, Frank. Perhaps I will have to now do something to prove it to you.' Then he hung up.

Frank slammed the phone down. He sat there for a few seconds, fighting the bile-black rage that threatened to envelop him, a rage that wanted to chew his heart and soul and mind to pieces. A hot coal burned in the pit of his stomach, churning, eating into his nerve-ends. He willed it away, eyes closed in concentration, sweat beading his hairline.

A noise startled him. His head jerked around in a blur of motion. Debbie was standing in the doorway. Her face was pale, one hand clutched to her throat.

'How long have you been there?' he asked.

Debbie was wearing his towelling dressing gown. She pulled it tight against her body, hugging herself, clearly distraught. 'Long enough,' she said. Debbie hung her head. Then added: 'In fact... too long, Frank. Way, way too long.'

Chapter Thirty-One

Laura raised her head from the soft pillow she had made from the pile of clothes. Her sleep had been fitful again, filled with terrifying images she could not remember clearly, but which had left her with an immense feeling of dread. A scuffle of movement outside the room had alerted her, and now both eyes were fastened on the door. Would one of them come for her now? Did it even matter? Perhaps she was already past caring.

She had no idea what time of day it was, and the rumblings in her stomach gave no clue. The deep growl was permanent – or so it seemed. She was constantly hungry, the meagre scraps they fed her barely enough to keep her alive. What little routine there was in this terrible place revolved around irregular meals and visits to the toilet. They would bring food and drink to her when they felt like it or thought about it. Some time after, one of them would collect the dishes. Later still she would be taken out of the room and led along a wide, bright passageway to the immense lavatory; the only other part of the building they had so far allowed her to see.

Mealtimes terrified her.

When the rattle of keys came in the lock, Laura's dulled senses seemed to kick in, releasing a flood of adrenaline. Anxiety took her by the hand. The trouble was, she never knew what to expect from either of them.

There was never much in the way of sustenance: a bowl containing a small amount of rice and a single potato; a thin soup, perhaps; watery porridge, which reminded her of the thin gruel her grandmother used to make when she and Gary stayed over at their grandparents' house. There was never any meat, nor bread. Even so, she welcomed any of these meals, and ate voraciously, all the while telling herself to slow down, to savour each mouthful, even as she shovelled it into her mouth with her fingers.

Occasionally, however, there would be an unwelcome surprise waiting for her. Rancid milk had appeared on the menu again. Once there was a thin gravy liberally poured over a dead mouse, its intestines bursting through a gash left by the spring-trap it had blindly wandered into. She didn't eat this, but the thought of the man forcing her to do so stayed with her for hours afterwards. Another time she had spooned into her mouth a quite presentable vegetable stew, only to discover that its ingredients included wood-lice and tiny spiders, some of which were still alive.

Her captors had scarcely spoken to her since the initial flurry of exchanges. The woman would study her more closely than the man did, her eyes roaming, exploring Laura's developing body. The girl felt unveiled by the scrutiny, its touch like the brush of a cobweb in the dark.

The woman worried her.

But the man petrified her.

He hadn't touched or physically abused her in any way, yet his presence filled her with absolute dread every time he entered the room. She wouldn't have been able to explain her terror to anyone, it was just instinctive, a sense of … of something evil and brooding and deadly. If he was in the room she had to be on her guard all the time, speaking only when he did, and only then after careful consideration. It demanded enormous concentration, and sometimes Laura felt it was beyond her. The man was unstable, seeming to teeter wildly on the edge between normality and madness. It was like being locked in a room with a rattlesnake, or a scorpion.

At one point, the growing stench of being unclean making her feel nauseous and degraded, Laura asked if she might have a wash. The man had turned his cold eyes upon her, a blank and glassy, pitiless gaze.

'Wash?' he said. It was as if the word meant nothing to him. 'You want to wash?'

'Yes, please.' Laura offered a tired smile.

Without a word he left the room, returning moments later with a large red pail, the word FIRE stencilled on its side. She thought he would set it down and leave her to it. Instead he launched its contents over her with one sudden movement, the icy water drenching her frail body, its impact stalling her breath. He then hurled the pail across the room and turned on her as it first smashed against the wall then clattered to the floor.

'Next time I'll hose you down, you little bitch. Would you like that?' He bent forward, glowering, spittle flying from his lips. 'Well ... would you?'

'No.' Laura sat there with water dripping from her nose and chin, hair plastered to her scalp, the thin cotton dress soaked through and clinging to her body.

'I guess you won't want to wash again, will you?'

Laura shook her head. Tears now rushed down her cheeks, merging with the foul-smelling, stagnant water.

'I didn't hear you,' he said melodically, almost singing the words. One hand cupped behind his ear.

'No. I won't.'

'No. Of course. I thought not. You sluts are all the same.' He shook his head as if disappointed in her, then stormed from the room.

After that she had to fight an inner battle to stop herself from flinching every time he came near. The trouble was she was unable to decipher his moods. Smiles were swept away in an instant, replaced by a savage intensity that threatened to explode at any moment. He seemed to bring a chill into the room with him.

And every time he left he paused at the doorway and asked the same question: 'Have you been inside my house?'

And always she would answer 'No'.

Now she heard the familiar jangle of keys once more. The lock snapped back. The door inched open. The girl swallowed hard. It was him. It didn't feel like mealtime, and she wasn't due to use the toilet. This just seemed like a different sort of intrusion from all the others. So, was this it? Had her time come? Was she about to discover the purpose of him taking her, the reason behind the slaying of her mother and brother?

She thought so.

As the door swung fully open and she saw the detached look on his face, she really did think so. And she hoped she would be strong enough not to beg for mercy.

Chapter Thirty-Two

Another deserted building. Another murdered child.
This time they found the body in a disused multi-storey car park next to an outdoor market in Acton. All gates leading into the car park were securely padlocked, but the lock of a door at the side of the building had been removed, and entry gained away from prying eyes. The corpse was left sitting propped against one of the concrete pillars, like a beggar waiting for the next handout.

Detective Superintendent Foster was conspicuous by his absence. Nicky Loizou had handled everything with the scene of crime officers, ensuring the chain of evidence, such as it was. Frank Rogers managed to stay in the background, observing from a distance, trying to remain objective if not detached. Geraldine McGiven was now confirmed as the second victim. If the monster was playing true to form, Frank thought, as he and Nicky finally left the SOCO to it, this would be Tracey Edmunds from Sheffield.

Sebastian Reeves was attending the scene of a fatal shooting in Finsbury Park, but Ernie Chalk, another pathologist well known to Frank, had arrived and would also be able to perform the post-mortem. More to the point, he was willing to do so even on a Saturday.

As with Geraldine, the girl had not been disfigured in the way the first victim had, yet there was something different about the body. The child's flesh was a little less decomposed than the others, but it hung on its skeletal framework like an ill-fitting suit. It sagged and drooped obscenely over her slender frame, and across her stomach was a gaping maw, out of which bulged the purplish remnants of her stomach and intestines.

* * *

Returning to the annexe from the scene, Frank and Nicky arranged to meet the following day. Nicky appeared exhausted from the now constant throng of crime scenes to attend, young victims to take care of, reports to complete, next of kin to inform, and identities to confirm. Frank was simply overwhelmed by all that his mind fed to him in a drip-feed of dark imagination. He was literally worn down by fear.

'You seeing Debs tonight?' Nicky asked. He now looked as crumpled as his clothing.

'I doubt it. I don't think I'll see her until Monday at the crematorium. I probably won't be fit company until afterwards.'

'You think it'll work out? You and her.'

Frank gave an expansive shrug. 'Who can tell? It's perhaps something and nothing. I can't see that far ahead.'

'But you like her, yes?'

'I love her, Nicky. We love each other, but sometimes that's not enough.'

'But it's a damned good start.' Nicky smiled. 'Just go with it. See where it leads.'

'Maybe. But I've got a bit on my mind just now, mate.'

'Debs is the kind of woman who'll understand. She'll give you all the space and time you need.'

'I know. She's good for me, and we get on really well. I just need to think about it a little more. I need to think about everything a little more.'

* * *

Frank did some of his best thinking out in the open air. Walking helped, too, he found. One of his favourite places was the public golf course overlooked by the Redbridge home, just a few minutes away from where he lived. Here he could skirt the holes, climb some pretty steep hills, cut through knots of trees, and casually observe people play a relaxing game while he, himself, tried to unwind.

The sun was high, but a gentle cooling breeze blew a welcome caress. The golf course was busy, yet he felt alone and miles from civilisation.

He was still there when Nicky called.

Having paused by a green while a golfer stood over a long putt, Frank wrestled the mobile from his jacket pocket. It only rang twice, but this was more than enough for the angry golfer, who muttered and shook his head in disgust. His partners, all of whom wore the obligatory red tops demanded by the course manager, did likewise.

Frank gave an apologetic shrug, then walked hurriedly away, across to a wide stretch of rough that separated the first and ninth holes. He stood behind a young tree whose thin trunk was shielded by wire, hoping to keep out of the way of stray drives.

'I think we may have caught a break,' Nicky told him.

The increase in Frank's pulse-rate was immediate. 'Tell me,' he said.

'We ran a check for any suspicious intruder or stranger reports in Paul Clarke's neighbourhood, going back three months. Nothing of interest came up. We did the same for the Redbridges and got a hit. Two nights before Karen Redbridge saw the man in her room, a woman in a neighbouring road called in shortly after midnight to report seeing a vehicle she didn't think should be parked outside her home.'

'Please tell me they got the plates.' Frank's tongue felt thick and heavy. The sounds and colours of the golf course, normally things he would have luxuriated in, now washed over him as he moved anxiously from foot to foot.

'They did. But it gets better. The vehicle was a van. And it had a clearly identifiable sign on the side.'

'Tell me it's a locksmith and I'll have your baby.'

'Not quite. And, that's an ugly thought, mate. No, the van belongs to a self-employed plumber.'

Frank felt a surge of disappointment. 'That's not exactly the trade we'd normally associate with this, Nicky. A builder, maybe, a chippy, for sure. But a plumber? What the hell do they know about doors?'

'It's a lead, Frank. You want to follow this up or not?'

'Of course.'

'You want me there?'

'No need.' He turned his head to look across at the road that swept alongside the first hole. 'Besides, I'm already here.'

Nicky gave him the name, address and telephone number associated with the van owner. 'Don't pick him up just yet,' Frank warned. 'But get him under surveillance as soon as you can arrange it. Your best teams, mate. I don't want this fucker spooked.'

* * *

Though the Redbridge house stood only a mile or so from his own home, the area might as well have been located on a different planet. The women in these houses were the kind to get together for coffee mornings and Tupperware parties, not in-depth discussions about the latest episode of Eastenders, and riotous Ann Summers evenings.

The three-storey house was an imposing presence, a large central gable flanked by two smaller ones, bay windows jutting forward as if keen to announce themselves. The exterior of the red-brick and sandstone house was as neat and tidy as the interior that Frank had seen on his previous visit. Dwarf conifers lined up in a row to separate the path from a gravel driveway.

Allison Redbridge was kneeling on the path working on the weeds when Frank got there. Mrs Redbridge looked surprised to see him, but smiled pleasantly as she brushed herself down and led him through to the kitchen.

'If you've come to speak with Karen, I'm afraid she's out shopping with her father,' she said over her shoulder. 'Can I get you a drink? Tea? Coffee?'

Frank shook his head. 'Nothing, thank you. I really just have a couple of questions for you, actually.'

'Fire away.' She leaned back against the sink unit, crossing her arms beneath her breasts. Her cheeks were flushed and shiny.

'Mrs Redbridge, when I was here before, your husband was asked whether you'd had any tradesmen working here during the previous few months. He said not. I can now be a little more specific, and wonder if you've had need of a plumber in, say, the last six months or so.'

Allison Redbridge shook her head immediately, and Frank felt himself tighten inside. 'No. Definitely not. We've not had any plumbing work carried out here for, oh, three or four years. And then it was Simon's brother who did the work. We had a new shower installed.'

Frank nodded, biting his lower lip. 'You're absolutely certain? No emergency work? Burst pipe, that sort of thing?'

'No. Sorry. Is this important?'

'I'm really not sure at this point. If you had employed a plumber, and it happened to be the person we're looking at right now, then …' Frank let it hang there, his mind already wondering what his next move might be.

'We really don't have many tradesmen working here, Mr Rogers. Simon's brother is quite handy with most things.' She smiled and rolled her eyes. 'Except some forms of carpentry. There we had him stumped.'

Frank, who had turned to leave, glanced across the room. 'What do you mean by that?'

She inclined her head towards the door that led out into the garden, the one whose lock had been removed by the intruder. 'It was that door, actually. Barry, that's Simon's brother, had one attempt at hanging it. He made such a poor job of it that we had to employ someone.'

'How long ago was this, Mrs Redbridge?'

Allison Redbridge screwed up her eyes. 'Oh, it must be nine months or so, now. Late September, I think it was.'

'Mrs Redbridge, can you remember who you used?'

'Oh, yes. I have his business card somewhere. He did a very nice job.'

She moved across to a cabinet on the other side of the kitchen and began rustling through the contents of the top drawer. Frank watched her with mounting interest. He and Nicky had made a mistake. The parameter they had used previously was within the past few months. The door had been fitted last year, and therefore had not crossed Simon Redbridge's mind. Even now, the penny was not dropping for Allison Redbridge.

Nodding to herself and smiling, she straightened and turned to him, arm extended. She handed him a beige card. Frank turned it over and read what was printed there in black letters.

The information Nicky had given him was: Alan Stevenson, Plumber.

The card read: Alan Stevenson, Joiner and Carpenter.

Frank ran it through in his head. A multi-skilled tradesman whose business image was that of master of one trade rather than Jack of all. A man who had fitted the very door used to gain unlawful entry. A man whose van had been seen two nights before the break-in.

A man Frank thought he should be more interested in than he actually was. What he'd heard was circumstantial at best, yet it was their first real lead. He knew he ought to be feeling something inside, something beavering away at his stomach. Instead he felt hollow. He would follow this development through, but having hoped for elation, he now felt merely curious. Frank had learned long ago to trust his instincts, and they were simply not convinced.

Chapter Thirty-Three

On another blissfully warm Sunday morning, Frank tended the garden as best he could. His mind afforded him no peace, yet it felt good to be focusing on something different, something natural and mundane. The borders needed tidying, plants required deadheading, and the mower and strimmer got a run-out. At lunchtime, he even cooked himself something, though nuking a lasagne in the microwave was hardly a stiff culinary challenge. But he ate it all, washed it down with a bottle of ice-cold White Stripe, and tried to keep himself busy.

Later that afternoon, as they made use of a local pub's garden furniture, Frank and Nicky discussed their suspect. 'I have a team at the address,' Nicky explained. 'It's a house, so he probably works from home as most of these tradesmen do. One team was in place yesterday evening, but his vehicle didn't arrive until near midnight. The driver matched the description Mrs Redbridge gave you. He may have been on a job earlier, or even out socialising.'

'Or with his victims,' Frank suggested. 'If he's our man, it's likely he spends as much time as he can at the place where he's keeping Laura.'

'We brought some extra teams in this morning, but he hasn't been out so far. A woman and a couple of young children have been spotted, so it looks as though he has a family. We'll sit on him until he moves. We'll have him, Frank. No problem. By the way, how did it all end up with Mrs Redbridge?'

'You know, it really didn't seem to register at first that Stevenson might be the man we're after. Then it suddenly seemed to hit her, and she was horrified. I tried to fend her off, lead her away from what she was thinking. I said we just needed to follow up a lead, but she's no dummy. To the best of her recollection, though, he wasn't a million miles away from the description Karen gave us.'

'That aspect has been bothering me. How come Karen didn't recognise Stevenson as the man she saw in her bedroom?'

'I asked Allison Redbridge about that. She said he was only there for two days, and both times he was gone by the time Karen got home from school. Karen may have seen him for a brief moment on the second morning, which would explain the sense of familiarity.'

'Stevenson is described as a little above average height, slightly built but strong, hair cut or shaved close to the scalp, yes?'

'Yeah.'

'Could look tall to a girl lying in her bed. Slightly built could be interpreted as slim. And if he does shave his head, perhaps he shaved it even closer for that visit.'

Frank nodded his agreement. 'I tried getting hold of the woman who called in that night, but she and her husband are away for the weekend. She may be able to give us a more recent description.'

'If she got a decent look at him.'

'Yeah. I suppose we'll have to bide our time on that one. So now we just wait for the teams to let us know when he's on the move. What are their instructions after that?'

Nicky pulled back his shoulders and rolled them. He was wearing sunglasses, but now he propped them up on his head, squinting. His skin prickled beneath the sun. He took a mouthful of his pint before continuing.

'The moment they spot him they call in an extra team. When he moves, three move with him, leaving one at the house. They circle and interchange; you know the drill. Their orders are not to approach him unless there's an immediate threat to Laura or any of the remaining girls. Once they have confirmation of Laura's whereabouts, they hold back and wait for a decision.'

'Which'll be made by Foster.' Frank shook his head in disgust.

'Maybe. Best wait and see on that one, Frank. There's some shit hitting the fan right now, so let's not jump to any conclusions.'

'And what if it all goes off early tomorrow? We'll be at the crematorium in the morning.'

'I know. The teams are aware of that, as a couple of them were due to attend. Again, let's see how it all pans out. No point in worrying unduly.'

'No. Agreed.' Frank held up a hand to shield his eyes from the sun's glare. 'Is it him, Nicky? Is this our man?'

'I really have no idea. Do you feel it?'

'You know, I'm not at all sure I do. I've got so much churning around inside me right now that I don't know how I feel about this man. All we have on him is that he works in the right trade and he was parked near a particular house days before that same house was broken into. It's worth a look, but it's pretty thin.'

Nicky gave a nod. 'Even so, it's still far more than we had before.'

'That's true. I realise this has to be taken seriously, mate, but if you backed me into a corner I'd have to say I'm not buying it. You know how I get, how my instincts take over, and I'm just not feeling it this time.'

'You're not infallible, Frank. You've been wrong before,' Nicky reminded him.

'I know. And I will be again. But Stevenson doesn't feel right. I need more convincing.'

He knocked back his drink and went to fetch two more. They spent the next few minutes mulling over the report that Nicky himself had collected from Ernie Chalk. The victim, confirmed as Tracey Edmunds, died the same way as victim number two: asphyxiation. Prior to her death, Geraldine McGiven had been injected with formaldehyde whilst still alive. Clear evidence of this had been found. Both men were appalled by the news, the child's pain unimaginable. This had not happened to Tracey Edmunds, however.

'Jesus,' Nicky said, reaching the final paragraph. He uttered a low whistle. His hand snaked out reflexively for his glass.

Frank looked up. 'What is it?'

'The bit about the flesh. No wonder it sagged.'

Frank huddled closer, running his eyes down the thin sheet of paper Nicky had laid out on the wooden table. Ernie Chalk's conclusion was that Tracey Edmunds had been skinned like an animal. Not well, and not effectively. Butchered may have been a better description. Either way, her flesh had been removed in an amateurish fashion and then later replaced over her skeletal framework. Because of the deep creases created by the sagging curtains of flesh, the thick welts made by whoever sewed the skin back together had not been obvious at the crime scene. According to Ernie Chalk, however, the body laid out on his stainless-steel counter had resembled a patchwork quilt.

Frank and Nicky swapped puzzled glances. 'Do you understand any of this?' Nicky asked.

'No. It beats the shit out of me. Why on earth would he skin her, then piece the strips back together again afterwards? It doesn't make sense.'

Nicky ran back through the report. 'Formaldehyde. Again. What is this crazy bastard up to?'

'Don't ask. I wouldn't want to be inside this one's mind for too long. He isn't like anyone else I've ever heard of. First, the period between his crimes *increases* instead of lessens, and second, the level of mutilation *de*creases. You can still see a natural progression, though. Each one has been in a different stage of...'

'Frank?' Nicky frowned at him.

'I can see it now,' Frank said eventually. 'I can see exactly what he's up to. But for the life of me I can't see why.'

'So, do I get let in on the secret?'

Frank swallowed. Cleared his throat. 'He's trying to stuff them. Human taxidermy, Nicky. I couldn't see it before because I was still thinking of the formaldehyde as more of an acid, as a method of torture. But as a preservative I'll bet it's used by amateur taxidermists, maybe even those in the profession. First, he tried injecting it into Jeanette Morris when she was already dead. That failed. He then injected it into Geraldine McGiven while the poor kid was still alive, hoping the natural blood flow would do the trick. Then I imagine he sought some advice, possibly looked at a book or two. I'll bet that was when he discovered that good taxidermy is possible only if you take the skin off first.'

Nicky gaped. 'You can't be serious.'

'Oh, but I am. I'll take any bet you care to wager.'

Frank could see a young couple at a table just behind Nicky looking in his direction. He realised his voice had grown increasingly loud.

'But how do we find out for sure?' Nicky asked him.

Frank gave a wry smile. 'We ask an expert.'

Chapter Thirty-Four

Frank was fortunate enough to locate a taxidermist who worked where he lived, and was actually at home on a glorious Sunday afternoon. Delighted to be of help, the man confirmed Frank's theory, explaining how the flesh had to be carefully peeled from the body, everything else but the skeleton itself removed, before replacing the skin over padding in the shape of muscles. And yes, formaldehyde was widely used by taxidermists, both amateur and professional. There was no elation at being proved right, just a growing sense of distaste and alarm.

Around eight-thirty that evening, Frank felt like getting out of the house again, so Nicky drove him to a bar in Highams Park; the type of drinking establishment where only members and their guests were welcome, and membership did not come without someone getting at least a monkey stuffed into their top pocket. Located opposite the level-crossing by Highams Park railway station, the door leading down into the basement bore no name, just the street number. A passer-by would have no idea that an illegal, subterranean bar was only yards away.

Soft amber lighting failed to cut through the thick cigarette smoke that hung in the air like a physical barrier. It was almost impossible to see further than five yards, an enforced myopia that suited the majority of patrons, many of whom were either villains, policemen, or alcoholics – some a heady cocktail of all three. Somewhere in the miasma, a solo guitarist worked his way awkwardly through his Hank Marvin repertoire.

'Jesus,' Frank said into his friend's ear. 'Both my hands have mild arthritis, I haven't picked up my guitar in years, and I can still play better than that.'

Nicky led them across to a booth. 'Want me to get you an audition?'

They were served by a semi-clad waitress who quite obviously wanted to sell them more than drinks. 'Two double Irish, and two of your famous mixed grills, please,' Nicky ordered.

'Uh-huh. Anything else you fancy?'

In her late teens, she wore a sheer blouse, through which her small breasts could clearly be seen. A minute G-string was the only other thing she wore, and it was obvious that not only her legs were shaved on a regular basis. Frank had never been inside the club before, but he knew exactly what she would do for an extra fifty pounds.

Both men shook their heads, and Nicky winked and said, 'Just the order, please, sweetheart. And don't send anyone else over, either. We're here for a drink and a chat.'

The young woman scurried away, hips swaying as she had been taught. Frank peered through the smoke, could hear the hubbub of voices, the clinking of glasses. His eyes came to rest on his friend, who gave a shrug.

'Nice place,' Frank said, rolling his eyes. 'How long have you been a member here?'

'A month or so. An informant of mine introduced me to the bar. Seemed like a place to come when I wanted to get away from it all, and whenever I felt like it. It's open twenty-four hours a day, apart from Christmas day.'

'Who's place is it?'

'It belongs to Victor Brown. He bought it from the Clay brothers a year or so back.'

'Vic the Whiff?' Victor Brown was a small-time thug with an aversion to bathing. 'Ten minutes in an interview room with him and you need to have your clothes fumigated and your body de-loused.'

Nicky grinned, nodding. 'I know. I swear he did it so that we'd toss him back onto the street more quickly.'

Their drinks arrived, the waitress not sparing them a second glance this time around. Nicky sipped from his and leaned forward across the small, rectangular table whose surface swam with spilled alcohol. 'I see your mob were lucky again last season,' he said. 'Boring bloody Arsenal.'

Frank raised his eyebrows, the poster above Gary's bed spearing into his mind. 'The more we win, the luckier we seem to be. Remind me how your team did again. Why do you support that bunch of pikeys?'

'Hey, I'm a Leytonstone boy. West Ham were my local club, and while we may have struggled a bit recently, good things are expected next season.'

'Yeah, like celebrating a corner.'

The two men shared several of the same interests, none more so than football. They attended as many clashes between their favoured teams as they were able, several England games, and a few neutral matches played at the grounds of other London sides. Work and family commitments often got in the way, but each game was a brief escape from the reality of the crumbling world they saw on a daily basis.

'I see that band you like, Steeleye Span, have another album out.'

Frank glared at his friend. 'It's Steely Dan, as well you know. Span are strictly folk music, and the only thing worse than folk music is the dead-dog, unfaithful-partner, train-wreck-of-a-life style of country music.'

Nicky was laughing now. 'I knew that'd get a rise out of you. You're so easy to wind up, which is strange considering your legendary patience and even temper.'

Frank smiled warmly at his friend. 'I know what you're doing, mate. And I thank you for it. Every time I reach the point where I think I can turn the release valve a little, something else crops up. I understand that you want me to get my mind off it for a few hours, but I really don't think that's possible right now. Sorry.'

Nicky wiped his eyes, which were already stinging from the smoke. 'That's okay. I think I was a bit naive to imagine you sitting here and chatting as though nothing was wrong. I'm concerned about you, mate, that's all.'

'I know that. It's just been a fucking awful week, and tomorrow doesn't even bear thinking about.' Frank swallowed. Already he could see himself standing over Gary's brass plaque. 'But I'll make it. With you and Debs, plus Peter Forsyth in my corner, I'll get through it somehow. I have no choice. Laura will need me.'

They ate their meal and polished off another drink, the topics of their discussion ranging from Kylie Minogue's rear-end, to war in the Middle-East. Though neither mentioned the investigation or the following day's ceremony, both were uppermost in their thoughts. Frank knew that life had to go on, but it would never be the same.

Nicky dropped him home then slipped away. His own flat in Woodford held endless possibilities with a flight attendant, he explained. If she was back from the Algarve, that was. He revealed that the two had been dating for a little over a month, having met as part of an investigation which was now over. Frank told him to switch off and enjoy what remained of the night.

The moment Frank stepped through his front door, he noticed something for the first time: since Monday, he had left the hallway light burning. Afraid of the dark? Or a guiding light for his daughter?

Oh, Laura. How is he treating you, baby bear? How are you coping? I know you're still alive. My heart knows it even if my head might suggest otherwise. But how do you get through each day, sweetheart? How?

It was almost midnight, but Frank went into his study, picked up the phone and punched in a speed-dial number. Debbie answered on the second ring.

'I need you,' he said simply.

* * *

They lay in bed together, Frank's arms wrapped around her, hugging her close. They had not made love. It wasn't something either of them craved this night. All Frank desired was someone to be with, the beat of another heart close to his own, the simple warmth of a body belonging to someone he loved a great deal. All Debbie wanted was to ease his pain.

'Did you have a good evening with Nicky?' she asked. Disembodied in the darkness, her voice whispered softly.

Frank told her about the club, the hooker-cum-waitresses, the splendid food, and the dreadful music. 'Why don't you play any more?' Debbie asked him. 'I remember you pulling out an acoustic at one of Janet's dinner parties, getting us all to sing along with 'American Pie', 'Hey Jude', and stuff like that. It was a fabulous night. You're good at it. You should keep it up, not let a talent go to waste.'

'You sound like my agent.' Frank moved his hand over the curve of her hip, caressing her smooth thigh. 'It's just something that doesn't seem to happen anymore. It wasn't a conscious decision, or anything like that. There just never seems to be time these days.'

'I would have thought there was plenty of time once Janet moved out.' Debbie's voice became tender: perhaps she didn't wish to invoke any bad memories.

'Too much. That's why I spent most of it either at work or in some boozer or another.'

'I didn't think you were the type to mind being on your own.'

'There's a difference between being alone, and being lonely. I was both, and hated being in this house during the week when the kids weren't here.'

Debbie nuzzled into him, her breath warm on his chest. Her fingers toyed with the hairs there, curling and twisting. 'You stopped living, Frank. For the past ten months or so you've existed, but not taken time for life.'

'There won't be much time for that tomorrow, either.' He didn't know why he'd said that, and wished now that he hadn't. It came back to him with a rush then, not that it had been too far away, out there lurking in the shadows, waiting for one little slip.

Tomorrow morning, while Laura was somehow pushing her way through each passing hour, her mother and brother would disappear from this earth for good. All that remained would be ashes and fine particles of bone.

'I need you to be strong for me tomorrow,' Frank said softly, his voice little more than a muted whisper. 'I need you to carry me through it.'

Debbie kissed his cheek, and then his lips. 'Whatever you need, Frank. Whatever you need.'

And when tomorrow is over, Frank thought but did not say, I'm coming for you, Laura. Daddy's coming, baby bear. Hold on. Just you hold on.

Chapter Thirty-Five

No sleet or snow, nor wind or rain befitting such a sombre occasion. Instead it was yet another fine summer's day when Janet and Gary Rogers were turned to dust at the City of London Cemetery and Crematorium in east London.

The ceremony itself was mercifully brief. Janet had not held any particular faith, and so the readings were more personal, a celebration of the two lives, the hymns chosen by the attending vicar. Heads bowed as the first casket slid from view. The second was smaller, so much harder to bear, but this time Frank did not lower his head. He watched stoically, whispered a final farewell, and promised to bring to justice the man who sent his son hurtling brutally from this life. Frank Rogers did not cry, but there were many tears shed around him.

He and Debbie stood together. At her side were Janet's parents. Both had mumbled words of apology and regret, which he did not need, but accepted nonetheless. He did so more for their sake than his own. To his right stood his own mother, whose presence had stunned Frank. The only dry eyes were hers and his own. Nicky was in the next row, directly behind Frank. Peter Forsyth, having arrived late, remained at the back by the door. There were other relatives, many friends, including a large group of men and women Frank had worked with down the years. Even Chief Superintendent Badger and Commander Allen were there to pay their respects. Frank was genuinely grateful to each and every one of them.

After the floral tributes had been placed within a brick quadrangle, other than a few lilies left inside glass vases beside the tiny brass plaques, Frank shook hands and said goodbye to those who had come to pay their respects. He accepted the obligatory platitudes with a smile and a nod, then made a point of seeking out his old mentor.

'Thanks for coming, Peter. It means a lot to me.'

Forsyth pushed away the offered hand, and instead pulled Frank into a warm embrace. 'If I can do anything, just let me know,' he said. 'And I mean anything. You want it, you've got it, my friend.'

Frank nodded. 'You still have influence, Peter?'

'Let's just say, I know which cupboards to look in for the skeletons.'

'One of these days you and I will have to have a chat about police corruption at the highest level.'

Forsyth patted his arm and turned to leave. 'Read it in my memoirs, Frank. But if you do need any leverage …'

The last to lay their floral tributes were Debbie and Nicky, and neither offered further words of comfort. No words could make this personal tragedy seem more acceptable. They left Frank standing alone for a time, deciding to wait for him in the car park. Birds sang in nearby trees, insects droned amongst the flowers, the sun beat down relentlessly. The sky was blue and clear and had no end. At that moment, he didn't care if he ever saw another. For him this would always be a summer of darkness.

Frank stared down at the brass rectangles. *There is no justice in this world,* his mind insisted. How could there be? An eight-year-old boy was dead, murdered in his bed, his last moments filled with more pain and terror than most people would encounter in a lifetime. What had he done in those few short years to deserve such an end? Nothing. Absolutely nothing. Life was unfair; that was accepted. But did it also have to be so cruel?

Shaking his head, Frank blinked back a fresh well of tears. He couldn't quite believe there were any more inside him to shed, but he somehow realised that what had gone before was merely the beginning. The real grieving, the real torment was yet to come. When this was over, when Laura's fate was also known, the protective walls he had erected would crumble and fall. He couldn't imagine what lay beyond, what might become of him then.

Several yards away, someone had tied balloons to one of the many other plaques that were laid out in neat rows, the ribbon fluttering in the light breeze. Frank moved across to take a closer look, and saw a small photograph attached to the ribbon's knot. A toddler, no more than two or three, Frank imagined. He checked the plaque, erected the day before according to the engraving. A little girl. Dead within thirty months of being born. What kind of God could allow such a terrible tragedy?

In the days and months and years to come, Frank knew there would be his own set of photographs to leap out at him unexpectedly, birthdays and Christmases to somehow get through. And when he had dealt with them there would always be an unbidden memory to catch him unawares. It was then that Frank realised something else: he was never going to be the same person again, the man he had been before that awful night. That Frank Rogers was gone for good. As dead and gone as his wife and son.

On the drive back to the house, he sat with Debbie in the rear of Nicky's car. No words were exchanged. No one else had been invited back. There would be no sandwiches, drinks and polite conversation. When they reached his home the two men embraced momentarily, before Nicky left them to it.

'I'll call you later,' Nicky said. 'Let you know how the watchers have got on.'

* * *

Inside the house there was no respite from the heat. Frank threw open the French windows, but there was little breeze, and the air remained warm and thick and moist. Debbie had switched the kettle on, and was washing two cups. Her black jacket lay over the back of a dining chair. Her crisp white blouse clung to her body, the slim-fitting skirt hugging every contour. She looked so much a part of the room, as if she had always belonged.

They sat at the table, Debbie slid a mug of tea across to him. They talked about the ceremony, agreeing how beautiful it had been.

'What is it with you and your mother?' Debbie asked. 'I mean, down the years I've known you, I picked up on the fact that you two don't get on.'

Frank snorted. 'That's the understatement of the year.'

'Still, I couldn't believe how cold you both were to each other today. I've never seen that side of you before. As for her, she slipped away without a word. I don't even know why she bothered to come.'

'I imagine she's grieving,' Frank said simply. 'In her own way. Gary was her grandson, after all. For all I know she may even be hurting. But she would never allow anyone to see behind the mask. Never show that kind of weakness.'

'And you? Could you not have reached out to her, today of all days?'

Frank hung his head. This was another cigarette moment, and all he had was lousy gum. 'Debs, you have to understand that the chasm between my mother and me can't be bridged by the death of someone she barely knew.'

Debbie stroked her arms and leaned back in the chair. 'What on earth happened? What was so terrible that it drove you two apart?'

Without looking up at her, Frank said, 'You could pick one of several reasons. The way she broke my father's spirit, for a start. He was a good man, an honest, hard-working docker. Tough as old boots. Except where she was concerned. He worshipped her; even as a kid I could see that. But she ground him down, Debs, little by little. She ridiculed him unmercifully in front of his friends, she laughed at his lack of education, mocked his job, nagged him day and night, and spent time with rather too many male friends. She wanted him to be a man of means, run his own business. She insisted he leave the docks and open a corner shop. That was the height of her ambition. But what did he want with standing in a shop serving customers all day?'

Frank shook his head, bitter thoughts rampaging through his mind. 'In the end he couldn't deny her, particularly when it became obvious that the docks were winding down. He left his job, a place where he was well-liked, respected, a man of influence. He became a shopkeeper, and I watched him die a little inside every single day. He was my age when he finally gave up. Slipped away in his sleep. Heart attack. At peace. At last.'

'And you never forgave your mother for that.' Debbie nodded. 'I can understand how you must have felt.'

Frank sipped from his mug, shaking his head. 'Oh, that wasn't the end of it. After a period of mourning that lasted about as long as took to down her first vodka, she began to party as if she'd been released. Reborn even. It was my old man who'd been released, but the irony was lost on her.

'Then came the different men, trooping through the flat above my father's shop without a care in the world. She neglected the business, the money dried up, she lost the shop, the booze caused her to lose what looks she had, and so the men stopped coming by. We were forced to live in a dive of a flat on a dive of a council estate, the type of place where the rats outnumbered the pets. Never one to blame herself, she turned on me.'

'It must have been awful for you.'

'I was fifteen by then. I could handle it. So, she began to take it out on my brother, who was far less able to cope.'

Debbie set down her mug, a look of astonishment spread across her face. 'Your brother? I never knew you had a brother. I thought you were an only child.'

'Even Janet didn't know. Maybe that tells you how close we really were. My brother was three years younger than me. The whole nightmare episode hit him very hard, and when she started on him, he fell apart at the seams. He was twelve when he ran away. I helped him pack, even gave him some money. I watched him slip away one night, and I haven't seen him since.'

'Frank, that's awful. Just awful.'

Frank moistened his lips. 'I like to think he's doing well. Living the good life.'

'You've never tried to track him down? With the contacts you've made, being a copper, it would have been easy enough. You must have been tempted.'

But Frank blinked and shook his head. His eyes met hers. 'Never. Not once. When he left I stuck around until I finished school and I was able to get out and fend for myself. It was imagining him living a better life that got me through the bad times. Imagining the very best. I've never wanted to ruin that notion with reality.'

Frank saw Debbie gather herself, clearly emotional. It had been a lot of information to absorb in one go. 'Everyone has a sob story,' he said gently. 'Mine's just another one.'

'What's his name? Your brother.'

'Jimmy. James, to be exact. But Jimmy to those who knew him. He was a smashing kid. Physically tough. Very bright.'

'You weren't concerned at how a twelve-year-old would cope on his own?'

'Those were very different times, Debs. To be perfectly honest, I was more worried at how he might end up if he stayed.'

'You didn't turn out too bad,' Debs pointed out.

He gave a short, humourless laugh. 'Yeah. Ex-cop, now a debt-collector. Failed marriage behind me. No, I wanted him to be better than I knew I was going to be. And he is. I just know it.'

Frank stood, walked behind Debbie and wrapped his arms around her. He buried his head in the nape of her neck. 'Some things are best left in the past,' he said. 'I scarcely ever think about those days. And I have other things on my mind right now. More important things.'

'Speaking of which, we haven't talked about the newspaper article,' Debbie said, looking busy as she did nothing.

One of the Sunday newspapers had run a small piece on how Debbie had been spotted entering and leaving Frank's house over recent days. A budding relationship had been suggested, as had nights spent together.

'Do we need to?'

She turned now. 'I'm okay with it, Frank. The tone of the article was accusatory, as if we were doing something wrong. But I'm ashamed of nothing.'

'Then that makes two of us. In fact, I'm far from ashamed. What we have right now is a good thing. Nothing squalid, nothing unsavoury. Good.'

'So … fuck 'em?'

Frank nodded. 'Fuck 'em all.'

He pulled her close, took her hands in his and breathed her in. The newspaper article was wrong. What he and Debbie had done was perfectly natural. And even though Janet had been dead for such a short time, their relationship had died long before. He was surprised, yet heartened to realise that he truly felt no guilt or shame.

'How about a kiss instead?' he said.

'How about a hug and a kiss?'

'How about a hug and a kiss and a bloody good cry?'

Debbie smiled, her eyes glittering as they lit up. 'Yes,' she said. 'That sounds just about perfect.'

Chapter Thirty-Six

First came the terror: the man stood in the doorway for several moments, staring at her the way a death-row prisoner might view their last meal. He then motioned with his fingers for her to join him. Laura rose unsteadily, not wanting to go so meekly to her death, yet too afraid to fight such a terribly one-sided battle. When she reached his side, all he did was lean forward and say, 'Soon, Laura. Soon.' Then he turned on his heels, closing and locking the door behind him once more.

Then came the relief: Laura stood by the door, staring at the spot where he had been, scarcely able to draw her next breath. So, what if he had said 'soon'. Soon wasn't now. Now she was still alive, all possibilities remaining.

Followed by the reckoning: on three more occasions over the next two days, he entered her room unexpectedly, and each time he left her teetering on the brink of madness by repeating the same simple phrase: 'Soon, Laura. Soon.'

The last time, late last night, as he turned to leave, Laura's mind unravelled and her will snapped like a dry twig. 'Don't do this to me!' she screamed at him, fear and dread spilling from her eyes in the shape of warm tears. Laura sank to her knees, head bowed. 'Please, don't do this to me.' Voice softening more with each word.

And, finally, the pain: Laura now lay face down across a pile of soft clothing, sobbing into her arms. She couldn't sit. Her buttocks were still striped with thick red welts where the man's belt had lashed into her tender flesh. The sting of it brought back the memory: no sooner had her words died than the man's large hand had arced down and slapped across her face with a force that sent her tumbling onto her back. A cry of shock died on her lips as he then stooped and flipped her over as if she were a toy. One hand covered her mouth, while the other yanked back on her left arm until it was up against her spine. She felt his breath wash over her. Her nose wrinkled at its terrible stench. He knelt and pressed his knee into her lower back, grinding it into her spine. She was helpless and in a great deal of pain. Tears glittered on her eyelashes.

'If you shout at me again,' he whispered in her ear, 'I'll get angry. You know how I feel about you, Laura, but you must be good. You really must. So … will you shout again?'

He released her arm, switched his grip to her hair, pulled it tight and moved her head in a fierce shaking motion.

'I didn't think so,' he laughed.

Laura paid dearly for that one errant outburst. Not satisfied with the level of pain and dread he had already doled out, he rucked up her dress, bent her over his knee, took off his leather belt, and used it with all his strength to beat her.

Laura cried throughout her ordeal. She sobbed, and offered a silent prayer. She didn't cry out again, though, even when he discarded her by throwing her to the ground once more. He stood over her and threaded the belt back through the loops on his trousers. Laura kept her head down, hair splayed out across the floor.

She heard the man's breath slow and become more regular. Then he spoke, seemingly from a great distance. 'You shouldn't have made me do that, Laura. I didn't want to hurt you. But you let me down, let us both down. You've been so strong … so right. Then you had to go and spoil it. You can't do it again, my love. I couldn't stand it if you ruined everything now.'

'I'm sorry.' Laura's voice was muted, so terribly sincere.

'Of course, you are. They all are after they've been punished. I thought you were better than that.'

Laura looked up at him for the first time since she'd been beaten. Her eyes were puffed and raw. Both cheeks glistened still.

'I am. You have to believe me. I am better. I am right for you. For you both.'

The words almost choked her. Mere words, yet they were so hard to say. For a child still shy of her teens, Laura was extremely bright. She recognised that the beating was only a first step. The next time would be so much worse. After that ... there may not be a third chance at all. The man was furious with her, his mood dark and oppressive. Unlike other such moods, it had not fizzled out quickly. She could still see the anger etched into his angular face, raging within him, able to erupt at the slightest provocation – real or imagined. She had to appease him. Appease him or die. It was that simple.

'I really am so very sorry,' she repeated. 'I won't do anything to upset you again. I promise.'

'You do?' He said it breathlessly. A voice full of wonder.

'I do.'

As he rested on his haunches, a smile spread across his face. He stroked her thin and dirty hair, coiling strands between his fingers. 'Good girl. Good girl.'

He cooed to her. Stroked. Cooed and stroked. The touch and the whisper of his words soothed her. Her eyes grew heavy, flickered briefly, and closed. Mentally and physically exhausted, Laura slept. When she awoke several hours later, he was gone. Laura instantly recalled the feel of his fingers slipping through her hair. Stark contrast against the pain from the beating. A pain she could still feel. She shuddered and bit her lip. She felt repulsed. But at least she was still alive.

Now that knowledge brought fresh tears from her eyes.

Chapter Thirty-Seven

Monday was over. The saddest day of Frank's life up to that point, and one he would never forget. But now it had to be part of the past. Frank was reminded of a scene from one of his favourite films. In *The Shawshank Redemption*, the main character, Andy Dufresne, considers the time he has wasted in jail for a crime he didn't commit, and says to his friend, Red: 'I have a choice to make. Get busy living, or get busy dying.' Frank considered that he, too, had that same choice. It would be easy to lie down and let life happen around him. But it was better to make it happen.

* * *

When Frank was first told that their suspect lived in a place called Grange Hill, he immediately thought of the old TV show, and imagined Nicky was pulling his leg. Frank had lived in London his entire life, a good deal of it in the East End, yet had never heard of this area tucked neatly between Woodford Bridge and Hainault. But he had located it on Google maps, and now here he was.

The narrow road was busy, crowded with cars parked on both sides, the residents obviously choosing to use public transport in order to get to work. Frank had found a space some way down the road from the official team's vehicle – the other two sat in nearby roads, pointed in opposite directions and ready to roll at a moment's notice. He could just about see the suspect's house, though, and this gave him a small measure of comfort.

He had been there for little more than ten minutes, when his car door was wrenched open and Nicky got in beside him. The car was instantly filled with the thick aroma of cooked food.

'Cup of rosie,' Nicky said, passing across a plastic cup. He waggled a small paper-bag, now spotted with grease. 'And one sausage sarnie.'

Frank nodded appreciatively. 'Brown sauce?'

'Of course. It's HP, too.'

'What are you doing here?' Frank asked. 'How did you know I'd be here, where I was?'

Nicky regarded him closely over the rim of his own cup, steam rising up before his eyes. 'This is you we're talking about. I knew you wouldn't be able to keep away, and I also knew you'd be in a position to see the house.'

'You know me too bloody well. Smart arse.'

They ate their food in silence. It was an unwritten rule when on a stake-out together that the last one to arrive found a nearby café and forked out for breakfast. Two teas, one sausage sandwich with brown sauce, one egg and bacon roll. Stake-out vehicles were imbued with many odours, several of which could be unpleasant, but that injection of greasy food of a morning always set the standard.

'Just like the old days,' Frank observed, using his nail to dig out a sliver of trapped food from his back teeth. 'I'd forgotten the simple pleasure a sausage sandwich could provide.'

'Nothing like it,' Nicky said around a mouthful of food. 'Forget all your nouvelle cuisine cobblers. Let that fat-tongued mockney produce something this good.'

Frank chuckled. 'Jamie Oliver, you mean? Hard but fair, Nicky. Hard but fair.'

Nicky's two-way radio hissed static. 'Barcode One. Suspect is on the move. I repeat, suspect is on the move. Heading ... north towards Chigwell.'

Frank looked up, but failed to see the suspect's van in amongst all the other vehicles. Nicky summoned the fourth team as Frank fired up the Renault and navigated his way out of the space and into the flow of traffic. He hung well back, allowing the stream of information emerging from the mobile watchers to guide their way. They slipped onto the A113, then turned and headed towards Junction 5 of the M11. Nicky's radio was alive with activity now.

'He's gone straight over,' Nicky said, intent on following the directions given by each team as they took it in turns at being the lead vehicle. 'Ignored the motorway and is heading towards Loughton. No, wait, he's cut back towards Buckhurst Hill.'

Frank was frowning. 'What's he up to? We just passed a road back at Chigwell that takes you straight to Buckhurst Hill.'

'I can't imagine he's spotted his tail, but he could just be taking precautions. If it is him, we know he's damn clever.'

'And if so, it suggests he could be headed for wherever his hideaway is.'

As Frank followed at a safe and steady distance, Nicky suddenly shook his head. 'No, he's turned right onto a narrow back road. Now crossing the A121 and pointing towards High Beech.'

'Jesus,' Frank sucked in a deep breath. 'I was there with Laura and Gary just the Sunday before last.'

'Several out-of-the way places in that neck of the woods,' Nicky said. 'We may be getting warm.'

They began winding through Epping Forest, the dense and tightly packed trees grouped around them like armed guards in camouflage, staring down implacably. The sun occasionally pierced the overhanging canopies of branches, slanting into Frank's eyes – diamond-like slivers of light, mottling the windscreen. Frank said nothing, his stomach a tight knot of anxiety. He still wasn't convinced about Stevenson, but this was one time he hoped to be proven wrong.

Nicky abruptly raised a hand. 'He's stopped. He turned off towards Waltham Abbey and the M25, but pulled up at a large house about a mile or so along the road. Barcode Two had to drive past and keep on going until they were round a bend and out of sight. Barcode One shot around to come the other way. They spotted our suspect lugging tools out of the back of his van. A middle-aged woman stood by the front door, a dog running around by her heels, yapping.'

Frank pulled the Renault over to the kerb and stopped. The road here was narrow with a grass verge on either side, little traffic on its smooth tarmac surface. He yanked on the handbrake, but kept the engine idling.

'He's at a job,' he said, resigned to the fact. 'Have someone check out the house, see who owns it, but my money is on a working day in store for our man.'

'You want to get closer?' Nicky asked. 'Get a look at him?'

'No. I can't risk him getting a glimpse of me. I want to, believe me. Seeing him might just give me a better feel for this. But I'm not willing to take a chance.'

'You don't think Stevenson's our man, do you?'

Frank felt the weight of his friend's scrutiny. He looked at Nicky and shook his head. 'He's been under surveillance since Saturday night. Sunday, he went nowhere, other than the pub for a few drinks. Yesterday he went to what turned out to be a job in Ealing, then straight back home at the end of the day. I can't believe he's holding his victims at home, in a house shared by a wife and two young children, which would mean he hasn't visited his victims in two whole days, and that's just not right. The man I've spoken to needs to be with them as often as he can be. It's what he lives and breathes for.'

'But he *was* inside the Redbridge home. He *was* in their street just a few days before someone let himself into Karen's bedroom. And for all we know his victims could be tucked away in a basement at his house.'

Frank was nodding. 'I admit there's some questions we need answering, and I understand that Stevenson can't be ignored – why else would I be here now? But there isn't enough to convince me, Nicky. Stevenson is not behaving like a man responsible for murder and abductions. He doesn't smell right to me.'

Nicky set his jaw. 'I think you could be wrong on this one, Frank. I think you're reaching for something that's not there. Stevenson is a solid enough suspect for the time being, and we know these bloody maniacs can act as normal as you and me half the time. We'd have had him in for questioning before now if it weren't for the fact that we need him to lead us to Laura. We'll have to agree to disagree on this one, mate. I think he's our man, and this surveillance op continues. Speaking of which, I'd better call the others.'

For a few moments after Nicky had issued several instructions to his teams, both men were silent. Then Frank glanced across at his friend, gaze narrowed, and said, 'Barcodes? What the hell is all that about?'

Nicky grinned. 'Just keeping it light. The surveillance liaison officer I spoke to in order to get hold of the team in Barcode Two, a DS by the name of Jarvis, is a Geordie. Newcastle play in black and white stripes, so they're known around the country as the …'

'Barcodes. I know. They hate it.' Frank shook his head in mild amusement. 'But ten quid and my left nut says your Barcodes aren't moving anywhere until around four o'clock this afternoon.'

He was out by thirty minutes.

When their suspect finally appeared at just shy of four-thirty, he headed back south down the A104, bought some plumbing supplies from a specialist retailer in Woodford, then went home.

He didn't appear again that day.

* * *

Long before then, Frank dropped Nicky off with Barcode Three, then headed home. On the way, he stopped only to pick up some groceries. Remembering something from his *To Do* list, Frank spoke to Tania Penny and arranged to meet her at the family home in Peterborough around one the following afternoon. Then he called Nicky and told him where he was going.

'I gather you don't want your trip on record,' Nicky said.

'You gather right. This is off my own bat. It probably won't get me anywhere, but you know me.'

'Yeah. You like to cover all the angles, leave…'

'No stone unturned. Right. They may be clichés to you, Nicky, but they're in my book of rules.'

'And I'd rather follow your rules any day, pal. Oh, by the way, Warren Capel spoke to a taxidermist as well. Judging by what we found, he agrees that someone is trying to carry out human taxidermy. But so far, they're making a real pig's ear of it. It seems to be a case of trial and error with each one.'

Frank thought about that. 'Would he have stopped if he'd got the first one right?'

'Exactly what I was wondering. And if so, then can we assume that he's still not got the knack. The taxidermist agreed that some people would use formaldehyde, but might not do other things such as scrape the inner skin off, take it off the bones, boil the bones, that sort of thing. Then it doesn't matter how cured the skin is, the rest will still rot.'

Frank immediately thought of Laura. He fought a constant battle not to imagine his little girl suffering the same fate as those already found, but there were occasions when the image came bursting through his defences. Now he saw his daughter's skinless body rising up before him, red and raw and inhuman, head thrown back in a silent scream. He saw birds and small animals, frozen in place forever, glassy-eyed, mounted on a wooden plaque. He saw Laura, frozen in place forever, glassy-eyed, mounted on a wooden plaque.

He shook his head. Nicky had said something that he'd missed.

'What ...? Sorry, mate. What did you say?'

'I said we're checking suppliers to see how easy it is to get hold of formaldehyde in large quantities. I also told you to take care.'

'Don't worry. I will.'

'I'll give you a buzz if anything dramatic happens at this end.'

'Yeah. You do that.'

There was a slight pause. 'Frank, are you all right? Not about to do something stupid, are you?'

'Me? No, not at all. I'm just getting busy living.'

* * *

The Swan in Wood Street, Walthamstow, was a typical East-End pub: big on atmosphere, small on frills, with watered-down beer and wall-to-wall villains, mostly minor, mostly legends only in their own simple minds. The kind who think selling stolen sports goods from holdalls made them gangsters.

Frank walked into the public bar a little after eight-thirty, ordered a pint of lager, waited for the man he had come to see to catch his eye, then wandered around the back to the toilets. Less than a minute later he was joined by a stocky little character with a spider web draped around his neck, a skull beneath each ear, and a bloody dagger slanting across his left cheek.

'Evenin', Mr Rogers. Thought we'd seen the last of you around this manor. What can I do for you?'

'How's tricks, Tattoo?'

'Mustn't grumble. I don't know that I've got much for you, though. A few dodgy mobiles, some phone cards, maybe.'

'I'm not after information.'

Tattoo ran a hand through his blond cropped hair, frowning. 'What is it, then?'

'I need a piece. And I mean a good one, not some reject that'll explode the moment I pull the trigger.'

The man's eyes narrowed, suspicious now. 'Oi, what's going on? You trying to set me up?'

Frank sighed. 'Don't you read the papers? No, of course not. What am I saying, you don't read, do you? I'm out of the business now, Tattoo. I work for myself, and I want a gun. No questions asked.'

'Okay.' The nervous man nodded thoughtfully. 'To hire or buy?'

Frank knew the market had changed, and that some people hired small arms specifically for certain jobs. 'To buy,' he replied.

'How much can you go to?'

'Whatever it takes. I want a pistol, a Browning or even a Glock if you can lay your hands on one. Something of that quality.'

Tattoo gave a low whistle. 'You are serious. The Glock's out of the question at short notice, but I do have a piece you'll like. Cost you four hundred.'

'Done. I want twenty shells thrown in.'

Tattoo smiled. 'You got the cash on you?'

Frank was wearing a lightweight windcheater jacket. He patted the breast pocket. 'There's a fifty here for your trouble if you can get it right now.'

'Give me twenty minutes.'

'Make it ten. I don't like this crap-hole of a boozer.'

* * *

Shortly after midnight, Debbie touched a cold sheet beside her. She wandered downstairs, found Frank in his study where she knew he would be, empty glass in one hand, a photograph of Laura and Gary in the other. His shoulders were heaving as tears streamed silently from his eyes. Debbie came up behind him, both arms embracing his chest.

'I had to look at this,' he explained without turning. 'I'd forgotten what they looked like, Debs. I'd forgotten what my children looked like.'

Later, after Debbie had gone back to bed, Frank took the gun out of his desk drawer and turned it over in his hands. He didn't feel like a criminal. In buying the gun he had committed a crime, but he genuinely believed his reasons for doing so were moral and just. It would be a heartless jury that would convict him if the gun was found in his possession. As for killing the man who had Laura … well, that was another matter entirely.

Chapter Thirty-Eight

At ten-fifteen on Wednesday morning, instead of driving north to interview Tania Penny as he'd intended, Frank found himself at New Scotland Yard, sitting in the large, exquisitely furnished office belonging to Deputy Assistant Commissioner Thompson. To Frank's right, was Nicky, and beside him sat Superintendent Foster, arms crossed, face turned away. The three were lined up on one side of a huge teak desk that was certainly not standard issue.

The DAC entered the room barking instructions to a young, bespectacled woman. She remained by the door, writing on a small notepad, nodding often, but saying nothing. She appeared to know when he was done, because without another word, she left the office, closing the door behind her.

Thompson took his place at the desk. The DAC, winding down his days prior to retirement, headed up the Met's Directorate of Professional Standards. Frank had never met him before, but knew he had a reputation for firm, fair handling of all matters. A large, silver-haired man with a broad, open face scored by deep lines that told of a career filled with grim and frustrating experiences, he eyed each of the three faces opposite before speaking.

'Five minutes ago, I terminated the surveillance operation on Alan Stevenson,' he said, his deep voice resonating around the room. 'I take it you gave the order for that operation, Colin?' His eyes bore into Foster.

Foster cleared his throat. 'Before I answer that, sir, I would like to formally complain about the presence of a civilian at this meeting.'

Thompson frowned. 'You mean Frank? Colin, he's here because he was ordered to attend. I should also remind you that he does have an official capacity at the moment. Your complaint is duly noted, but let's push on. Now, did you give the order or not?'

'Actually sir, it was DCI Loizou who was in charge of the surveillance.'

'I'm perfectly aware that Nicky was the one who wanted and suggested the op, but you would have given the final order, would you not?'

Shifting uncomfortably in his seat, Foster met DAC Thompson's stare for the first time. 'I have complete faith in DCI Loizou, sir. I trusted him to have done all that was necessary. I understand the costs of maintaining such a surveillance, but I was assured that an operation like this would reap dividends within twenty-four hours.'

Thompson nodded and clasped his hands before him on the desk. 'And were all necessary checks and clearances made prior to giving the go-ahead for the op?'

'As I said, sir, I had faith that the DCI would have done all that was required.'

Nicky remained stoical throughout this exchange, but Frank could see the set of his jaw, and imagined his friend would be inwardly fuming. Without knowing why the surveillance had been pulled, Foster was passing the buck. This came as no surprise to Frank. Still he was furious.

'This is complete bollocks,' he said, looking directly at the DAC. 'Sir, the surveillance had to be arranged at short notice. I urged immediate action, but I know Nicky went through all the correct channels, including obtaining approval from his senior officer.'

Thompson blinked at Frank and grunted once. 'Your reputation for speaking your mind precedes you, but even though your status is temporary, I'd appreciate a little respect for my rank.'

Frank nodded. 'I'm sorry, sir, but it grinds my gears when I hear people trying to wriggle out of their obligations.'

'All the same, hastily arranged operations, particularly surveillance ops, often go awry, and a little more time ought to have been put into this one.'

'Exactly,' Foster remarked, nodding his head sagely.

'By the officer with overall responsibility for this case,' Thompson added, his voice growing louder with each word as his attention swung back to Foster. 'Namely, you, Colin.'

'With respect, sir, I may not have been given all the facts.' Foster was determined to stand his ground. He adjusted the glasses on his nose. 'The DCI and Frank Rogers are thick as thieves, and have little respect for authority.'

'Perhaps it depends on who wields that authority, Colin. And how.'

Frank, whose main concern was that their suspect now had no one watching him, leaned forward and said, 'Sir, why exactly did you cancel the op?'

'We had a complaint, Frank. One we had to act upon.'

'A complaint? From who?'

'Alan Stevenson himself.'

Frank glanced across at Nicky, who seemed shocked by this revelation. The surveillance had been spotted after all.

'Stevenson is not a happy man,' Thompson continued. 'DCI Loizou, were checks made on Stevenson's background?'

'They're on-going, sir. They were ordered right away. I have to confess that I haven't taken time to follow up my request. But as Frank has pointed out, we couldn't afford to wait.'

'That's as maybe, but you wouldn't have found a criminal record.' He glanced down at an open folder of notes, and raised his eyebrows. 'Though that may have been a close call. What your checks may eventually have come up with, however, is that until three years ago, Alan Stevenson was a sergeant with the Vice Squad.'

'He's one of ours?' Nicky could hardly believe it.

'Was. He left under an enormous black cloud, however. Allegations of corruption, a bit too familiar with the women on his patch, a little heavy on the violence, that sort of thing.'

Frank snapped his fingers. 'I remember the stink it created,' he said. 'The name meant nothing to me, but I do recall the rumour-mill going into overdrive.'

'No wonder he spotted the surveillance,' Foster said. 'A sloppy arrangement all round if you ask me.'

Frank glanced across at him and shook his head contemptuously. The man didn't appear to realise he had no allies in this room.

DAC Thompson stood and walked across the royal blue carpet to a narrow window, hands clasped behind his back. Bathed in sunlight, he peered out for a few moments, as if gathering his thoughts. When he turned around, his face was grave.

'Stevenson is a bitter man. If he can get his own back on the force, he will. He's threatened to sue us if we go anywhere near him again. Harassment, he will allege. Given the way he was forced out of the job, and the current litigious climate, he'd probably win. Therefore, he's out of bounds from now on, gentlemen.'

'But, sir, this changes nothing,' Nicky protested. 'In fact, this makes me suspect him all the more. Whoever is responsible for the murders and the abductions is very clever; he leaves us nothing to work with. Who better than a fellow cop? Even his desire for revenge makes sense of why he's now toying with us.'

'That's one way of looking at it, chief inspector. And if you want to follow this up, then you must do so. But you go through all correct procedures. You dot every i and cross every t. What you do *not* do is go anywhere near Alan Stevenson unless you are prepared to make an arrest. And if you do that, you'd better be bloody sure about your evidence. Understood?'

'Yes, sir.'

'How about you, Frank?'

'I'm with Nicky as always, sir.' This was neither the time nor place to reveal his lack of conviction.

'Then do what you can, people. But do it the right way. By the book. And keep away from the man.' The DAC gave a single nod. 'That's it then, gentleman. Thank you for coming.'

As they all got to their feet, Thompson retook his own seat, held up a finger and said, 'Superintendent Foster. A word please.'

As Frank and Nicky filed past him, Foster glared at both men. Perhaps the penny had finally dropped. Frank deliberately met the glare, held it for a second, then winked. The look on Foster's face made him want to laugh. He managed to hold back until he and Nicky were way down the corridor.

* * *

They sped back through the city, taking the Embankment alongside the Thames, heading east towards Blackfriars. A multitude of vessels made their way across the gleaming water in both directions, many of them containing tourists. London, and its river, were doing the visitors proud today.

'Where do we go from here?' Nicky asked. 'How do we dig into Stevenson's life without him finding out? It only takes one word in the wrong ear.'

Frank agreed. 'I'm not even sure he spotted the surveillance. He may still have friends in the job, someone who tipped him off about the op.'

'Perhaps. Our man is one tricky fucker, and he always seems to know what we're thinking. Who better than a cop to know what's inside a cop's head? What I know for sure is that we now have to investigate him with both hands tied behind our backs.'

'Not quite. If he was the bad apple they claim, he's bound to have left enemies behind somewhere.'

'But those are in his past,' Nicky argued. 'We need to know what he's up to now.'

'You're right. But you know how I feel about Stevenson. It would suit me if you put a DS on this and let them run with it.'

'Stevenson is our only suspect. I still like him for it, despite what you say. You go with your gut feeling as always, but I'm looking at the evidence. And that tells me we can't drop this. The problem is, without surveillance we're blind.'

Frank heard the matter-of-fact tone, but saw something completely different in his friend's pensive features. 'Let it go, Nicky. Have him checked out thoroughly, but don't do what I think you're going to do.'

Nicky glanced at him. 'You know what I'm thinking?'

'No. Tell me.'

'What if you're wrong? What if Stevenson is our man and we let him slip through our hands?'

'But I don't think I am wrong.' Frank gave a thin smile.

'And I don't think it's a risk worth taking. I'm surprised you do.'

'Are we going to fall out over this?'

Nicky smiled and ran both hands down his cheeks. 'I doubt it. But you never can tell.'

'No,' Frank agreed, matching his friend's smile. 'You never can.'

Chapter Thirty-Nine

'Go back home, Frank. Go to the annexe, go anywhere; do anything but stay here.'

'I'm keeping you company,' Frank insisted. 'And that's all there is to it.'

'You believe you're right and I'm wrong, and you don't really want to be here. You shouldn't be here, because if this goes tits up, you need to stay with the investigation.'

Frank gave Nicky a hard stare. 'Then just you make sure it doesn't go tits up.'

The two men stood in the cool shade of a stand of trees on the golf course opposite the road where the Redbridge family lived. They were less than a hundred yards from where Frank had been when Nicky called to tell him about Stevenson. As the pair spoke in hushed voices, their eyes were fixed firmly on Alan Stevenson's van, parked just around a corner less than a hundred yards away.

'What's he up to?' Frank wondered aloud. 'What's he doing back here?'

'I can't work it out. First of all, he sat for a few minutes doing nothing. When he finally got out of the van he was acting ... furtively, I guess. You know, looking around him, anxious, nervous even. He then walked up to the corner of the Redbridges' road, peered around a hedge, ducked back sharply. A couple of minutes after that he went back to his van and climbed in. Same pattern on two more occasions since you turned up. Makes no sense. Now he's back in the van, just sitting there waiting.'

'Yeah. But waiting for what?'

Frank had posted himself close to Alan Stevenson's home just after five that morning, guessing that Nicky would be parked up somewhere close by. At seven-ten, Stevenson came out, got into his van and drove off. Frank smiled to himself as Nicky's Mondeo slipped away from the corner of a side street to follow. Frank sat three vehicles behind him all the way to Chingford, becoming more thoughtful as he realised where they were headed. Frank found a space and waited for his friend to position himself and settle down to watch Stevenson. Less than ten minutes later he was creeping up next to him.

Frank smiled at the memory of how startled Nicky had been. Then had come the explanations, Nicky pleading with him to leave.

'I still can't believe you didn't spot me tailing you,' Frank said now, grinning and shaking his head.

'And I can't believe you were stupid enough to follow me here.' Nicky rolled his eyes. 'If Foster could see us now he'd be rubbing his hands with unrestrained joy.'

'Fuck Foster.'

'Yeah, fuck Foster,' Nicky agreed. Then he nodded and pointed. 'Heads up. He's on the move again.'

Stevenson was out of the van once more. Aside from a postman and a lone dog walker, the pavements had been clear for almost an hour, yet still the man appeared edgy. Looking about him, he walked slowly to the corner of the road, then craned his neck to peer around the hedge. This time he didn't make his way back to the van. Instead, he strode purposefully towards the Redbridges' house. Looking back over his shoulder, he paused for a moment as if uncertain how to proceed now that he'd reached this point.

'This is not right,' Frank said, concerned by what he was seeing. 'Our man would never attempt this in broad daylight. He's strictly an early hours man.'

'Maybe he's casing another house.'

'The man we're hunting wouldn't need to, surely. He's been down this road several times before. I don't like it, Nicky. Something's wrong here.'

'What do you want to do, Frank? I'm beginning to wonder about this myself. I'll back your decision either way.'

'I don't know what to do. Just sit tight for now.'

'What if he's looking to silence witnesses?' Nicky offered. 'The Redbridges may actually be in danger here, Frank.'

'I can't believe he'd be that stupid. He knows he'd be the prime suspect.'

'All the same, if he does something, we may have no alternative but to go in. He may be dictating the terms here, not us.'

Frank nodded his head, squinting across the road. 'I wonder if that's it. What if he's banking on someone still watching him, and he's trying to force our hand? Make us snatch him when he's doing nothing wrong. Wouldn't do his harassment case much harm, would it?'

Just then, Stevenson turned on his heels and nipped through an open gate, walking briskly down a path alongside the house next door to the Redbridges'.

Frank cursed and moved away from the cover of the trees. 'We have to get closer. Once he's out of sight we have no way of knowing what he's up to.'

'Don't rush him, Frank. We have to let him get inside, if that's what his aim is.'

'I know. But we have to find somewhere where we can see down the side of that house. He may be waiting there for us to steam in and nick him. On the other hand, he may be breaking in right now.'

As the two men trotted across the first hole fairway, over an embankment, and out onto the street, Frank was convinced this wasn't the way their man would act. Not once had he gained entry to a house during the day. *Not once that we know about,* Frank corrected himself. *It's not as though we understand everything about this man.* But again, that nagging feeling persisted. Something was wrong here. Terribly wrong.

At that precise moment, an explosion of movement stopped both men in their tracks. As if from nowhere, armed officers burst into the open and ran towards the house, which Stevenson had by now disappeared behind. Cries of 'Armed police!' shattered the stillness of the morning. And as the men sped from view, Detective Superintendent Colin Foster emerged from an unmarked vehicle that had just screeched to a halt, brushing himself down, wearing his best suit and a superior smile.

As he walked past the two stunned men, he shot Frank a look, and winked. 'Thanks, Rogers,' he said. There was no mistaking the vindictiveness in his tone. 'Let a professional take it from here.'

* * *

Frank and Nicky watched the interrogation on a monitor, a camera perched high in one corner of the interview room filming the entire process. Once back at the Francis Road station, Foster had insisted on conducting the initial interview himself, allowing only DC Capel into the room with them. For the benefit of the camera and the audio recording, Foster re-read the suspect his rights.

'Just tell me what the fuck this is all about!' Stevenson roared, cheeks pinched red with fury. 'Why the fuck have you arrested me? I've done nothing wrong.'

'Would you like to wait for a solicitor to be present?' Foster asked, studiously adhering to the rule book. 'We can arrange one for you.'

'I don't need no fucking brief. Tell me why I'm here.'

'We'd like you to answer a few questions. Help us with our inquiries.'

'Help? So, I can leave if I want to?'

'Uh, no. You are under caution, and we are detaining you without charge for the time being. The sooner you help clear this matter up, the sooner we can all go home.'

'Right. So again, tell me why I was arrested.'

'Why don't you tell me why you were in the garden of a house that is not yours, sneaking alongside and heading towards the back door.'

Stevenson screwed up his face. 'Is that it?' He appeared shocked and a little relieved. 'Look, I'd rather not say why I was there, but it's not what you were thinking. I wasn't going to turn the place over. I'm not a fucking thief.'

'He's good,' Nicky said, looking across at Frank.

'Not really. He's not our man.'

'He'd better be, for all your sakes.'

Frank and Nicky turned, unaware until that moment that they had been joined by Deputy Assistant Commissioner Thompson. He studied them closely.

'Before you both plead total innocence, you should know that I'm aware that Superintendent Foster made the formal arrest. But I have a sneaking suspicion you two played a part in this.'

No way was Frank going to get himself too deeply involved at this stage. He looked back at the monitor. 'I have no idea why he was there, sir. But for my money, he's not our man.'

Nicky held up a hand. 'Hold on a minute. You don't know he's not the one. Let's find out why he was there, see what reason he comes up with.'

Foster had already informed the man that his word counted for nothing. 'You must tell us why you were at that particular address, Mr Stevenson. Please, it can only help if you talk to us.'

The man reached up to scratch behind his ear. Tall and thin, his ropy muscles appeared taut beneath a grey T-shirt. A fine stubble spread across his head, and Frank could see a shaver's nick where he had trimmed too close to the scalp. It could look completely bald to a young girl woken from her sleep in the dead of night.

'This is harassment, Foster. I'll have you for it. You and the lousy Met.'

'I don't think so.' Foster's smile was smug, self-assured.

'We'll see. Anyhow, I'm surprised Angie hasn't already explained,' Stevenson said.

'Angie?' Capel interjected, provoking a scowl from Foster. 'Who might that be?'

'The owner. The woman who lives there, at the house.'

'And what do you think she might have to tell us, Mr Stevenson?'

The man spread his hands and put back his head. 'The reason I was there, of course. I've been slipping her one, haven't I? I had to wait for her old man to leave this morning, but as soon as I saw his motor had gone, I nipped in. Didn't she tell you?'

Foster shook his head, pushed back his glasses. 'Quite the opposite, in point of fact. Mrs Reed told us she had never seen you before, and could not account for you being on her property.'

In the next room, Frank swore. 'Shit! This is why Foster should've waited. If Stevenson breaks in, we have him. If he's invited in, we have a different story altogether.'

Stevenson's mouth had fallen open. 'You what? Never seen me before? Are you having a laugh? I mean ... oh, hold on. I know her game. She's obviously shit-scared of her old man, and doesn't want to get involved in anything to do with you lot. Can't say I blame her, mind, the way you treat people.'

Foster paused, his fingers tapping anxiously on the desk before him. He looked concerned by the suspect's confidence. He leaned over to Capel and whispered something in his ear. Moments later, Capel appeared in the room in which Frank, Nicky, the DAC and, by now, a handful of other officers were monitoring the interview.

'The boss is going to suspend things for now,' Capel said to Nicky. 'He'd like you and Frank to talk with Angie Reed. See if you can clear this up.'

'Stupid bastard shouldn't have given the order. It was too soon.' Frank almost snarled his outrage.

'I think he may just have realised that. See what you can do, eh?'

As they left the station, Frank was shaking his head bitterly. 'In the end, I thought he was trying it on. Baiting us, wanting someone to arrest him in order to claim harassment. And all the time he was porking some housewife.'

'You believed him, then?' Nicky seemed uncertain.

'Yeah. I did. Didn't you?'

With obvious reluctance, Nicky nodded. 'Looks like you were right yet again. Stevenson's not our man.'

'No. But right now I'd give anything to have been wrong about him.'

* * *

Angie Reed chain-smoked throughout the entire conversation. At first, she kept to her original story, denying all knowledge of Alan Stevenson. It was Frank who pointed out that the man had carried out some work in the very next house, at the back door, directly opposite her own, that her story could be verified. At this point, the woman seemed to sense that she had backed herself into a corner from which she could not escape.

'That's how we met,' she said at last.

In her mid-thirties, Angie Reed was a plump, somewhat plain woman. Her T-shirt was a little too tight for her over-developed breasts, her denim skirt a little too short for her heavy legs and thighs.

'I came out into the garden while he was putting on their door. He's got the chat, and made his interest in me all too obvious. I made him a few cups of tea, he came indoors for one on the second day, and things sort of took off from there.'

'You started an affair?' This from Nicky.

'Yeah. Off and on Alan would pop round. We never went out anywhere. It was just sex.'

'And your husband knows nothing of this?'

The woman shook her head forcefully. 'Christ, no. He touches me about twice a year, but he don't want anyone else sniffing around. He'd kill me. Kill us both.'

'Which is why you lied earlier,' Frank said.

'Yeah. I panicked. Didn't know how to get out of it.' Her gaze narrowed then. 'Why did you arrest Alan, anyway? What's he done?'

'I'm not sure he's done anything. So, this affair has been going on since last year, and he sneaks around as and when he can. Is this only during the day, or has he been here of an evening, too?' Frank was remembering the report of Stevenson's van being seen after midnight.

'He's been here a few times of a night. My old man works away sometimes. Alan never stayed all night, though.'

'What's the latest he was ever here?' Nicky asked.

Angie Reed stopped to consider. 'Ooh, must have been around one in the morning. Wasn't often he stayed that late, but he did a few times. I hope you're going to tell his wife, too. I don't see why I should be the only one to suffer.'

Frank decided he'd had enough of this woman. He and Nicky excused themselves, and for a time sat out in the car. 'I should have listened to you,' Nicky said miserably. 'I was taken in by coincidence, just wanting so much to nail this fucker. I'm sorry, mate.'

'Don't worry about it. Stevenson had to be investigated. He was. Now we can move on.'

'I expect you'd like to come back with me, do some gloating when I tell Foster?'

But Frank was shaking his head. 'No, you break the good news,' he said. 'Savour the moment for me. I'm going home.'

'Thompson's going to hit the roof.'

'Maybe Foster's actually screwed himself this time.'

'I wouldn't bank on it.'

'No. Me neither. Oh, and Nicky, you're bound to be asked what we were doing there today. So, this is what you tell them: we were out taking a walk on the golf course when we saw the armed boys steaming in. We stepped up to see if we could lend a hand. We had no idea Stevenson was still under surveillance. And by Superintendent Foster of all people.'

Nicky grinned. 'You think Thompson will believe that crock?'

Frank shook his head again. 'No. But I'll lay odds he'll want to, just for the sheer pleasure of sticking it to that prick Foster. I got the distinct impression that he likes the man about as much as we do.'

Chapter Forty

The drive up from Chingford took little more than an hour and a quarter. Orton was south of Peterborough city centre, minutes from the main A1(M) route. An attempt had been made by the developers to give the place an identity, where flats and both small and large houses were jumbled together, some with wooden cladding exteriors, others bricks and mortar. But whichever way you cut it, there was no mistaking the uniformity of another local authority estate. Bland and run down, it stood as testimony to naivety and waste.

Following the Alan Stevenson fiasco, he'd gone home feeling pretty low. Not at all sure how to proceed. The only thing he was certain of was that he needed a drink. Tania Penny's phone number was stuck to the fridge door by a magnet, and he saw this when he reached inside for a beer. It struck him immediately that not all leads had been followed up, and this would be one way of maintaining some kind of momentum.

He had two choices: sit there and mope while getting slowly drunk, or move on to the next lead.

It was a no-brainer.

Tania Penny was waiting for Frank Rogers outside the three-storey house that had once been her family home. It was a featureless place, but Frank noticed that the grass was trim, net curtains gleaming white and windows sparkling. Tania got out of her small ten-year-old Volvo as Frank drew up. She had not been waiting long; the Volvo's cooling engine was still ticking like a time-bomb.

The young woman was tall and willowy, with mousy hair tied up and clipped neatly in place. She wore a baggy T-shirt that hung outside a tight pair of cut-off denim shorts. The weather had turned a little cooler, and Frank noticed goosebumps rising on her tanned legs. She would have been stunningly beautiful had she not been so laden with sadness. It seemed to pull at her resolve, ageing her prematurely.

'I couldn't wait for you inside,' she explained after they'd introduced themselves. Her voice was thick with the sound of the Fens. 'I haven't been anywhere near the place since ... since I found them.'

Frank understood. 'I'm sorry. That must have been an awful ordeal for you.'

Tania shook her head at the memory. 'You have no idea.'

'Unfortunately, yes I do. My wife and son were killed by the same man. He now has my daughter.'

The young woman put both hands to her mouth as if in prayer, features crumbling. 'Oh, damn. Now it's my turn to be sorry. I should have thought ...'

Frank raised his hands. 'No need. Look ... if you really don't want to go inside, perhaps we could talk elsewhere.'

Tania turned her head toward the house, its window panes darkened by shadows. 'No. I must go in there. I need to. Now seems like the right time, with someone beside me who can understand how I feel. I just couldn't face it alone.'

They strolled slowly across to the house. Several children played on the path, unaware of life's vagaries and deceptions. Frank envied their innocence. 'How has the place been kept so clean?' he asked Tania.

'The rest of my family take it in turns. You know, uncles, aunts. They all muck in once a week.'

'How about the upkeep? Must be a strain paying rent for a place you don't even live in.'

She smiled briefly and shook her head. 'Oh, no. My parents bought the house off the council. The insurance paid off the mortgage, and the place was left to me.' Her voice seemed to break as she spoke.

Frank stopped and reached out to grasp her forearm. His grip was tender. 'Look, if this is going to be painful, if it's too much for you, tell me. I really only need to see you, not the house itself.'

'I know. But like I said, now is as good a time as any to face up to it. It is mine now, after all. And Samantha's ... if she comes home.'

Frank said nothing. His reassurance at that moment would have sounded hollow and unconvincing. Tania turned the key and pushed, pausing on the doorstep. He saw her jaw stiffen determinedly. Then she was inside, walking around the house in complete silence. Frank remained in the hall by the front door, allowing the girl her privacy. He felt for her. She wasn't much more than a child herself. It wasn't right for the young to die, but it was no more right that they should be left behind to mourn and grieve. And this poor girl had more than that to contend with, for she had actually discovered the bodies. How was that affecting her life?

Frank took in all that he could. The hall and stairway carpets were obviously new. Blood could be scrubbed away, but no amount of cleaning could expunge the memories held in each fibre. For the first time he thought of Paul Clarke's relatives, and how they were handling the cleaning up. The man may have stolen his wife, but Frank would never have wished such an end on anyone.

When Tania was finished with the rest of the house they moved into the kitchen. She took a bottle from the fridge and poured them both a tall glass of sparkling mineral water. 'I've nothing stronger. My parents weren't really drinkers. And there's no milk for tea.'

She led them into the living room, where the shadows lengthened and time slipped by unnoticed as they talked. Like the rest of the house, the room was too clean, too tidy. It had the air of abandonment. Frank's heart reached out to the young woman, but although he asked all the right questions, she really had nothing new to offer.

Tania had stayed the night with a friend, returning the next afternoon to find her family slaughtered, Samantha missing. She could not recall seeing any strangers in the area, nor had anyone worked on the house, her father being a keen and excellent all-round building tradesman.

Frank was on the point of excusing himself when he noticed her moist eyes locked on the wall to his right. He turned and saw two framed photographs. One was of Tania herself, posing on a beach, her bikini the same shade as her flesh. The other portrayed a girl several years younger, with the same exquisite bone structure and fledgling beauty, smart in her school uniform.

'Poor Sam,' Tania whispered. 'I hope she isn't suffering. I think I'd rather she was dead than that.'

Frank edged forward to give her hand a gentle squeeze. 'She's a lovely looking girl. My daughter had just had her school photograph taken, too. She ...'

His head snapped back to the photograph. He got to his feet abruptly, spilling the glass of water across the carpet, oblivious to it. Slowly, as if with great reluctance, he inched his way across to the wall. This time he ignored Samantha Penny's face. This time he saw only the background behind her. He closed his eyes and drifted back eleven days.

Laura coming into the kitchen early on Saturday morning. Laura handing him a large envelope. Laura eyeing him nervously as he pulled out the photograph. Frank squeezed his eyes tight, then tighter still. He saw Laura clearly, her face looking out of the photo, the image of her mother. Then he saw the background. A peach and beige marble effect, more luxurious than the standard backdrops, yet with a curious defect in the marbling that made one section look like the face of a cartoon dog.

He opened his eyes and looked beyond Samantha Penny. Peach and beige. Marbling. Defect. Not in precisely the same place, but the seating would never have been exact. The picture faded out and re-emerged as Laura once more. Her school photograph.

School.

Her favourite place?

Not a chance. Laura's response to the question about her favourite place had been a clue after all. The best she could think of giving.

'It can't be,' he muttered, shaking his head slowly. His mouth was dry, heart clamouring. All moisture seemed to have seeped into the palms of his hands.

'What's wrong?' Tania asked. While he had been standing there, she had fetched a cloth from the kitchen and was on her knees mopping up the water. She looked up at him, wary and a little anxious.

'It just couldn't be,' he said again, as if he hadn't heard her.

'Sorry?' Tania turned to him, concerned now by his behaviour. 'What's wrong, Mr Rogers?'

Frank turned, face clearly registering his shock. 'Oh. Nothing. Sorry. I just ... I just thought of something I need to do. Urgently. Look, Tania, I have to go.' He picked up the framed photograph. 'May I borrow this? I can't tell you why I need it, just that it will help.'

Tania Penny nodded. 'Of course.'

'Thank you. Are you going to be all right here?'

Tania nodded, bewildered by his strange behaviour. She dug her hands into the pockets of her jeans. A girl more than a woman. 'Yes. There weren't any ghosts.'

'Is that what you were afraid of? Is that what you were expecting to find?' He lowered his gaze, remembering. 'Yes. Me, too. But you know what, Tania, if they do come, you have no need to be afraid. They'll be a comfort, believe me.'

She got to her feet. 'I'm sorry I wasn't much help.'

'No problem. I really do have to go right now, but I'll be in touch as soon as I have any news. I promise.'

Tania blinked. Her eyes appraised him frankly. A weight had been lifted from them, as if shutters had been thrown back, allowing her natural beauty to come flooding out once more.

'There won't be any,' she said simply. 'Not any good news. Not for me. I've resigned myself to that now. Right from the moment you started finding the bodies. But I hope it's not too late for you and your daughter.'

Frank shook the girl's outstretched hand. 'Please, don't give up on Samantha.' He felt like a charlatan even as the words left his mouth. False hope was a sore that never healed.

Tania smiled. 'Do me a favour.'

'Anything.' He meant it, too. She was so vulnerable, so brave, so alone. He wanted to hold her, to protect her, to be with her when the news came.

'Get him for me.'

'That's another promise.' And then he did hold her, because it was what they both wanted. She seemed to crumple into his embrace. Her head rested against his shoulder as she sobbed. Frank stroked her hair, offering no words of comfort, because they would have been shallow and meaningless. They both knew that Samantha Penny wasn't coming home.

Tania saw him back to the Renault. 'Thanks,' she said, looking a little embarrassed. 'I must have needed that more than I realised.'

'It's okay. I knew exactly how you were feeling.'

'You're a nice man, Mr Rogers.'

'And you're a very nice girl. And please call me Frank. Listen ... you have a future ahead of you, Tania. You may not think much of it right now, but please don't let the past hold you back. You can't change anything that's gone, but you can still shape your own destiny. Try not to be bitter, try not to feel guilty that you didn't suffer with them. Mourn, because that's right. But only for a time. Then let it go and get on with living. It's what your family would want. It's what they would expect of you.'

Tania broke into a bright, wide smile. She leaned into the car and kissed Frank on the cheek. 'Good luck. If I need to talk, can I call you?'

'Sure.' He took out a business card. 'Use my home number. The business is taking a back seat for a while.'

'Thank you. I hope things turn out all right for you.'

'So do I.' He patted her hand, gunned the engine, and left her standing by the kerb. Still alone, still sad, but he hoped no longer afraid of the dead. He had a feeling that she too was going to get busy living.

Chapter Forty-One

Nicky Loizou looked up as Frank burst through the annexe door. 'No luck with those formaldehyde suppliers, mate,' he called out. 'We're still checking, though. How'd you get on?'

Frank brushed by him and strode wordlessly over to the incident boards ranged across the far wall. The unit was bustling and noisy, telephones ringing, printers chattering, a hubbub of voices.

'You know something,' Nicky said. It wasn't a question.

'Yes.'

'So?'

'Look at the boards, Nicky. Tell me what you see.'

Nicky's gaze moved from Frank's troubled eyes to the boards. Seven innocent faces peered down at him. At least three of them no longer breathed. None of them told him anything new.

'Tell me what you think you know, Frank.'

'Just over an hour ago I saw Samantha Penny's photograph. It wasn't like the one we have here on the board, it was a more recent one. But its background was not only highly unusual, it was also exactly the same as the one in Laura's recent school photo, the smaller version of which is here.'

He rapped a finger on the board.

'And here's another one just like it. Look for the abnormality. A rip in the fabric that makes that part of the pattern look like a cartoon dog. Same rip. Same background.'

Nicky looked at all of the photographs again, including the framed one of Samantha Penny that Frank held in his hands. He looked at them all one more time. Frank followed his friend's eyes. Behind three of the girls there was the same curious marbled background, the same irregularity. No mistaking it.

'This could be it, Frank,' Nicky said, looking intently at him. 'It's been there all the time. I just never saw it.'

'You were looking at the faces. Just like everyone else.'

'Except you.'

'I stumbled across it, Nicky. Pure luck. But when you put this into the overall picture it becomes so clear. That's how he finds them, gets to know them. Before he does the shoot, he puts the girls at their ease. How? By asking them questions they can easily respond do.'

'Like, do you have a pet? What's its name?'

'You've got it. He then finds out where she lives. If he does shops as well as schools, then the address will be given by the parent. Otherwise he probably asks other questions, putting them in such a way that the girl gives the information without even realising.'

Nicky nodded excitedly. 'Then he takes a few sweeps of the area, decides how to get in.'

'Or *if* to get in. Some places will be too difficult, alarmed, not secluded enough to cover his entry, using double-glazing. So, he simply moves on to the next. He's taking photographs all the time. He must have a list as long as your arm.'

'You got him, Frank. You got the bastard.'

A huge cheer went up, and hands rapped against desktops. All around the two men, activity had ceased long ago. There had been total silence for several minutes. Now for the first time since the investigation had begun, there were smiles on every face.

But Frank's gaze narrowed to slits, and he shook his head. 'Not until the cuffs are on, Nicky,' he cautioned. 'You know better than that.'

Nicky acknowledged the rebuke with a shrug and a guilty grin. 'Sorry. I suppose I was a bit previous. Carried away by the break.'

'So, what happens now? I suppose you really have to let Foster know what we have. Technically it's still his case.'

Nicky's grin widened. 'Now it's your turn to be wrong about something. He's taken a leave of absence. I gather it was suggested to him by the DCA. I think the phone trace Foster ordered, plus the incident with Stevenson, made him surplus to requirements.'

Frank gave a cry of triumph and slammed a balled fist into the meat of his palm. 'Now that's the kind of news I've been waiting for. So, I suppose you're in charge.'

'At present. There was talk of bringing in a new super or a more experienced DCI, but I pleaded to have the case. Together with you, of course. This break will give me even more time to get a result.'

'Could be the making of you, mate. Superintendent next stop.'

Nicky pulled a face. 'So, let's get the ball rolling. We have to find out who took these photographs.'

'I can give Laura's school a bell. They'll have the name, address, the lot.'

'Right. Oh, how about a call to the Redbridge home? Find out if Karen Redbridge has had her photo taken lately. Ask if the man who took it and the man who came to her room could have been the same.'

'It will be. But I'll confirm it anyway.'

Nicky thumped his friend on the back. 'This is great, Frank. I can't tell you how pleased I am.'

A shadow of doubt passed across Frank's face. Nicky, as ever attuned to his friend's feelings, raised an eyebrow. 'What? What's the problem?'

'Nothing. I just ... I'm a bit nervous. We're close now. Close to getting him. Close to finding out whether Laura is still alive.'

'You know she was, just three days ago.'

'Yeah. I just hope he calls again soon. Today. That way I'll maybe still have some chance of getting through the night.'

Nicky inclined his head. 'Make that call. Be busy.'

Frank nodded and turned. And turned back again sharply. There was a terrible look on his face. 'Oh, Jesus, Nicky,' he said. 'Oh, Jesus.' He plumped himself down on the edge of a desk.

Alarmed, Nicky dropped to his friend's side. 'What? What is it, Frank?'

'I know what he wants them for. When we talked about it before, we assumed that he was doing these terrible things to the girls because they were either giving him trouble or he was getting fed up with them. But I see it now. It explains why only one was disfigured. He did lose his temper with her … but he was always going to perform the taxidermy. That's the reason he takes them, why they're all so similar. He wants to preserve a child just as she is now, but none of them have turned out right so far, which is why he's still doing it.'

Nicky was nodding excitedly. 'Yes. That's it, that's it. But why are you so down about it? It's another break for us.'

'But don't you see?' Frank lowered his gaze. 'Until now I thought Laura might be safe just as long as she kept her cool, didn't upset him. But if I'm right, then he was always going to kill her. Nicky, if we don't get to her soon, Laura *will* die. There's no doubt in my mind about it now. No doubt at all.'

Chapter Forty-Two

The man and woman rose early that Friday morning. She made him a light breakfast while he bathed and dressed. When he was ready, she came to him and they embraced warmly. 'Have you got everything?' she asked.

'Of course. Do I ever forget anything?'

She smiled and pecked his nose. 'Silly me. Are you going into the office today?'

He gave her a quizzical look. 'What's wrong with you this morning? Don't I always go into the office first thing?'

She stood back, brushed away an imaginary thread from his impeccably ironed shirt. 'I don't know. It's just a feeling I have. I had a bad dream, and you know I think bad dreams are ill-omens.'

He laughed at her. 'Nothing's going to go wrong, you stupid woman. They can't trace me. They have no idea how I operate. Now look, we have our pretty girl to cheer us. Last night she saw the error of her ways. She'll be thinking about that. Soon she'll be wanting to sip from us. And no one is going to stop that from happening.'

The woman nodded and kissed his cheek. 'Like I said, silly me. Have a good day.'

He patted her behind and winked. He tugged his baseball cap forward on his head. 'Of course. And don't worry about a thing. I'm better than they are.'

After he had left, the woman smiled to herself, licking her lips in anticipation. After ten minutes, when she was certain he would not return, she ran across to a dusty mirror and gazed at herself for a few moments. She ran stiff fingers through her matted hair, pulling it back behind her ears. It had been some time since she'd had need of preening herself. Larry took her anytime, no matter how she looked or smelled. But now she had someone else to impress. She took one last look, then she smiled again and went to Laura.

* * *

Frank had watched the dawn approach, slowly touching the day with its gentle light. A late night, followed by little rest and an early rise, had left him feeling weak and stiff, eyes scoured with grit. The couple of hours' sleep he had managed to grab were spent alone. Debbie had understood. As Janet never had.

Today could bring about the final conclusion of the investigation, and it had always affected him this way. This time, though, the jangling nerves and heightened senses were all the more acute because of Laura's involvement. He was close. Too close to switch off, too close to sleep. Close enough to have the stench of possible failure in his nostrils.

At six, Nicky and Tom Whelan called to collect him. They drove across London through the light early-morning traffic to a street close by a four-storey building in Hammersmith. There they met up with Capel and a team of constables as happy to be in plain clothes as they were with the overtime. They grouped together around Nicky's car, while he outlined the operation.

'The man we're after is known here as Mr Tanner, though I can't imagine it's his real name. No first name available. He leases a couple of rooms in this building. Frank contacted Laura's school yesterday afternoon. They gave him the name and this address as the one supplied by the photographer they used. It checks out with other inquiries we've made, particularly with Mr and Mrs Redbridge. Have no doubts, this is the right man.

'Yesterday evening we located the owner of the building. According to him, Tanner comes in every weekday morning, first thing, to sort through the post and no doubt set up more photo shoots. The rooms he uses are made up of an office area, and a developing room he put together himself. We have a warrant, and the building caretaker is going to let us into the office.'

'How're we going to hit him?' Whelan wanted to know. His face was firmly set, eyes cold and unforgiving. He was known in the Met as a hard man, particularly in cases where children were the victims. Frank could almost see the adrenaline pumping through the sergeant's veins. Tom would like nothing more than for their quarry to resist arrest.

'Simply,' Nicky replied. 'We have team A down here in the observation van, in contact with team B – me and Frank – inside the office. The caretaker will be with the observation team. He will pick our man out as he approaches and enters the building. Warren, who will be in charge down here, will radio through to me and Frank when our man is on his way up. We have to let him use his own key to get inside the office before we take him out.

'Tom, you'll be in another room with team C at the end of the hall. Through a peep-hole you'll see him coming, and you can let us know when he's close to the office door. You're there with the plain-clothes unit as back-up if he resists me and Frank. The moment he steps inside the office, you come running. Warren's team will spread out to cover front and rear exits as soon as our target enters the building. The door at the rear opens from the inside only, so we're secure there.'

'Sounds watertight,' said Frank.

'It is. Once inside, there's no way out for him.'

'Then why aren't I convinced?'

Nicky offered a wry grin. 'Because you're an old sceptic and a worrier. Relax. If he comes into work today, we'll get him.'

Frank rubbed his sore, bloodshot eyes. 'And what then? What if he doesn't cough? I still think it would be better if we let him come and go and put a trace on him.'

Nicky frowned, but said nothing. Frank had discussed the plan with him during the journey across town. It was only on this point that they had differed, but it was such a vital element. Nicky gave orders for everyone to take their positions. After a moment or two, he and Frank made their way to the third floor, where the caretaker was waiting for them.

In the lift, Nicky said, 'Listen, Frank, I know your feelings on the matter, but I simply can't take the chance of him getting away. We may never have a better opportunity of nabbing this fucker. If we decide to follow, he could be lost.'

'Not if you put enough bodies onto it.'

'Frank, you know better than anyone else that there are no guarantees. The best watchers in the world aren't infallible. We may only get one shot at this. If he tumbles us, he won't be stupid enough to come back. I have to call it, and the way I see things is that we grab him while we can.'

Frank turned his head away. They were silent for a few minutes. The caretaker let them into the office, moved along the corridor to let Whelan and his team into the one at the end, and then joined the observation team in the specially equipped white Ford Transit. In that time, Frank changed his mind entirely.

'You're right,' he said to Nicky, who sat calmly at a cheap wooden desk. He turned away from the office door. 'I wasn't thinking straight. Laura's safety blinded me. It's a tough choice, but you made the right one. A bird in the hand, eh?'

Nicky smiled and winked. 'Take the weight off your feet, Frank. We might have some time to kill.'

Frank pulled out a chair from the other side of the desk. Absently, he began tapping his fingernails on Nicky's radio set, which lay between the two men. After a while he looked up and laughed nervously. 'How the hell can my heart beat this fast without exploding?' he said, shaking his head miserably.

Nicky smiled at him. 'Frank, take it easy, mate. You need to keep a cool head when this fucker gets here. It only takes one moment of madness to kill, and we're going to need him alive…and well.'

'I know, I know. It's not easy, but I'll be fine. Honestly.'

'You think we should go through the office?' Nicky asked, pulling open one of the desk's three drawers. It was empty, apart from a stack of pens.

'Later. When it's over. We may yet need some clearer evidence on this one. What we have so far is pretty circumstantial. DNA aside, that is. Even then, he has to volunteer a sample.'

'We're going to get him, Frank. One way or another.'

Frank lowered his gaze. 'I don't know, Nicky. You know me – a pessimist'

'Anxiety.' Nicky waved a dismissive hand. 'That's all.'

'Perhaps you're right.' *But your tone lacks conviction,* Frank thought. *I know how much you've come to trust my instincts.*

The radio gave a bark of static. The two men locked eyes as stags lock horns. Neither moved or even blinked.

'Warren to Nicky,' the disembodied voice drifted out of the tiny speaker. 'We have our man in sight now, boss. Approaching the building from the north by foot. He's wearing a grey windcheater over a white shirt, blue jeans, white trainers. Oh, and a plain blue baseball cap. I'll let Tom know it's a go.'

Frank had an almost overpowering urge to race to the window. He held himself in check. The silence in the room was complete. Neither man even took a breath.

The radio squawked again. 'Warren to Nicky. He's inside the building. He's all yours, guv'nor.'

Chapter Forty-Three

Frank and Nicky stood behind the door, bracing themselves against the wall. Nicky had inserted an ear-piece to keep any radio transmissions to himself. Frank watched him closely, tense, nervous, overwound.

'Warren to Nicky. Target has entered the lift. We are about to surround the building.'

Nicky depressed the button on his radio. 'Nicky to Tom. Target in the lift.' He described their quarry, then added, 'Make sure everyone is absolutely clear about what they have to do. And for God's sake, don't jump the gun. He must be allowed to enter this room.'

'Tom to Nicky. Understood, boss. Will let you know as soon as we have eyeball.'

Nicky blew out his cheeks. He caught Frank's scrutiny, gave a nod and a wink.

It seemed an age before the ear-piece hissed again. 'Tom to Nicky. Target has just stepped out of the lift...'

Nicky grasped Frank's arm. He put a finger to his lips. Both men held their breath.

'... moving down the corridor ... slowly ... taking something out of his jacket pocket ... okay, here we go ... it's keys ... putting one in the slot ... turning ... he's all yours, boss.'

What followed took only a matter of seconds. The door opened inwards. A tall figure stepped over the threshold, his shadow spilling across the beige cord of the office carpet. Frank heaved his shoulder against the door, sending the figure crashing against its frame. Before the man could recover and react, both Nicky and Frank were all over him.

Nicky went for the man's upraised hands. Frank threw himself forward, hitting the man's chest with his forearm. The man went down with a gasp that sounded like a broken air-line. No sooner had he hit the floor than Frank fell forward, ramming his knees into the nape of the man's neck. Nicky crouched low, pulling the flailing hands together, reaching for the plastic cuffs in his back pocket.

It was no contest. Frank rolled the man over as Nicky began to read him his rights. Long before the figure was secure, Tom Whelan had appeared at the door with his team in tow. They stood back, ready to act if necessary.

It wasn't him. Frank knew right away. He knew as soon as he looked into the man's terrified, bewildered eyes. Knew long before the man's cap was torn off, revealing a mop of gelled hair, pulled back and tied in a small pony-tail.

***

Vincent Tanner sat at the office desk, sore and bruised, but mostly undamaged. Around him, Tom, Warren, Nicky and Frank paced uneasily. They had been firing questions for a little over an hour, and each of them knew in his heart that the man was telling the truth.

'One more time,' Frank said. He stopped pacing, looked down at the man, thankful that his inner fury hadn't taken a hold at the wrong moment. This man would be dead, otherwise.

Tanner looked up. His mood had turned from fear, to incomprehension, to anger, and finally to outrage. 'Again? How many more times? You say I'm not under arrest, but you won't let me go. I have rights, you know.'

'Mr Tanner,' Frank sighed. He felt so weary. 'Terrible crimes have been committed. Vicious murders. The man responsible is either you or the person you claim to work for. Now, I'm telling you that I believe you when you say you are innocent of these crimes, but we have to be absolutely clear in our minds about everything before we can let you just walk away. So, you can either sit here and go through it again, or we can bring you in for questioning and hold you in a cell for the next thirty-six hours. Which would you prefer?'

He didn't like bullying Tanner. The man had received a big enough shock already. But time was wasting, and it was too precious a commodity to let trickle away on posturing.

'You can't treat me like this.'

Nicky stepped forward and slapped a hand down on the desk. His face was creased with anger and frustration. 'Look, Mr Tanner. For all we know you could be a part of it. You could be the front man or his partner, so don't think you're off the hook. Now, run through it again, or we'll do it down at the nick.'

Tanner gritted his teeth, but nodded. 'Okay. About a year ago I answered an advertisement for someone wanting a photographer. Old school. None of this digital lark. Proper film. I was interviewed at one of his shoots at a Mothercare in Southall. I was told that I would be shooting kids at shops, doing my own developing, virtually being my own boss. The money was good, the hours suited, so I took it.

The guy told me he would be travelling all over the country for long periods, so we established a routine. He asked me to set up an office and darkroom, which he paid for. He would come and go as and when he could, would leave me a schedule, I would do the jobs, develop the shots, and he would see to the business side of things. I was told to leave the weekly prints in an envelope which would be collected from this office. Once a month an envelope would be left for me. He paid cash, making me self-employed. He also left the money for the rent, though it was paid in my name for tax purposes.'

'What did he look like?' Tom Whelan asked.

'Jesus! I've told you ...'

'So, tell me again.'

'He was a big guy. Six-two, maybe taller. Skinny. Like me he wore a baseball cap, but it looked as if he might be bald underneath.'

'Scars? Any other distinguishing marks?'

'Yeah. He had a scar just under his left eye. About an inch long.'

Frank sat down opposite Tanner. 'Okay. How many times have you met with your boss since you started?'

Tanner crossed his arms. 'Not once. Haven't seen him since that day I was interviewed.'

'Talked with him?'

'Many times. If ever I had a query I used to leave him a note. Sometimes he would call me about it.'

'Didn't you think it was a peculiar arrangement?' This from Nicky.

Tanner nodded and shrugged. 'Sure. But when you have a good deal like I have, you don't rock the boat. Know what I mean?'

'About that interview. Where was the job advertised?' asked Frank.

Tanner stroked his chin. 'You got me there. I was out of work, so I was scouring all the papers and websites. Could've been from anywhere.'

'Think harder,' a thick Irish brogue insisted. Whelan moved a little closer, his presence intended to intimidate.

'I don't know. I can't remember.'

Frank leaned back in the chair. He closed his eyes. Nicky took over. 'Okay, Mr Tanner. So, you have this nice little earner, the boss is a bit peculiar, but you don't care as long as you get paid. Nothing wrong in that. You said he wanted you to do shops. Tell me, did you ever do schools?'

Tanner frowned. 'Funny you should ask that. I never did. I wondered about it. I used to do a similar job some years ago, but then I did shops, playgroups, schools, Santa's grotto … you name it. With this job, I only ever did shops and department stores.'

'Did your boss ever ask you to sound the children out?'

'I don't know what you mean.'

'Well, for instance, did he ever ask you to find out whether the children had any pets?'

'No …' Tanner shook his head thoughtfully. 'Not really. He said that I should put them at their ease. You know, talk about things they enjoyed. Get them in the mood. But never any specific questions.'

Frank rubbed his eyes. Tanner's response worried him. They now knew that out of the seven girls, five had their photos taken at school shortly before being abducted. That still left two taken in shops. He flipped open his notebook. 'Tell me, Mr Tanner, are your negatives and customer records stored here?'

'No. Whoever collects the weekly contact sheets, also takes the negs, prints, and does all the business records elsewhere.'

Capel cursed. 'So, you have no direct way of contacting your own boss, and we have no way of tracing him.'

Tanner nodded. 'That's about it.'

Frank got up and walked across to the window. The traffic outside was stalled, steaming in the ever-increasing heat. There was a smell of hot oil and muted irritation. He pushed up the lower sash, but only warm air wafted in. There was no breeze. He turned slowly.

'You can go,' he said to Tanner. 'Carry on with your schedule as if nothing had ever happened. Do so until we advise you otherwise. What day does he come to pick up your weekly output?'

Tanner got to his feet, dishevelled and still simmering. 'Monday mornings. I get here first thing as usual, drop everything off. Tuesday morning they're gone.'

'Okay. Now this is very important, so listen close. If your boss calls, you don't breathe a word about this. It never happened, okay?'

'Sure.'

Frank stood right in front of the man, locking eyes. 'I mean it. I know you're not happy about this and you may feel like getting back at us, but that would not be a clever thing to do. You warn him off and I'll see you inside as an accessory. I'll also make sure that you get placed inside a very hard jail, and then I'll make sure that every con on your wing knows that you sided with a child killer.'

Tanner nodded once, mute with fear. Nicky showed him out. Someone said 'Bastard.' All eyes turned to Tom Whelan, who slammed the door shut behind Tanner. 'Fuck it!' he added.

'Well, lads,' Nicky said, now perched on the edge of the desk. 'It looks like we bring the whole show back on Monday.'

'Too long,' said Frank. He looked as if he had aged five years in the past few hours. 'Three days is too long. He'll call before then. And my little girl is running out of time.'

'Not a lot else we can do, Frank,' Whelan said. His whole frame indicated his state of mind far more eloquently than words ever could. His shoulders were slumped forward, chin down, muscles relaxed. 'This is the only place we can trace him back to. If he doesn't pick the stuff up himself, someone else must. Eventually something or someone must lead back to him.'

After a final search of the premises the four men left the office, disenchanted, frustrated with life. Frank wished he shared Tom Whelan's confidence. Whoever their man was, he was cunning. He had himself covered all the way, leaving the police to chase their tails. If he had slipped up so far, Frank hadn't noticed. Why should he slip up now?

Too long, he thought again. *By the weekend, he'll give us another gift. And this time it could be Laura.*

Chapter Forty-Four

His name was Lawrence Swain, and the office he visited that morning had no connection whatsoever with either of the two so far uncovered by the police. He leased the entire top floor of a three-storey corner building just off Great Eastern Street in Shoreditch, EC1. It was where he kept all his records and negatives, where he did all his own developing.

The floor had once been leased by a printing company. It comprised three partitioned offices, a wash room and toilet, and an open-plan room where the marks of old machinery still lingered on the vinyl floor. It was a vast area, yet just about every inch of wall space was now taken up by photographs of varying sizes. In the largest of the three offices, a life-size print of Laura Rogers hung on the back of the door. It was a shot he had taken at the school with a small Olympus as she had settled herself before the backdrop. In it, Laura was sliding onto the stool, and her grey skirt had hitched up. It revealed a tantalising glimpse of her thighs.

He spent no more than an hour there. He didn't have far to travel that morning, and wasn't supposed to begin snapping until eleven.

Since taking Laura, he had made sure that his work was confined to the London area. He no longer had any desire to travel great distances, to stay overnight in towns he did not know and did not feel welcome in, not when his Laura waited for him at home.

Today was a simple four-hour appearance at a major newsagent chain at Euston Station. Easy money, and maybe even someone to replace Laura if and when she had run her course. If he needed a replacement at all.

Swain was confident that once he had sucked Laura's marrow dry, she would be his best work yet. Taxidermy, he had discovered to his distaste and enormous discomfort, was not an easily acquired art. He had made such elementary mistakes with the first few. Eventually he had sought professional help, had learned enough to make his amateur attempts better each time. The last three were holding together very well, yet he still had not been pleased with them. They weren't quite right to begin with, he ecided.

Laura was.

Would be.

She would be perfect. Finally. But first he would enjoy her body. The thought left him short of breath.

Having arrived at Euston a little after ten-thirty, he did not get away until almost four. During that entire time, he was the consummate professional, casting all thoughts of Laura aside. Face set into a smile, mind attuned to children and parents – mainly mothers. Boys and girls ranging from toddlers to those just entering their teens sat before him.

The little darlings, his understanding smile said throughout.

Little spoilt bastards was what they mostly were. Whining little shits who got their own way simply because their parents couldn't be bothered to deal with them, to instil a little discipline. Lawrence Swain knew how to deal with the little darlings. Fucking right he did. They could all go and ask Laura Rogers her opinion as to whether he knew how to deal with children.

These thoughts chased across his mind, but he continued to treat the little darlings as if they were fragile glass. He made them laugh beforehand, putting them at their ease, caught a smile each time he depressed the shutter button. Any girl aged between eleven and thirteen he took particular notice of, although outwardly his demeanour remained exactly the same.

But none was Laura. None came anywhere near. In a way, he was glad. Laura would live a little longer. And he wanted to enjoy her to the full.

When the last of the little darlings had gone, he packed away the backdrop, tripod, lighting rig, the reflectors, three different cameras, various lenses and filters. Then he set off through the growing throng of traffic, the day's heat dying quickly with the onset of a cool westerly wind that hurried through the streets as if fleeing something monstrous. He wondered how Tanner had fared today, whether he had managed to capture another Laura. Just thinking about her made him smile and sigh.

* * *

Laura said nothing as the woman paraded around the room, pausing every so often to strike a pose, attempting to tease with her body. Laura let her do all the talking.

'Has my Larry told you how much we love you?' Her mouth was curled into a smile, but her eyes were distant. 'Because we do, you know. We both love you so very much. We're so glad you decided to come home, that you came back to us. You were away too long, you naughty girl. We missed you terribly.'

Laura stared back at the crazy woman. She had revealed the man's name, a slip quite out of character. Laura smelled the man on her, a sweet, pungent odour that was disturbing more than it was unpleasant. But her words didn't make any sense. The woman was looking directly at her, but seeing someone else entirely.

One of the other girls? A friend, perhaps?

Laura stayed quiet. There was nothing she could say. At least not yet.

'Now that you're back with us,' the woman went on, 'we can play games again. We can have fun just like we used to. Would you like that? Of course you would. Our little Princess loved playing games, didn't you? Ah … we had such fun. It wasn't the same while you were gone.'

Her head suddenly snapped to one side, her gaze narrowing as she stared hard at Laura. It was as if a storm-laden cloud had passed across her face.

'You really shouldn't have left us, you know. We were very unhappy. Larry was miserable, and took it out on me. And it was all your fault.' She stepped closer to Laura, hands raised as if to strike out, her fists balled.

Laura didn't move, didn't even flinch. She saw the woman's right fist arc in a wide loop, arrow down, grow larger until it filled her vision. It took a moment to realise that she had actually been struck. Then a bolt of pain shot between her left eye and the prominent cheekbone beneath. Her head jolted back and rocked unsteadily. There was a brief explosion behind her eyes, like the opening volley of a firework display. And although the woman now stood with a mortified expression on her face, both hands raised to her open mouth, Laura felt as if the hard bones of the woman's knuckles were still buried in the side of her head.

She had no time to react before the woman dropped to her knees and wrapped both arms around her neck. She felt the woman's stale breath whisper against her skin, the caress of her wispy hair, the touch of dry lips against her brow. The woman's body reeked with stale sweat, and something sweet and nasty that seemed to lodge in Laura's throat. Her nose wrinkled in disgust as the woman rocked back and forth, sobbing now.

'I'm sorry, I'm sorry, I'm sorry,' the woman moaned, her voice cracking and pitched so high the sound hurt Laura's ears. It was almost a squeal of pain. 'I didn't mean to hurt you. Honestly I didn't.'

She pulled back, and Laura could see her eyes brimming, red lines swarming all over the whites. 'Please forgive me,' she begged, the expression on her face was one of utmost mental agony. 'Please, please, don't tell my brother.'

At first Laura continued to say nothing, but her mind began to work once more. The woman was distressed beyond all reason. She was scared. More, she was terrified. *But of what?* Laura asked herself. *Or ... of whom?*

Him, of course. 'Your brother?' Laura said, her voice cracking through lack of use. 'I thought he was your partner.'

'And so he is in many ways. We're very close. Closer than usual, maybe. But please say you won't tell him I hit you. Not even that I was in here.'

She's terrified of her own brother, Laura thought. *She doesn't want him to know what she did. She's terrified of him and what he might do if he finds out. I'm special to him, and that worries her.*

The woman's hands were caressing Laura's face now, taking care as they slid across the tender spot of redness that was beginning to swell a little. Laura locked eyes with her defiantly. It occurred to her that a subtle shift in the balance of power had taken place. The woman had been so sure of herself, so confident. Now she was subdued. The blow had not been that hard, the pain had come and gone in an instant, yet Laura sensed that she now had some leverage. Her silence in exchange for …

She smiled at the woman, who smiled back, hope radiating in that single expression. 'I do wonder if I should tell your brother what you did to me,' Laura said softly. 'I do think he deserves to know.'

Colour bled from the woman's face as if her blood had been drained. 'No.' She shook her head violently. 'No, don't do that. There's no need. Really. I … I could get you some nice soothing cream for your bottom. I know it must still hurt where he beat you, and we don't want it infected, do we? And we could keep this little secret just between the two of us.' She nodded encouragingly.

Laura felt as if her heart might burst. Here was the opening she had been waiting for. 'Maybe. It might be good to have our own secret.'

'Yes. Yes, it would.'

'But … you would have to be good to me.'

Laura's captor frowned. 'I would? In what way?'

'For a start, I don't think you should hit me again.'

'Oh, no. No, I never will. I promise.'

'And I don't think you should touch me, or kiss me, or do anything wrong to me.'

'But what if Larry wants me to?'

Laura considered only for a second. She couldn't push this too far. A little at a time. Gain the woman's confidence. 'Only if you have to,' she said reluctantly. 'But if we're going to have a secret, if I'm going to trust you, at least tell me your name.'

The woman frowned in a slightly amused way. 'It's Violet. You should remember that, Princess.'

'Violet.' Laura gave a huge grin. 'Okay, Violet. It'll be our secret. I won't tell, just as long as you're good to me from now on.'

The woman breathed a long sigh. She got to her feet. 'I'd better be going now.'

'Yes.' Laura nodded, and her eyes hardened. 'I think you'd better. And, Violet … don't forget that cream.'

Moments later, Laura, too, heaved a heavy sigh. She had gained a small measure of control. Now all she had to do was think how best to use it.

* * *

Lawrence Swain entered the room some time later, carrying a bucket of Kentucky Fried Chicken. He crouched down and set it on the floor by her side. 'Dinner,' he said. 'A treat for you.'

'Thank you.'

He gave a surprised smile. 'There's a good girl. Now, isn't that a whole lot better than making me angry?'

'Yes.' Laura took the lid from the bucket and pulled out a piece of greasy chicken. He looked on as she ate hungrily. Although her meals were better of late, her stomach had not yet acclimatised to the lack of in-between meal snacks. She knew she had lost some weight, and felt weakened by it.

'Good?' he asked.

'Wonderful.'

He put a hand on her shoulder, squeezing it tenderly. It was all Laura could do not to scream or shudder at his touch. 'I feel that things are improving, Laura. I really do. I shouldn't wonder if you are getting to feel something for us. Perhaps it won't be long before you love us like we love you.'

Laura pulled out a second piece of chicken. She managed to give one of her prettiest smiles. 'I do like you. I like you both. Especially when you're nice to me.'

The cream now spread across her buttocks soothed her wounds, the relief filling her with even more confidence. But confidence had caused her guard to drop.

Larry inclined his head, frowning. '*Like* us? *Like* us both? So, what the fuck happened to love? And what's this shit about being nice to you? You should love us no matter what. That's what fucking love is all a-fucking-bout!'

The change had come over him in an instant, every little feature of his face hardening. She had lost him. Now she had to bring him back. She lowered her gaze and saw his hands hanging loosely, the fingers beginning to curl into fists. The thought of touching him made her want to bring the chicken right back up. But there was no other way.

Survival.

Laura dropped the chicken piece back into the bucket. She wiped her fingers on her dress, then slowly reached out. Her hand slipped into his, between the curling fingers. She saw something come back into his eyes, like a spirit re-entering a body. He was hers again.

He looked down, then across at Laura. She smiled. He smiled.

Please don't hold me, her mind screamed inwardly. *I don't know if I can take that.* But he did. He pulled her to him and hugged her close. Laura closed her eyes and reached inside herself once more. She didn't know how much more she had to give, but her reservoir of strength had to be almost dry. Still she drew from it. Perhaps for the last time.

Survival.

That was all that mattered.

Chapter Forty-Five

Frank lay awake in bed, blinking sleep from his eyes. He hadn't taken a single drink last night and was astonished to discover just how clear his mind was this morning, how sharp and keen his senses were. He stretched and yawned, breathed the morning air. Then he sat up. A once-familiar smell drifted up to him from downstairs. It had been a long time. He smiled and swung his legs out of bed.

Debbie had come over again the previous evening. They'd slept together, but hadn't made love. They held each other all night, though, their heat spilling out onto the sheets. As midnight became just another memory, he spoke of the bitter defeat he and Nicky's team had experienced. She stroked his chest and soothed him, telling him it would be all right. Telling him until he too finally came to believe it.

'Breakfast,' she called up the stairs.

'I'm on my way.' He scowled at the overcast sky, pulled on his dressing gown, and padded downstairs.

Debbie was already showered and dressed, fresh and glowing. The place in his heart that wasn't confined to his son and daughter ached for what she meant to him.

'My God,' he said, registering what was on the table. A heaped plate waited for him: Sausage, bacon, mushrooms, fried egg, beans, fried slice. 'It's enough to feed an army.'

'Tuck in.' She kissed his cheek. 'You need a good start to the day. It'll help keep you going.'

Frank grinned crookedly as he sat down. 'I can think of a better way.'

She laughed. He loved to hear her laugh. It was melodic and refined, a sound of genuine happiness. 'You need to keep your strength up if you want to do that sort of thing. Eat first. If you're still in the mood after, maybe I'll see if I can fit you into my busy schedule.'

'Oh, but—'

'Eat! I'm not that easy, you know. You think you can just flutter those long lashes of yours and I'll crumble.'

He tried. Debbie waved him away and plunged her hands into a bowlful of soapy dishes. Frank shook his head and tucked in. His plate was half empty when the phone rang. Debbie reflexively picked it up and gave the number. At first, the ensuing silence sounded completely natural, but then he began to wonder why he couldn't hear her voice. He turned his head to look at her.

Debbie was pressed up against the wall, the receiver hanging loosely from her hand, her mouth open in a silent scream. He jumped to his feet, snatched the phone away from her and demanded to know who was on the line. His only reply was static, not that he'd needed an answer.

Frank slammed it back into its cradle. Then he took hold of Debbie's hands. 'It was him, wasn't it?' His voice was low, choked. Was there no end to this madman's intrusion into his life?

'He … he said he was happy to speak to me at last,' Debbie said finally, stumbling over her words. Frank led her across to the table and sat her down. She put her hands to her face and wept.

'Oh, Frank. His voice was so cold, so chilling. Just hearing it terrified me.' A thin trail of mucus ran from her nose. She cuffed it away angrily.

'What did he say?' Frank gently stroked her hair, his own fingers shaking with rage.

'He said he wanted to taste me. He said he wanted me to experience pain for him, so that he might discover another level of existence. He said he thought I would enjoy him, too. And then I would know the wonder that is death.'

Frank pulled the trembling woman close and held her tight against his chest. His head ached with pressure, needing to vent his anger at someone or something. The bastard had entered someone else's mind now. By involving Debbie, he had changed the rules, and was now playing a different game altogether.

The phone rang again. Debbie jumped as if scalded.

'Let it ring,' he whispered, stroking her fringe back from her face. His hands came back moist. It fuelled his anger all the more.

'No,' Debbie said quickly. 'He might have another girl for you.'

'It doesn't matter. We can't do anything for her now.'

'Frank.' She pulled him to her, lips brushing his. 'You have to answer it. You know you do. I'll be all right now.'

He cursed and snatched the phone off the wall. 'You lousy bastard!' he spat venomously. 'This has nothing to do with her.'

'Tut-tut. That's not very civil, is it? Don't speak to me like that again, Frank. Or maybe I'll have to take it out on your little girl. How would it be if I sprinkled crushed glass into her eyes? His voice was calm and horribly reasonable.

'No!' Frank cried out. He gripped the phone so tight that he thought it might buckle under the pressure. *Calm yourself, damnit. Calm yourself. Laura's life is in your hands now.* 'No ... don't do that, Oscar. There's no need. I ... I'm sorry.'

'And so you should be. I wouldn't want to ruin Laura's eyes. They're really quite beautiful. And so wide open to everything I have taught her. Quite the young lady she had become.'

Frank jammed his eyes shut.

'Your little girl isn't any more, Special Detective Rogers.'

He felt as if he'd been struck. *Isn't! Isn't what?* 'What do you mean?' he asked, his voice sounding small and pathetic.

'I mean she is no longer a little girl. None of them are, once they've been introduced to the pleasure of me. Once they've felt the delights a real man can offer. No more cherry for Laura. No white wedding for this one, Frank.'

A low moan escaped Frank's mouth. 'Oh, you haven't. Tell me you haven't. Please.'

He was begging, pleading with this beast, and he hated himself for it. It was all wrong, but the words had escaped as if they had a life of their own. Tears flooded his cheeks. He wanted to climb through the telephone line, wrap the cord around the throat he found there and tighten it until the madman's face turned black.

A chuckle, a practised sound. 'I'll just have to let you sweat on that one, Frank. Leave it in the pot … let your mind give it a stir from time to time.'

'Do you have any further proof that she's still alive?' Frank didn't want to know. Not really. Not in the place where his heart was darkest.

'Actually, I do. Your little girl and I were enjoying a rare feast last night. We pulled a wishbone and I asked her what she'd wished for. You know what, Frank? She didn't say she wanted to be with you. Didn't say she wanted her mummy and her brother back. She said she'd like to be in Disney World.'

'You could have got that from her at any time.'

'Well fuck you, you cock-sucking motherfucker! I've had enough of this fucking bullshit. I'm going to fetch her now, bring her to the phone. I'm going to break her little fingers one by one while you listen to her cries. I'm going to pull your fucking daughter inside out, and what I'm not going to do is listen to any more of your crap!'

'All right, all right,' Frank said hurriedly. He'd pushed too far this time. Damn Nicky and his bright fucking ideas. Laura might not be dead but her clock was ticking away. 'Take it easy. I won't ask any more. I promise. From now on you talk and I'll listen.'

His breath came in laboured gasps. Pain rippled through his chest. He felt the beginnings of a cramp in his left arm.

Oh, Christ. The ultimate irony. Laura gets rescued only to find out that her old man has died of a heart attack. He slowed his breathing.

'Please, Oscar,' he said weakly. 'I'll do anything you say, but please don't hurt her. Hurt me all you like instead.' He shot a glance at Debbie, who sat as if in a trance, tears drying on her cheeks.

Silence.

He's put the phone down on you. You went in too strong. You didn't know him well enough. Laura's going to die right now, and it's all your fault—

'Very well, Frank. I'll give you a chance to redeem yourself.'

'Thank you.' The words stuck in his throat. He thought: *There was a time I would have been willing to let you go, let you have your day in court, let justice take its natural course. Not now. Oh, no. Because now it doesn't matter what else happens – you, my friend, are going to die. I am going to kill you.*

'I suppose you can guess why I'm calling?'

'You have another gift for me.'

'Precisely. It's a rare pleasure dealing with you, Frank. I like to think we are both professionals, but pleasant also. People are either charming or tedious, I find. I haven't quite decided which you are. Laura, however, is unquestionably charming.'

Frank's head squeezed tighter still. Something the man had just said triggered an alarm in his head. What was it? What? He couldn't latch on to it, so let it go. Instead he debated whether to let Oscar know that they were onto the taxidermy angle. After a brief search of his instincts, he decided against. Who knew what it might trigger inside the monster's mind.

'Tell me where to find my gift, Oscar,' he said.

The man gave him the address. Then he said, 'Don't cut me off yet, Frank. We both know it isn't going to help her now.'

'You want to talk some more, Oscar.'

'Yes. But not to you. I want to talk to Debbie again.'

The blood seemed to ice over in Frank's veins. He looked across at the already shattered woman he had come to know and love as much as he had ever loved anyone in his life. Her face was white, both hands held against her brow were shaking uncontrollably.

Frank swallowed. 'I … I can't do that, Oscar.'

'Can't? Or won't?'

'Won't.'

'Very well. How about if I hurt your lovely daughter some more, Frank? How about if I record her screams and play them to you? Is that what it'll take?'

'I can't. You must know that. You've upset her enough. She won't come to the phone now.'

'Okay, Frank. The next time you hear from me, your pretty little girl will be dead, and her screams will haunt even your dreams.'

Frank broke down then. His resolve was forgotten. He wept like a baby and slumped against the wall, forehead cool against the ceramic tiles. His shoulders heaved and his pain came out in huge wracking sobs. He had heard of heartbreak, had scoffed at the thought, but now he felt the pain as his heart tore apart at the seams. He was struggling to compose himself one last time when he felt a tug against his fingers. Debbie was trying to take the phone from him.

He shook his head wildly, eyes wide and glazed.

'Yes, Frank,' she whispered. 'I can guess what he's threatened. Better I hear what he has to say than he hurts Laura.'

'I can't let you do that for me.'

She shook her head. 'No. But you can let me do it for her.'

He looked for a second into her eyes. What he saw there astounded him. He saw the kind of strength only a woman is capable of, the kind a man can never conceive of. It came from a place found only inside a woman who loves.

He relented.

Debbie took the phone from him, steeled herself, and spoke. 'Hello, Oscar. I believe you wanted to talk to me again.'

* * *

Holly Stevens. Barely twelve when she was taken like the others. They found her body in a deserted railway yard, right by the sidings. She shared her fate with those who had gone before. Once SOCO had allowed the photographer and police doctor their time, Frank and Nicky saw all they needed to, then left. Nicky suggested they stop off for a drink, hoping to wind down before they returned to the normality of familiar surroundings. Frank agreed: he didn't want to take another little girl's tortured body back to his home; did not want Debbie to feel its horrific touch.

As they drank bottled American lager with whisky chasers, the two men spoke in hushed voices. Frank felt numbed by all that had happened that day, his senses twisted and scarred beyond all recognition. He could not comprehend a mind capable of carrying out such atrocities, let alone enjoy doing it. And that same creature had his little girl.

Monday was still almost two days away. The monster was purging himself one child at a time, and Frank could only pray that killing Laura was not part of that plan for a while yet. The clock inside his head chimed away another hour of her life.

Frank mentioned his fears briefly. Nicky tried to assuage them. They would have the man behind bars soon enough, he insisted. If they had to, they would deal with him for Laura's life. Hope bloomed like a flower in Frank's heart. Yes. Let them deal. Let him give Laura's location. Then let him die. Just a few seconds. That's all it would take.

Bang, bang. You're dead.

Frank told Nicky about Debbie's astounding composure earlier. Nicky nodded and said, 'She's a tough one, Frank. You could do a whole lot worse for yourself when all this is over. What did the sick fuck say to her the second time?'

'More of the same. Described in detail all the things he would like to do to her. She just listened until he was through, then said goodbye. Told me it had been like listening to some pervert making a dirty phone call. I asked how she knew about such things, we both laughed, and that was it. Neither of us mentioned it again.'

'He won't get to her,' Nicky said. 'He won't have the chance.'

'I want him.' Frank hadn't meant to say it aloud.

Nicky shook his head.

Frank tossed back a shot of scotch. 'I want some time alone with him. He'll never bother anyone again.'

'I can't do that, Frank. You know that. My balls would be in the mangle if I left you alone with him.'

Frank nodded. 'I understand. Too much to ask of even our friendship. But if Laura dies, Nicky, I'll come through you to get to him if I have to.'

'Laura dying would change everything, Frank. If that happens, I'll happily stand aside.'

Chapter Forty-Six

Lawrence Swain did not consider himself to be either a madman or a deviant in the way that Frank Rogers thought of him. Indeed, during the time he spent outside the nightmare of reality that seemed to be expanding every single day in order to swallow him whole, Swain considered himself to be just like any other ordinary man. An ordinary man with desires that were just ... different.

In the swarm of darkness that enveloped him from time to time, however, there was no clear idea of exactly how he thought of himself. In the darkness, there was only the rush and blurring of time, wave upon wave of ambiguous emotion and movement. Everything was distorted, twisted out of shape, a surreal life run at double speed. Moments in time he had no control over.

He was a haunted man. Haunted by those he had killed, and by the unbidden thoughts raging inside his mind. Voices cried out, others whispered, each insinuation like a dagger to his heart. They waged a war inside his head and would not let him be. Worse still, they were gaining in strength, voices becoming louder, like a hurricane tearing its way through his soul.

Soon, he thought, *I will be taking Laura into the darkness with me. Just like the others.* And afterwards it would be no surprise at all to discover that he had emerged from it alone. As he had on six previous occasions.

Laura's time had just about run down. He would use her, abuse her, and dispose of her. That was his way. It was a kindness. The same kindness he had demonstrated when disposing of the girls' families. No child would want to live having been used and abused by him and Violet. It would have been heartless to have left them alive, agonising, waiting for the hammer to fall. Surely no one could fault him for that. He knew that society would scorn him for the incestuous relationship he shared with his sister, but they had no idea. Violet was the only one who truly knew him, the only one who would understand why he did the things he did.

There was a time when he had actually considered Laura to be almost as perfect as his sister. The one he had been waiting for all this time. Had she been, well, his mission now would be so different. She was close. Oh, she was so close. But ...

Today, at the department store in Kensington, more than fifty children had sat before the almighty Nikon. Little more than half had been girls. Of these, only four were the right approximate age. Two had been dark, one a red-head, but the other, oh, the other was the most magnificent creature he had ever seen.

Stacey Kimble.

Even the name sent a shiver through him.

Thirteen years old. Strawberry-blonde hair, long and lush and flowing. The face of an angel, cast from the finest alabaster. He had almost swooned when he saw her approaching. But he was nothing if not professional. One day, perhaps, he would slip into the darkness while working. If he did that in the presence of those children and parents, he was going to be caught. He would take a few of them with him, of course, but it would be over. Somehow, immense pride in his work dragged him through, even when the darkness seemed to linger close by, beckoning. Stacey had been put at her ease with a smile and a silly joke, and while her mother hovered in the background, she had given him all he needed. Except for the phone number and address, and those came straight from the mother's lips.

Stacey lived in Winchmore Hill, with her parents, a younger brother, their pet dog Dougal, and a hamster called Roland. The dog was a small King Charles spaniel, instantly loveable no doubt, and easily destroyed. Stacey's room was lilac, with pink curtains raised against a window that overlooked the back garden. Now,

Swain knew where to look and what to look for when he drove past the Kimble home – which he would do several times before reaching a final decision.

He had also to see if the house was alarmed, to make sure that entry to the rear was possible, that he could park close by without leaving any tyre depressions. All this he would do soon, maybe even on Monday after he'd been to the Hammersmith office. If all went well, there would be a new girl to take Laura's place within a fortnight.

First, he and Violet had to have their fill of Laura. They would enjoy her in so many different ways. He would allow himself to taste her pain. Then he would get down to the more serious work.

These thoughts and more raged through his dizzy head as he lumbered home in the rush hour traffic. It was another sweltering afternoon, the open window afforded little breeze, and a band of sweat collected around the edge of his baseball cap. He idly tapped his long fingers on the steering wheel. Today he would not lose his temper with other drivers. Today he was at peace with himself and everyone around him.

Except for Laura.

His expression changed dramatically when he thought of her. He'd done everything possible for that fucking little bitch. He'd changed his working schedule so that he wouldn't have to stay away from home. He'd shown her what aesthetic wonders lay in store for her, the beauty of a true artist's work, he'd treated her fairly, with enormous kindness, hadn't even starved her like the others.

And for what?

So, the devious little bitch could go behind his back, so the little bitch could make pacts with his own fucking sister. So, the little bitch could try to escape.

As the sweltering metallic line edged forward, Swain's face grew darker still. He could feel the empty husk of the darkness moving closer, looking to swallow him whole. Soon it would be time to enter it again. For once, he would welcome it.

Chapter Forty-Seven

Laura didn't know how long she had to live. What she did know was that soon, very soon, she would have crossed over into a realm where madness reigned. She had moments of delirium, experienced passages of time where she seemed to float out of her body. Several times lately when her mind had snapped out of a self-imposed unconsciousness, she had found herself shambling around the room, uttering incomprehensible sounds to the rhythm of both hands slapping against her bare thighs. Not soft taps, either, but hard smacks that left behind obvious marks.

She had taken to squatting in one corner of the room for hours at a time, twisting her greasy strands of hair, winding them around her fingers, and yanking on them until she cried out in pain. On other occasions she would gasp suddenly, look down at her arm to see that she had been scrubbing at it with her nails, the skin raw and red and unsightly. Left unattended, these sores wept a watery pus, then scabbed over, only to be broken by her nails again soon after.

All were rare moments laid against the broader canvas of her day, but their frequency and momentum was increasing. She was becoming unhinged, and there seemed no way of preventing it from happening.

During her most lucid hours over the past few days, Laura had sensed a shift in the atmosphere. The woman, Violet, was just plain crazy and unreliable. But the man was now subject to constant fierce mood swings, turning three different ways almost in the same breath. He was unstable, unpredictable, and therefore by far the more dangerous of the two. A human time-bomb waiting to detonate.

The swings were escalating daily. The mental violence had become physical, culminating in a further beating with his belt. Now she sensed there were sexual overtones in everything either of them said or did. The more Laura considered these things, the more she brought them into sharper focus, the more she was convinced that it was steadily building to a climax. Before long, one of them was going to take matters too far. One of them would seriously damage her, perhaps even kill her in one frenzied moment.

As soon as Laura worked this out, she decided there were only two courses of action open to her. She could give up, become their punchbag, accept anything that came her way, until the final welcome oblivion.

Or she could fight.

The first alternative meant death. Eventually, death was a certainty. But before that there would be a great deal of pain, she was sure. Pain she did not want to endure. The second option, fighting, meant trying her damnedest not to be around when that time came. It meant escape. And even if she were caught, what more could they do to her than kill her?

Laura had always known she was wise beyond her years. She believed she had figured things out well, that she had coped admirably for a girl her age. And for the most part, this was true. But in her thoughts, there was still much naiveté, for Laura simply could not imagine anything worse than death.

The truth was so very different.

Late on Saturday afternoon, Laura decided to fight. It was either that or succumb to them or the onrush of madness. By then she had worked it all out. The door was far too solid, but there were other exits; means of escape she had not considered before because they were out of sight. The room had four wooden shutters, beneath which were four windows. The shutters were nailed to the frames, and she had no tool with which to prise them loose. Except for just one faint hope.

With one of her long fingernails, Laura managed to ease out a screw that held the blade of a pencil sharpener in place. The blade was small, but it was unused and therefore still sharp. She ran down to the shutter furthest away from the door and, the blade pressed between forefinger and thumb, began to cut into the first of five wooden slats that comprised the shutter. Beneath the grimy surface, the wood was almost white. Laura cut into it again, as if peeling an apple. Her intention was to create a large enough gap so that her hand could slide between the slats. If she could prise just one away using some leverage, the others would surely yield.

In this way, Laura worked steadily for hour upon hour. She sliced into the wood until her finger and thumb became swollen and sore, then took a brief rest. She couldn't allow blood to be drawn, but she thought she might get away with the odd blister. And all the time she kept one ear cocked for the jangle of keys, terror spurring her on to greater efforts.

Since she'd begun, Violet had brought in her lunch a few hours ago and the man had brought in her tea. There were two visits to the toilet, also. Alerted by the keys each time, Laura had been sitting playing quietly by the time the door had swung open, the blade carefully hidden. Although she was living with constant fear, Laura was proud of herself. She was fighting back. Not only that, she was winning. And neither he nor his sister had any idea of her intentions.

So, Laura carried on attacking the wood, blissfully unaware of the video cameras watching her every movement.

Chapter Forty-Eight

Each digital memory card lasted a day before it needed replacing. Lawrence Swain went through them three times a day: before he left for work he took time to study the previous night's output; when he got home he would look at what Laura had been up to while he was out; and last thing at night, before he turned in, he would run through her evening's exertions.

Swain kept his video equipment in the room directly behind the doll's house. There were three cameras, cabled together and timed so that when one tape finished another began. He had done all the wiring himself. There was a machine for editing, and a TV with a 32-inch screen. When he wasn't at work or with his sister, Swain spent much of his time in this room.

It would have been impossible to sit and study every frame of film, of course. Swain reviewed them all at twenty times normal speed, slowing the film only when something noteworthy caught his attention.

At first, he had selected moments such as the times when Laura first saw what they had given her to eat. Then there were the regretfully few occasions when the girl changed her dress. It was as if he had captured the moment a butterfly emerges from its pupal state; the girl emerging as a woman, the butterfly beating its wings for the first time. There were times when he simply wanted to watch her at play.

But then there were other, more important selections. He slowed the recording when his sister unexpectedly wandered into view. He watched as she paced the room, saw the blow, the caress afterwards. A specially rigged microphone secreted next to one of the ceiling lights picked up every whispered word. By the time Violet left the screen, Swain's face was pinched tight by fury.

It was some time before he noticed exactly what Laura was doing at the far end of the room. At first, he thought she was merely playing a game, then it occurred to him that she might be trying to force the shutters open. Finally, after rewinding, he saw her hide something small and shiny just before Violet came into the room with a tray of food.

The next time he glanced at the screen, the recording had ended. He looked at his watch, astonished to discover that three hours had gone by. Hours when he had no doubt drifted back into the darkness. He hadn't left the room. If he had, Laura might already be dead. Then he remembered what he had seen on the monitor.

You ungrateful little bitch. I treated you better than any of them, and how do you repay me? After conspiring with my own sister, you try to escape. You actually try to escape. You insult my fucking intelligence, that's how you repay me is it, you little horror? You think your damned freedom lies behind those shutters? Do you? You think I'm that fucking stupid?

He felt betrayed, and not by Laura alone.

Now, as afternoon merged with the evening, Swain smiled to himself and chuckled. He'd fully intended to end Laura's miserable life tonight. But now he had other plans. He'd fucked with the father's mind and found it hugely entertaining. He saw no reason to deny himself a little more fun before the hard work began all over again. No, he was going to fuck with her mind. Let her fingers get sore, let them blister, let her heart misinform her. Let her believe the pain was worthwhile because escape was just a few scraps of wood deep.

* * *

Around seven-twenty that night, the man brought Laura her tea. Meatloaf, new potatoes, processed peas, gravy. No surprises. The best meal they had served up in almost two full weeks. He chatted for a while, his mood seemingly lighter, for which she was thankful. She managed to keep her hands out of sight for much of the time.

She ate heartily, waited for the tray to be cleared away, for Violet to escort her to and from the toilet. Then, when the key was turned for the last time that night, Laura went back to work. She had already created a chink of fading daylight. Within an hour she found purchase for one finger. The breakthrough made her work all the harder.

Chapter Forty-Nine

Frank and Debbie lay curled up on the sofa together. For him, it was a delight to feel this close to someone again. Yet his heart sank as he spoke, fearing he was about to blow it yet again.

'You know I have to be on my own tonight?'

'I do. You want me to go home?'

'No.' He shook his head, pecked her cheek. 'You take the bed. I'll stretch out on here. I won't sleep anyway.'

'You might surprise yourself. You may find sleep comes naturally tonight.'

But Frank knew he would spend the darkest hours lying wide awake, thinking about the morning, running the possibilities through his head. It was his way, always had been, and he was too long in the tooth to change now.

'I'm sorry,' he said. 'I'd rather be cuddling up beside you than sprawled out here on my own, but I'm not good to be around at those moments. I can get a little manic, a bit self-involved.'

Debbie brushed his arm with her soft hands. 'Shhh. It doesn't matter. You're the one who has to be in the right frame of mind in the morning. Do whatever it takes, Frank. We'll keep.'

The phone rang, its strident tone causing Frank's heart to lurch, his flesh to crawl. Was this him now? Was he about to give up another body? And would he stray from the chronological order he'd maintained so far and deliver up Laura?

The relief he felt when he heard Zoe's voice was palpable. Frank felt a trickle of sweat slip from his brow even as he started to smile. Zoe wanted to know if he would be going into the office the following morning, her bouncy manner a stark contrast with his own.

'Not tomorrow, Zo. I have something on in the morning, and I'll be tied up all day. If things go to plan, I may see you on Tuesday.'

'Okay.' She sounded flat, dispirited for the first time. 'I don't know how much longer I can hold the fort on my own though, boss.'

'I'm sorry.' Frank looked to the ceiling, tried to think. 'Listen, I promise you this: if I can't make it in, I'll send someone else in my place. Someone will be there first thing Tuesday morning. Give them all my usual calls.'

'What about any new business?'

Frank made a snap decision. 'You handle it.'

'Me? Frank, they're not going to want to see someone like me. They want to see the boss.'

'You're my assistant. Assist. Take whoever I send with you, so they can see we have the necessary muscle. But you know how the business works, Zo. I have faith in you.'

'But I'd have to wear ... normal clothes.' She sounded doubtful.

Frank recalled the cremation ceremony. Zoe had looked good in black after all. 'Get yourself a nice suit,' he said. 'Charge it, and let me know how much it comes to. You can do this, Zoe. It's not rocket science.'

She laughed then. 'Just try to be here yourself. So how are things?'

'Not too bad. Debs is here with me, and things are moving on the investigation. It may all be over tomorrow.'

'Oh, Frank. I hope so. For your sake. For Laura's sake. And for my sake.'

'Your sake?'

'Yeah. I mean, me in a suit?'

* * *

Debbie stayed up with him long into the night. They talked about all manner of things, none of which were to do with the case or anything that had happened to Frank's family. He played a little music, keeping the volume low, looking for a mellow sound to complement his mood. They held each other for hours, polished off a bottle of Merlot, before Debbie eased herself away.

Kneeling in front of him, she kissed the tip of his nose and said, 'I love you, Frank. Take care of yourself tomorrow.'

'Of course. Sleep tight.'

'You, too. And Frank, don't lie here all night winding yourself up. The last thing you need to do tomorrow is what you'd actually like to do to this man.'

Frank leaned up. 'What d'you mean?'

'I mean, don't work yourself up so much that you hurt him more than you need to. He's no good to you dead, Frank.'

'But I wouldn't ...'

Debbie put a finger to his lips. 'Yes. Yes, you would. All I'm saying is, think of the bigger picture. You need him if you're going to get Laura back. Just remember that.'

He nodded. Debbie stood, both knees cracking, and moved to go upstairs.

'Debs,' he said.

She turned. Smiled at him questioningly.

'I love you, sweetheart,' he went on. 'When this is all over, how about you and me sit down and talk about our future together?'

It may have been the dim light, perhaps even a trick of the eye, but for a moment Frank thought he saw Debbie's smile falter. For a few seconds she made no reply, then her voice came out of the shadow.

'The future starts tomorrow, Frank. As it does every single day. Take care of that. We'll see about the rest afterwards. Just concern yourself now with getting our girl back.'

It was fully ten minutes before he realised what she'd said.

Our girl.

Chapter Fifty

Brother and sister basked in the afterglow of their lovemaking. Violet was sore all over. Larry had pinched her flesh too often and too hard this time, his hips had pounded her with the intensity of a piston. He had used her, but she did not mind. Her Larry was still the best thing in her life. She adored him, would do anything for him, and he knew that. So, she was shocked more than hurt when he suddenly squatted above her and slapped her face.

The sound as his open palm met her cheek was like a gunshot. Violet's head snapped to one side, and a trickle of blood ran down from the corner of her mouth. As she parted her lips to speak to him, another blow threw her head back the other way. Then he was kneeling on her stomach, raining blows upon her, both open-handed and close-fisted, onto her face and chest. She howled in pain, tears forced from her eyes, but not once did she reproach him or plead with him to stop. She knew either would serve only to fan the flame of his anger.

When his rage was spent, and he sat above her, shoulders and chest heaving, sweat dripping from his forehead, Violet closed her eyes and prayed for the pain to lessen. When she opened them again, Larry was staring at his hands, knuckles smeared with her blood. She felt the swellings begin to rise on her flesh, and she felt sick. Not physically, but sick at heart.

And when she somehow managed to dredge up the strength, she asked: 'Why, Larry? Why?' The words leaked out through her swollen, cut and heavily bruised lips.

By this time, he had moved away from the bed. Naked, he sprawled across their small sofa. He looked at her as if she were demented.

'It's one thing for that little bitch to think me stupid,' he said. 'But entirely a different matter when you do.'

Violet shook her head. The movement sent tiny sparks dancing before her eyes. 'I don't understand.'

He sat up, spine rigid. He reminded her of a cobra about to strike. 'Secrets,' he said softly. 'All of a sudden you like secrets. Well, I'd expect nothing less of her. She, after all, knows nothing of the cameras and the microphone. But you do, Judas. You do. And still you made a pact behind my back. A pact with that filthy piece of garbage, and not a piece of silver in sight.'

Tears dribbled between the swiftly closing slits of Violet's eyes. 'I wasn't thinking straight. You must have known that. I wouldn't really keep anything secret from you, Larry.'

He got up, walked across the floor to stand over her. 'But you didn't tell me, did you? You didn't tell me that you went to her. That you struck her, that you made a bargain with her. Why didn't you tell me, Violet?'

The woman sobbed, shrinking away from him. 'I didn't think. After I'd left the room it was as if nothing had happened. I couldn't remember any of it until you just mentioned it. Honestly. How could I lie to you, Larry? I love you. I love you.'

His face softened. Creases stretched across his forehead as he surveyed the results of the beating he had administered.

He'd gone too far this time, Violet realised. The darkness had swallowed him whole. It wasn't supposed to happen with her. His very own sister. She wasn't supposed to fear him in this way.

It was Laura's fault. Fucking little darling she turned out to be. The worthless piece of shit was nothing but a troublemaker. Her and her blonde hair with strawberry tints. So proud of it once. Now it hung on her like a nest of rats' tails. She would cut the lot off, shave the girl's head with an open razor until her scalp bled. Then she would cut out her tongue.

No. No, that would all have to wait until after Larry had recorded Laura's screams. Screams he would later play to Frank.

Special Detective Frank Rogers. Hear your little girl one last time, Frankie. Hear her last pleas for mercy.

'I'm sorry, Violet,' Larry whispered, his face turned to the ceiling. 'I'm so sorry.'

She smiled up at him. On her battered face she was sure it must look obscene. 'That's all right, Larry. Come to bed. Make love to me. Fill me.'

Yes. That was better. He was calm now. She would keep him that way for the night. In the morning he would get to know Laura in that special way. And after that he would wrap his hands around her neck. And finally ... well, then he would kill her, of course.

After that, who knew what he might do to pass the time?

Chapter Fifty-One

Frank Rogers was a tight bundle of nerves, strung out through lack of sleep, nervous tension exhausting him all the more. Yet still he could find no way to rest. After three sweaty hours tossing and turning on the sofa, he spent the remainder of the night sitting at his desk in the study.

A police artist had visited Karen Redbridge, hoping to elicit an approximate likeness. According to the report Frank read, Karen gave her all, but the impression was vague at best. When the artist had finished, Karen stared at the drawing for a moment before shaking her head. It wasn't him, but she couldn't give any more.

So, the spectre inside Frank's own head had no real features still, other than that it was tall, with no hair with which to restructure its appearance. It was just a shadow, permeating Frank's every waking thought.

Light crept into the furthest reaches of the sky, sending shadows scuttling and hurrying across the land. Frank stared out through the study window, watching dawn's steady approach. And he wondered how his little girl had fared during those hours of darkness, whether she was able to see the frigid light, whether she could feel the gradual warmth upon her flesh. For a time, he put his head in his hands, all out of tears, but sorrow seeming to seep from his pores into his palms. When he looked up again, he knew it was time.

Again, it was Nicky and Tom Whelan who called for him. Their journey across to the other side of London was busier than it had been three days earlier. The atmosphere and tension inside the Ford Mondeo was almost physical, an entity all three men thought they could touch. Its fog clouded their thoughts and clogged their throats.

As they drew behind the observation vehicle, Frank swivelled in his seat. His eyes switched from Nicky to Tom, as if reaching into their souls. Finally he nodded. 'Are we all ready for this?' he asked.

They were.

***

Slice.

Three fingers.

Laura was actually able to put three fingers into the gap she had created. Her fingers and thumbs were beyond pain, both wrists ached terribly, and her nerves were coiled like a spring as she strained to listen for the keys. It would take only one lapse. One lapse, the door opens, one of them catches her at it. But that lapse was never going to happen.

Three fingers.

When she could put four in with any amount of comfort, that was it. She would yank on that board with all her might, she would summon up every single ounce of power within her slight frame. And if justice and willpower had anything to do with it, that board would fly off in her hands.

Three fingers.

One more to go.

Slice.

***

The same three teams positioned themselves in much the same way. Everyone remained perfectly calm on the surface. But beneath this thin veneer, their nerves jangled and their doubts began to gnaw. Several of the more experienced men knew something big was about to happen. What they didn't know, couldn't be sure of, was the outcome. They were all so on edge. What if their target spotted the observation vehicle? What if someone gave the game away? What if someone scared him off? What if Tanner had already betrayed them to his boss?

Nicky Loizou had no time for these thoughts. Although every single one passed through his own mind, he showed them the back door. Only positive thoughts were needed here. He glanced up at Frank. His friend's face was cadaverous, teeth fastened together, lines taut, eyes narrowed. He was ready. They both were. The trap was set, and the beast was on its way.

* * *

Slice.

Four fingers.

The sun had risen just above the horizon, and she could now put four fingers into the space. She forced them in, the wood smooth where she had shaved it. The grip was good. She gave an exploratory tug. The boards seemed to move almost by will alone. She pulled, tensed her feet against the wall beneath, pulled harder still. One slat detached itself so suddenly that Laura fell backwards to the floor. She stared at it for a moment, not quite able to comprehend the enormity of what had happened. She hardly dared believe that she had done it. Then she sprang to her feet with a stifled cry of triumph.

Using the first piece of wood as a lever, the rest of the slats gave way easily, affording her a glimpse of a blue sky for the first time in many days. She placed each strip of wood on the floor with care. Now was the tensest moment of all. At any time before she could have moved away, even denied all knowledge, blaming the cuts on some previous occupant. But now the shutter was down. If someone came into the room, she was done for.

Shit or bust.

It was one of her father's favourite expressions, one her mother had often chided him for using in the presence of her and Gary. But in the circumstances ...

'Shit or bust!' she said. And felt better for it.

Laura had prepared a small box to stand on. She'd already tested her weight upon it. Now she hefted it across and clambered on top. She reached up to find the window's lock. It was the type that simply swivelled open. There were husks of dead insects there, bound with spiders' webs. She ignored both the touch and the thought, pushed the metal lever with her thumb, and offered another prayer.

The prayer worked, and so did the lock. It gave a tiny squeal and swivelled open. Laura felt her heart about to burst out of her throat.

This was it. She was almost free.

Now. If only the window hadn't been painted closed. She pushed up the lower sash. At first it resisted, but on the second attempt it moved grudgingly on tired cords. Fresh cool air rushed in through a six-inch gap, its touch a distant memory. Laura drew it into her lungs, tears filling her eyes. She knew she was up at least one flight of stairs, but didn't give a damn at that moment. She was going to jump no matter what.

Laura hefted herself up onto the ledge and peered out.

She looked down upon what appeared to be a car park. A high wall with a trim of barbed wire stretched around its perimeter as far as she could see. Beyond the wall was a large expanse of open scrubland that led to a light commercial development. The wall was a barrier she hadn't considered, but in no way, did it detract from the feeling of euphoria that had swept over her. She was going to be free.

Free.

Then she leaned forward and heaved the window up some more. Except that it didn't move. Laura pulled on it again. Put her back into it for a third time. Only then did she notice the wooden blocks screwed to the outside, preventing the window being raised any higher than it already was.

The gleam of victory was snatched from her eyes as if it had never been. A feeling of utter hopelessness filled Laura's heart. A black wall of frustration descended upon her, crushing her spirit with its bulk.

She had dwelt upon the fact that the man might sneak in and catch her at the window. Had considered so many times what she might find behind the wooden slats. What she had failed to take into account was the sadistic nature of her tormentor and captor.

There was no escape after all.

The fresh air of a new day meant nothing, the sunshine meant nothing, the cloudless sky meant nothing. Not if she had to remain in this room. There was to be no escape after all. Merely a choice of deaths.

Laura slowly got down away from the window, put both hands to her head and opened her mouth to scream. That was when, in the periphery of her vision, she noticed the door to the room standing ajar. And when at the same time she felt sour breath upon her neck.

Chapter Fifty-Two

Though later that day, Nicky Loizou would blame himself for poorly planning a straightforward operation, it was mostly due to circumstance and sheer bad luck that it all went so badly wrong. None of which was any comfort to the distraught DCI, his thoughts burdened with the deaths of two officers, a third with critical injuries, and one who would probably never walk again.

It had always been Lawrence Swain's custom to travel to the Hammersmith office by road, leaving his van in a small car park directly opposite. Had he done so again, he would have been in full view of the observation vehicle from the moment he drove up. This morning, however, buoyed by a wonderful start to the day, he decided he wanted to spend some time in the West End. There were music, book and video stores he wanted to visit, a play he wanted to see. He would turn himself off from everything else for a few sweet hours.

He had driven himself to the nearest underground station, where he took the tube. Because of this, he arrived at the building from the rear. As on Friday, Warren Capel's team would only move around to the rear of the building *after* their quarry had entered through the front doors. The rear of the building had been checked over, but its single door was for emergency use, and should have opened from the inside only.

It was not an entrance. Only an exit.

Perhaps the check had been too cursory. During the inevitable resulting inquiry, investigators would discover that the door had been rigged to open from the outside as well. That the man they were hunting had previously demonstrated a knack with door locks was something that had not been considered during the tense moments of planning.

It was to be a costly error.

No one saw Swain enter, so no one was aware of him as he came up in the lift. No one was aware of him as he strode briskly along the passage. And because no one knew he had entered the building, Tom Whelan spoke into his radio without a second thought.

Nicky had not yet plugged in the ear-piece. There hadn't seemed any need. Tom's sharp voice came bursting out of the radio's speaker. Outside in the passage, Swain couldn't hear the message that passed between the two officers, but he could tell that both the voice and the static burst had emanated from inside his own office space.

Swain froze. His mind threw a thousand questions at him, a thousand separate answers. Finally, it screamed at him to get out of there. He turned sharply and, as he moved, his rubber-soled Reeboks squeaked on the cold marble floor. The sound echoed along the passage like the wail of a banshee. As the sound reverberated down the short corridor, Swain forgot all about stealth. Instead he bolted.

Frank Rogers heard the harsh squeak. His head jolted up. Nicky heard, too, and reached for the radio. 'Tom, what the hell was that?'

Whelan put his eye to the door's spy-hole. He was in time to see a fleeting figure duck through the door that led to the stairway. A figure wearing a baseball cap.

'Target sprinting away from you,' he snapped into the radio.

Frank was already up and running. He and Nicky raced into the passage moments before the sergeant and his entire plain-clothes team hurtled through. Tom was screaming into the radio. 'Warren, who came into the building? Did you see anyone? Anyone at all?'

'Negative. No one's been in or out this morning.'

'Bastard came in the back way,' Tom bellowed. There was no need to use the radio now. He and his four-man team were in the wake of Nicky and Frank as they leapt down each flight of stairs, heedless of the potential dangers.

Frank couldn't see their man. The sound of running feet was so loud in the confined stairway that he couldn't even be sure there was still anyone in front of him. It didn't matter. He didn't need any audible confirmation. The man had come, now he was going. Frank had to get him before he was gone for good.

As they raced down the stairwell, Warren Capel and his team came across to the front of the building. All were armed, as was every other man there that day except for Frank. Capel sent three men around the back, before arranging those who remained with him. They spread themselves out across the pavement, crouched low and sideways, pistols and semi-automatic H&K assault rifles extended in standard firing position. No one was slipping out this way.

* * *

Swain was grateful to any god who cared to listen that he was the sort of man to keep himself physically fit. He felt good, he felt strong, and he felt fleet of foot. No one was going to catch him. If he kept his wits about him he was going to make it away from this place safely. Despite his confidence, he wondered how the hell he had so nearly been caught.

Tanner? Had the man somehow suspected? If so, Mr Tanner is going to get an unannounced visit one of these nights. He is going to discover the true meaning of pain and misery, and then he is going to die screaming.

Swain burst out of the same rear door through which he had so recently entered, his legs pumping high like those of a sprinter as he headed down the narrow alleyway that took him back out onto the streets.

It was impossible, but the doors seemed to fly open again only seconds later. Surely no one could have caught up with him so quickly. He was too big, too strong, wing-heeled like a god. As he ducked into a turn that emerged into the street from an archway, he risked one swift glance back over his shoulder.

The shock almost caused him to lose his balance and stumble. Frank Rogers.

Overweight and long out of shape, Special Detective Frank-fucking-Rogers.

You knew he was good, Larry. You knew as soon as you saw his photo in the paper. A worthy adversary, I believe was your initial impression. Worthy? A little more than that, wouldn't you say?

Shut up!

He snapped the voice off. It wasn't a phantom speaking into his mind this time. It was the voice of his father. His father, who had never once had a good word to say for his children, never praised their achievements, then wondered why they stopped attaining anything. His father ... the dead man.

Absurdly, Swain began to laugh as he ran, lips curled back, teeth bared in a wicked snarl.

The street's pavements were mercifully deserted, the way ahead clear. Swain ran through his mental street map. He had to keep off the main routes for as long as possible, out of the public's reach. He had to keep on running, keep on thinking. There had to be a way out of this.

* * *

As Nicky maintained a steady half-dozen paces behind Frank, he barked directions into his radio. Capel and his men had scampered back to the van, its engine screaming in protest as they hurried to head off their quarry.

'He's heading north into Brackenbury Road.'

'Take a right,' Capel said instantly to his driver. Then into his radio: 'We're turning into Dalling Road, Nicky. It comes out at the top of Brackenbury. I sent a team around back but they would've been far too late to even see him.'

'They're in pursuit with us.'

Static for a moment. Then: 'He's turned east ... into Coulter Road.'

Warren Capel cursed. They would now emerge too far north of their man, and his knowledge of the area was limited. 'Right at the top,' he said to his driver. 'We'll follow them instead.'

Because the van was used for observations only, it had no siren or flashing lights. It gave no warning of its high-speed approach. As it flew out into Brackenbury Road it was confronted by a Luton Transit that seemed to fill its windscreen. Ben Watkins, Capel's driver, swung the wheel hard to the left. But the van wasn't a squad car, wasn't nearly so well-balanced or built for such a manoeuvre.

Watkins felt it slide first. He had time to utter a cry before the van flipped over and, sliding along the tarmac on its side, ploughed into a line of parked cars. Its initial speed kept it going, metal screaming, engine still racing, until finally it rolled over one last time and buried itself halfway inside an open-top Morgan.

The engine snapped off. The revolving tyres eventually came to a grudging halt. For a full minute before the first cries of pain, the silence of death filled the street.

* * *

Frank felt his entire body protest. His head felt swollen with pain, blood thumping in his temples like a hammer-drill. Across his shoulders and chest there was a fire raging out of control, and its flames licked inside his throat and worked their way down into his lungs. Cramps tore at his legs, insisting he stop using the muscles, or at the very least, slow down. But out of necessity, Frank had found that place beyond pain that great athletes force themselves to strive for. It consumed him, but he was able to ignore it.

He wasn't gaining on the bastard, but he wasn't getting left behind, either. The man's baseball cap had flown off, and his gleaming dome of a head was like a beacon to Frank. It was all he could see, all he needed to see. It was his way back to Laura. His only way. If the man escaped, Laura was dead.

The man weaved back and forth, finally heading south again toward the Hammersmith flyover and the underground station.

Once there he could be lost. He couldn't allow the man to make it that far, but couldn't see any way of catching him.

Where the hell was Capel?

He could hear Nicky breathlessly snapping out road names, but they had been running for several minutes now, and the van had to be close. Had to be ... or the madman would be swallowed up by the subterranean railway system and lost forever. With him he would take Frank's heart and soul. His reason for living.

Sweat blinding him, Frank asked even more of his body. He begged and pleaded for one last surge. But within seconds he knew there was nothing left to give. The tank was empty. And as his eyes fixed on that head of flesh, it seemed to draw away from him.

He gave a cry. It was filled with pain and anguish. And the desperate sense of loss.

Chapter Fifty-Three

Perhaps the only thing that saved Warren Capel from greater injury was his instinctive reactions when entering a vehicle of any description: he had put on his seat-belt.

Ben Watkins hadn't been so sensible or so fortunate. The whole of the van's off-side was just about gone, but where the door had crumpled like an aluminium can, Watkins had crumpled with it. His body was grotesquely twisted, limbs jutting at obscene angles, and his face had almost been shredded of flesh by the road surface and the collision with the other vehicles.

Capel saw this in glorious technicolour close-up, the van's momentum having pressed him tight against the still-warm body. Hearing a shrill cry of pain, the Detective Sergeant tried to look back over his shoulder to see how the two men in the back had fared, but as his head swivelled, an explosion of pain rose up from his neck. Bile rose with it, shock settling on him like a nest of rattlers. He began shaking uncontrollably.

Don't move your neck again, he told himself. Something's wrong there. One more twist and you could be a vegetable for the rest of your life. Just keep still and wait. Ignore the cooling body next to you. Forget the fact that the petrol tank may have ruptured, that you're sitting in a perfect incendiary device. Just close your mind to it all. Help must be on its way.

He began surveying the damage to the rest of his body. Careful to move only his eyes, he saw plenty of blood spattered over his clothing, though he couldn't decide whose it was. Then his glance travelled down and he saw a curious thing. His left leg was stretched out straight, but the area from his knee down to his ankle hung at a right-angle. It was an impossible angle. The joints simply weren't designed that way. Unless ...

He swallowed thickly. Through the torn material of his trouser leg, splintered bones jutted like jagged strips of driftwood. He stared at them, so white they seemed to glow with an eerie phosphoresce. Warren realised that his fibula and tibia had somehow been thrust upwards with such brute force that they had slammed through the patella. His knee was shattered, his entire left leg ruined.

'That's bad, Warren,' he said to himself. 'That really is bad. But it can be fixed. I'm sure it can. And if not ... so what, you're breathing. Be grateful for that. Ben would be right now.'

And then something else struck him. He felt something shift inside his stomach, a tight knot forming there. His neck was obviously in a bad way, his leg in an even sorrier state. So why wasn't he screaming with the pain of it? Why could he feel no pain at all below the waist?

He tried to move his shattered leg, perversely hoping that the sudden jolt would send a shock of blinding pain through his system. Nothing happened. He tried moving the other leg. Same again. He had to move them somehow, had to feel a glorious flash of pain. Had to.

A figure suddenly appeared at the side window. The Luton driver. His face visibly paled as he saw what had become of the two men in front. 'Okay,' he said to Warren. 'Help is coming. Hold on.'

Capel turned to him. 'Please,' he whispered. 'Let there be some pain.'

* * *

Out on the main road, the pavements were more liberally sprinkled with human flotsam and jetsam. A couple of filth-encrusted winos scrabbled through rubbish bins fixed to street lights, last night's chip wrappers containing a meagre source of cold nutrition. A young shirt-sleeved postman gave them a wide birth, while a female jogger, wearing only a tight pair of shorts and a vest, thundered past, oblivious to everything but the music playing on her iPod. The postman glanced at her heavy breasts bouncing beneath the thin material. He continued to look back at her, not watching where he was going, and so the sudden jolt of fourteen stones of speeding muscle knocked the wind out of his lungs and sent him flying.

Swain had rounded the street corner with no thought for other pedestrians. He and the postman hit the ground with a solid thump, the latter's head striking the pavement so hard it opened up in a wide gash and let loose a torrent of blood.

You buffoon, the voice of Swain's father roared at him. *You can't even get this right, can you?*

'Get the fuck out of my head!' Swain yelled as he scrambled to his feet. He looked around, eyes wild and staring. Frank Rogers was only yards away, bearing down on him like an express train. To his right, several other figures were hammering down the pavement toward him; they had come another way to cut off his escape. That left the road or …

Yards away there was a small butcher's shop, cuts of fresh meat already hanging from sharp and shiny hooks in the window. At this time of morning it was the only shop open along this stretch of road. There was no more time for thought, only reaction.

* * *

Frank had him, looming large right in front of his eyes, and then he was gone in a puff of smoke. The tall, lean monster swivelled to one side, out of Frank's clawing reach, and dashed through the open doorway of a shop. Frank slid on the pavement as he turned and saw the window display. He wondered at the irony that had sent such a vile beast into a place like that. It was so fitting.

Frank quickly weighed up the situation, glanced down at the postman who lay groaning and twitching on the floor. No time for him. Had to get the madman. Had to get him before he could arm himself. But when he looked up again at the shop, the door was now closed, and beyond its glass pane stood the monster. And the monster was smiling.

The man held a meat hook in his right hand, swinging it by his side. And his smile was getting broader with each passing second.

By now the pavement around Frank was bustling with activity. Nicky, Tom and his men had arrived. Two men were attending to the stricken postman, Tom was bawling into his radio. Nicky drew in great lungfuls of air, hands resting on his knees.

And the monster was still smiling.

'Warren's had an accident,' Nicky gasped. 'Don't know how bad. But we've got this fucker cornered now.'

Frank's body felt as if it wanted to either burst or expire. The commotion around him was like a distant throng, Nicky's words a vague drone. It took a moment for their meaning to seep through the whirring cogs.

Yes.

The man was cornered. But like an animal, he wouldn't come out of that corner without a fight. The butcher's was open. Someone had to be inside. Maybe several someones. They weren't visible right now, but how long before they discovered their intruder? If the madman got hold of them there would be carnage here.

And the monster continued to stare directly at him, the smile growing impossibly broader still.

Frank shook his head. No. It wasn't going to happen that way.

He took a single step back, then charged at the shop door and threw himself forward through the air. Even as he hit the sparkling pane his mind was telling him it was only in films that people didn't get hurt by glass. In real life, people got badly hurt. Often, they got themselves killed. But by then he was through it and he had delivered himself into the arms of fate.

The single pane of glass shattered with the sound of a small explosion. Frank had thought to shield his face with his arms, but the backs of both hands and forearms were now shrouded with slivers of glass, blood welling from the wounds. His only saving grace was that he had landed at the feet of the madman who, caught unawares by the sheer stupidity of the attack, had been sent sprawling backwards.

Frank was the first to react.

As he stumbled to his feet the soles of his shoes slid on the debris of shattered glass and he pitched forward again. He felt the bite and tear as more broken shards found purchase in his flesh, but the greater urgency came when he saw the man rising up like some vengeful demon. The bald head looked immense, both eyes filled with hate and grim purpose.

Still on his knees, Frank scrambled wildly, seeking to gain a foothold without slipping. He couldn't. He could do nothing but give a guttural cry as the madman stepped forward and brought the gleaming hook down into the meat of his shoulder. Frank's next cry was one of immense pain, the hook biting deep into cartilage and muscle and sinew, narrowly missing the collar-bone. Through a gathering mist of confused agony, he saw the monster's triumphant expression, a gleam in those cold eyes that would not be denied.

The pain increased alarmingly as the madman wrenched the hook around, trying to pull it free. All he managed to do was drive the sharpened point deeper into the wound. In the midst of this, an absurd thought ran through Frank's mind: *if this is how a fish feels when it's caught, I'm never going to hook a carp again.*

As the world began to diminish around him, Frank's survival instincts took over. It was the one advantage he had over this monster. He reached up to the hook, clasped his own hands over the other man's, and yanked as hard as he was able back towards himself.

His opponent hadn't expected this. He wasn't balanced, wasn't prepared, and so his whole weight dipped forward. As it did, Frank allowed his legs to collapse, and the man went over his back and out across the threshold of the doorway.

All this took place inside ten seconds. It was the longest ten seconds of Frank's life. It had given no time for Nicky or any of the others to react. But when the monster came rolling back out of the doorway, they moved as one. He was pounced upon, boots and knees and fists unconcerned about where they landed. His hands were gathered behind his back, wrists cuffed and he was then rolled onto his side. The meat hook lay behind him, a generous portion of Frank's shoulder still attached to it.

* * *

His wounds temporarily tended from items taken from the shop's impressive first-aid box, Frank allowed Nicky to help him back out onto the street. A large gathering had now surrounded the shop, and somewhere in the distance sirens heralded the approach of emergency vehicles. Tom Whelan and the other officers stood around the kneeling man, who hadn't said a single word since his capture.

As they walked past him, Frank had to look. Down there, the man didn't look like any monster. Or madman. He looked just like any other criminal in similar circumstances: frightened, frustrated at being caught, wary.

Frank stood over him and glared into the man's eyes. 'What have you got to say for yourself now, you fucking lunatic?'

The monster's mouth stretched thinly. 'I had your darling little daughter, Frank. Used her, abused her. Then I disposed of her.'

And then he laughed.

He kept on laughing while Nicky and Tom Whelan fought to keep Frank from killing him there and then.

Captured at last, the monster laughed until he wept.

Chapter Fifty-Four

Frank realised he must look as if he'd been in a car wreck. His hands and arms were swathed in bandages, as were his legs beneath a fresh pair of trousers. The bulge of padding and even more bandages was obvious beneath his shirt. Various cuts and abrasions littered his face, and bruises were beginning to attain angry colours. He looked so badly wounded that when he was brought back to Leyton police station where the prisoner was being held, Nicky immediately pulled him to one side.

'Are you sure you want to do this now?'

Frank nodded. 'When else? We have to find out where Laura is.'

'But, Frank. He said—'

'And I can't afford to believe him.' The voice was a hard rebuke. 'I take it you found nothing of use on him.'

'Not a thing. He had a mobile, but it was the one we'd already traced. We checked it out; last calls made, last calls received, everything. It was all wiped clean. He must do it after every call, covering his arse every step of the way.'

'We can get those details from his provider, though, yes?'

'In time. It's a delaying tactic, nothing more.'

Frank nodded. 'The sooner I get in there, the better, then.'

'But are you fit enough? You lost a bit of blood back there, mate.'

Frank lifted his head. 'Stop mothering me, Nicky. I'm okay.'

'I suppose you heard about the obs van.'

'Yeah. Shit, what a fucking mess. It's early days, but they reckon Warren may be paralysed.' Frank shook his head wearily. 'I don't know who was luckier.'

'We've tried talking to our man, but he won't have it. He'll speak only to you.'

Frank nodded. 'That's the way I want it.' His voice was cold and hard.

'How are you going to play things?'

'As coolly as I can. If Laura is dead, then I can't help her now. If she's not, then we have a little time. I can't steam in, bully him for information, or he'll just clam up and play more games with me. He'd enjoy that. I have to develop some kind of rapport with him, let him loosen up, even pander to his ego a little. Most of all, I have to get him to talk. If he opens up about what he did to the girls, he may just say enough for us to establish where he's keeping Laura. It's the only way. For the time being.'

Frank was nowhere near as calm as he pretended to be. In all likelihood, Laura was dead. He felt in his heart that this was true. His every instinct told him that the monster had much to gain by lying, but had used the truth as a weapon.

Since the day she'd been taken, Frank had felt Laura's presence. It was nothing he could identify, just a feeling, a sense that she was still alive and guiding him. Now he felt nothing but a cold isolation, no voice telling him it would be all right, that he still had time. Laura might well be dead, but he refused to believe in the truth. It was the only way he could get through these next few hours.

And he had to get through. Because there was someone waiting for him. Someone he had to talk to. Someone he would eventually kill.

* * *

The prisoner sat in the interview room fingering the neck of the paper suit they'd given him to wear. His clothes were already with forensics. The three police officers in the room were all armed. Tom Whelan stood directly behind him. Another DS stood beside the door, his eyes never straying from the bald-headed man. They waited patiently for Frank Rogers to appear.

When he finally entered the interview room, Frank felt himself guided into a chair opposite the prisoner as if he'd been blinded.

Frank commented on this in a dry, hushed voice, and the two men exchanged uneasy grins.

Frank sat across the table from the man he had come to think of as a monster. So ordinary-looking, yet this man had murdered children in a variety of despicable ways, had tortured, and had disfigured their small corpses. A sick, perverted killer. He surely couldn't be human, with a human heart, a human soul, human feelings. Was he capable of love? He must certainly be capable of hate. The two men locked eyes.

'You understand that this interview will be recorded?' Frank said to him. He wanted to reach over, to wrap his fingers around that solid neck and squeeze until his energy was drained.

'I do.'

'And even though you have been advised of your rights, you still do not want to be represented by a solicitor?'

'It would serve no useful purpose.'

'Okay. Well, let's get on with it.'

The bald head shook. 'No. I want them out of here. I want to be alone with you.'

Nicky took a step forward, arms folded across his chest. 'I'm afraid that's out of the question. You two cannot be left alone together.'

'Cuff me again,' the man said, smiling. 'I won't hurt him.'

'That wasn't quite what I had in mind.'

The prisoner's smile broadened defiantly. 'Oh, Frank won't hurt me. Will you, Frank? You want to know if I was lying about Laura. And until you're certain, you won't let anything happen to me. No, I'm perfectly safe, DCI Loizou.'

Nicky cleared his throat. 'Even so. Someone has to be here with you.'

For the first time, their suspect wrenched his gaze away from Frank. He fixed Nicky with a tight glare. 'If I don't speak to Frank alone, I don't speak at all. I'll go to my grave with the truth untold.'

Nicky gave a curt nod, and said, 'Let's step out of the room a moment, Frank.'

Outside the interview room, Nicky met Frank's curious gaze. 'This is one tricky son-of-a-bitch,' he said in a low voice. 'Now he has me trying to work out which is the lesser of two evils: not having him talk, or having you alone in there with him.'

'We need him to speak. I need him to.' It was as simple as that.

'Promise me you won't lay a finger on him. I mean it, Frank, one blow and you're out, friend or no friend.'

Frank gave a wry grin. 'You have my word.'

'Very well.'

The two moved back inside the room. Nicky looked across at the prisoner. 'I would like you to repeat your request on record, so as there's no redress later.'

'Whatever it takes.'

They went through the ritual of identifying those present for the recording devices, and their suspect repeated his request. He was then cuffed and the room was cleared. As Nicky left he patted Frank on his good shoulder. 'I'll be just outside in the corridor. Use the panic button if you have to.'

The prisoner gave a dry, harsh laugh. 'He'd never have time,' he said smoothly. 'But don't worry, it won't come to that. I mean him no physical harm.'

When it was just the two of them, Frank began the interview recording once more, again naming himself. His prisoner had so far refused to give a name, so he was simply an unidentified suspect.

Frank took a sip from a plastic beaker of water, then clasped both hands before him on the table. 'Right,' he said. 'Let's get down to it. First off, I'll ask you once more to give me your name.'

'Lawrence Wilde.'

Frank raised his eyebrows. 'Why did you refuse before?'

'Because I felt like it.'

'I see.' Frank got up and opened the door, whispered a few words to Nicky, then returned to his seat.

'Off to see if I have a record?' The prisoner shook his head. 'So predictable.'

'That's right. Standard procedure, Lawrence.'

'Call me Larry. We're friends now, after all.'

Frank ignored the sarcasm. 'Larry it is. Why did you ask me to call you Oscar before? Any significance?'

The man smiled that same confident smile. His eyes never rose above freezing-point. 'Work it out, Frank. You can, you know. Now that you have the full details. Don't ask me anything else until you have.'

Frank edged forward. 'More games?'

There was no response. Frank nodded reluctantly and set his mind to work. *Now that he had the full details.* Well, the only extra detail he had now that he didn't have before was the name. Lawrence Wilde. His eyes opened wide. Wilde. Oscar.

'Of course. How stupid of me. All those annoying little sayings of yours. You sounded so clever, and yet you were using someone else's material. They're all from works by Oscar Wilde. I have a feeling you even used perhaps his most famous line, "I have nothing to declare except my genius". But it was the last one that triggered something in my mind: "People are either charming or tedious". It rang a bell, but I couldn't put my finger on it at the time.'

The prisoner looked impressed. Frank felt his loathing spring to the surface once more. He held it in check. 'So, Larry. You're a fan, I presume.'

The man dipped his head. 'I have that honour. Your little girl was, too, I think. After a time.'

Frank's eyes narrowed dangerously. 'Was?'

'I told you, Frank. Used. Abused. Disposed of. Now, I may well be lying. Then again, I may not. That's for me to know and you to find out. You're the detective, after all. So, detect away. It suits my purposes for the doubts to slop around inside your head. Wouldn't want you to do anything silly, would we?'

Frank took a breath. *Don't lose your temper,* he told himself. He repeated the words silently like a ritual chant. *Not until you know for sure.* The bastard is cuffed and on his way to a life sentence, and still he has you by the balls. Just don't allow him the pleasure of giving them one last squeeze.

'In what way might Laura have become a fan of Wilde?' he asked.

'I left books for her to read. One contained several of his works. I believe she read it.'

Frank nodded. 'Okay, Larry. Let's talk about the gifts you left me. The girls.'

'Girls? Gifts? I have no idea what you're talking about.'

Frank stared hard at him. The bastard actually looked bewildered. 'Larry,' he said, shaking his head, 'we have you cold. You were good at not leaving fingerprints, or anything else for us to trace. It was smart going into the houses naked. We've seen that you are completely shaved, so no hairs, no fibres. But you did leave something for us at each house.'

The man's features did not alter in the slightest.

'You left your semen. You're a clever man, Larry. All that business with the offices and Tanner and the photographs was inspired. Oh, yes, we know all about that. But giving us your DNA was a bit careless, don't you think? And of course, there's your voice. We have it on record, telling us where to find the girls. Did you know that each voice has its own characteristics? Each has its own peaks and troughs when analysed. Each one is unique. That and the sperm samples place you at the homes and with the girls, Larry. In short, you're fucked.'

Then the man did something Frank wasn't expecting. He began to snigger. 'Oh, Frank. Do you really believe any of this matters?' He gave an exaggerated yawn. 'Yes, I did it. I killed them all. But I'm not going to prison for it, Frank.'

'You angling for a plea of diminished responsibility and a psychiatric ward, Larry? I don't think that's going to work.'

'No, no. What I mean is, I won't even be charged. You'll be letting me go.'

Frank's face set hard. 'The only things I am certain of right now are that you *will* be charged, you *will* be found guilty, and you *will* be sentenced. Don't kid yourself otherwise.'

'We'll see.'

Frank didn't like the smug certainty of that face, that smile, the air of calm indifference. He didn't like it at all. He dismissed it, though, and got back on track.

'Larry, we have to establish a few more details. You have murdered many people, for which you will later be charged. And so far, you have given us four of the seven girls you abducted. The condition of those girls will also be discussed at length later on. But tell me, Larry, where are the others? Anne Smith, Samantha Penny, and … Laura Rogers.'

Again, that icy, lupine grin appeared. The suspect glanced up at the ceiling as if trying to remember. 'Who can tell?' he said finally. 'What may be considered a state of death to some may be seen as perfect, eternal life, for others.'

'You don't deny that you abducted them?'

'No. I don't.'

'But you won't tell me what has become of them.'

'No. I won't.'

'We know about the taxidermy, Larry.'

For once the smile and the confidence was wiped away. It was only for a second, less even, but it was enough for Frank to know that he had struck a blow.

'You do?' Larry said, and the smile returned. 'Good for you. A certain fictional detective from Baker Street would have been proud of you. You were responsible, I take it? Yes. Had to be you. You're so very clever. In another life, you and I could have been close.'

In the next life, maybe we will be, Frank thought. *But you'll be getting there ahead of me.* His head was reeling with the conversation. He had no plan of attack, but he wanted to shy away from discussing Laura. The only way through was to keep the man off guard, let him trip up over something less direct.

Frank's hands and shoulder hurt like hell. The legs weren't so much of a problem, though he knew he'd he hobbling for a while yet. He noticed the prisoner moving his neck against the paper collar, something he'd been doing throughout. The room was stifling, yet Frank felt cool. Almost cold. He looked at the man just a yard away and realized that the monster's evil was emanating from his pores, emerging as a chill essence. *How did you get this way?* he wondered. *How have you come to this?*

'Let's start again,' he said. 'We know that you and Mr Tanner, your employee, took photographs, and from these you chose certain girls as your victims. You broke into their homes, murdered their families, took them from their beds. The first victim was tortured and mutilated before you killed her. Another three have also been found murdered, and you attempted to perform human taxidermy on them all. Why don't you tell me, in your own words, how it all happened?'

'Are you pandering to my ego, special detective?' The smile was now coy. So cool.

'I think you have a story to tell. I'd like to hear it.'

The man opened his mouth to speak, and as he did so the door flew open. Frank turned quickly. 'Out!' he snapped angrily, not knowing who stood there, seeing only his daughter's life dangling from a thread.

It was Nicky. 'You'd better come,' he said. 'We have something interesting.'

'So do I.'

'Frank … just come.'

And when he looked into his friend's eyes, he saw a glimmer of hope. It was more than he'd seen in the monster's glassy orbs. 'I won't be long,' he said to his prisoner. 'Don't go away.'

As he reached the door, he heard the man say, 'Hurry back, Frank. We don't have much time.'

Chapter Fifty-Five

All the way along the dim corridor and up one flight of stairs to Nicky's office, Frank fired questions. 'Wait and see,' was his only answer. When the two men reached the office, an elderly woman sat at the desk waiting for them, a uniformed PC standing by her side.

'Thank you, constable,' Nicky said, nodding his appreciation. 'Mrs Shaw will be fine with us now.'

The PC smiled and excused herself from the room. Nicky shut the glass-panelled door before taking his seat. The office was a testimony to Nicky's lack of organisation; files and documents either scattered across the grey cord carpet, or stacked in towering piles that looked as if a single gust of wind would send them crashing. Two tall windows would have provided a good source of light, had their blinds not been drawn.

Frank remained standing, leaning back against the only wall to contain shelves, arms folded across his chest. Nicky looked up at him and said, 'Frank, this is Mrs Irene Shaw. She has some information for us.'

The woman glanced at Frank, nodded once, before turning her attention to Nicky. Irene Shaw was in her late sixties, Frank guessed. Smart and upright, well-groomed with plump, sanguine cheeks. She had the kind of face you could easily see advertising home-made apple pie.

'It's about a letter I received,' she began. 'From my county council. It referred to my time with social services. I worked with the welfare department.'

'And you have something to tell us, something you feel may be important,' Nicky said. He snapped a glance at Frank. Smiled briefly.

'Yes. At least, I think I do. The letter outlined a particular set of characteristics, asking whether I recalled any similar cases during my time as a social worker. I don't remember many, I must admit. They were all pretty run-of-the-mill, as I never rose to a senior position. But this one particular case did stick in my mind.' She shook her head briefly. 'Hard for it not to.'

Frank came forward and perched on the edge of the desk. 'You mean you were able to match some of the characteristics?'

The woman beamed, eyes still alert behind her glasses. 'Not some. *All*. I remember it vividly, because it was one of those dreadful cases that went terribly wrong. The managers tried to hush it up, tried to shift the blame, as they do. But I was there, and I remember it like it was yesterday.'

Frank nodded eagerly. 'Go on. Please.'

The woman folded her hands on her lap. 'It was twenty-two years ago. Due to a number of complaints, a family by the name of Swain were investigated by my department. The initial investigation told us that the father was a joiner, mother a housewife. They had a boy and a girl, both of whom showed all the signs of being both mentally and physically abused. Too many bruises in the wrong places, extremely non-communicative, demonstrating aggressive behaviour, that sort of thing.

'The father was arrogant, volatile, a heavy drinker. Something of an enigma, because he was also devoutly religious. The mother was quiet and down-trodden. After a thorough investigation, the children were taken into care for observation. There we discovered burn marks on the boy's body, and tiny little nicks, like paper cuts. Many were on his ... his genitals. The girl had been abused also, and sexually molested, though not raped. When questioned, however, they maintained that their wounds had either come about naturally or were self-inflicted.'

'Self-inflicted!' Frank cried. 'Surely your people didn't believe that.'

'At the time, no. Later, however, it was thought that some of their claims may have been true. Anyhow, they were seen by a child-psychologist. Both children displayed a total apathy for life, but not once did they ever accuse their parents of anything untoward. There were many verbal traps laid, but neither child fell into them.'

'So, they were returned to their parents,' Nicky said, shaking his head in disgust.

'Yes, I'm afraid so. You must understand that child welfare wasn't as advanced in those days. It was always thought that the parents had a priority, and if the children weren't going to admit anything, there really wasn't much we could do.'

'But something else happened,' said Frank. He knew the best – the worst – was yet to come.

'We were summoned to the house by the police after a neighbour called in, distressed at what she was hearing from the Swains's home. By the time the police got there, they found the mother and father both dead, a twelve-year-old girl also lay dead by their side.'

'And the boy?' Frank asked. This was important. The boy was their very own monster. Had to be.

'They found him inside a tiny cupboard. With his sister.'

'Sister? But you said she was alongside the parents, dead.'

The woman shook her head. 'No, you see, there was another daughter. We had no record of her, had no idea she even existed. She must have been born at home and never registered. It was she who died, while the twins survived.'

'Twins!' This was Nicky. 'They were twins?'

'Yes.'

'And the boy, presumably, had murdered them.'

'Not exactly. From the boy, we got absolutely nothing. He refused to utter a single word to anyone, just kept drifting away somewhere inside his head. But from his sister we did learn one or two things. Evidently, the other sister had been kept inside the same cupboard for just about twenty-four hours a day. She was fed irregularly, and often with ghastly things like spoilt milk, mice or rats, insects. She was treated terribly. The only times she was allowed out were when her parents needed … well, needed to use her.'

Frank hung his head, eyes closed tight as if to ward off the brutal reality of what he was hearing. The entire human race was shamed by such people. 'The poor little mite,' he muttered.

The woman shuffled her legs and shook involuntarily. 'Not only that, but the twins were forced to watch every despicable act. Finally, it seems that their parents did it one time too many. The girl, Sophie, died after a fierce beating. The boy, Lawrence, got hold of his father's tools and killed both his parents with them. Then he took his sister into the cupboard, where they were found.'

Nicky blew out his cheeks. 'My God. It sounds like the worst nightmare imaginable.'

Frank's features were drawn and stretched tight across the bone beneath. 'The boy was called Lawrence. That matches with the name we've been given by someone in our custody. The sister … what became of her?'

'Both Lawrence and Violet were institutionalised. Both were rehabilitated and released into the public when they reached the age of eighteen.'

'That's why he's so cocky,' said Frank.

He slammed a heavy fist down against his side, grunting as a jab of pain reminded him of his wounds.

'All along we've had thoughts only of him. One man. One suspect. But we were wrong all the time. There are two of them. We have Lawrence Swain, but sister Violet is still out there. Somewhere.'

'Don't ask for any forwarding addresses,' Mrs Shaw said, her eyes sadly reflective. 'Once out in the big wide world the twins simply disappeared.'

'So where did all this take place, Mrs Shaw?' Nicky asked.

'Hove.' It was Frank's voice.

The woman stared up at him in surprise. 'However, did you know that?'

'He went back.'

Nicky nodded solemnly. The monster's first victims lived in Hove. The scene of Lawrence Swain's childhood horror show.

Frank's entire frame seemed to shrink in on itself. He'd thought they were nearing the end. Instead, they were only at the beginning. They had the man who'd taken Laura, but if she was still alive then someone else now held her captive. He reached down and patted the woman's liver-spotted hands.

'Thank you for coming forward,' he said, managing a thin smile of gratitude. 'Many people wouldn't have bothered. You've confirmed who we're dealing with, at least. Hopefully we can use the information you've given us.'

Irene Shaw looked up at him. 'Lawrence is the serial killer, isn't he? The one that's been in the news lately.'

'I'm sorry. I can't answer that at the moment.'

She smiled. 'That's all the answer I need.'

Frank grew more serious. 'Please understand, anything you've said here today should remain between us for the time being. If the press find out what you suspect, they may alert our suspect's accomplice.'

'Yes. Of course. I won't breathe a word to anyone. But you know, Violet was every bit as peculiar as Lawrence. Perhaps not as violent, but definitely a strange little girl.'

Chapter Fifty-Six

Frank returned to the interview room some forty minutes after he'd been summoned away by Nicky. The officer guarding the suspect left the room, leaving Frank and the prisoner together once more.

'Let's establish something right away,' Frank said immediately, taking his place at the table. 'Would you like me to carry on calling you Lawrence Wilde, or would you prefer I use your real name?'

The man tilted his head, frowned. 'My real name?'

'Yes. Swain. Lawrence Swain.'

There was a slight pause. Just a beat, but it was enough for Frank to realise that his revelation had struck home.

'How did you manage to stumble upon that?' Swain asked.

'We're detectives.' Frank flashed an icy grin. 'We did what we do best.'

'It's not important.' Swain let his eyes roam the interview room.

'Of course not.' But it was, and Frank could tell the man had been rattled. Now he was wondering what else they knew about him. 'So why hide the fact? Why not tell me the truth right from the beginning?'

The prisoner stared at him. 'This isn't getting you back your little girl, Frank. Don't you want to see Laura again?'

'You told me she was already dead.'

'So I did. I also made it clear that I consider there to be various levels of death. Laura may be still warm and breathing and praying for her daddy to arrive on his white charger. You wouldn't want to disappoint her, would you?'

'Are you going to tell me where she is?' Frank asked.

'Of course, I'm not. What would be the fun in that?'

'Then there's nothing to keep me from snapping your neck here and now. If you won't give me the information I need, you're of no use to me.'

The madman chuckled softly. 'Oh, Frank. You know you won't do that. You have to hold on to the small glimmer of a chance that I'll suddenly capitulate, spill the beans ... cough. It's a fair cop, guv, and all that sort of thing. You kill me and you've no hope.'

Frank closed his eyes for a moment. He had to shut out that grinning, evil face. He was drifting away when he heard the rattle of steel and his eyes sprang back open. Swain laughed, his broad shoulders rocking.

'Made you jump, eh, Frank? You never know when I'm going to shrug these cuffs off. I know I said I wouldn't harm you, but really ... shutting your eyes like that. One can only resist temptation for so long. In fact, I can resist anything except temptation.'

'Another Wilde quotation? Let's not regress here, Swain. By the way, did you change your name from Swain to Wilde by deed poll?'

'Oh, what's in a name, Frank? You know, my father named me Lawrence after our greatest actor.'

'Olivier. So, your father was a fan of the arts, too. Did he like Wilde?'

'My father was a failed actor. He built stage sets, but his dream was to tread the boards. He did once or twice, but he wasn't any good. He took his bitterness out on us.'

Frank stared at the man who sat across the table from him. There was not the slightest sign that this man wasn't every bit as normal as the next. No tell-tale tics or glares or twitches. He could be a solicitor, a banker ... a copper. Instead he was a madman. And Frank wanted to know why.

'Us?' Frank said, feigning interest.

Swain nodded, blinking rapidly. 'My mother and me.'

'Ah. I thought you may have meant you and your sister, Violet.'

This time, Swain's disquiet was all too obvious, his features reflecting alarm. Frank saw him look up, perhaps trying to work out where this information had come from, or maybe wondering if he himself had erred in any way.

'So, you've discovered a few things,' Swain said eventually. He smiled, but it was transparently forced. 'So what? You don't yet know what you need to know. But what you must have realised by now is that my sister is the reason you will let me go. You have me, but she has Laura.'

Frank leaned back in his chair. He raised his eyebrows. 'And Violet may not be as cunning as you, Swain. She may not be able to cope with your absence. Violet may be a person we can deal with.'

Just as Frank was feeling good about sowing that little seed of doubt in the man's head, Lawrence Swain said something that made the hair on Frank's neck stand tall, a chill to move down his back.

'Oh, Violet won't be able to cope with my absence, Frank.' His eyes became slits of triumph. 'She's liable to do anything. Absolutely anything. Poor Laura. I wouldn't want to be in her shoes when Violet loses it.'

Frank realised his own attempt at mind games had backfired. Swain was obviously disturbed by what had been discovered, but his words held far more weight and dread for Frank.

'Tell me about your life,' he said, needing to get back on track.

'Why? What possible interest could my life be to you, Special Detective Rogers?'

'I'm interested in you. I'm curious as to what made you the way you are today.'

The bald and shiny head shook. 'No. That's not it. You want to see if you can trip me up. See if I'll give anything away. I won't, you know. I'm too good. Too bad.' He chuckled again.

'What were your parents really like?'

Something moved across the man's eyes, like a series of low-scudding clouds slinking across a late-autumn sky. A raw nerve touched. Aggravated. Frank mentally scored another point for himself. Even so, he was losing by a mile.

'Tell me,' he insisted.

The man took a deep breath. When it came back out through his nose it sounded like a distant whistle. 'My father was a complete bastard. You may well know that already, depending on where you've gained your information. What you may not know is that behind her docile facade my mother was every bit as bad. Our other sister, Sophie, was locked away from us until my father wanted to have her. They did it in front of me and Violet. Every sordid little act. Sophie just lay there and let them get on with it. She was like a doll, but one who lived and breathed. My mother joined in fairly regularly. She also stood by while that miserable bastard did as he liked with us. It was a living hell.'

'That doesn't excuse you for all that you've done.'

Swain smiled wistfully. 'I never said it did. I'm not seeking to justify myself to the likes of you. You asked, I answered. I thought a cliché might add a little colour to the proceedings.'

'Okay. So, this went on for some time, I gather.'

'Yes. I sometimes think it would have gone on forever had I not killed him.'

When Frank failed to react, Swain gave a stifled laugh and nodded. 'You knew that, too. I suppose you must know all the relevant facts. But facts don't tell the whole story, do they?'

'No.' Frank agreed. 'So, tell me more. Make me understand.'

'Why not? I'll give you an insight into what life was really like, Frank. When I was almost ten years old, my father sent me to buy a box of Tampax. I had a vague idea what they were, and of course I was embarrassed. But I went all the same. My father wasn't the kind of man you argued with, as I'm sure you've realised by now. When I came back I gave them to my mother. But my father took them from her. 'They're not for her,' he said. 'They're for you.' I looked blankly at him. I thought that my mother bled sometimes and needed these things, I knew that Sophie had also recently started to bleed. But I wasn't bleeding.'

Swain paused. He stared deep into Frank's eyes.

'You know what they were for? Do you have any idea?'

Frank said he didn't have a clue.

'Well, they *were* for me. And they *were* to stop my bleeding. After my father took hold of me, laid me across the end of my bed and sodomised me, he used the little white mouse to plug me up. Believe me, after my father had been there, there was plenty of room.'

Frank lowered his gaze. He couldn't imagine a life anything like the one this man had endured as a boy. But it was no excuse. It could never be.

'When did you become like him, Swain?' he asked. 'When did you become your father?'

Eyebrows angling toward the bridge of his nose, the man considered the question carefully. Eventually he shook his head. 'I never did. I told you once before, I am unique. Okay, so I may have lied once or twice. I did mistreat pets. We didn't have any, and when I was finished, neither did many of our neighbours. But I was always better than my father.'

Frank shook his head. 'I don't see it that way.'

'You wouldn't. You're a philistine. You have no class.'

'Class? You call what you do class? Any fool can murder unsuspecting people. Any fool can terrify innocent little girls. But why did you take them? Why did you want to keep one for yourself?'

The man sat back. Little of what had so far taken place seemed to have disturbed him. Even his trip back in time hadn't affected him in any noticeable way. He remained perfectly calm and reasonable, completely unruffled. He began moving his head from side to side like a metronome.

'Think about it, Frank. You're good at that. Why should I furnish you with all the answers?'

Frank shook his gaze from the hypnotic movement. Deliberately he closed his eyes. He was not at all afraid of what Swain might do. Not here. Not while he was trapped. Frank wiped his mind clean. *Think. Think.*

Think.

It took a minute or so, but the answer came to him so completely that he was drawn to the wonder of it rather than the horror. 'You wanted a replacement for Sophie. Your elder sister was twelve when she died—'

'When she was murdered.'

'Right. Now, I'll bet she was of slim build, had dark blue eyes and strawberry-blonde hair, worn long.'

'I knew you'd get there eventually, Frank. You're almost clever enough to be me.'

'Oh, I wouldn't want to be you, Swain. I like being human.'

This elicited only another smile. 'Oh, dear. I thought you would be beyond that. You disappoint me.'

'That's too bad.' Frank sighed. This was all grist to the mill, but it wasn't taking him any closer to Laura. He had to find out where Laura was being kept.

'The girls,' he went on. 'You took them to replace Sophie. But then you discovered that they weren't interested in playing your games. They wouldn't *be* Sophie. So, the first time this happened, with Jeanette Morris, you hit upon the idea of taxidermy. That way you could keep Sophie forever.'

'Exactly so.'

'So, tell me about it.'

Swain put back his head, focused on the ceiling. 'The clock is ticking, Frank. Don't you want to know about Laura? What I did to her? Whether I killed her or not?'

And then suddenly Frank did know. It explained the man's confidence, it explained his words. *The clock is ticking.* That meant he, Frank, was running out of time. Yet if Laura was already dead then time was of no consequence. The bastard was eventually going to admit that Laura was alive, and then he was going to barter for that life.

For an instant, Frank thought he was going to keel over. He felt far too hot all of a sudden, the walls of the interview room were closing in, the ceiling light glowing like the brightest sun. His eyes refused to focus. He had to get out, had to get away from this man for a while. But he couldn't allow the bastard to know what he had come to understand.

'I need a break.' He rose quickly, the chair screeched and tumbled to the floor. The door was yanked open and Nicky appeared on the run. Frank held up a hand, then turned to Swain. 'You'll be taken back to your holding cell for the time being. This interview will continue in the morning. When I am ready, we will discuss Laura. And then you will tell me whether she is alive or not.'

'Will I, Frank? I wonder.'

His laughter filled the room and raced down the corridor, filtering into every room as it went, like a poisonous toxin, the essence of pure evil. Not a single person who heard it failed to be chilled by its sound.

It was the sound of madness.

Of something inhuman. In human form.

Chapter Fifty-Seven

Frank was dropped off at home by an unmarked squad car just before eight-fifteen that evening. A few journalists had gathered outside his house, but he brushed them off with a recommendation that they study the official press release.

He knew he looked battered, but only realised how bad it might actually be when he saw Debbie's initial reaction. He'd expected shock, maybe even anger, but no sooner had her eyes taken him in than Debbie reeled back against the hallway stairs and sobbed, arms wrapped around herself, shoulders heaving.

It took several minutes to convince her that he looked a great deal worse than he felt, and that none of his injuries were too serious. Helping her into the kitchen, Frank made light of what had happened in the butcher's shop, preferring instead to focus on the positives.

Through ragged breaths, Debbie explained that she'd been frightened by the gathering outside, the fragmented information gleaned from their barrage of questioning. TV coverage had highlighted the struggle between Frank and a suspect, the injuries sustained, the need for a visit to hospital, yet failed to mention how badly he'd been hurt. By the time she'd contacted the hospital, he'd discharged himself, and this had eased her worries. Messages left at Francis Road had failed to earn a return call.

'I'm sorry, sweetheart,' he said, head pressed against hers. 'I never got any messages that you'd called.'

'I thought about driving over, but I didn't feel at all well.'

'No? What's up?'

Debbie shook her head dismissively. 'I had a really bad pain that started just beneath my chest and wormed its way down to my stomach. I'm sure it was just nerves. Tension.'

Frank narrowed his gaze. 'You don't look yourself, that's for sure. How are you now?'

'I'm fine. My belly's grumbling, but I'm doing great compared to you.'

'Oh, don't worry about me. I feel terrible for not calling you. I guess I wasn't thinking too clearly, got caught up in the whole sorry mess. I am fine, honestly. But I should have phoned, should have let you know I was okay.'

'Okay?' Debbie pulled back, held him at arm's length. 'Have you seen yourself, Frank?'

He managed a weak smile. 'Actually, no I haven't. Not properly at least. I haven't dared look in a mirror.'

She shook her head. 'Oh, Frank. I was so worried.'

He held her again, saying nothing this time. A meal and a few drinks would relax them both. Enough, he hoped, to take her mind off what might have been.

* * *

Now Frank sat up straight in the bed, his pillow wedged against the headboard. Debbie lay by his side, arms wrapped around his waist, one leg draped over his. As they relaxed together, Frank told her about Lawrence Swain, his voice almost a distant whisper.

'He sounds odious,' she said, feeling goosebumps rise on her flesh despite the night's sticky heat.

'It was like being in the presence of a devil.' Frank stared straight ahead, barely conscious of Debbie's fingers on him. 'I've never felt anything quite like it before. I suppose it was the same for the guys who had to interview Sutcliffe, West, Shipman, and people like that. Men so ordinary, yet so inhuman at the same time.'

Debbie lifted her head, eyes reflecting her obvious concern. 'He really got to you, didn't he?'

Frank grunted. 'In more ways than you can imagine. I'm pretty sure now that Laura is still alive, but I also know she's still in a great deal of danger. I know I shouldn't, but I can't help but wonder what he's done to her. Him and his damned sister.'

'Just concentrate on getting her back alive.' She pressed her lips against his arm.

'Easy to say. He wants to trade. He'll offer a deal, along the lines of, if we don't let him go, his sister will kill Laura.'

'And?'

'And what?'

'Will you let him go?'

Frank reached up to push his hair back. It was slick with sweat. 'I have no choice in the matter, Debs. He stays behind bars, no matter what.'

'And if it was your decision alone?' Debbie released her grip and sat up. Their eyes met in the darkness.

'It would have to be the same. I would be putting Laura's safety above that of other girls he might snatch in the future.'

Debbie was silent for a while. Then she said, 'Even saying something like that takes a lot of strength. I don't know if I could be so rational.'

'It comes with the territory. Once a copper, always a copper. But perhaps it makes me less of a father.'

Debbie pulled his head down into the crook of her neck. 'No, don't say that. Don't even think it. You're doing all you can, and no one can ask more of you. Do you think you can find Laura, Frank? Is there a way?'

'It's possible ... but not likely. We tried to trace him and his sister through every means at our disposal. There are a few Swains around with the right first names, but they're not the ones we're after. They simply don't exist under those names. We tried under the name of Wilde, too. Again, no joy. We tried to trace them through the photographic company, but it's not registered, and its banking facilities led back to false names and a false address.'

'He's one slippery bastard, isn't he?'

'The man is completely amoral. He either knows what he's doing is wrong and doesn't give a damn, or he's not even aware of it. My guess is it's a combination of the two. I'd say he normally knows he's doing wrong, but then he's overcome by another side to his personality that has no idea he's even doing these dreadful things.'

'Jesus.' Debbie shivered and Frank knew that she was thinking about such a man wandering the streets, totally out of control. It was unnerving. It was something she'd have read about, or had seen at the cinema. It just wasn't supposed to ever come close enough to touch.

Frank rolled over and switched on the bedside lamp. He pulled open a thick blue folder and extracted typewritten sheets of paper and a bunch of photographs. He scanned the reports one more time, glancing occasionally at a photo. Every now and then he shook his head and muttered to himself.

He felt Debbie's close scrutiny, and there was a measure of comfort in realising that she would be acutely aware of his pain. But he was close to breaking, and nothing she could say or do could prevent it.

'Why don't you leave it for now, Frank?' Debbie's voice was gentle, no hint of a rebuke.

'I just want to give this lot one more go. I keep thinking there must be an answer in here for me.'

'Not exactly ideal bedtime reading.'

He smiled. Not feeling much like it, but knowing it was what she wanted. 'You can say that again. You know, he was improving with the taxidermy. The first two were total botch-ups, the third better, and the fourth a staggering improvement. He obviously didn't use enough formaldehyde with number three, because all the signs of decomposition were there.'

Debbie sat up, drawing the sheet around her. 'Tell me about it. Explain it to me.'

'You must be joking. You want nightmares?'

'I take it there are female pathologists?'

'Yes, but …'

'Tell me, damn you.'

'Okay. You asked for it, remember.' He pinched the bridge of his nose. 'After a couple of days, you get green and purple staining, and the body begins to distend. A week or so after death the body swells with gases and the skin blisters. Three weeks in and the blisters burst, tissue softens, organs and cavities burst open. A week later the tissue liquefies. No more real changes for a few months, but if the body is kept in water or in damp soil then adipocere – which is the human fat becoming hard and suety – forms on the face and head. Later it forms on the trunk, too.'

'And this ... adipocere was present on all the girls?'

'Right. Because they were immersed in water they were also more discoloured, and the nails and hair are quite loose.'

'But the fourth girl wasn't so bad.'

Frank nodded grimly. 'She was in good shape, actually. Of course, she hadn't been dead as long, but decomposition had barely begun, due to the taxidermy process.'

'And all to replace his sister.'

'Yep. Crazy, but it also has a certain kind of logic. No girl is going to remain with them willingly, so to keep their 'sister' with them, taxidermy is the ideal solution.'

Debbie shot him a frosty glance. 'You sound almost as though you understand him.'

'In a way, I do. Oh, I don't approve, but if I'm going to wear him down, I must understand what makes him tick.'

He stuffed the papers back into the file and snapped the lamp off again. 'Looking at those poor kids makes me think of Laura all over again.'

Squeezing his arm, Debbie whispered, 'I know. I wish I could take those thoughts away for you.'

'Perhaps I can get some proper sleep. At least then my mind shuts it out.'

'Early start?'

'I have to see him again. Today I'd had all I could take, but tomorrow the show goes on. I have to get close to him, Debs. It may be the only way of getting him to slip up. I have to reach out for him, go across to his side of the fence.'

'Just as long as you can cross back, Frank.'

He said nothing, but as his eyes closed he began to consider the implication of her words. To understand Lawrence Swain's kind of madness might induce the very same thing in himself. He swallowed thickly, a dry, acrid taste filling his mouth.

He recognized it at once.

It was the taste of fear.

Chapter Fifty-Eight

The tape was running, the room was again stifling, the air tainted with one man's evil.

'So, Swain,' said Frank, rubbing his chin thoughtfully. 'We know how you abducted the girls, and we know why. What I still don't understand is why you had to torture the first girl.'

Lawrence Swain still wore the white paper suit. His bald head was slick and shiny, a stubble beginning to form around his neck, chin and cheeks. According to the night-shift records, Swain had not slept, yet his eyes were wide and alert and devious.

'Oh, that should be easy for you to work out, Frank. Still, I'll give you this little snippet. I took her because I wanted to replace my sister. But then I discovered something in her that was wrong. She simply wasn't up to scratch. And so ...' He raised his eyebrows and grinned.

'And so, she had to pay,' Frank finished for him. 'You believed she had deceived you. So you punished her.'

'Of course. What else does one do with a naughty child? For all his sins, my father had the right idea where discipline was concerned.'

'But you killed your father for what he did to Sophie.'

Frank sucked in his breath as he saw a look of genuine disconcertion pass across the man's features. Swain was clearly troubled by what had been suggested. But it was only a second or two before he recovered.

'He deserved to die. It's one thing to destroy strangers, another to destroy your own.'

'I see. You know, perhaps you're right.'

The man's eyes opened wide. His astonishment was obvious. 'You see it too, Frank? Do you? Maybe we're more alike than I thought.'

'Maybe. And perhaps we can be more so if I get to understand you better.'

Nodding eagerly, Swain said, 'I'll be your tutor, Frank. And you my trusty pupil. Together we can be an unbeatable team. Astaire and Rogers, Butch and Sundance … Mickey and Donald.' He laughed at his own absurd joke.

'Okay,' Frank said. 'So, I'm with you so far. After you'd killed the first child you hit upon the taxidermy angle. But why attempt the taxidermy on those girls who weren't worthy of preserving? Why not wait until you found the right one?'

Swain shook his head slowly. Mocking. 'Oh, Frank. How obtuse of you. Don't belittle yourself. You know why as much as I do.'

'Maybe. But I want you to confirm it.'

'Very well. I needed the practice. It's that simple. I had only the vaguest notion how to perform taxidermy, and I couldn't be at all sure if it would work with humans.'

'And so, your first attempts were botched.'

Swain chuckled. Not his carefully conceived chuckle, but one of genuine humour this time. 'You could say that, yes.'

Frank glanced down at the open file on the desk. 'Jeanette Morris was injected with formaldehyde.'

'That's right. I wondered whether it could be done after death, and with the skin still intact on the body.'

'Geraldine McGiven was also injected. This time while she was still alive.'

'Ah, yes. Geraldine. She was quite sweet, but not at all suitable. Dreadful voice. It grated so.'

'You knew what injecting formaldehyde into her body would do?'

'I had a good idea. Acid in the bloodstream. It was fun. How she screamed.'

Frank closed his eyes for a moment, the image Swain had created too much to bear. 'So, after you failed with Geraldine you knew you had to take the skin off,' he said.

'That's right. I wasn't at all bothered by having to do so, as you can imagine. The thought was quite appealing, actually. However, it proved to be a real fucking nightmare.'

'Is that so?' Frank was surprised at the profanity. It was a chink in the cool and calculated veneer.

'Yes. I still had no idea how to proceed. I didn't want to buy the books, not wanting to leave any trace, you see. So, I stole one from a library, flicked through it, and thought I knew it all.'

'But again you failed.'

Swain closed his eyes for a moment and nodded. 'It was a bastard. On Tracey, I think it was, I cut myself several times with the scalpel. I got that from an artists' supplies shop, by the way. I cut the skin too thick in places, too thin in others. Worst of all I accidentally cut through her stomach lining. Oh, Frank…the smell was awful. The gasses were like the worst farts imaginable. I was actually sick, threw up until I was empty.'

'How awful for you.'

Swain missed the sarcasm. 'Quite. But the real agony was yet to come. I was so eager to get it done that I hadn't bought myself proper protective clothing. When I put her skin into the bath of formaldehyde and water, some of it got into my scalpel cuts.'

He closed his eyes and put back his head 'Oh, Frank, Frank, Frank. I can't begin to describe the pain. I washed it out quickly, but it burned like hell.'

'I don't suppose it was much fun for Tracey, either.'

Swain waved a limp hand in his direction. 'Don't toy with me. Tracey was far beyond caring by then. You know that.'

'Of course.'

Frank took a drink of water. He hoped Swain hadn't noticed how dry he'd become. The conversation was starting to get to him again already. There was only so much of this madman he could take. Yet somewhere inside that deranged mind was the place Laura was being kept. And while the monster was talking, there was always that one chance that the location could slip out. One chance in how many?

'I did it wrong again, though,' Swain went on, eyes narrowed now. 'It took only a few days for her skin to start rotting.'

'But you did improve.'

Yes. This was the way. The odds were good that Swain had done all this in the same place he kept the children. The more he spoke about it, the better idea they would get.

'Oh, yes. I eventually found out all I needed to know. You've seen only my failures, Frank. I have some real beauties back home.'

Back home. He said 'back home'. So, he was keeping them close by. Same place as he carried out the delicate operation. Had to be. Same place he was keeping Laura. Frank's heart skipped several beats.

'Tell me about your successes, Larry. Tell me how you finally got it right.'

At that moment, the door was opened. It was Nicky, who had again been standing outside in the corridor. 'We need to talk,' he said to Frank.

Frank released a lungful of air. It wasn't exactly perfect timing, but he could do with another break. Time to regroup, gather his wits once more.

'Okay. Interview suspended for a ten-minute break. Prisoner will remain here in the presence of two police officers while Frank Rogers leaves the room.'

He got up slowly, not trusting his legs. He felt weary, exhausted merely by being in the man's presence. His thoughts were becoming increasingly unclear. Outside he gave a wry grin. 'The bastard's not as clever as he thinks he is. He's ...' And then he saw how Nicky's face was set, and knew immediately that something was wrong.

'What is it?'

'It's the sister, Frank. She's on the phone. Wants to speak to you.'

Chapter Fifty-Nine

Violet Swain had not begun to worry about her brother until midnight had come and gone. As she lay fully clothed on the stained bedsheet, questions started to arise in her mind. Why was he not yet home? Where had he been all day? Had he left it so late that the underground had stopped running? Surely not. Not Larry. He was a perfectionist. So, where the hell was he?

Perhaps the play had gone on later than he'd thought, maybe he'd chosen to stay in town for the night. But if that were the case, why hadn't he called? Her mobile was right there on the table.

Glancing down at it, Violet stifled a gasp. She had forgotten to re-charge the damned thing. It had probably run down so low that it wasn't working. Larry had been trying to get through all the time and now he was stuck somewhere and he was going to blame her and he would hit her just like he had the other night and ... But when she tried the power-indicator button it beeped cheerfully and flashed a strong red light. *I'm fully armed,* it said. *Ready to go.* He just hasn't called, that's all.

So, where was he? Since Sophie had come back to them he hadn't been away for a single night ... Violet blinked and frowned. Sophie? No. Not her. Laura. The girl was called Laura. Had to remember that. Larry would beat her again otherwise. But what if Larry was wrong? What if it really was Sophie?

Larry's never wrong. Wash your mouth out with soap and water, before he does it with sulphuric acid.

Violet tried to shake these unwanted thoughts aside. Larry wasn't here. That was the important thing. It didn't matter about Sophie, didn't matter at all that she had come back after all these years ...

Laura. The girl's name is Laura.

... right, Laura it is. But where was Larry? Why hadn't he called?

Because they have him. The answer broke through her fragile defences. *Because they have him.* That man he was taunting, Sophie's father (no, not Sophie, Laura ... Laura's father), he'd caught up with Larry, had thrown Larry into a cell and tossed the key down the toilet. Hadn't Larry always told her that's what they'd do if they caught up with him?

She'd gone to bed some time later, but only drifted in and out of sleep. Early in the morning she'd rushed to turn on the television and switch to the news channel. When she found it, the screen screamed its headlines at her. She sat perched on the edge of her seat, listening to the item. They hadn't mentioned Larry by name, of course, but she knew what 'helping with inquiries' meant. It meant slamming the cell door and tossing away the key, that's what it meant.

And all because of Sophie. If he hadn't ...

Not Sophie. Laura. Laura. It's not Sophie. You must remember that.

... been so keen on her none of this would ever have happened.

It was then that she felt as if she had emerged through a thick fog, and it occurred to Violet that Laura was the real key. The one to the cell door could be thrown away, but the girl was the one to open it again.

Chapter Sixty

'I'm looking at a photograph of you now, Frank Rogers. Your voice suits you.'

My God, he thought. *They're both the same. Both calm and deadly and utterly without compassion.* 'What do you want?' he asked, not without difficulty. 'I'm rather busy at the moment.'

'Oh, I bet you are. You have my brother, don't you? You'd better not hurt him. I know what you people do in those cells of yours.'

'Yes. We're the bad guys here.'

'Don't fuck with me, you prick. Don't fuck with either of us.'

'I don't think you're in any position to make threats.'

'Really. Let's see, shall we?' There was a second of silence, followed by a loud, piercing scream. Frank went cold, instantly rigid.

Laura. Laura in pain.

'Now will you answer me?' Violet asked in a manic voice.

'What did you do to her?'

'I asked first, Frank. I think you'd better answer me now.'

He glanced across at Nicky, who'd heard the entire conversation through the office speakers. He licked his lips. 'Yes. Yes, we are interviewing your brother. Now tell me what you did to my daughter.'

'I slapped her. Hard. With the phone. She didn't seem to enjoy that. Perhaps I should do something else. Something even more harmful.'

'No. No, you don't have to do that, Violet.'

'Ah, so you do know my name, then. I see.' She paused, obviously considering this fresh information. 'Well, no matter. You still don't know the most important details. Such as where I'm keeping Sophie.'

Frank almost missed it. He was about to respond when the anomaly snagged. 'Sophie?' he said. For a further moment, the name didn't strike any chords.

'Did I say Sophie? I meant Laura, of course.'

Frank tossed the name about. Then he had it. 'But you did say Sophie, Violet. Maybe it is her, after all. Perhaps you don't have my daughter at all.'

The laugh that rattled down the line made Frank wince. 'Don't be absurd. Of course, it's your little bitch of a daughter. Sophie left us a long time ago. She won't be coming back.'

'Violet … why did you call? What do you want from me?'

'Larry, of course. I want my brother back, safe and sound. I get him, you get Laura.'

Frank shook his head. Telling this woman the facts of life wasn't going to work. She had already proved she could be violent. Telling her now that her brother was going to stay behind bars and rot there for the rest of his life could only make matters worse. Frank had to stall, give himself some time.

'That's going to take some time to arrange, Violet. What you're asking me to do is not all that easy, and I can't make the decision on my own. I need a few days, at least.'

'You've got twelve hours,' she said. Then the line was dead in Frank's hand.

* * *

'Quite a family,' Nicky said, slumping into a chair opposite his friend. He leaned back and shook his head despondently. 'I thought that sick fuck downstairs was bad, but she sounds every bit as crazy.'

Frank nodded thoughtfully. 'Yeah, but is she as clever as him? She's confused, badly disorientated. When she said she had Sophie, she really did mean her sister.' He stroked his chin and closed his eyes. 'Nicky … I get the terrible feeling that in her own way, she's even more dangerous than her brother.'

'Why? Because of what she just did to Laura?'

'Partly. But he was content to toy with us, me in particular. The taunting was a pleasant distraction. The kind of violence he's into is final, no coming back from it. When he means business it's all over. Since snatching Laura he's decided to fuck with minds, and obviously gets a real kick out of it. But his sister is not in control of herself like he is, therefore she's more likely to do something stupid. Like hurt Laura badly ... or worse.'

Nicky leaned forward. 'Frank, I don't want you jumping down my throat for saying this, but I think the time is right for you to come off this case. They're using you, and it's got you stuck between a rock and a hard place. You're going to have a breakdown, because you're emotional and you know we have fuck all to go on. Each hour that slips by will eat you up, mate. I don't want that to happen.'

Frank thought about it. He knew how close he was to the edge, thoughts swimming in ever decreasing circles. Soon he wasn't going to be of use to anyone. He admitted as much to Nicky.

'But,' he added, 'I need to see this through as far as I can take it. Realistically, the only chance we have of finding them is to break that evil fucker downstairs. I'm the only one who can do that now.'

Nicky had to allow the argument. It was their only chance. 'I'll have someone contact BT to find out where that call came from. You never know. Meanwhile, are you ready to go back in there?'

'Not really. But the clock is running.'

'Twelve hours. You think she'd do something the moment her deadline is up?'

'Yes I do,' Frank nodded adamantly. 'I think she's the type to send us a finger or an ear or something equally repellent.'

Nicky stood up. His features were grim as he headed for the office door. 'Yes,' he agreed. 'I think you could be right.'

Chapter Sixty-One

'How did you enjoy talking to my sister, Frank?' was how Lawrence Swain resumed the interview.

Frank tried hard not to show his surprise. His eyes betrayed him this time, and the prisoner chuckled.

'What makes you think I spoke to Violet?'

'Frank, my dear fellow, neither of us is a fool. My sister's no fool, either. It wouldn't have taken her long to piece it together. What's more, the good Chief Inspector Loizou's face was all too easy to read.'

There was no point in denying the fact. Frank shrugged and said, 'She wanted to know how you were.'

Swain's eyes narrowed. For perhaps the first time since he'd been taken into custody he was showing some anger. 'Don't fuck with me, Frank. I thought we had some kind of an understanding. The smell of bullshit doesn't appeal to me. Now, either you talk straight, or I stop listening.'

With enormous effort, Frank resisted the urge to strike out. The arrogance of the man was astounding. It didn't matter that he was being held, that his clothes had been stripped off, that he had been subjected to a none-too-delicate body search, or that he had admitted to murdering innocent children, because as far as the madman was concerned he still held all the best cards.

Frank had to make an instant decision. He couldn't think of a single reason to tell Swain about his sister's deadline, but in the back of his mind, he wondered whether this was a prearranged plan in the event of Swain being captured. The trouble was, he didn't want to tell the man a thing about it, didn't want to give him any more reason to feel superior and secure.

'Violet has given us a deadline,' he said finally. 'Either she has you back within twelve hours or she does something to Laura.'

'Does what exactly?' Swain asked, the beginning of a smile playing across his lips.

'She didn't specify.'

A frown. 'How very disappointing. My dear sister is not as accustomed to boring into people's minds as I am. Such a waste of a conversation. She could have tasted your pain, too. We could both have recalled it in our twilight years.'

'You would have painted a picture for me.'

'Most certainly. So where do we go from here, Frank?' He sat back in the chair, the frame groaning beneath his weight.

'You go nowhere. You stay right here.'

'But your little girl, Frank. Your little precious, the fruit of your loins. What will become of her?'

'I have no idea. Whatever the outcome, I'll have to live with it. The simple fact is, even if I wanted to let you go, I don't have the authority.'

'And if you did ...?'

Frank recalled Debbie asking the same question. 'I still wouldn't let a sick fuck like you back on the streets.'

Swain nodded appreciatively, eyebrows raised. 'That's honest enough. I admire that. Between us, my sister and I have fucked up your entire life, yet you stick to your principles.'

Frank shook his head, snorting contemptuously. 'I wouldn't let people like you ruin my life. I'd never give you that satisfaction. The most important thing is never allowing you to win. My family has been devastated, my daughter may yet die, but you will ultimately pay the price for your crimes. You and your sister both.'

Behind his back, the handcuffs rattled as Lawrence Swain gave a brief burst of mocking applause. 'Bravo, Special Detective Rogers. A fine and noble speech, to be sure. But we both know what will actually happen. If I were in a country where the death penalty was still in existence, then indeed I might well pay the ultimate price. But we're in England, Frank. The last civilized country in the world, so it is said. Who am I to argue? No, I will either be placed into some kind of institution, where I will eventually convince any amount of head doctors that I am sane and able to be released back into society, or I will serve my time in solitude, with a colour TV, hi-fi, books, and just about anything my heart desires to keep me company. Whatever the outcome, the one thing you can be sure of is that I will not suffer for my crimes. Now, does that sound as if I'll be paying the price?'

The terrible thing was, Frank knew the man was right. The punishment would never fit the crime, would never come anywhere near making amends for the wasted lives, the pain, the misery that Lawrence Swain had inflicted. But beneath the madman's smug grin of self-satisfaction, there was something he had not considered: Frank would not allow him to go on living.

He couldn't say for certain when he had arrived at that decision. It had always been his intention to kill the man if Laura perished, but now he was going to do it, whatever the outcome. In general, he was not altogether convinced about the need for a death penalty, but when you were dealing with a mind like this, you simply had to eradicate it completely.

'Justice will be seen to be done,' he said. 'The deadline is irrelevant to this interview. So, shall we move on?'

'By all means. It's your time we're wasting. Your little girl's time. But listen, Frank, if I'm going to trust in you, I have to know you better. Why not tell me a little about yourself?'

'Later. Maybe. If I choose to.'

But Swain was shaking his head and tut-tutting. 'Oh, no, no, no, Frank. I thought we were agreed on this matter. You may have me handcuffed and incarcerated, but I still call the shots. You will tell me about yourself when I choose.'

'Or you'll say nothing at all.'

'You've got it. But for now, I'm happy to continue.'

'How considerate of you. So, back to taxidermy. How did you manage to get it right in the end?'

Swain gave a broad grin. 'It was so easy. I merely telephoned a taxidermist, told him I was an author researching a new novel, and that I wanted to pick his brains. The man I spoke to was only too eager to impart his wisdom.'

'So how was it done?'

'Briefly, you take the skin off in one piece. Slit the carcass up the front or rear, between the legs up to the chin or back of the neck. With the arms, you cut from wrist to chest and across to the other wrist. Legs are slit from the ball of the foot up the thighs, around and back down again. There is little blood, because it will have coagulated by the time the first incision is made, so it's not all that messy.

'You sound as though you enjoyed yourself,' Frank said, interrupting the flow of words.

'And so I did. Very much. Once the skin is off, you then have to skin that …you know, get rid of the surplus, pare it down. Then it is placed in a bath filled with water and formaldehyde. While this is soaking, you take the flesh off the bones and then boil the bones. After, the bones can also be soaked in the bath. Later they are taken out to arrange once more into a skeleton. Onto the skeleton you must rebuild the shape of the muscles and that sort of thing. That was done by binding wood wool onto the bones to form a rough mannequin. Over this goes a mixture of papier mâché and plaster, to smooth and shape the muscles and develop the shape of the body more fully.

'This takes two or three days to dry. When it is, the skin can be washed in undiluted formaldehyde and then sewn onto the mannequin. As this dries, it must be pinned because of the shrinkage. It takes roughly ten days to dry properly, depending on ventilation. When it's ready, the pins come out and all the minor imperfections, stitches and cracks are filled in with beeswax.

'The flesh is discoloured, of course. It's a kind of green, off-white, and blue colour. To look right it must be made-up with cosmetics. Then the hair goes back in place. I use the real hair if I can. Finally, we pop in the glass eyes. Job done.'

Frank had hardly dared to breathe while the prisoner was speaking. He could just as easily have been talking about performing taxidermy on an animal or bird, and Frank found it almost impossible to imagine this happening to a human child. He sat looking at the monster for several moments, unnerved by Swain's complete lack of compassion for his victims.

'How many were successful?' he asked eventually.

'Three.'

'And they're at home still.'

'Two of them. Where I can see them. Where they can see me. I gave you one.'

'Of course. The formaldehyde … Where did you obtain it?'

'Various places. Mostly farm suppliers.'

'And the other materials are presumably just as easily purchased.'

'Yes.'

'Except for the eyes,' Frank said as it came to him. 'Not exactly the kind of item you pick up at your local Tesco.'

'They can be found if you know where to look. Now then, Frank,' Swain said, leaning forward. 'Tell me, how did you feel when you saw Gary lying in the mortuary all cold and dead and useless?'

The sudden change of tack threw Frank for a moment or two. Swain was quick to latch on to his disorientation. 'Come on, Frank. Picture his innocent little face, eyelids gummed together so they couldn't spring open and shock you, no breath escaping his colourless lips, no heart beating beneath his ribs.'

Frank clamped his teeth together. Through them he hissed, 'You bastard. You had no need … no right to take his life.'

'No need, no right, just something to do, Frank. Some men like train-spotting, others enjoy a few pints and a game of pool with the lads. Me, I like masturbating over women who are being fucked, sticking something sharp into defenceless flesh, taking little girls out into the dark night and scaring the crap out of them. These are a few of my favourite things.'

Frank stood up and moved away from the table. He rested his forearm on the brick wall and leaned against it. He felt the acrid taste of bile rising up into his gorge, and his entire body seemed as if it were jerking, spasm after spasm, wave after wave of anger so black it fogged his vision. Behind him, Swain hummed softly to himself.

Frank wheeled. From where he stood he glared across at Swain. 'Your father masturbated over Violet's face as he watched you and her fucking, didn't he?'

The question didn't require an answer. Frank just knew.

'He came into your room at night and took Violet out, and you always thought he would put her in the cupboard with Sophie. And whenever he felt like it he would cut you, cut Sophie, cut Violet. And he would use a tool from his carpenter's kit to do it with.'

Lawrence Swain jerked back in his chair as though physically stunned by the tirade of words. His eyes narrowed menacingly. 'Don't think you can fuck with *my* mind, Frank. Believe me, you don't want to join me here in this kind of darkness.'

Frank held his gaze. 'There are many degrees of darkness, Swain. You have no idea how dark a world I'm prepared to inhabit if it gets me what I want.'

'But you would need some light to guide your way back. Without it you could lose yourself in there for good. That's the difference between us, Frank: I don't need to come back.'

'Perhaps not. But I can come deep enough to reach you. As deep as I need.'

'Nothing can get through to me. Nothing at all. When I'm attacked I simply clear my mind and enter a different world. A world of aesthetic wonder, where the likes of Wilde are not vilified because of their sexual preferences. A world I can actually go to any time I like because I can create it with my bare hands. Laura's been there, Frank. She's seen my other world, been a part of it.'

His eyes were big and round and bulging with a rage he was desperately trying to control.

The two men stared at each other for some time, neither willing to break the contact first. But then Frank let the twisted bastard enjoy a moment of juvenile victory.

'Interview suspended,' he barked. 'Frank Rogers leaving the room. Prisoner to be taken back to his cell.'

Puzzled, Swain shifted angrily on his seat. 'You can't leave now,' he cried. 'I was just warming up. There's so much more where that came from, Frank. Let me tell you about Laura. Let me tell you about how I—'

But he was talking to an open door, two burly constables filling the empty space. 'Come back here, Frank!' he roared, as the two policemen took hold of him. 'Come and hear all about how I punished your daughter for trying to escape. Hear how I tore her apart, Frank.'

Swain's voice seemed to follow Frank as he fled along the corridor and up the stairs two at a time. The monster's taunts echoed in his head as fresh tears blurred his vision.

Chapter Sixty-Two

They sat in the doll's house, Violet lying on her side on the single bed, Laura perched on the edge of the chair directly opposite. Since her desperate and ultimately futile attempt at escape, Laura had been waiting patiently to die. The man had laughed at her tears of frustration, then he had left her alone with the promise that he would kill her upon his return from a business trip. He had made the threat so casually that Laura was convinced of its sincerity.

She was going to die.

Time had passed quickly at first. Now that she had light spearing into the room, she was able to follow the passage of the day. She was a little surprised when no food came at midday, but decided that he was punishing her. She fully expected him to come for her before twilight, but then dusk came, followed by the kind of city darkness that is never complete. And still he hadn't shown. Even the woman had not come into the room.

Laura slept badly that night, but was amazed that she had managed to sleep at all. Daylight again. The sun was rising on the other side of her prison, and she watched as the shadows grew shorter. Hunger pains gnawed at her stomach. At one point, she wondered whether this was the way he'd intended to kill her, by starving her to death. But even at her tender age, Laura was aware that a man like her captor needed death to be violent and bloody and personal.

Just before the sun reached its zenith, the familiar sound of keys jangled in the lock. Laura stiffened. She was afraid to die, terrified of the way it was likely to happen, but was too exhausted to fight. Her mind flashed visions of her mother, brother and her father. They'd let her down. Between them, they had failed to protect her. It wasn't their fault, but the failure was theirs all the same.

But it was the woman this time. Violet. She locked the door behind her and came over to squat by Laura's side. In one hand she held a knife, in the other a mobile phone. She made a call, and Laura was shocked to hear her father's name mentioned. She hardly dared breathe, intent on listening to every word spoken. It seemed impossible for her father to be so close and yet so far away. The blow with the hard edge of the phone came from nowhere, causing her to let out a yelp of pain. She could only imagine what might have happened if Violet had used her other hand. When the call was ended, Laura was even more convinced that she was never going to see another day.

For a few minutes after the telephone conversation, the woman walked in tiny circles, muttering to herself. Then, after a brief pause, Violet walked purposefully across the room to the doll's house and silently beckoned Laura to join her.

Another shock awaited Laura when the door was flung open. The girls were gone. The dead girls. Had they taken their leave of their own free will, just got up and walked away? Nothing made sense any more. Nothing was what it seemed. By now she should be dead. Instead, the woman was here, the dead girls were gone, and the terrible man was with her father.

'Well, this is cosy,' Violet said. She patted Laura's thigh. 'As we have a few hours together, I thought we should use it wisely.'

The knuckles of her right hand were white as she gripped the carving knife, whose blade was now pressed against the mattress.

'Remember what we agreed,' Laura said, thinking quickly now. She swallowed. 'You mustn't do anything I don't like. Larry wouldn't care to find out about our secret.'

But Violet slowly shook her head and said, 'Oh, it's far too late for that now. How do you think I got these bruises?' She indicated the purple and yellow marks on her arms and legs. 'You see, I'm so fucking stupid I forgot all about the cameras, the ones that have been watching every move you've made since you came back.'

Laura blinked. 'Came back?'

Violet smiled, a grim slit in her face. 'That's right, Sophie. You came back to us. After all these years. After all we suffered because of you.'

Laura's mind whirled. That name again. Sophie. Which was it better to be? Clearly the woman was deranged, and couldn't be trusted not to react against either name, but it seemed as if she had a particular dislike of this girl called Sophie.

'But I'm Laura,' she said, offering a tentative smile of her own. 'You remember. Larry took me away from my family. My name is Laura Rogers.'

Violet waved a dismissive hand. 'Silly girl, don't you think I know my own sister?'

'But I'm not Sophie,' she insisted, shocked by what the woman had revealed. 'I'm Laura. You must remember. Ask Larry if you don't believe me.'

Violet's face darkened alarmingly. 'Larry's not here as you full well know,' she said through a stiff jaw. She set the phone to one side and reached out a hand to stroke Laura's hair. 'And please, I don't want you to confuse me any more, Sophie.'

'I keep telling you, I am not Sophie!' Laura's voice rang out harshly.

'But of course you are. And you used to enjoy these kinds of games. Daddy and Mummy and you. You used to squeal with delight. So, don't play the innocent with me.'

'You're mad. I'm not Sophie, and I'm not playing your games.'

Violet looked at her for a few moments, saying nothing this time. She blinked a couple of times, shook her head as if to clear her thoughts. When she looked at Laura it was as if she were surprised to see her sitting there. In a quick, jerky movement, she shot to her feet. She stood looking down at Laura. Her mouth twisted into a thin sneer.

'I'll leave you to it. For a while.' She walked across to the doll's house door, pausing on the threshold. 'Oh, and by the way, don't get carried away by the thought that the call I made will be traced. Larry knows all about these sort of things, and we have more phones than we know what to do with.'

Laura felt one more faint sliver of hope slip from her grasp.

Chapter Sixty-Three

The inside of Nicky's office was sweltering, despite the windows having been thrown open. Frank sat in a chair opposite his friend's desk, shaking his head, trying to come to terms with his failure to break Swain.

'I can't get him to slip,' he said. 'Or if he has, I haven't spotted it. Nicky, where the hell is that fucker holding my daughter?'

His friend gave a grim shrug. 'Nothing so far from his clothing, particularly no traces to indicate a farm or something similar. He may have yet another office somewhere where he does his developing.'

'The photography is the only thing we can trace back to Swain, and though it's his way of getting to the girls, I just don't see that being enough for him.'

'But there are no records of either Lawrence or Violet Swain ever being employed. No trace of a driving licence for either of them, no tax records, no bank details. It's as if they don't exist. How can they afford to live off his meagre earnings?'

'I wonder if they inherited any money,' Frank said.

'I guess we can check. Perhaps they got the proceeds from the house when they were eighteen, though I doubt he would have profited from his crimes. I know there was a huge element of diminished responsibility, though, and maybe it was the sister who got the money.'

Frank nodded. 'Yes. There never was anything against her, so she may well have received proceeds from the sale of the house. Problem is, I still don't know how any of that will help. This freak must have a weakness I can work on now, today.'

'Why don't you speak to Irene Shaw again? She spent time with him, knew more about him than we know now.'

It was an excellent idea. A few minutes later Frank had located the number and had punched it in. He explained to the ex-social services worker what he was seeking to do. 'It's my belief that he and his sister must have some weaknesses from their past that we can exploit,' Frank went on. 'Would you think that's possible?'

'Anything's possible, Mr Rogers. But I can't think of anything off the top of my head'

'What about their desires? An unfulfilled desire can create weakness.'

'Lawrence would have wanted to succeed where his father failed. That, in itself, could be considered weak.'

Frank nodded to himself. 'I don't suppose he ever gave any indication of what he wanted to do, where he wanted to go when he grew up?'

'I'm sorry. I really would like to help, but I simply can't remember. We discussed so many things. His likes, dislikes, loves, hates.'

'His fears?' The question was out before Frank had really formed it in his mind.

'His fears? Yes, of course, Mr Rogers. I had completely forgotten about those conversations.'

Frank licked his lips and lowered his voice almost to a whisper. 'Tell me, Mrs Shaw, what did Lawrence Swain fear?'

* * *

When Frank put down the telephone he sat lost in thought for some time, eyes closed, breathing calm and steady. Finally, he opened his eyes and asked Nicky to fetch him something from a particular shop in nearby Walthamstow.

'Are you sure about this, Frank?' Nicky asked. He gave his friend a quizzical look. 'Sure this is the way you want to go?'

Frank nodded. 'Absolutely. You up for it?'

Nicky wet his lips. 'I don't know about that, but I'll do it.'

Frank headed back down to the cells, a spring in his step for the first time. The custody sergeant unlocked the door without delay. Normal procedure had been waived the moment Lawrence Swain had opted not to have a solicitor present.

Swain sat upright, spine pressed against the painted brick wall. Its gloss finish reflected his paper suit; a ghostly companion by his side. He was smiling. As usual.

'I hope you're in a better frame of mind than you were last time,' he said without looking at Frank. 'You were unnecessarily rude, Special Detective Rogers.' He made to move off the narrow, steel-framed bed.

Frank held up a hand. 'No, don't bother. Stay where you are. We're not going to the interview room this time.' His manner was deliberately easier. It was part of his plan to put the madman at his ease for the time being.

'No interview? Oh, what a shame. I do so enjoy our little chats.'

'Me, too. I thought we'd make it a little less formal.'

The madman's face brightened considerably. 'Good. I like a man who's not afraid to step out of character.'

Frank leaned against the doorframe, arms folded. 'Comfortable?' he asked. 'This cell?'

'It's not so bad. Hardly the Savoy, but I suppose it will have to do. For the time being.'

'Oh, yes. You think you're getting out.'

'I am getting out, Frank. It's just a matter of time. We both know that.'

Frank bit down on a retort. There was time for that later. 'Look, let's not fight. I'm sorry for what I said before. Sophie must have meant a lot to you. Tell me more about her.'

'What is there to tell? She lived, she died.'

'And you loved her.'

'Yes, I did.'

'More than anyone? More than Violet, even?'

'Yes.' His eyes shone as he looked deep within himself. 'You're good, Frank. But you must pay a price, as I do, for the curse of insight.'

Frank wasn't sure about that. Later he would have to give the matter some consideration. 'What are you keeping from me, Swain?' he asked. 'I sense a lot more than you're telling me.'

'Like what, for instance?'

'Oh, I don't know. There's a sadness in you. You loved Sophie. Your father took her away, so you killed him. It all sounds so … contrived. Too easy to believe, an excuse for the way you are now. Somehow I feel there's more to that story than meets the eye.'

Swain grinned and shook his head in admiration. 'Clever, Frank. None of them were as clever as you. Even as a child I had no equal, and there were many fools who believed they were my betters. Fools who tried to see inside me, open up my head to see what made me tick. Only you come close, Frank. But even you aren't good enough.'

'What do you mean?' In spite of himself, Frank was interested.

'I'm going to tell you something I've never told anyone, Frank. My father didn't kill Sophie. I did.'

'You! But why … if she meant so much to you?' Frank was astonished.

'*Because* she meant so much to me. They had taken her out of the cupboard yet again, stripped of her few dirty rags, and then took off their own clothes. Violet and I were in our usual place, sat before them like we were waiting for a show to begin. But this time it was different. For all she'd been through, Sophie always complained, even tried to fight them. Only that day she came without a whimper, even got on her knees so that our father could take her more easily. There was no fight left in her. She was empty. I knew then that she was lost.'

'So, you murdered your parents.'

'It was the first time that I became aware of how much power I actually had.'

'Power?'

'Over life and death, yes. I don't know where such recognition comes from, but I felt it creep over me that day, and it took control. While my father was enjoying himself with Sophie, I slipped off the sofa and went to his toolbox. Using the tools he was so proud of seemed like the right thing to do. I killed him first, just came up behind him and slit his throat with a chisel. Then I killed my mother. And then it was Sophie's turn.'

The madman lowered his eyes. Frank looked into them and what he saw there stunned him. Sorrow. Immense sorrow. Human sorrow.

'But why kill Sophie?' Frank wanted to know. 'Once your parents were gone, she was safe, surely.'

'Physically, yes. Oh, her body was ruined, but I knew it would heal in time and at least it would never be abused by either of them again. But in here,' he tapped the side of his head, 'she would never be safe. There's nowhere to hide from what's inside your mind, Frank. You must know that by now. She was a hollow shell. There was nothing left of the Sophie I adored. For her there could never be any escape from the horrors of her memory. All that they had ever done would stay with her for the rest of her life. No, Frank. She would never be safe again.'

'So, you killed her out of a sense of ... compassion.'

'Compassion? Yes. But most of all, love.'

For several moments, Frank felt something stir within him that was at once confusing and disturbing. He felt sympathy. Lawrence Swain had not been born a monster, had not begun life as a madman. His evil had been forged by evil parents, who no doubt had their own tales of woe to tell. Parents who had forced him to endure a childhood of physical, mental, and sexual abuse. Parents whose actions had led him to take three lives while he was barely into his teens. And so, Frank was able to sympathise with the boy who had taken those lives. Yet through this surprising sensation leaked the images of families murdered in their beds, of little girls whose lives were equally wasted.

Sympathy, yes. But not forgiveness.

It was time to go on the offensive.

'I had a conversation with someone who knows you,' said Frank. 'Knew you, I should say. Knew you as a boy, before and after you murdered your parents.'

'Really.' Swain had quickly recovered his composure. He yawned hugely. 'How dull for you.'

'Swain, you remember how I only needed to hear your voice to know you were the man who had murdered my son and wife?'

'Yes. What of it?'

'Well, now I need only to see your eyes to know when you are concerned or disturbed about something I mention. Something about my discussing your past worries you. Don't tell me otherwise.'

Swain pursed his lips, took care to maintain control over his breathing. Frank saw now that it was all an act. And if none of it was natural, the facade could be pulled to pieces.

'Very astute,' Swain said at last. 'But you still don't know the thing you need to know most. You still don't have a clue where Laura is.'

'That's right. I don't. But you're going to tell me.'

'Dream on, Frank.'

'You may not think you will, Swain. But I can assure you, before I leave here, you will have given me the address and precise directions if I should need them.'

Lawrence Swain laughed. Gone was the dramatic chuckle. Another falsehood uncovered. The veneer was peeling back all the time, revealing something spectacularly ordinary beneath.

'You can't get to me, Frank. My mind is closed to the likes of you.'

At any time before, Frank would have believed him. Now he saw the madman as just another criminal. Vile and vicious, despicable and base, a man without a conscience. But nothing special. Nothing special at all. Just a ham who blew his lines.

'You're a bad actor, Larry. I'll bet you're every bit as bad as your father was.'

'You leave that bastard out of this. You …' Swain faltered, smiling weakly. 'You won't get through that easily, Frank.'

'No. I didn't expect to. I have something else in mind.' Frank felt a tug on his sleeve. It was Nicky, standing just behind the doorway. Frank smiled. 'Put it on the floor,' he whispered.

Nicky grimaced. 'You bet I will. Then I'm getting the fuck out of here.'

'I don't think I'll be long.'

'I hope you know what you're doing. It's my neck on the block.'

'And it'll be safe. Believe me. I needed to know him, and now I do. There's really nothing to fear.'

When Nicky had gone, Frank edged back inside the cell. Swain was still on the bed, but had shifted forward a little. The brief exchange had intrigued him. Frank remained close by the door, his own smile broad, a glint in his eyes.

'Your father used to lock you up in the dark,' he said quietly. 'Down in the small cellar beneath your home. There was no light, it was cold and damp and dirty in there. That's why you sometimes think you are the dark. You believe it entered you, became a part of you. It twisted your mind, Larry. It did some crazy things to you.'

'You have been busy. Someone has a big mouth. Whatever. I lived through it. I'm still here.'

'But it must have been terrifying, down there in the dark. What did you hate most about it?'

Swain frowned, and his eyes became wary. The question had obviously unsettled him. A memory he would rather have not recalled. Sweat sprang from his scalp and trickled down the side of his face.

'Just the dark,' he said. 'That, and being alone.'

'Really? Yes, I can see that being left in the dark for long periods must have been harrowing. Loneliness, too, is a terrible thing. I bet you got the odd rat down there, too. Not very nice having one of those running about, eyes gleaming, chattering.'

'Yes. They were very unpleasant.'

'But then what about the spiders, Larry? What about the monster spiders you used to get down in that basement?'

A tremor. Two eyes widening. For the first time, Swain's tongue snaked out to wet his lips. 'What about them?'

'Oh, just something I heard.'

'Such as?'

'Such as, when you were small you used to have a bed much like the one you're on now, with steel strips down the sides. Such as, one night you were looking at a comic and it dropped down the side, and in order to get it back you had to go to the end of the bed and crawl all the way under. Such as, when you turned back, you came face to face with an eight-legged monster, a monster you had never seen the like of before.'

A single bead of sweat began to trickle down the madman's brow, curving into his eye. He blinked, tongue now highly animated, eyes open wide. He said nothing, but his head began to slowly shake. Mute denial.

'Such as,' Frank went on more forcefully, 'you screamed the house down, woke your father, who wasn't at all pleased. Such as, when he found out why you were screaming, he picked up the spider, made you crawl out and get back into bed, and then he tossed the spider under the covers with you and held you there. Such as, when he locked you up in the dark, you were driven crazy by the thought of another of those monsters creeping up on you unseen, crawling up your trouser leg, or across your hand, or one falling from the ceiling onto your head.'

'Bastard!'

Swain got to his feet. His teeth were bared, like a wild animal about to strike for fresh meat. His head of flesh was slick now, a thin moustache of moisture above his upper lip.

'You're trying to fuck with my mind, Frank. But I'm better at it than you are. You tell me about the spiders, and I'll tell you how I took your daughter and had her begging for more.'

Frank didn't even blink. 'We have to talk about the spiders, Larry.'

'Laura liked calling me Larry, too. 'Take me again, Larry,' she'd say. 'I really enjoy it, Larry."

Frank stepped behind the door for a moment. He stooped, and when he straightened, he held a glass container in his hands.

Lawrence regarded him with amusement. 'What, you bought me a fish, Frank?'

'It is like a fish-tank, isn't it, Larry? But as you can see, there's no water in it. But you know what else they keep in these kinds of tanks, Larry? Tanks with lids? It's from an exotic pets centre I know. Give you a clue?'

Swain backed away. His legs struck the edge of the bed and he fell back onto it. He scrambled back into the corner, knees raised against his chin, both arms wrapped around them. 'Take it away,' he said. 'Take it away.'

But Frank didn't take it away. Instead he put the tank on the floor, shifted the glass lid to one side, and dipped his hand inside. He laughed as he stood up straight. Laughed as he took a step closer to the prisoner. Laughed as Lawrence Swain screamed. Laughed as the brown and black tarantula on the palm of his hand began to move.

Chapter Sixty-Four

Hands to his eyes, Swain continued to moan and rock back and forth. 'Take it away, take it away, take it away.' He said it over and over again, voice raised to fever-pitch. He refused to look at it. He made a choking sound in the back of his throat. His eyes were wide and wild.

But Frank came closer until he was standing by the bed. 'Come on, Larry,' he said cheerfully. 'His name is Tiny, and he wants to play. Just look at how he fills even my big hand, see how furry he is. Quick bastard, too, I would imagine. All those thick, hairy legs.'

'I won't look, I won't. And you can't make me.' He wrapped both arms across his face.

And then Frank appeared to relent. 'Okay, Larry. I'll take him away. Look, I'm backing off now, back toward the door.'

'I won't look, you bastard.'

'All right. In fact, it's probably best you don't look.'

'Why?' Suspicious now.

'Because now I'll tell you what I'm going to do if you don't tell me where to find my daughter. I asked you if you liked your cell, Swain, and you said you did. But you will have noticed that it's an internal cell, which means there's no external light. So, when I close the door, I'm going to switch off your only light source. Believe me, it's so dark in here you won't be able to see your hand in front of your face.'

Behind the arms, Swain uttered a long moan of terror. He was clever enough to understand what was coming.

'And after I've turned off the light, Larry, I'm going to put Tiny here through the viewing flap in the door.'

The moan was cut off, replaced by the sound of stifled weeping.

'Just imagine that, Larry. You and Tiny together in a pitch ... black ... cell.'

Now the man was sobbing, shoulders heaving as he coughed up his emotions.

'But the best thing is, Larry, that you and Tiny won't be alone. See, my friend didn't just fetch one spider from the exotic pets shop. No, he got five more of the big buggers. So now imagine that, Larry. You and Tiny and five of Tiny's pals – all of whom are bigger than him, by the way.'

'Oh, God, no. *No!*' Swain cried, and his sobs echoed around the cell. He began to whine and howl like a tormented animal.

'You won't know where they are because you won't be able to see them. But if you listen close enough, you might just be able to hear them scuttling across the floor. Oh, but you'll feel them, Larry. No mistaking the touch of a spider this size, Larry. And they'll make the monsters of your childhood look like money-spiders by comparison.'

Swain looked up. His eyes were already swollen with tears, red and puffy. Frank could see that the man had bitten through the paper material of his white suit, and had drawn blood from his own arm. His head shook maniacally.

'You won't do it. You can't. You're not allowed. You have to play by the rules. I know you have to.'

'But there's just me and you down here, Larry. Apart from Tiny and his friends, that is. No one else can hear what's going on. And even if they could, you really think they'd care?'

Through his sobbing, Lawrence Swain continued to shake his head. 'I don't believe you. It's a bluff. I know it is. Has to be.'

'If you'd ever played cards with me, Larry, you'd know I never bluff. And don't forget, I'm not a copper any more. I have my own rules for dealing with people like you.'

But Swain had dredged up some resolve. He sat upright, chest thrust forward. 'Fuck you. You and your mind games. I'm better, Frank, and I know just how far you'd go.'

'Okay, Larry.' Frank stepped out of the room and slammed the cell door behind him.

'Come back,' Swain cried. 'You crazy fucking bastard.'

'Give me the address, Larry.'

'Fuck you.'

The naked bulb recessed into the ceiling, protected by a steel cage, suddenly winked off, and the madman was plunged into darkness. 'No!' he roared, his voice rising in pitch and timbre. 'No. You can't do this.'

'The address, Larry.'

'Fuck you.' He sobbed again. 'Fuck you.'

The steel rectangle in the door was lifted. Light flooded through the opening. 'Here comes Tiny,' Frank said. Something passed across the band of light, and then came the distinct sound of something soft being dropped onto the cell floor.

'No. Let me out, let me out!'

Frank imagined the man getting to his feet and standing on the bed, toes curled into to the thin mattress. Perhaps Swain's bladder giving way and a stain spreading swiftly across the crotch of his white overall.

'You can't do this. Oh, please, no. *No. No. No!*'

'The address, Larry.'

'Take it away. Turn on the light and take it away.'

'The address first, Larry.'

'Fuck you.'

'Okay.' Frank lifted the flap again. 'Here comes number two.'

They were up to number four when Lawrence Swain finally broke down and gave the address.

***

Nicky and Frank sat in the back of the speeding squad car as it thundered across the capital, sirens blaring. Neither man had trusted himself to drive. At that moment, several other units were heading west, out of London toward Slough. A disused theatre, once a cinema and bingo hall, and more recently the lair of a monster, was just off the main A4 road that cut through the urban development.

As the high-powered Volvo sliced through the traffic with ease, Nicky turned to his friend and laid a hand on his shoulder. 'I heard most of what went on in there, Frank. Tiny was the only spider we had, but Swain believed there were more. You ... you used his own methods against him. You terrorised the information out of him. Doesn't that disturb you?'

'No.'

Nicky studied his friend's face for a second or two. Then he grinned and nodded. 'Yes, it does.'

Frank sighed and turned to his friend. 'Yes, it does,' he admitted.

'That's just as well. Otherwise you'd be no better than him. My God, did you see the look on the custody sergeant's face. He was terrified of you, looked at you as if you were the devil himself.'

'It needed to be done. He would never have broken otherwise.'

'Sure. I know that.'

'Even so, it leaves a nasty taste.'

'Can you live with it?'

'I'll learn to. I have no other choice.'

'Was it all deliberate, Frank? All thought out? You played good-cop, bad-cop all on your own. You softened him up with all that business about Sophie, found old sores and opened him up, then went for the jugular. You attacked his fears, his weakness. It was ... well, I don't mind telling you, mate, it was fucking chilling. You were so bloody cold. For a moment there, I almost forgot who was the psychopath.'

'It worked, didn't it?'

'Yes, it worked. But like the nut-job said, there's a price to pay.'

Frank turned away. His features were impassive as he stared out of the window at the city. He swallowed once and said, 'Then I'll just have to live with that, too.'

Chapter Sixty-Five

When their squad car screeched to a halt outside the theatre, there were several other cars and vans already waiting. None had used a siren, and no vehicle had its lights flashing. The three-storey theatre, in which Lawrence and Violet Swain had lived for more than a decade, cast a deep shadow across the corner of the street and the steps leading up to its imposing entrance were almost lost in the gloom.

The entire area was cordoned off with blue and white tape, keeping back the usual gathering of onlookers who exchanged rumours excitedly. As Frank and Nicky got out of the Volvo, a cop wearing blue body armour rushed up, holding out two more of the protective chest pads.

'DS Coleman, sir,' he said. 'We were the first to arrive at the scene. We've already secured the area.'

Nicky took his armour and began strapping it on. 'Good. Any sign of movement in there?'

The tall and wiry young officer shook his head. 'Nothing. We have our tactical weapons officers positioned on all sides, but there aren't all that many windows left un-shuttered. Through one they've seen what appears to be a room recently lived in.'

'What about a vehicle?'

Coleman gave a single shake of the head. 'Sorry, sir. No sign.'

'No van?' Frank asked. Lawrence Swain must have had something in which to transport both the tools of his trade and the bodies of his seven victims.

'Not here. I have officers scouring nearby streets.'

'We're too late,' said Frank. His voice was low, imbued with immense frustration. 'Violet's not here anymore.'

'You can't know that,' Nicky said. 'Not for sure. She might have just moved whatever vehicle they have, dumped it somewhere.'

Frank looked up at the grey-brick building. So cold, cheerless. Just right for its inhabitants. 'They won't find Violet Swain in there. The question is, did she take Laura with her?'

Nicky looked at Coleman. 'I assume your men are ready to go in.'

'Yes, sir.'

Nicky scratched the back of his head. 'I was going to take some time to get the feel of the place, see if she's still holding them. But…' He turned to look at Frank.

'No,' he said grimly. 'Let's get in there.'

Nicky gave a single nod, and then DS Coleman gave the word to go.

***

The breach went according to plan, with armed officers from the SO19 Tactical Firearms team swarming into the building and swiftly examining each room in turn. Frank was in the building's auditorium, marvelling at the stage and its equipment, some of the sets he assumed Swain had built, when one of Coleman's DC's came for him.

'Skipper says you should come upstairs, sir.' The young Detective Constable looked concerned.

Frank's heart lurched. Something was up. Something or someone had been found. *Please,* he begged. *Don't let it be my little girl. Please.*

He followed the constable up to the room where it became instantly clear the Swain twins had kept Laura for two full weeks. The door to the doll's house was open wide, and Frank could see a cluster of bodies grouped around something on the floor. Again, his heart kicked.

A sharp cry gave him a jolt. 'Over here, Frank. Quickly.'

Frank saw Nicky beckoning him over. He barged his way through the group of men and into the doll's house. On the floor, pinned to the bare wood with a narrow carpenter's chisel, was a single sheet of paper. Taking care not to touch it, Frank read:

My sweet Larry

If you are reading this then hopefully all is well. I hope you understand why I had to leave without you. If you can bring yourself to forgive me, I hope you will join me at the place we both loved most of all when we were children. Whatever you decide, I love you, Larry. I always have and I always will.

No matter what.

Frank exhaled deeply. 'You won't find Laura here,' he said softly. 'Violet has her.'

'But where? Their favourite childhood place? That could be anywhere, damnit.'

Frank shook his head, eyes narrowing. 'No. Not anywhere. Somewhere specific. Violet and Lawrence Swain grew up in Hove, remember. Think about it, Nicky. If you lived in Hove, where would you like to spend your childhood summer days? Where would you go to escape your misery?'

Chapter Sixty-Six

Violet's mood was almost ecstatic. Her hands gripped the steering wheel at the regulation ten-to-two. She kept her speed in line with whatever restrictions were signposted. She checked her rear-view mirror constantly, and her eyes read the road ahead. She was relaxed, confident. She had everything in hand.

'We're going to have such fun,' she said, glancing across at Laura.

The sun was sliding over to her right, beating down on the tarmac. Her weary-looking Ford Focus broke through barriers of shimmering heat-haze as it ate up the miles. The afternoon was glorious, and Violet was clearly ready to become a child again.

'When I was a girl I used to escape as often as I could,' she explained. 'I'd walk the couple of miles or so into town, or if I had a little money I'd get a bus. I'd walk around the centre and the piers for hours. Did you know they had a palace there? Well, they do. It has funny-shaped domes ... they look like onions. But it's a beautiful place. Truly beautiful. You'll love it, believe me.'

Laura said nothing.

'Right near the palace are a lot of old narrow streets. Once the cottages used to belong to the fishermen, but that was long before even I was born. Walking through the place is like going back in time. That's one of the reasons I used to go there so often. There I could lose myself for a while. A different place, a different time. A different life.

'There's a waxworks, too. Have you ever been to a waxworks museum? I used to sneak in the back way without paying. It was creepy, but I loved it there. The pier was wonderful, too. But best of all was the doll's museum. Dolls in Wonderland, I think it was called. It's such a long time ago now. But I used to adore walking around, looking at the dolls. And you know what … there was even a post-box for Father Christmas. Every year I would post my letter to him. And every year he would let me down. He never did take my mummy and daddy away. Not until much later. When it was too late.'

* * *

Laura's eyes were open, vacant: she heard every word, but her mind had switched off.

She sucked on her thumb as she had done many years earlier as a toddler. Her senses were operating perfectly, perhaps more so now than at any time before, but her brain was refusing to accept any of their signals. Even the muted voice by her side was a puzzle. But not one she wanted to decipher. There was no life outside her own body now.

There was only her thumb, and the beat of her own heart.

Chapter Sixty-Seven

They were almost ninety minutes behind as their car flashed along the same route that Violet and Laura had travelled. They took the M25, cut off onto the M23 past Gatwick Airport, before hanging a left onto the A23 heading towards the south coast. The siren and lights were used only in dense traffic, while out on the open road speed limits were ignored. Frank and Nicky shared the car with the same two uniformed officers from Leyton station. Their expressions were equally grim and purposeful. Frank guessed his own would also betray anguish.

'I hope you're right about this,' Nicky said, letting go a soft sigh.

'I am.' Frank turned his head and smiled soberly. 'You know I am. If you were a kid brought up in a madhouse in Hove, where your very life was threatened on a daily basis, you'd have to seek some relief or go crazy at an early age. The Swains would have gone exactly where I would have. Brighton is a couple of miles away, and it has the pier, the amusements, the kind of glamour that would appeal to a child. Most of all, it has a means of escape.'

Nicky could not argue with that kind of logic. He had already contacted his own superior, who in turn had called ahead to Sussex Police. Now there was little he could do except wait the journey out. A message for him interrupted the silence.

'Yes?' he said into the communication device strapped to his body armour.

'It's DS Coleman, at the theatre, sir.'

'Yes, Coleman. Go ahead.'

'We've turned up some good hard evidence, sir, including the missing girls, other than Laura Rogers. They're dead, sir, have been for some time. It ...' His voice faltered momentarily. 'It's the most incredible stuff, sir. In the basement, we found the baths where our man must have kept his victims' skins. There's a lot of flesh and hair and nails scattered around. The baths are, well, they have tide-marks of dried tissue.'

'Okay, sergeant. Take it easy now. Have you found the tools he killed them with?'

'Yes, sir. He hadn't cleaned them. Both power and hand tools are smeared with blood and tissue. We also broke into a room and found some pretty expensive video equipment. There were photographs there, too. Terrible, awful photo—'

The man broke off to utter a stifled sob. In the front of the car, the driver shook his head slowly, while his companion chewed into his bottom lip and stared at the countryside flashing by.

'Sorry, sir,' Coleman said, his voice strong again. 'We also have the audio recordinlgs. Everything we need to convict the bastard, in fact.'

'Good work. Look, sergeant, arrange to have everything taken to our operations annexe in Leyton once forensic are done with it. And…get yourself off duty, make sure you have a drink or two before you go home.'

'Yes, sir. Thank you, sir.'

Nicky blew hard and turned to Frank. 'We've got him, mate. He won't be going anywhere for quite some time.'

Frank rubbed his eyes. 'You better believe it. He has to pay for all that, Nicky. Did you hear that poor bastard's voice? What he's seen today will stay with him for the rest of his life. Later, maybe tomorrow, maybe the day after, you and I have to prepare our case. We have to listen to those recordings, watch every video, study every photograph. My own daughter will be on some of them. You think there's any chance we'll be the same people afterwards?'

It wasn't a question that needed any answers. The two men turned to look out at the scenery. Not another word was spoken until they reached Brighton.

* * *

As Violet and Laura walked side by side along the seafront, occasional gusts of wind toying with their hair, Violet supported the girl with one hand, while the other arm stretched out across her shoulders. They drew stares as they made their way along the promenade and down to the shingle beach: the young girl with the glazed expression, wearing only a flimsy checked dress that was far too short and tight for her; the older woman, buoyant, smile wide and dazzling, wearing a green ankle-length dress and carrying a backpack over her shoulder.

People on the beach assiduously avoided the two figures – they must have looked out of their heads on either booze or drugs, Violet guessed. But that was perfectly all right by her. She was glad of the space as she approached the cool shadows stretching out from the pier.

'I told you this was a wonderful place,' she trilled. She hugged Laura closer, their gait becoming more awkward. 'I'm sorry I couldn't find Dolls in Wonderland, though. Maybe it isn't open any more. Maybe I was looking in the wrong place. It's been a long time. Still, there's a lot of new things to see. That marina wasn't here before. All those boats ... so beautiful. The amusements are better, too. And the aquarium. I don't remember it being that good before. If it was even here. This is such a wonderful place. Don't you just love it?'

Laura said nothing, and if she heard and understood Violet's words, there was no outward sign of it. She hadn't uttered a single word since they were in the doll's house together. Violet glanced at the girl and smiled as if she had responded anyway.

As they stepped beneath the pier, Violet allowed herself a stifled cry of triumph. She had made it this far. Now there was no turning back. The plan had sneaked into her mind the moment she realised that Larry probably wasn't going to be coming home to her. The warm sensation that had crept over her was so powerful, so intense, so rich and rewarding, that she thought for a second she might faint. Bright stars flared before her eyes, her stomach gave way to convulsions.

This was what Larry must have been feeling all along. Every time he cut one of the girls, every time he peeled their flesh, every time he drilled into their very souls. No wonder he felt so good afterwards, no wonder he hadn't allowed her to experience it for herself. He was greedy, selfish. He ought to have shared the pleasure. But now it was her turn to be greedy, too.

She set down the backpack and rummaged around inside for a few seconds. She'd brought several tools with her, and was now having trouble selecting just one. In the end, she chose the simplest of them all. Larry had experimented with a whole variety of tools, so opting for the standard carpet knife seemed like the best thing to do. He would despise her for what she was about to do, but he would appreciate the irony.

Yes, Larry had killed so many. Had drawn ultimate pleasure from so many, but he had been forced to do every one of them away from the eyes of an unsuspecting world. He had skulked in darkness, lacking the strength of conviction necessary to reveal this remarkable sense of completeness in public. His power was now hers, but she was willing to take it one step further. About as far as it could go.

Out in the open.

In broad daylight.

Beneath a fading, but still most potent sun. In full view of whoever wanted to share her experience.

First, she would make sure all eyes were fixed upon her, and then she would use the sharpened tool to take the girl apart piece by bloody piece. She would both laugh and weep as she did so, drawing strength from the horror-stricken faces around her, the sheer incredulity. It was going to be the ultimate rush of power.

Larry had never attained such perfection.

But she would.

* * *

They drove to the front, where they were met by a local CID officer. 'They've been spotted,' he said as Frank and Nicky clambered out. 'Along the beach, towards the pier.'

Nicky grasped his friend's arm. 'She's alive, Frank. Laura's still alive.'

Frank didn't trust himself to speak. It was more than he could ever have hoped for. He told their driver to stay with the car should it be needed in a hurry. The other officer had to remain on the promenade in case Violet Swain managed to slip away and scramble back up from the beach. Then Frank and Nicky, together with the armed officer from the local station, hurried down a concrete ramp to the shingle below.

* * *

Out of the cool shadow. Up a rise of stone steps, cluttered with litter discarded by ignorant fools. Onto the pier. The boardwalk was bustling with activity, and if anyone noticed the woman carrying a razor-sharp knife, if anyone thought her odd, none of them stopped to question her.

Violet led Laura further down the pier, heading out toward the incoming tide. When they were halfway along, she stopped, grabbed hold of Laura's shoulders, and turned the girl to face her.

'Our time has come,' she said, leaning forward. Her voice was brittle with emotion. 'We're on the brink of a very special moment. I'm so glad you're going to share it with me.'

She raised her hand to show the girl the Stanley knife. 'The eyelids first, I think,' she said, her tone now distant, absorbed in the majesty of what she was about to do. 'So, you can't close your eyes to the pain or the beauty of what follows. One of Larry's little tips.'

Laura stared at her. She said nothing. But in the back of her throat a low moan began to rattle.

* * *

They were a hundred yards away from the pier when Nicky's radio crackled. 'Loizou,' he snapped. 'What have you got?'

'Woman and girl matching your descriptions spotted on the Palace Pier, sir.'

Nicky looked around, uncertain. 'Where is that?' he asked, thumbing the transmit button on the radio.

'Right in front of you, sir. Sorry, it's marked 'Brighton Pier' now. You want us to join you?'

'No. You keep looking in your area, just in case it's a false alarm.'

Frank was already off and running, the armed officer by his side. Nicky caught them up easily, and together they moved back up onto the promenade and across to the pier. As they hammered onto the boardwalk, Frank stopped in his tracks and pointed.

'There,' he said.

His eyes zoomed in on his daughter, now just fifty yards away. She was locked in eye contact with Violet, who held something in her hand. Sunlight glinted off its metallic surface. Laura did not appear at all frightened or even concerned. She just stood there as if she were in some kind of trance, waiting for the woman to strike her down.

'Let me go on my own,' Frank said over his shoulder. 'Let me try to talk her out of whatever she's planning to do.'

Nicky nodded reluctantly. When Frank was out of earshot he spoke into the radio once more. 'All officers in attendance. This is DCI Loizou. Targets located on Brighton Pier. Move in on this area and surround the area. And bring up the sniper team.'

* * *

The woman's hand was raised, the blade now just inches from Laura's face. She turned her head slowly, lines converging into a frown in the centre of her forehead as Frank stepped into view.

'Please don't do that, Violet,' he said.

Frank swallowed back his terror, relieved to have gained her attention. Though his hands hung loosely by his side, implying no threat to her, he felt prepared to move given the slightest opportunity. He was close now. Close enough to hear Laura's insistent low moan and ragged breathing.

'You don't have to go through with this, you know,' he went on. 'There's no need, Violet. Not now.'

'Yes,' the woman said, the frown deepening as if she were trying to locate some lost memory. 'Yes, there is. Larry's always had it all, everything his own way. Now the only chance I have to...appease him for what I've done is to experience the thrill and the incredible charge for myself, while also finishing the job he started. Only I'll be putting it on display for all to see. Everyone will be able to share my finest moment. He'll be in awe of me, then. He'll never touch me again.'

'But he won't ever touch you again anyway. We have him in prison. Locked up in a cell. He'll never get out, Violet. Never.'

She narrowed her gaze and glared at him. 'Liar. You're all liars. This bitch pretended she was Sophie, but I remembered what happened to Sophie. She made me remember, and then had to pay for lying to me.'

'And she will pay. But she doesn't have to die. And we can't tie you to anything your brother has done, so even though you may think you have nothing to lose, you really do. You haven't murdered anyone, Violet. So why go through with this now? We know it was all Larry's doing, that he was responsible for them all. He's the one we wanted, Violet. Now we have him, and you can be free.'

A war of emotions tugged at the woman's features. All at once she looked old before her time, haggard, the violent years she had endured catching up with her in an instant.

'I don't know,' she muttered softly. 'Maybe you're still lying, trying to confuse me.'

When she looked at him again he was startled to see tears glittering in her eyes. Gently he said, 'No, Violet. I wouldn't trick you. We know what you've gone through all these years. You're a victim as well. Larry is the one who will have to pay. You can still be helped. We will help you. But not if you hurt my daughter.'

Violet shook her head, swinging the blade back and forth. Beyond her, people backed further away, drawing closer to the sea beyond the end of the pier.

'Maybe I don't want to be helped. Perhaps it's better for everyone if I do this.'

She blinked back the tears and shook her head as if to force away any negative emotions.

'I mean, look at your little girl. She's a fucking zombie.' Violet shook the knife in front of Laura, and yanked on the Laura's arm to pull her even closer. 'But you know what? She's *my* zombie. *My* puppet. I yank on a string here, she moves; pull on a string there, she moves again. She's not yours any more. Don't you understand that?'

Frank raised a hand, palm out defensively. 'I do. I do understand you, Violet. But this needn't be the end for you. There's so much you can do, so much waiting for you out here. Don't waste the rest of your life, Violet.'

With each statement, he inched closer to them. His eyes never left Violet's face, though Laura continued to claim his attention. Since he had begun talking with Swain, he was aware of Laura only peripherally, standing there like the blurred edge of a photograph.

'But it's not a waste,' Violet argued, her voice softer now. 'With Larry gone I have nothing.'

'No, just the opposite. With Larry gone you have everything.'

'You wouldn't understand. For the very first time I am in complete control.' She turned to glance at Laura, and when she switched back to Frank she was grinning. Confidence renewed. 'Larry only ever wanted to be better than our father. I want to be better than them both.'

Violet moved to one side and jabbed her arm forward, the blade almost touching Laura's left eye. Laura neither moved nor blinked. She stood perfectly still, thin bare arms by her sides, shoulders sloping. By now, police officers had circled them and were pushing back the crowd of onlookers that had gathered at both ends of the pier. Those members of the public who refused to look away, gasped or cried out in horror as the blade cut the air.

Frank somehow stopped himself from leaping at the woman, but the muscles in his legs coiled in anticipation. 'No, Violet!' he shouted, both hands now raised. 'If you do that you will be shot, believe me.'

She stood sideways on to him, her gaze switching between him and Laura. 'You think that bothers me?' She laughed, as if the very thought were absurd. 'Kill me and I'll be with Sophie once more.'

'And what if you're only wounded instead? You'll go to jail, Violet. You know what they do to child killers in jail? They beat them. Beat them every day. That's when they're not raping them with anything that comes to hand. They'll make you wish you'd never been born. How is that better, Violet? Tell me. How?'

When she looked at him this time he saw doubt in her eyes. Fear, too. He knew the moment was upon them: she would either relent or strike. He had seconds; not even minutes.

'Let her go, Violet,' he said in a soft, low voice. 'Let her go and learn to live. Then come with me and you can do the same.'

Frank saw the anguish and confusion in her face, distorting her features. He knew her mind would be awash with lies and deceit, her brother's words and violent acts, that images of brutality would add weight to his own words. But he also knew that a mind so unbalanced could shun logic and reason, opting finally for an action that would bring about closure. Frank watched the woman's inner struggle with a sense of impotence, an acceptance of one simple truth: if Violet Swain decided to strike, to thrust that blade up and into his daughter's eye, even his swiftest response would be too late to save Laura.

Please, he silently implored a God in whom he did not believe. *Please make this woman see reason. Allow my little girl to live.*

For a moment, time seemed to move out of sync. The world beyond their small group went about its business, yet for them it paused for breath. Then Frank saw something pass across Violet's eyes, and the woman's shoulders wilted in the sunshine. She nodded and shook her head at the same time, strange little circles.

'Take her,' she sighed. 'Take her now.'

'Laura,' Frank said, blood roaring in his temples, his heart hammering to be free. He held out a hand. 'Laura, come to Daddy, sweetheart.'

But his little girl didn't move, didn't even turn to face him. She simply stood there looking up into Violet's eyes. Frank walked forward, slowly, edging his way to his daughter's side. Violet's head was lowered now, chin tucked way in, her hair hanging in thin, dirty ropes. Frank kept one eye on her as he reached out to take his daughter's hand.

And as his fingers locked with hers, Laura threw back her head and screamed. In that same instant, Violet moved with incredible speed. Frank's eyes were off her for only a split second, but it was more than enough to miss the blade slashing up toward his unprotected face. Its finely-honed edge gouged into his chin and moved up along the cheek, missing his eye by a hair's breadth along its path. It sliced through to the bone, and as his head jerked back reflexively, blood spurted out of the flapping maw she had created.

With one hand, Frank pulled Laura behind him, while the other came up before his bloody face. He stared in horror as the blade arced down at him once more, but before it could bite deep into his flesh again, a hole appeared in the centre of Violet's forehead.

As she stumbled backwards, another bullet took her just beneath the chin. Behind the shock so evident in her eyes, there was also a moment of agony as she realised she had been cheated of her ultimate moment. And then there was nothing to be seen in them at all.

Violet Swain's body was spun around by a third bullet. As she fell she twisted sideways, her back arched, and she toppled over the pier rail to the shingle beach below.

Frank sank to his knees and wrapped both arms around his daughter. He held her tight as he wept with relief, face still streaming blood.

'It's okay, sweetheart,' he whispered through his tears. 'Daddy's here now. Everything is all right again.'

Laura Rogers just went on screaming.

Chapter Sixty-Eight

Frank wanted to personally inform Lawrence Swain of his sister's death. He wanted to see the man suffer as he himself had been forced to suffer. But when he was done he merely felt shabby and unfulfilled.

Swain said nothing at first, betrayed no outward sign of emotion. He lay back on the narrow bed inside his cell, staring up at the ceiling as if the news hadn't affected him in the slightest. After a minute of silence, a crooked smile appeared from nowhere. He sat up, swivelled round and placed his feet on the floor, stared into Frank's eyes.

'That face of yours looks painful, Frank. Violet did a good job on you.'

Frank's wound had been sewn back together during surgery that lasted more than two hours, with only some slight nerve damage to consider for the future. That, and a nice scar.

'Even better than you did. She won't be doing it again, though,' Frank reminded him spitefully.

'Oh, no. She may be dead in this life, Frank, but her spirit exists in another. I know that for a fact. And I will join her there, together with Sophie.'

'Sooner than you may think.'

Frank leaned forward and put his head close to Swain's, their eyes locking. The gun in his jacket pocket felt heavy. His desire to end this man's life was now overwhelming.

'You and your sister have taken too much away from me. More than I can bear. Your sister had a bloody end, and I wish I had pulled the trigger. Now it's your turn. There's no one else down here with us, Larry. No one at all. Custody sergeant is away from his desk. So, there's nothing to prevent me from killing you right here and now.'

Swain closed his eyes and sighed. 'You can't rattle me, Frank. You seem to forget that.'

'Oh, I think I can, Swain. Remember Tiny, my hairy eight-legged friend?'

Swain visibly paled. His face lost its arrogant sneer, torn away in a single moment of recollection. 'So, you won that one. You're still lagging behind, Frank. That minor triumph doesn't compare with what I've done to your head.'

Again, the weight of the gun pressed against Frank's chest. It would take only seconds to pull it and fire, empty the clip, end this bastard's miserable life. Seconds out of a whole lifetime.

'How can I allow you to live, Swain? How can I allow you to live and breathe while my son is no longer able to?'

Swain smiled at him. 'Because you haven't got the balls.'

Frank returned the smile, hardening his eyes. 'Really? Are you sure about that?'

'Oh, I'm certain. It takes strength to do what I do, Frank. The kind of mental strength you simply don't have. If the roles were reversed, you'd be dead already.'

'Are you baiting me, you prick? You want me to prove I have what it takes?'

'Anytime you're ready, Frank. Here I am, waiting. On the other side, I will have my dear sisters with me. You can kill me, Frank, but you can't hurt me. And you know what else?' His eyes gleamed triumphantly. 'You can't possibly win.'

Frank straightened, looming over the man. He glared down at him for several seconds, his hand itching to move to the inside pocket of his jacket. He wanted this man punished. But how do you punish a man who seeks death? The question hung before his mind's eye. And then suddenly the way ahead was so clear he almost stopped breathing.

'You're wrong,' he said flatly. 'I've been agonising over this, Swain. One minute I want you dead and I want to be the one who wipes you off the face of the planet, and then a voice reminds me that I have a daughter who needs me more than ever before. An accident? A little fall down the stairs? I've considered that, too. But that isn't personal enough. Shooting you would be the easiest thing in the world, and we both know you deserve it.'

Frank paused, turning it over in his mind. 'You said I can't win. I believe I can. I want you gone, but the truth is I want you to suffer the way my daughter suffered. To feel terror, fear and pain. It occurs to me now that the real fear, the real suffering for you would be to carry on living in this world, locked away from your desires, locked away inside your own mind.'

The madman's eyes flew open. His face had now taken on a bleached-white pallor. 'You don't mean that, Frank. You can't. What about what I did to your son and daughter? You can't allow me to live after all I've done to you and your family.'

'Swain, if that's what hurts you the most, then that's how I'm going to have it. Killing you now would give me pleasure for a moment, but forcing you to live will provide satisfaction for the rest of my life.'

'You don't know that. You can't. If you have a gun, Frank, use it now. That's the only way you can be certain of my suffering.'

'I don't think so. Not now. I don't think you want to be locked up in a small cell all by yourself. It gets dark in those places at night. I could even drop one of the screws a few quid and have him slip something into your cell the way I did.'

Swain's flesh now pressed tight against the bone beneath, his neck and cheeks drawing colour from rage. 'Your son begged for mercy, Frank. Laura, too. I tore your boy to pieces, and I screwed with your little girl every chance I got. What kind of man are you? What kind of man would let the person who killed his son and ruined his daughter live a single day more?'

His words echoed, lingering in the room like uninvited guests. Frank looked deep into Lawrence Swain's eyes, and saw not his soul but what lay in his heart. 'The kind of man who is better than you,' Frank whispered. 'I know you now, Swain. I know you don't want to live. You will die some time, but not today. And not by my hand.'

'Coward!'

'Enjoy the next forty years or so, Swain. And remember something while you're sitting in jail: I'm the man who put you there. Think of that every minute of every day.'

'No. That's not the way it's meant to be. Kill me, Frank. You have to kill me.'

'I don't have to do anything of the sort. Do you appreciate the irony of that, Swain?'

The man shook his head, sitting upright now, face creased in abject misery. 'I can't be allowed to live. You must want me dead. You must.'

'And I do. So much more than you can possibly believe. But only after you've felt the fear your victims felt. Only after you've been left to rot in your own stench, knowing that I could have killed you and chose not to.'

'But that's not the way it was meant to be.'

"Meant to be'?'

'Yes. Let me quote you something: 'I only knew what haunted thought quickened his step, and why, he looked upon the garish day with such a wistful eye. The man had killed the thing he loved, and so he had to die." He nodded frantically. '*Had* to die, Frank. *Had* to.'

'Another gem from your idol, eh, Swain. *The Ballad of Reading Gaol*. Did you imagine yourself ever being in jail like him?'

And then the absolute truth dawned on Frank. So clear, so bright, so obvious. He'd missed it all along.

'Yes, that's it. Of course. You have imagined it. You wanted this, didn't you? You killed Sophie all those years ago, and when you found you couldn't really replace her, you convinced yourself that you had to die for it. *The man had killed the thing he loved, and so he had to die.* That's why you involved me. You could have gone on taking girls indefinitely, but you changed your MO. That's also why you left Karen Redbridge alive. Another lead for us. You wanted to be caught, didn't you, Swain?'

'No.'

'You're lying. I can tell, you know that by now I'm sure. Your subconscious was telling you all along that you had to die. You killed Sophie – the thing you loved most – and so you had to die. You couldn't kill yourself, that would have taken far too much courage, so you had to get someone to do it for you. It just happened to be me. After you'd taken Laura and you realised who I was, you started setting it all up. You knew that if you hurt me by hurting my family, that I would want you dead. Isn't that right, Swain?'

'No. No, you're wrong.'

Frank took a step forward. 'Isn't that right, Swain?'

'No. No, no, *no*!'

'Larry?'

Silence. Then: 'Yes.'

'And you wanted to die like those men described by Wilde.'

'For my sins. Yes. I killed the thing I loved, Frank. I killed her over and over and over. I have to die. You have to kill me, Frank.'

Frank's grin had turned icy. He stared down at Swain as if looking at an insect. 'You'll rot inside a cell, you bastard. And you'll know pain every day for the rest of your life.'

'No!' Swain howled. He got to his feet. 'You can't do that to me. You must kill me. Think of what I did to Laura, to Janet and Gary. They're inside my head and I can't get rid of them. They haunt me, Frank. Sophie, all the others ...'

Frank moved slowly back outside the cell. 'Suffer,' he said. 'Suffer, because a monster like you deserves to.' And then he slammed the cell door shut.

As he walked unsteadily along the corridor he heard the madman's cries. This time they were not triumphant. This time they were cries of terror and utmost misery.

Chapter Sixty-Nine

Frank felt as if he ought to have a season ticket to hospital. Two recent visits to have his own wounds tended, Laura still being observed in a specialist unit in Fulham, and now yet another trip to a private room in which the woman he loved struggled to regain her health following several days in the intensive care unit.

On the same day that Laura had been rescued, a ruptured appendix had almost cost Debbie her life. Frank was acutely conscious that he had spared her little thought and less time in the days that followed, Laura's condition having demanded most of his attention. Today he brought fruit with him, but mostly he was laden with an overwhelming sense of guilt.

Debbie was sitting up in bed when he arrived, some colour having returned to her cheeks. She'd lost a good deal of weight, and only yesterday had cracked a joke about the 'near-death' diet. Frank took his usual place by her side, perched awkwardly on the edge of the bed. He kissed her lips, and smiled as he recognised a familiar taste.

'You're wearing lipstick,' he said. He studied her closely. 'And is that a little blusher and eye-shadow I see?'

Debbie gave a wide grin. 'It is. Some of the doctors here are hot, you know.'

He winked. 'Some of the nurses, too, if you're that way inclined.'

She ran a hand down his stitched cheek. The wound was still fresh and ugly. Her other hand reflexively sought her own wound. She shook her head and managed a weak laugh. 'Aren't we a couple of fine specimens? A pair of disfigured book-ends.'

'A damaged-yet-perfect pair,' Frank said. 'How do you feel, sweetheart?'

'I feel stronger, Frank. Strong enough for you to tell me what's been happening the past few days.'

He nodded and took her hands in his. He told her about Laura's lack of real progress, the misery of seeing his daughter in an almost catatonic state, about the clamour of media attention he'd received, and then spoke about Lawrence Swain for the first time since his last visit to the man's cell.

'I wanted to kill him, Debs. But not just shoot him in the head and have done with it. No. No, I wanted to put a bullet in each knee, then one in each elbow. I wanted him to feel some pain, the kind of pain he's been dishing out. Then I wanted to gut-shoot him and let him bleed out, because I know it's a slow and excruciating death. I wanted him to suffer before dying. But most of all I wanted him gone.'

Debbie was regarding him as if she barely recognised the man sitting by her side. 'Then it's a good job you came to your senses,' she said, her voice flat and uncertain.

'It was nothing to do with senses. I simply realised what would torture him more. And that was living with it. With all those voices inside his head, eating away at him each and every day.'

Frank realised his grin was becoming fixed in place, but he couldn't help himself.

'How exactly did you find out where Laura was being held?'

Frank told Debbie about Swain's fear, and how he had exploited it. The look of horror on her face disturbed him, but in his own mind he knew that what he had done could be justified.

'It was either that or claim Laura's body later,' he finished weakly. 'He would never have told me otherwise, and we would never have found out without him telling us. I had to find a way inside his head, Debs.'

'Oh, I think you did that, Frank.'

He nodded. 'You sound almost as if you wished I hadn't. Ask Laura if she agrees with you.'

Debbie snatched back her hand. 'I'm tired now,' she said. 'I think I'd like to rest for a while.'

Frank realised he'd been unkind. As he got to his feet he held up his hands. 'Okay, I apologise for that crack about Laura. I can see how repulsed you are at the tactics I employed to get that information out of Swain, but surely you can understand why I did it. One man's brief few moments of terror in exchange for a life has to be worthwhile, Debs. Particularly when it was my daughter's life. Why can't you accept that?'

Debbie held his gaze. In her eyes, there was sadness and regret, where minutes before there had been joy and hope.

'It's not that I can't accept it, Frank. I understand why you did it, of course I do. But you don't seem to appreciate the cost.'

'What cost? I got Laura back. She's safe now. Where's the problem?'

'The problem is that you crossed over into the abyss, Frank,' Debbie said, lowering her head. 'And I'm not at all sure that you will find your way back.'

Chapter Seventy

When Debbie called at the house it was something of a surprise. She had been out of hospital for a few days, but had not wanted to see him. Frank had respected her wishes, despite not knowing exactly what had gone wrong between them. He had telephoned her a couple of times, but their conversations had been stilted and one-sided.

Laura had recently moved out of her self-induced coma-like state, so he'd had other things on his mind during that time. The look of joy on her face when he slipped her stuffed Tigger into the bed alongside her, reminded him that despite Laura's age, she was still a child at heart. It felt like a lifetime ago since he had removed the toy from Paul Clarke's home, not knowing at the time whether Laura would live to enjoy it. Yet here she was. His baby was unwell, but she was safe. Nothing else seemed to matter.

Now he and Debbie sat together in the garden, sipping sparkling white wine; uncomfortable, seemingly out of reach of one another.

'I had to come,' she explained, managing a weak smile. She shifted uncomfortably on her chair, winced. He imagined her stomach would still be tender. 'I had to see you. Talk to you, face to face.'

He lowered his eyes so that she would not see his pain. He could guess what she was about to say, had known it since that day in the hospital.

'You've come to say goodbye,' he said.

Debbie nodded. 'That is why I came here today, yes. There was so much going for us before ... before all this. It's not your fault that things have changed, that we have changed, but it's not mine either. I feel so desperately sorry for all that you've lost,

Frank. And for how things are with Laura, of course. It must be so difficult for you to have saved her from that woman, only to have her so badly traumatised. Unimaginable. But one day, she'll come all the way out of it. One day you'll have her back.'

At that moment, Laura was still lying in a hospital bed, wide awake yet completely unaware of her surroundings. She had recognised Frank when he'd seen her last, but had spoken less than a dozen words to him. She remained under constant observation, but he had been warned not to expect a swift recovery.

'Maybe,' he said. 'Maybe she'll come out of it. But even if she does, I doubt she will ever be the same little girl.'

'So, you have to be there for her. Make it up to her somehow, lead her out of the darkness.'

'But you won't do it with me?'

'I don't know if I'm strong enough, Frank. I have to be this honest, because I think so much of you. You come with a lot of baggage, that's for sure. But it's not even that. The fact is … you frighten me.'

'I know.' He looked away.

The garden was warm and welcoming, as it had been throughout the entire summer. But at that moment it felt cold and lonely.

'Something inside you died, Frank. There's a huge piece of you missing now. I worry that what happened squeezed all the goodness out of you. You say that Laura will never be the same, well, neither will you. I've seen signs of that already.'

Frank nodded. His heart, already incredibly burdened, grew heavier still. 'You need to bear in mind my emotional state that day at the hospital. And how it was when I did those things to Swain. None of that was entirely the real me. But you're right, even so. I know you are. I know that I have to get my life in order, and then somehow get my little girl back. I just didn't want to face all that without you.'

Debbie wiped a stray tear from her cheek. 'You must think me heartless.'

'No.' He shook his head, shifted sideways and took her hands between his. 'No, Debs, you're the one thinking straight. Perhaps there can be no future for the two of us, when I'm not even certain of my own.'

Frank closed his eyes as the conversation paused. There was no Gary to break the silence. Never would be again. Laura would be home eventually, but in his heart Frank believed he had also lost his daughter for good. And now Debbie.

He had a life to be getting on with, a business to resurrect, a little girl to help through the bad times – out of the darkness, as Debbie had put it. Perhaps if he kept busy enough he would somehow stop himself from reflecting on how empty his life was going to be, and how desperately lonely he already felt.

This was just all so damned wrong. After he had been through so much, overcoming the worst life has to offer, there seemed no point in not taking one more step. He looked into Debbie's eyes.

'Do you love me?' he asked.

She nodded. 'I do. Of course, I do.'

'Then can you really see no way past this, Debs? Sure, we have fences to mend. They may be badly broken, but are they so completely irreparable? So insurmountable?'

Her gaze narrowed. 'I honestly don't know, Frank.'

He squeezed her hands tighter. 'Which to me suggests we still have a chance.'

'You may be right. Thing is, Laura will need you soon. All of you, if she is going to recover.'

He nodded. 'I realise that. I just happen to think that what she really needs is a happy me. And you make me happy. With all that I have lost, I genuinely believe I still have a shot at being happy.'

'And you deserve to be, Frank. You so deserve to be.'

'Then please don't give up on us, Debs. Even if you have to walk away now, don't make it for good. I'm not stupid enough to believe you won't struggle to get past what I did. But I also believe that, given enough time, you may come to understand my reasons and accept that I am never going to be that person again. How awful it would be, for all of us, if that were to happen too late to rescue everything we have.'

Debbie shook her head and smiled at him. 'You do make it so bloody hard to be angry with you, Frank.'

He matched her smile. 'It's one of my many virtues.'

'I came here to end things between us,' she reminded him. 'Now you've got me all turned around. I don't know what I'm doing anymore.'

'I'm a battler, Debs. I was never going to let you walk away without a fight.'

She stood. Smile still in place. 'Will you give me time, Frank?' she asked him.

'Of course. Take as much as you need.'

'Will two minutes do?'

Frank pulled his head back, frowning as he rose from his chair. 'I don't understand.'

'I have an overnight bag in the car,' Debbie said. Her smile widened. 'I came here to end things, Frank. But I also came here hoping you would persuade me not to.'

THE END

Acknowledgements

I would like to thank everyone at Bloodhound Books, especially Fred and Betsy for once again putting their faith in me. Also to the editor on this one, Clare Law, who helped me improve my work. And to the bloggers out there who did a magnificent job for me in reading, reviewing, rating and publicising my previous book, *Bad To The Bone*. As for my family and friends, well, it's a given that I acknowledge your love, friendship and support. Finally, to you – my readers. I'll be forever grateful.